The Key to Genius

The Key to Genius

D. Jablow Hershman and Julian Lieb, M.D.

PROMETHEUS BOOKS

700 East Amherst St., Buffalo, New York 14215

Dedicated
to those who have known
the torments and triumphs
of manic-depression
and creativity

Published 1988 by Prometheus Books
700 East Amherst Street, Buffalo, New York 14215

Library of Congress Cataloging-in-Publication Data

Hershman, D. Jablow.
    The key to genius: manic-depression and the creative life/ by D. Jablow Hershman, Julian Lieb.
        p.   cm.
    Bibliography: p.
    ISBN 0-87975-437-0
    1. Genius and mental illness. 2. Manic-depressive psychosis.
3. Genius and mental illness—Case studies. 4. Manic-depressive psychosis—Case studies. I. Lieb, Julian. II. Title.
BF423.H47   1988
153.3′5—dc19   87-32900
                                                                       CIP

Contents

1

A Dissection of Genius

GENIUS AS A RELATIONSHIP

We define genius as the proven ability to produce artistic, scientific, or other intellectual work that is considered supremely valuable during or after the lifetime of the producer. Certain qualifications must be met in order to achieve recognition of the work done. The candidate for genius must produce, perform, discover, or invent something that is highly valued. If this work is too far ahead of its time, it will be ignored or derided; unless the work can be preserved to be appreciated later, recognition may never come.

The most favorable chance for recognition comes to those whose work relates in some significant way to the needs and spirit of their contemporaries while the producers are still living and can make their work public. Once the producer has died, even if he or she was highly acclaimed, the remaining work may go unpublished, as was the case with Leibniz. The work of those who die without reputation is usually lost to posterity.

The title of genius is not inalienable but varies over the years with the number and fervor of one's appreciators. William Hogarth, the eighteenth-century painter, thought that some of Michelangelo's work verged on the ridiculous, but Hogarth's Romantic successors worshipped the sculptor. Furthermore, one's reputation as a genius varies in longevity, depending on the field of endeavor. The philosopher and mathematician may wear their crowns for centuries; the actor is quickly forgotten, buried under changing styles. One's claim to genius also depends on the credibility of those who promote it.

Genius, therefore, is not an attribute: it is a dynamic relationship between its possessor and society. It indicates, in a general way, what society expects of the genius and how it responds to that person. There are always geniuses in potentia; but there are no unrecognized geniuses. A genius is someone who is acknowledged as such, even if only by those who work in, or have been trained in, his field, and who pass their verdict on to society.

The title of genius can be temporarily won for reasons that have little to do with the quality of one's work: a colorful life, timely publicity, and a personality that fits the stereotype of genius can distract society from the absence of talent. However, the person who has a more lasting claim to that designation has won it by other means, and it is this individual with whom we are concerned. The genius we have defined has done work that is of importance or value to society and has produced it with unusual skill. Work that is a lucky accident does not earn lasting respect for its producer. Furthermore, outstanding ability wasted on trivia does not lead to recognition of genius. According to our definition, outstanding ability, work of high value, and recognition are essential elements of genius.

THE MAD AND MELANCHOLY: FROM THE CLASSICAL GREEKS TO THE ROMANTICS

The traditional view of genius has its roots in classical Greece. Aristotle associated great ability with depresssion: "All extraordinary men distinguished in philosophy, politics, poetry and the arts are evidently melancholic." Socrates and Plato stated that genius, among poets at least, was inseparable from madness. Socrates said that the poet has "no invention in him until he has been inspired and is out of his senses," and Plato claimed that the poetry of sane men "is beaten all hollow by the poetry of madmen."

Marsilio Ficino, a Renaissance philosopher, linked Aristotle's concept of melancholy genius with Plato's idea of inspired mania and thus was the first to associate genius with what is now recognized as manic-depression.

Eighteenth-century rationalists, though honoring both sanity and high intelligence, continued to attribute the latter to temporary insanity. The poet Diderot stated: "These reserved and melancholy men owe their extraordinary, almost god-like acuteness of insight to a temporary disturbance of their whole mechanism. One may notice how it brings them now to sublime and now to insane thoughts."

ROMANTIC GENIUS: THE MODEL MANIC-DEPRESSIVE

The novelist George Sand proclaimed, "Between genius and madness there is often not the thickness of a hair." The Romantics were quite enthusiastic about both genius and madness. Charles Lamb wrote to one of his friends, "Dream not, Coleridge, of having tasted all the grandeur and wildness of fancy till you have gone mad." Lamb had no need to patronize Coleridge, who was an opium addict. Coleridge's fellow Romantics used alcohol, drugs of all kinds, and even hunger, thirst, and illness to silence reason, paralyze conscience, and break down familiar patterns of thought in the search for inspiration. Hallucination was considered the most fertile condition for the artist.

"I should have taken more opium when I wrote it," remarked Friedrich von Schlegel after having written an unsuccessful play. De Quincey's fame derived from his book on the experiences he had under opium. The poet Byron declared: "Man, being reasonable, must therefore get drunk. The best of life is but intoxication." During the part of his life in which he was writing poetry and taking drugs, the poet Rimbaud went about in a state of delusion and hallucination. To him factories appeared to be mosques, and carriage traffic rolled by in the sky. Many of the Romantics complained of severe depressions, so they may have resorted to drugs and alcohol to relieve their suffering as well as to stimulate creativity.

The Romantic concept of genius is a catalogue of manic-depressive symptoms, perhaps derived from such leading manic-depressive Romantics as Rousseau, Byron, and Goethe, as well as from large numbers of Romantics who also had the disorder. According to the Romantic view, there was no genius without the manic-depressive's wide-ranging and unbearably powerful emotions. The writer Goethe lamented, "I am not always in tune for great emotions, and without them I am negligible." The writer Victor Hugo said: "What in fact is a poet? A man who has strong feelings and who expresses them in impassioned words."

Liszt's portrait of his fellow composer Chopin as a Romantic genius may be exaggerated, but it does enumerate some of the manic-depressive symptoms that were expected: "Chopin was . . . of an intensely passionate, an overflowing nature. . . . Every morning he began anew the difficult task of imposing silence upn his raging anger, his whitehot hate, his boundless love, his throbbing pain, and his feverish excitement, and to keep it in suspense by a sort of spiritual ecstasy—an ecstasy into which he plunged in order to . . . find a painful happiness." The writer Carlyle insisted that the genius experience both extremes of mania and depression: "A great soul . . . alternates between the highest height and the lowest depth."

Continuing the tradition with antiquity, the Romantics coupled severe depression with genius. Liszt wrote to his competitor Wagner: "Your greatness is your misery; both are inseparably connected." Romantics, however, also looked for signs of mania such as excitement and hyperactivity. The philosopher Schopenhauer stated, "The lives of men of genius show how often, like lunatics, they are in a state of continuous agitation." Francis Galton, in his book *Hereditary Genius,* identified inspiration with two other manic symptoms, the rapid and copious flow of ideas and willfulness. "If genius means a sense of inspiration, or of rushes of ideas," he wrote, ". . . or of an inordinate and burning desire to accomplish any particular end, it is perilously near to the voices heard by the insane, to their delirious tendencies, or to their monomanias."

Although Romanticism had waned by 1889, its concept of genius held sway. Accordingly, the playwright Anton Chekov believed there could be no genius without intense emotion and two manic symptoms: insomnia and immense productivity. He confessed: "I lack the necessary passion—and therefore talent for literature. . . . The fire in me burns in an even, lethargic flame; it never flares up or roars, which is why I never find myself writing fifty or sixty pages in one night."

The Romantics added to the classical insistence on madness the idea that the genius pays in suffering for exceptional ability. Heine stated, "The history of great men is always a martyrology"; the novelist Flaubert insisted, "There never was . . . a great man who has not been pelted with potatoes or struck with knives." This point of view is a distortion of history. As a rule, extraordinary ability enabled people to rise to a social and economic class higher than that from which they originated, making a corresponding improvement in their lives. The sufferings of the successful were as nothing compared to the sufferings of the vast impoverished majority that they had left behind. Paranoia and the despair generated by depression inspired much of the Romantics' feeling of martyrdom.

TWENTIETH-CENTURY OPINIONS

Several people have espoused the idea that manic-depressives have been disproportionately numerous among people of high achievement. In 1931 Ernst Kretschmer published *The Psychology of Men of Genius,* in which he identified manic-depression not only in men of genius, but also in their families. He said that there was a resemblance between mania and periods of creative productivity, while depression is similar to periods of sterility. He concluded that, while severe states of manic-depresssion were counterproductive, talent could not achieve the level of genius without assistance from the milder states of the illness. In words that foreshadowed recent findings about the biochemistry of manic-depression, Kretschmer said: "The spirit of genius . . . is no free-floating, absolute power, but is strictly bound to the laws of blood chemistry and the endocrine glands."

In 1960, Lord Russell Brain, in *Some Reflections on Genius,* retreated somewhat from Kretschmer's position, stating only that manic-depression and genius were "closely related."

The most recent discussions of manic-depression and creativity have been more limited in that they have not addressed the question of genius or distinguished between the lower and the higher levels of achievement. Nancy Andreasen, who investigated fifteen writers, confirmed Kretschmer's conclusion that severe states of the illness interfered with work or decreased its quality. She found that milder manic and depressive states enhanced specific aspects of creativity. She also attributed Martin Luther's role in history in part to his manias and depressions and concluded, "A variety of artists, writers, statesmen, philosophers, and scientists have suffered from disorders of mood."

In *Moodswings,* Dr. Ronald Fieve commented that mild mania enhances creativity, and that many of the eminent people in various fields have been manic-depressives. In common with Kretschmer, he concluded that mania and depression are similar to creative fertility and sterility but denied that creativity required manic-depression.

GENIUS AND MANIC-DEPRESSION

Kretschmer, Brain, Andreasen, Fieve, and others who have written about creativity and manic-depression have investigated important elements of the relationship between the disorder and genius, but the subject still requires clarification. The central question remains unanswered: Is manic-depression an essential element in genius? Additional research will provide copious examples of creative manic-depressives in various fields. The value of this information is limited: counting case histories can never conclusively determine whether or not manic-depression is present in most cases of creativity and genius. It is not possible to determine which living creative people and geniuses have the disorder, for there is no general agreement on who is creative and who is a genius. Assessing the incidence of the disorder among the dead results in an additional problem: one can never be certain of having all the relevant information about them.

However, given correct premises, logic can lead to information that is inaccessible to statistical methods. We claim that manic-depression is almost indispensable to genius because of the advantages it can supply, and that if there have been geniuses free from manic-depression, they have been a minority.

The premise that manic-depression can provide specific advantages has been supported by Kretschmer, Brain, Andreasen, Fieve, and others. Assume that two people of equal talent and training graduate from a music conservatory with the intention of becoming composers, and that one of them is a manic-depressive. The composer who works harder, has more ideas, is more original, and is also a perfectionist will produce better work. Depression can make one a perfectionist and mania can provide the other assets. If the composer also has tremendous faith in his talent, is more ambitious, more charismatic, and indefatigable at promoting himself, he will be more likely to achieve recognition for his work. Mania will provide all of these characteristics too.

Similar cases can be made for the other fields of creativity. It follows, therefore, that the manic-depressive has a better chance of winning the title of genius than someone of equal talent and training who does not have the disorder. Consequently, having bested their competitors, manic-depressives will constitute the majority of geniuses.

It is conceivable that a few individuals may possess talents so extraordinary that they can successfully compete for recognition as geniuses without the assets provided by manic-depression. For this reason, we believe that manic-depression is almost, but not absolutely, essential in genius; however, it is not the only important element. Manic-depression is no substitute for either talent or training, and it can interfere with both. Not every trained, talented manic-depressive becomes a genius. The degree of talent, the quality of training, and the type of manic-depression are all decisive to the outcome.

The disorder can be a disabling illness that prevents the accomplishment of anything, and it can make life unbearable. The Romantic poet Heine asked: "What is the real reason for the curse which hangs over all men of great genius?" While it does not hang over all of them, there is some truth in the Romantic idea that genius is paid for by suffering. The suffering, however, is caused by manic-depression, not by the possession of talent per se.

The illness has negative as well as positive effects on the lives and works of creative people. It can enhance the talent of one person and destroy the productive capacity of one equally talented. What happens depends on the severity of the illness and the course it follows. The illness can range from states that appear normal to psychotic states that require hospitalization. Manic-depression may also predispose people to abuse alcohol or drugs, frequently with a destructive effect on both their work and lives. A creative life may be cut short by suicide before significant work is done. But, for a few, during some part of their lives, the disorder does confer assets that can lead to incomparable achievement.

Prometheus, according to Greek mythology, stole fire from the gods and brought it to mankind. Zeus responded by chaining him to a mountain, to suffer the punishment of having his liver eternally devoured by an eagle. The Romantics made Prometheus a symbol of the martyrdom of genius. The myth could also symbolize the creative manic-depressive who brings his gifts to mankind at the cost of a painful and tragic life.

DEPRESSION AND THE CREATIVE "BLOCK"

The "blocks" and periods of "inspiration" that creative people experience are not simply, as others have claimed, similar to or parallel to periods of depression and mania: they are the manifestations of depression and mania as they appear in the course of creative work.

In deep depression, intellectual processes become impaired and slowed down. Memory, the capacity to solve problems and to generate ideas, comprehension, the ability to think, and even the ability to form complete sentences eventually become minimal. Until he reaches an extreme state, the depressive is still able to function and can perform what is routine and mechanical, but the quality of creative work done in this state is relatively poor. The depressive feels lethargic, tires quickly, and needs more rest and sleep. He loses the will to work and becomes reluctant to exert any effort whatsoever.

Before depression has diminished the capacity for work, motivation for work may disappear completely. The depressive loses his capacity for enjoyment, including his pleasure in work, and eventually nothing interests him. He becomes overly critical of what he is doing and may abandon it as worthless or may destroy it. Depression often brings despair, which makes one pessimistic about the outcome of whatever work is in progress. The depressive may also develop the conviction that his talent is illusory or that it is gone forever.

Periods of creative sterility are caused by the loss of energy, motivation, and by the decline in intellectual function that depressions can engender in anyone, regardless of occupation or profession.

MANIA AND INSPIRATION

Philosophers, mathematicians, scientists, and others in scholarly professions receive from mania a general heightening of intellectual processes, including the ability to remember whatever they need, an abundance of insights and original ideas, seemingly effortless comprehension, and the capacity to construct and work with complex structures of thought. All of this happens at increasing speed. Mania endows the writer and poet with greater access to their vocabularies, with spontaneous similes and metaphors, with an expanded imagination, and an augmented native eloquence. Manic artists experience increased sensitivity to the visual qualities of the outer world and in their own work. Whatever the sphere of creativity, the manic may benefit from all of these gifts, not only from those particularly helpful in his own metier. Mania also bestows abnormal energy and an insistent urge to do something. In the creative individual this is experienced as a need to work, as the "creative urge."

Manics who are not in creative fields also experience increased energy and a need to do things. They think fast, have better recall, use unusual words, are flooded with ideas, and have intensified sensory perception. However, lacking the talent, training, and motivation of creative people, they do not necessarily focus these assets on a single activity. The creator, on the other hand, uses mania's excitement, energy, speed, and rush of ideas on his work and calls his conditon "inspiration."

RECRUITMENT FOR CREATIVITY

Several studies have shown that people who have achieved eminence in the arts and sciences were often shy, solitary children who felt different from the children around them. In many cases the feeling of being different surfaced before the child displayed any unusual ability. Shyness and aloofness may have been signs of depression. In some cases a bad temper and an egotistical, dominating personality, both indicators of manic-depression, may have added to social difficulties, and the illness in itself would suffice to make the affected child feel different. Whatever the cause, children who shun games and playmates to lead more inward lives, who satisfy their needs in their own activities, develop habits and attitudes that can prepare them for the sacrifices required by creativity.

Unless his gifts have made an early appearance, an adult who chooses to embark on a life of creativity must gamble on possessing sufficient talent before beginning the training for his career. As the painter Chardin noted, "Talent does not declare itself in an instant." Whether or not one takes the gamble may depend on being manic, for it is mania that provides the conviction that one possesses untried talent. Flaubert had what was needed. He speaks of "a great confidence in myself, splendid leaps of the soul, something impetuous in my whole personality."

MAINTAINED BY MANIA

A benign grandiosity, a belief in oneself regardless of the opinions of others, may be required to keep one working long enough to achieve anything. Most creators and intellectual pioneers have periods during which they are not appreciated or understood or financially rewarded for their work. Sometimes these discouraging years last their entire lives. What sustains them amid a storm of criticism or in the silence of neglect may be a grandiose self-image. The poet Stephen Spender noted, "It is evident that a faith in their vocation, mystical in intensity, sustains poets." This is true in other fields as well.

Mania can supply another incentive for pursuing the creative life without external encouragement. Creative work can induce a euphoric mania that, although not reliable, can keep people addicted to their work.

DEDICATED BY DEPRESSION

One is more likely to create great works of art or make significant advances in the sciences if one feels that one's work is the most important thing in one's life. It is not necessary to go as far as Van Gogh, who declared, "My work is my body and soul, and for it I risk my life and my reason." However, without devotion to one's work, the daily time and effort required for high achievement will not be spent. Depression can bring a fear of rejection, difficulties in communicating with people, and a need for solitude that impels people to substitute creative work for the pleasures of a more sociable existence. With few exceptions, only a person wary of love and friendship, as some depressives are, will divert the compelling needs for affection and companionship into creativity. Wagner expressed it thus, "My burning need for love, unslaked in life, I pour into my Art."

The pain caused by depression can reinforce dedication to creativity. When one is too depressed for creative work to induce a manic state, keeping occupied distracts from misery. Therefore, if the depression is not incapacitating, the sufferer may work even when he does not feel like it and believes the results will be worthless, so long as he can thereby reduce his suffering. He may come to fear leisure and develop an emotional dependence on working that will not let him rest. The composer Tchaikovsky claimed "Without work life has no meaning for me" and called music "a true friend, refuge and comforter for whose sake life is worth living." Creativity may feed on desperation.

Depression can also keep the creative person from activities that interfere with work. The painter Vasari noted, "He who takes the study of art should flee the company of men." Most creative work requires solitude, and cooperative efforts, such as those in the performing arts and some sciences, are not social occasions. The gregarious creator runs a risk: he may spend too much time and energy enjoying himself with his friends while neglecting his work. It is not unusual for manic-depressives, depressed and hard working as unknowns, to lose their incentive when success makes them manic. Mania can induce too much sociability, so that the energy mania brings is spent on amusement. These are the creative people whose productivity declines when fame and friends arrive.

THE DRIVE TO EXCEL

The poet Alexander Pope said, "Self-confidence is the first requisite to great undertakings"—optimism is perhaps the second. The manic, well endowed with both, is also blind to difficulties or, if he is aware of them, sees them as a challenge. The painter Chardin remarked: "He who has not felt the difficulties of his art does nothing that counts." Sensible people do not even consider undertaking the complex and difficult projects that manics conceive and execute. Very often the sensible people are right but occasionally the manic accomplishes what seemed impossible, and mankind takes a leap forward. Mania makes people headstrong, rebellious, and daring. When they are creative also, they make innovations that advance civilization. The genius often defies authority and tradition, blazing a new trail for more reasonable people to follow.

Competitiveness is often part of the manic character and can motivate the creative individual to take on work of major importance, though it is dauntingly difficult. The mathematician Morris Kline, speaking of his profession, attests to the role of competitiveness in creation: "I think that in research you want to satisfy your personal ego. You want to know that you did it before the other fellow. . . . The history of conflicts and arguments among mathematicians' dissension about priority of creation . . . is enormous."

The grandiosity of the manic, so long as it does not destroy his critical judgment, drives him to attempt to surpass not only others', but also his own, past achievements. Claims such as Gibbons's "I am the greatest historian that ever lived" are also demands on oneself to remain the best throughout one's life. No one with an ego of that size willingly slackens his effort and allows others to rise above him.

Depression makes different contributions to the pursuit of excellence. When it is not severe enough to reduce intellectual functions, it can improve creative work. It supplies the critical judgment needed to correct the extravagances of mania. It also promotes the calm, patient, disciplined effort, the revision and polishing, that is an essential ingredient in most kinds of creative work.

The novelist I. B. Singer states: "Nobody could write without suffering. . . . Suffering is almost identical with life itself." Depression can give emotional depth to an artist's work and provide him with themes that speak to the experience of all mankind. It may compel him to try, through art, to transcend the evils of the human condition and the terrors of death.

Many of the questions that philosophers address are inspired by the depressive's need to understand the reasons for his own suffering. Depression leads people to ask ultimate questions about life, death, good, evil, the nature of man, of the universe, and of God. The mutable moods, perceptions, and opinions of the manic-depressive may lead him to philosophy in order to determine for himself what is real. His yearning for a stable, reliable way of interpreting reality may lead him into science and mathematics.

EVIDENCE FROM EXPERIENCE

The following chapter presents the most salient facts about manic-depression. The rest of the book, save for the final two chapters, examines the impact that manic-depression has had on the lives of geniuses by looking into their lives. The protagonists express their own versions of events; those who best knew these luminaries add more objective points of view.

We have selected as subjects men who were considered geniuses during their lifetimes and/or posthumously. They represent a variety of national origins, cultural and economic backgrounds, periods, fields, and experiences of manic-depression. Our discussion uses exclusively masculine pronouns for simplicity's sake. Women were not included among our subjects only because of the scarcity of biographical information about creative women, compared to that generally available about such men.

AUGMENTING CREATIVITY

Problems in the lives of creative people can diminish both their productivity and the quality of their work. The biographical material available on European artists since the Renaissance indicates that their lives were filled with suffering and misfortune that in great part resulted from their emotional difficulties. There is no indication that artists differ in this respect from other creative people. Our concluding chapter, "Augmenting Genius," addresses the internal problems that limit the potential of creative people.

2

Manic-Depression

The earliest mention of mood disorder of which we have record is from classical Greece. Hippocrates, in the fifth century B.C., was aware of both mania and depression as medical problems, and he recognized their chronicity, but he did not know that they are phases of the same illness. In the second century B.C., Areteus, an eminent Greek physician like Hippocrates, recognized that mania and depression could alternate in the same person. He described the personality types that accompany the moods: the self-sacrificing, pious, guilt-haunted sufferer of depression; the gay, obstreperous, rash bon vivant of mania. After Areteus the concept of manic-depression disappeared from medical writings until the nineteenth century, when French psychiatrists reported the existence of a cyclical disorder of mood. The man who formally described the illness and gave it the term "manic-depressive insanity" was Emil Kraepelin, a German psychiatrist. In his *Lehrbuch der Psychiatrie,* published in 1889, Kraepelin provided an almost-complete description of the moods, behavior, and thought patterns of manic-depressives. The novel data on manic-depression that have appeared since Kraepelin are the sociological, biochemical, and pharmacological studies of the past three decades.

The American Psychiatric Association's diagnostic and statistical manual of mental disorders describes manic episodes as follows: "The essential feature is a distinct period when the predominant mood is either elevated, expansive or irritable and when there are associated symptoms of the manic syndrome. These symptoms include hyperactivity, pressure of speech, flight of ideas, inflated self-esteem, decreased need for sleep, distractibility, and excessive involvement in activities that have a high potential for painful consequences,

19

which are not recognized." In depressive episodes, by contrast, "The essential feature is either a dysphoric mood, usually depression, or loss of interest or pleasure in almost all usual activities and pastimes. This disturbance is prominent, relatively persistent, and associated with other symptoms of the depressive syndrome. These symptoms include appetite disturbance, change in weight, sleep disturbance, psychomotor agitation or retardation, decreased energy, feelings of worthlessness or guilt, difficulty concentrating or thinking, and thoughts of death or suicide or suicidal attempts."

Mild or moderate forms of manic-depression may imperceptibly shade into normalcy and, as such, are often not recognized by the layman. Paradoxically, when the illness is so severe that it reaches medical attention, it is often misdiagnosed as schizophrenia because of the dogma that catatonia, hallucinations, and delusions, particularly paranoid delusions, are diagnostic of schizophrenia. Consequently, many manic-depressives have been deprived of the striking benefits that antidepressants and lithium can offer.

A factor that has often interfered with the identification of manic-depressives is that culture and contemporary values strongly influence the way that people evaluate and judge behavior. Thus, behavior that is regarded as deviant in one era may not only be tolerated, but even extolled, in another. In contemporary western society hallucinations are held to reflect illness, but some primitive societies continue to value the ability to hallucinate. Social role imposes yet another influence on the perception of behavior. As in the case of Napoleon, manic behavior can propel an individual to a great military career, but the self-aggrandizement and disregard for others that occur in a manic can severely handicap a physician, a teacher, or an attorney.

A psychiatric text never describes manic-depression in terms of a logical exposition of syndromes: each manic-depressive has a unique personality and history. However, similarities and patterns are recognizable in the lives and personalities of all manic-depressives. The emotional manifestations of manic-depression run the gamut of human experience and are primarily distinguished from the emotions of normal states when they are inappropriate and/or unusual in intensity and/or duration. Rage, anxiety, fear, sorrow, joy, excitement, jealousy, sexual passion, ambition, discouragement, boredom, inspiration: this is only a partial list of the intense feelings manic-depressives may endure. Manic-depressive behavior is similarly inappropriate to the circumstances in which it occurs, and it also ranges over the entire spectrum of normality. In extreme stages the illness passes far beyond the normal to include such pathological acts as self-mutilation, random violence, and suicide. Manic-depressives may enter into the realm of delusion and express abnormal thoughts and beliefs. Hallucinations may occur in both the manic and depressive states.

The characters and personalities of manic-depressives generally fall within the range that is considered normal or, at worst, somewhat eccentric. Most manic-depressives have periods of normalcy, and some manage their lives so that they have little contact with people outside of those periods. Many, particularly those suffering from milder forms, do not realize that they have the disorder. Most manic-depressives never become noticeably bizarre nor do they suffer enough, or trouble those around them sufficiently, to require hospitalization. It is not uncommon for a manic-depressive to react with astonishment at learning of the diagnosis, and with outrage when lithium therapy is recommended.

Attacks of both mania and depression can begin gradually, over days or weeks, or can erupt precipitately. Changes in the severity of an attack, for better or worse, may occur slowly or suddenly. Mood cycles can alternate between mania and depression every twenty-four or forty-eight hours, but such regularity is rare. Some people, like Tolstoy, have seasonal variations of mood, while others have annual cycles. Women may have episodes of depression and mania synchronized with their menstrual cycle. Manic and depressive spells range in duration from a few hours, days, or weeks, to as long as fourteen years.

Depression is not always followed by mania, nor mania by depression. Periods of normalcy may intervene, and the duration of remission is as unpredictable as the lengths of mania and depression. Episodes of mania and depression generally alternate; depressions may be long and intense, with manias brief and insignificant, or more rarely, the reverse may be true. Every conceivable variation between the two extremes can occur. A common pattern is a period of normal mood, followed by mild or severe depression that changes into full-blown mania, followed by depression, and then normalcy. Or, there might be several successive attacks of one kind, with one of the opposite type intervening at some point. Within an attack of depression there may occur a sudden interlude of mania. Patients who are in apparent remission may still be troubled by symptoms: poor judgment, insomnia, irritability, and difficulty in concentrating. Some patients never feel completely well between their attacks, though their symptoms may not be obvious. Some episodes of mania and depression appear to be triggered by events; in many cases episodes occur "out of the blue," with no obvious precipitant. When mania appears after depression, it is frequently mistaken for recovery because all the symptoms of depression vanish: the patient loses his melancholy and glows with vitality; his anxiety and pessimism change into optimism and gaiety. Having been listless, he is now charged with energy and ready to take on the world.

Less severe forms of mania are termed hypomania. The term cyclothymia is applied to individuals who have mood swings that are of reduced intensity compared with those of manic-depressives. In its milder forms, hypomania is difficult to distinguish from normal happiness and excitement. Mild depression is equally misleading because it can be initiated by such antecedents as infectious diseases and endocrine disorders. Tchaikovsky was one of the many manic-depressives who think that their depressions are some kind of illness or character defect, and that their manic periods are simply those times when they are well and functioning at their best.

There is no reliable way to predict who will develop manic-depression. The only indicator of high risk is knowledge of a blood relative who has mood swings or is a known manic-depressive—this imposes on an individual a fifteen times greater-than-average chance of becoming manic-depressive. The mode of inheritance is not simple, and no formula can predict who will also be affected in a family with a manic-depressive history. Nonaffected people also appear in manic-depressive families, and the disorder can skip a generation.

Alonzo Graves, a manic-depressive patient who wrote about his life and his manic-depressive episodes, was born into a family in which everyone was affected to some degree, which is not uncommon. According to Graves's description, his father is typical of the functioning manic-depressive who never sees a doctor for his illness and is never diagnosed as sick: "He had literally demonic energy." "Repose, relaxation, reflection were alike foreign to his temperament." "He would imagine all the desirable results to be attained in advance from a new embarkation, and seemed to wear out its attraction in a few months, and to be tormented with the necessity of getting clear of it." Graves lists fifteen separate financial enterprises undertaken by his father. They range from raising Shetland ponies, to mining, to a bicycle repair shop; only one of these ventures broke even. Graves's father was also "a bad judge of character," and "he likewise surrendered utterly to every woman who saw fit to focus upon him." He had many brief depressions or "fits of discouragement." However, somewhat out of character for a manic, he spent little care and money on his own appearance.

Graves's mother had fits of "hysteria" and spent most of her time in bed with imaginary heart disease after her oldest son died. His older sister married a man who had "nervous breakdowns" and she, a gifted musician with a talent for languages, attempted suicide and was hospitalized after the birth of her first child. The sister had a manic personality: "exceptionally energetic, socially capable and resourceful in her professional activities, being in addition notably self-willed and independent. She was inclined to talkativeness, and had a disposition to dominate her younger brother and sister." Graves's younger sister had a series of hospitalizations after the birth of her first child and had delusions of receiving "communications from some esoteric other-world source."

The families of manic-depressives are more likely to have members who are suicidal, addicted to alcohol and other drugs, or compulsive gamblers than other families. These behaviors are often simply the most obvious expression of underlying manic-depression. The alcoholic and gambling relatives often show the same symptoms that occur in pure manic-depressives, with mood variations that in some cases fit the rhythm of their alcoholic binges, or the rhythm of their gambling gains and losses. Some manic-depressives use alcohol to relieve chronic depression; others use alcohol as a sedative during manic attacks or drink during mania to release their inhibitions, to prolong euphoria, or simply to celebrate. In the nineteenth century alcohol was the sole remedy for mood swings; in this century, many mood-altering drugs have become available. Alcoholism, gambling, and the unpredictable variations of mood that go with them often cause severe marital problems and family chaos. Manic-depression itself is a significant cause of marital and family conflict.

The successful use of lithium carbonate and antidepressants in treating both phases of manic-depressive disorder has directed research into the biochemical causes of depression and mania. It now appears that several sets of chemical control systems in the central nervous system are involved in regulating mood. Initially, a disturbance in catecholamine metabolism was held to be the key factor in causing mania and depression, but it is now suspected that prostaglandins, cyclic nucleotides, and calcium also play critical roles.

HYPOMANIA

The distinction between hypomania and mania is essentially quantitative. The two states share many symptoms in common, but in mania the symptoms are more intense, the patient is not amenable to reason, and psychotic symptoms such as delusions or hallucinations are usually present. When hypomania is integrated into the personality, rather than occurring in discrete episodes, the individual is said to have a hypomanic temperament or personality.

Hypomania is often a social and financial asset. Some hypomanics work long, hard, and intensely because they cannot rest and so get credit for their "diligence." Since they think and react at high speed, they appear clever and astonish people with their work output. Neither setbacks nor disappointments slow them down for long. Their infectious good spirits, friendliness, and lively interest in others may make them popular.

Both businessmen and people in the arts can profit from the hypomania's good memory for detail, but this vanishes in acuter stages when distractibility makes the hypomanic absentminded. The hypomanic is self-indulgent, elated, euphoric, or irritable, and has moderate pressure of speech and heightened activity. He may be talkative to the point of betraying tightly guarded secrets. He is often the picture of good health and may radiate well-being. Unlike the acute manic, the hypomanic remains amenable to reason.

Hypomania can foster a lively attention to everything. Some hypomanics react rapidly and see connections between ideas that others do not notice. This is of special value to poets, humorists, entrepreneurs, inventors, scientists, and others whose work requires creativity or diagnostic acuity. Hypomanics have a facility for telling jokes and making witty remarks. They are cheerful, eager, and undaunted by big, difficult projects.

But all is not roses. The hypomanic individual, driven by impulse, insists on getting his needs or desires satisfied immediately and has a "will of iron." Hypomania loosens the bonds of self-restraint, and discipline surrenders to spontaneity. Good manners give way and the hypomanic may become known for his lack of conventionality. Hypomanics tend to be sloppy, rushed in their work and uncritical about the results. Hypomanics do mainly what they like and tend to neglect boring or unpleasant duties. Their opinions can vary from one extreme to another without their knowing it, for they often forget what they thought before. They may impress people as being inconstant and unreliable; often there is not much continuity in their activity. They may flit from thing to thing, person to person, and may abandon what they are doing because they lack the patience to finish it, or because something more attractive has come along. Some hypomanics yearn for variety and love change. They are in the vanguard of many new movements—the first to join and the first to leave. Their restlessness and quick satiation with situations or projects may cause them to pursue novelty, be it by changing jobs, sexual partners, or domiciles. This may rob them of the recognition that their accomplishments deserve. Sometimes they fail by taking on too many things at the same time, yet they rarely learn from their failures.

Some hypomanics cannot sit still and may do a lot of pacing. This kind of behavior is suitable to some businessmen and professionals, and goes unnoticed in them, but it is detrimental to any pursuit that requires prolonged concentration. Some hypomanics have sufficient self-control to overcome the flux of their impulses and ideas. They are able to accomplish structured and coherent work despite their inner and outer distractions. Paranoid hypomanics, by contrast, are often involved in strings of lawsuits. They resent being admonished, corrected, or given orders and may respond with anger. They ignore regulations and defy those who have authority or power over them.

Although an infectious gaiety is diagnostic of hypomania, the condition is more enjoyable to the person living in it than to those living with it. The hypomanic is not always pleasant company. He can be extremely touchy. The least slight to his ego, the smallest frustration, can suddenly end his good humor and make him very disagreeable. In his good moods he is often insensitive to the opinions of his listeners and to his effect on them. Hypomanics often behave with inappropriate familiarity toward strangers and toward superiors. They appear to make friends easily and are given to both self-revelation and enticing revelations out of others. The hypomanic tries to win large amounts of admiration, and his interest in others and in the world at large is frequently limited to how much he can control them and profit from them; his altruism is often a front for self-display. Hypomanics can be skilled at manipulating the self-esteem of others and may have an uncanny knack of sensing the vulnerabilities and conflicts within a group. Their arrogance and self-righteousness may prompt them to meddle and to dominate. Insight into their own condition is often almost nonexistent: how can anyone who feels so marvelous be aberrant in any way? Although they may see themselves as paragons, some are ruthless and lie easily. Many high-ranking executives and people successful in politics are hypomanics. Their drive, imagination, charisma, and other hypomanic virtues are known, their problems hidden.

Some people would have no friends at all if they did not have hypomanic periods. The hypomanic commonly becomes extremely sociable and insists upon being in the company of others. John Constance, a manic-depressive, describes how it feels to be this way and, as many hypomanics do with their symptoms, makes it appear both rational and admirable:

> The sense of communion extends to all fellow creatures with whom I come in contact; it is not merely ideal or imaginative but has a practical effect on my conduct. Thus when in the manic state I have no objection to being more or less herded together—as is inevitable in Public Mental hospitals—with men of all classes and conditions. Class barriers cease to have any existence or meaning. Sometimes, it is true, I get cross with one or the other of my fellow patients, but I find no difficulty in making up the quarrel almost at once. I seem to be filled with a sense of universal benevolence and constantly bear in mind the text "Love your enemies."

Rebelliousness, distractibility, and lack of self-discipline may create trouble in school for hypomanic children. These children are often disorderly and may become ringleaders of the disaffected, a role that they may continue as adults. Playing truant, having to change schools, and failing to study and pass examinations are characteristic of hypomanic children. The most gifted end up educating themselves in bursts and snatches. Acute perception notwithstanding, their learning is patchy, their logic is slipshod, and those who are not highly gifted develop a rather shallow understanding of the world. They cast judgments too quickly, are too impatient to wait for the results of their efforts, and will impulsively tear down what they or others took great pains to build.

In comparing one hypomanic with another, it may be hard to believe that they are suffering from the same illness. One will be given to profanity, while another gives out pictures of saints. One will become notorious for his sexual excesses, while another will crusade to clear the streets of prostitutes. One will be witty, another quarrelsome; one will travel, another indulge in shopping sprees; one be seductive, another jealous.

MANIA

If you receive a long-distance phone call in the middle of the night from someone who has nothing important to say and is bubbling over with good humor when there is nothing to laugh about, you should suspect that your caller is manic. Insomnia, euphoria, sociability, and pressure of speech, assisted by impulsiveness, produced the phone call. The manic has an intense need to communicate, primarily by talking, which he will do even if alone or too hoarse to be heard. He constantly interrupts others and becomes irritated if they insist on talking. He feels that he cannot stop from saying everything that pops into his head, and he cannot control his thoughts. This may create embarrassing situations. Manics are extravagant not only in the amount of their verbalization, but also in its style, which can be showy, ostentatious, conspicuous, grandiloquent, bombastic, and contain abstruse phraseology: a veritable cornucopia of foreign words and phrases; spectacular metaphors; strings of words and nouns and adjectives; a plethora of synonymous terms; and a virulent rash of exclamation points!!! Speech may be both loud and rapid. Manic musicians tend to play louder and faster than when their mood is deflated. Mania also triggers floods of letters, and the writing of fiction, articles, and diaries.

The heightened sexuality of some manics is expressed in a variety of behaviors. Some people merely experience arousal. Others, particularly women, believe that they are in love with or are loved by individuals who may be indifferent or hostile, total strangers, or famous people. Some manics experience and may act out incestuous impulses, while others just think and talk about sex excessively. The manic may increase his sexual activity to the point of promiscuity, and some heterosexuals become homosexual during mania. In milder cases manics may believe themselves to be loved by or in love with some likely individual and disbelieve it during depression. It is not always possible for an observer to find out which belief is delusional.

One of the earliest symptoms of mania, and one of the last to leave, is the flight of ideas that increases in severity with the manic's total disintegration. The manic has difficulty concentrating and cannot keep his mind on one thing. Too many extraneous stimuli bombard him and he cannot shut them out, even as his own disordered thoughts crowd him, demanding attention. The manic's conversation jumps from topic to topic without much logical sequence, and he is not able to follow a train of thought. Often he is incapable of narrating any fairly complicated event, unless he is brought back to the subject by interruptions and questions. Manic speech is called "circumstantial" because it repeatedly talks around the point, rather than logically developing an argument.

In mania there is an increase in bodily as well as in mental activity, restlessness, and a need to be on the move and doing things. To keep still is as difficult as it is for a squirmy child. The manic is impatient and finds confinement and restraint intolerable. He wants to work, though he may be too mentally disorganized to work effectively. He can work much longer than normally without feeling any fatigue, and he will also have little awareness of other forms of physical discomfort: heat, cold, hunger, thirst, or pain.

The manic sleeps very little but is slower to feel the effects of insomnia than others. John Constance enjoyed his manic insomnia. "For several weeks I believe I did not sleep more than two or three hours a night. Such was my state of elation, however, that all signs of fatigue were entirely absent; and the sustained and abnormal mental and physical activity in which I then indulged has left on my memory no other than a series of very pleasant impressions." Perhaps he would have felt differently if he suffered the ordeal of a patient who did not sleep for seven nights running and remained sleepless for two more nights after admission to the hospital. Soporifics may have no effect on manic insomnia, depending on its degree of severity.

In the early phases of the disorder, the manic may enjoy food and gain weight. This stops as his metabolic expenditure increases, and when it outstrips his consumption, he starts to lose weight. At that time he may be indifferent to food, too excited to eat much, or fail to notice that he has missed meals.

Mania is noted for quick changes of mood. In the blink of an eye the manic may become tearful or angry. A change to irritability is the most common departure from euphoria. Opposition to the manic's wishes or opinions, pressure to do something he does not want to do, or even mild criticism can turn his good humor into rage. The irritable manic is dissatisfied, intolerant, faultfinding, and prone to violent outbursts of rage. He may destroy objects and beat his wife and children. The angry manic is out of control and cannot restrain the expression of his hostility and rage, no matter how much he may regret it later. Enraged manics may threaten homicide or commit it.

PSYCHOTIC OR DELUSIONAL MANIA

The delusional manic usually shows some degree of grandiosity, ranging from simple overconfidence, to the complex delusions of acute mania in which the individual believes himself to be some famous person or religious figure. The manic may repel people or encourage them to worship him and accept his domination, as Johnson did of Boswell. The manic may believe that he was chosen by God or Fate and so predestined to accomplish some historic or superhuman mission. More commonly, the manic's overestimation of his own importance, capacities, and good qualities has disastrous consequences for himself and those who naively believe him and are foolish enough to depend on him. Grandiose people make good salesmen, swindlers, and demagogues. The grandiose delusions may take on religous overtones: the manic may believe that he can drive out the devil or has a divine mission to rid the earth of drug addiction. He may be convinced that the pope is coming to visit him or that he is going to father the Messiah. The paranoid delusions of a manic frequently have a grandiose tinge: he may be convinced that *his* shortwave radio is monitored by the KGB or that UFOs have *his* house under surveillance.

Along with grandiosity some manics experience "ideas of reference." Manics may believe that many people are interested in them, that events have something to do with them when there is no connection, that people's remarks refer to them when the subject is something else, even that statements about them appear in books written by people who never heard them. Clifford Beers gave his "ideas of reference" a religious coloration: "I now interpreted the most trifling incidents as messages from God."

When a manic develops delusions and visual or auditory hallucinations, severe confusion, and only a dim awareness of reality, he is said to have acute mania or manic psychosis. In this state he is subject to many manic emotional states and conditions, and capable of being ecstatic, erotic, anxious, enraged, even despairing. Removed from any kind of stimulation, he may be briefly quiet and then scream when addressed. Flight of ideas becomes a hurricane of simultaneous thoughts and impulses. The acute manic may pray, do senseless rhyming, or show the waxy flexibility of catatonia. Overactivity in hypomania becomes devastating in acute mania. The acute manic may disrupt a performance, sing or scream on the streets, or give military salutes. The acute manic generally makes trouble. He cannot be reasoned with, will not accept the authority of another, and is prone to violence. The manic occasionally turns violence against his own body. Manics may inadvertently hurt themselves because of their poor judgment and insensitivity to pain. They may subject themselves to heat prostration, sunburn, or frostbite and may risk their lives for trivial objectives. In time of war this is mistaken for courage.

DEPRESSION

Depression refers to a constellation of symptoms and behaviors that develop either "out of the blue" or in response to stress, usually in the form of a major loss. When symptoms of depression are chronically woven into the personality, the person is said to have a depressive personality. A person with a depressive personality is more susceptible to acute depression than a person with a normal personality, although the latter is by no means immune.

The depressive personality, or chronic depressive, is the antithesis of the manic personality. He tends to be quiet and reserved and likes to remain in the background. He cannot enjoy life to its fullest and is given to perceiving events and people in a negative light. He tends to be pessimistic, easily moved to tears, lacking in self-assertiveness, conscientious, long-suffering, shy, timid, and anxious. He avoids rather than participates.

MILD STATES

Depression, like mania, runs the gamut, from mild states that are often mistaken for fatigue, laziness, or the onset of a physical illness, to psychotic states in which the depressive enters either a state of devastating anguish or catatonic stupor. The earliest stage of depression may be devoid of any feeling of sadness. Often the first change depressives notice as they cross the border into depression is some difficulty making choices or decisions. They may feel some reluctance to do anything unfamiliar or tiring. The thought of visiting or entertaining friends loses its appeal, and they would rather spend evenings at home than go out. They notice that their work is boring and the people at work irritating. They realize that happiness is passing them by, that they lead a monotonous existence, but no remedy appears attractive. The people they care about seem to be losing their importance. As they recede into indifference, it is difficult to have any meaningful communication with them. The past may seem much better than the wearisome present, and the future seems to hold no promise. Depressives begin to wonder if they are capable of meeting people's expectations and demands. Every little thing seems to go wrong, and there is more to worry about every day. These fretful interpretations of reality grow darker and more anguished as depression intensifies and sadness becomes a dominant feeling.

SEVERE STATES

The appearance of a depressive is quite different from both his normal and his manic self. Facial musculature often loses its tone and the corners of the mouth may turn downward. The eyes are dull, the skin may be dry and rough, and nail growth often stops. In contrast to the youthful appearance of the manic, the depressive may look prematurely old. Depressives frequently lose their interest in and motivation for grooming and may wear the same garment day in and day out.

Depressed mood is often associated with a variety of physiological maladies, and many depressives are burdened with an assortment of ailments ranging from migraine, colitis, and allergies, to endocrine disorders and menstrual disturbances. They often lack energy and stamina. With all of this cast against a background of worry and pessimism, it is easy for depressives to become hypochondriacal, and many of them do.

Many depressives experience a daily fluctuation of mood in which depression is most intense during the early part of the day with some improvement occurring in the evening, or vice versa. Depression can impede insight and judgment, and it is not uncommon for depressives to deny that they are ill and blame their difficulties on stress, marriage, job, or children.

Most depressives experience some degree of melancholia, and many are easily moved to tears. Some can weep for hours over minor disappointments. The depressive may feel as though life is slipping away. Depression robs one of interest in events, in work, in other people. Hobbies, whatever else was once amusing, are now boring or meaningless. The withdrawn depressive no longer wants to see friends. He has nothing to say to them, and he is afraid for them to see him as he is. Often the depressive's libido diminishes; he has no appetite for life, no motivation, is incapable of enthusiasm, and sinks into himself. Only solitude is safe.

Attacks of anxiety and apprehension are often a component of depression and may precede it. Anxiety may be experienced emotionally as worry, apprehension, or fearfulness; physical manifestations of anxiety may take the form of diarrhea, sweating, or palpitations. Depressive anxiety often manifests itself as phobias, which are unfounded fears of situations, people, places, or animals. Panic is the most extreme form of depressive anxiety. Some anxious depressives experience a feeling of unreality about themselves or about the outside world. The former condition is termed depersonalization, the latter derealization.

The anxious depressive worries incessantly about what has occurred in the past, what is currently occurring, and what is likely to occur in the future. He is afraid to test himself in novel situations, and he damages his career and social prospects by his inability to assert himself and by his tendency to avoid conflict and be passive. He tries to please, to be liked, and is easily hurt when rejected. The hostile depressive may be anxious, but his depression brings out a critical, judgmental, morally superior view of his fellow man. He is petty and vengeful, bears grudges, and is critical of virtually everybody and everything.

"Agitated" depression is characterized by agitation and insomnia, while "retarded" depression is marked by slowed mental and physical processes and increased sleeping. The insomnia of the agitated depressive appears in the form of difficulty in falling asleep, frequent awakening during the night, waking early in the morning without being able to resume sleeping, or all of the above. The wakeful nights of agitated depressives are often haunted by anguished thoughts and ruminations about real or imagined misdeeds in their past, or by frightening, discouraging apprehensions about the future.

In retarded depression the sufferer usually has trouble concentrating; his thinking lacks clarity and it begins to slow down. The combination of lack of confidence and difficulty in concentrating can saddle the depressive with yet one more deficit: indecisiveness. Memory loss, particularly of recent events, is common in depression. Sometimes mental inefficiency and failure at familiar tasks such as reading precede all other symptoms of depression. Speech slows down, and the voice may lose expression, even drop in pitch. Sentences may be left unfinished and answers may come after some delay. Here the depressive is at the opposite pole from the manic, whose "flight of ideas" crowds his mind with racing thoughts. The depressive may most acutely notice his thinking disability in company, when he is unable to contribute to conversation because his brain is, quite literally, empty of thoughts. This blankness is called "poverty of ideas."

Alonzo Graves gives the following "Evidence of mental deterioration in Myself" in his account of a retarded depression.

> My own tests of the loss of capacity are these: Concentration upon written matter, habitual in former occupation, is relatively poor. . . . In conversation there is a lapse of attention. . . . I note that my memory is only with ease capable of carrying a single date, a single set of symbols, a single name. . . . Formerly I could carry a full set of familiar material, I believe. . . . I am clumsy, slow, and liable to come to full stops in the performance of the most mediocre household duties, unsure of the next step, and at the opposite of deftness in technique.
>
> My impression is that of slowed mental operation. Underlying the process, a matter of volition, is a distaste for activity, the symptoms of which are submission to the will of others in details of living, so long as others choose to exert will, and a basic distaste for the effort of continuing life on any plane that is open to me.

When depression is severe, the sufferer may be unable to care for himself, conduct his daily business, or perform simple household tasks. His helplessness may be coupled with expectations that others take over his responsibilities. Self-esteem is usually lowered in depression, along with self-confidence.

Depression ruins many lives. It saps energy, interferes with sleep, destroys the capacity to experience pleasure, and often disrupts concentration and memory. For those who do not respond to pharmacological treatment, it can be a debilitating disorder. The obvious hazards of depression include alcoholism, drug addiction, and suicide. Less obvious, but of increasing interest to researchers, is the frequent coexistence of depression and defective immune function.

Of all the factors that contribute to suicidality, depression is by far the most potent. Freedom from physical illness, a supportive home environment, and absence of alcoholism are some of the factors that militate against suicidality, while recent loss, a family history of suicide, and a hostile temperament militate for it. Among depressives, the hostile, agitated, delusional depressive carries the greatest risk for suicide.

Although depression and mania are each other's antitheses in most respects, they do have some symptoms in common. Like mania, depression that does not end with suicide is often self-limiting. In both mania and depression there is difficulty in concentrating and work is done less efficiently than normally. In both conditions insomnia, anxiety, agitation, irritability, and rages can occur. In extreme states of both, paranoia, delusions, hallucinations, and catatonic stupor may emerge. Both mania and depression are variable in development, intensity, duration, and groupings of symptoms, with no individual having all the symptoms of either state at any time.

PSYCHOTIC OR DELUSIONAL DEPRESSION

In depression thinking often takes on a negative hue. Positive thoughts about one's self, the outside world, and the future change to despair about everything. Out of the negativity may emerge unrealistic and unshakable beliefs that are termed depressive delusions. Many depressives develop the delusion of being fatally ill. Even in their misery death may be terrifying; to others who passively accept its imminence, it is an appropriate punishment. Some depressives have a conviction, which they cannot explain, that death is near, though the belief vanishes as the mood improves. The depressive may conclude that he is in desperate financial straits despite evidence of comfortable circumstances and become afraid to spend money, even for necessities. Delusions of sin and guilt can augment the misery of depressives. They may see themselves as failures who not only did evil, but omitted to do good, and carry a deep and unrelenting feeling of being flawed or tainted, or unfit to tread the earth with the rest of humanity. Delusional depressives may think of themselves as "bad" or "beneath contempt." Some groundlessly accuse themselves of ingratitude to parents, neglect of children, betrayal of God, responsibility for a war, or the most reprehensible sexual behavior. Sufferers bearing such convictions of sin and guilt may feel that only extreme punishment might cleanse them.

Hypochondriacal delusions persuade the depressive that his occasional headaches are caused by brain cancer, or that a rash must indicate the presence of syphilis. The depressive who believes that his bowels are rotting and that his brain is turning into dust is experiencing somatic delusions. Hallucinations can merge with somatic delusions, and the psychotic depressive may believe that parts of his body disintegrate, rot, and fall off, or change grotesquely.

Some delusional depressives experience negative ideas of reference. They feel that certain events, even distant ones, are somehow aimed against them. Thus, the fact that a neighbor wears a tie every day may, through a series of inferences, be interpreted as revealing the neighbor's malevolent intentions. Ideas of reference may be part of the general hopelessness or may have paranoid aspects. Some depressives feel that specific people or groups are out to get them or, if they develop a negative grandiosity, attribute all of life's disappointments to persecution by God.

In the most extreme forms of depression, there is no longer any question that something terrible is happening. Not only do all the symptoms of depression intensify to an unendurable degree, but hallucinations, catatonic stupor, and suicidal behavior may also appear. If the sufferer falls into stupor, his awareness of his environment becomes vague and his speech, if any, becomes confused. In catatonic stupor the patient may retain an uncomfortable attitude because it may not be possible for him to change position. Some patients have relentless, petrifying hallucinations. Here is Clifford Beers's descent into hallucination: "A crumpled pillow is quite an ordinary everyday object, is it not? One looks at it and thinks no more about it. So is a washing rag, or a towel tumbled on the floor, or the creases on the side of the bed. Yet they can suggest shapes of the utmost horror to the mind obsessed by fear. Gradually my eyes began to distinguish such shapes, until eventually, whichever way I turned, I could see nothing but devils waiting to torment me, devils which seemed infinitely more real than material objects in which I saw them." Some people hear the voices of the dead, some see them too. Such hallucinations can bring on violence. This is what George Sand saw Alfred de Musset go through while they were in Venice:

> Once, three months ago, he was as though mad for a whole night, as the result of great anxiety. He imagined he saw phantoms around him, and cried out in fear and horror. Now he is always uneasy, and this morning he hardly knows what he says, or what he does. He weeps, complains of a trouble without name or cause, wants his own country, and says that he is near death or madness. [The following day she writes:] Last night was horrible. Six hours of such violent frenzy that, in spite of two robust men, he ran naked up and down the room. Cries, songs, shouts, convulsions. Oh! my God! what a sight! He nearly strangled me by kissing me. The two men could not make him let go the collar of my dress!

ON BEING A MANIC-DEPRESSIVE

Many of the contrasting symptoms of mania and depression often exist in the same person, either alternating or in combination, with either manic or depressive characteristics predominating. In some manic-depressives such as Howard Hughes, manic grandiosity and depressive withdrawal from society coexist; in others there is a combination of depressive pessimism with manic impulsivity.

Mood changes may be beneficial. Mild depression may foster empathy, sensitivity, and the discipline needed for work; mild hypomania can be conducive to both productivity and creativity.

Artists may undergo changes of moods depending on where they are in their projects. George Elliot and Charles Dickens began their novels in states of depression that lifted as the books progressed. Dickens became manic upon finishing his books but Elliot apparently did not. Artists, writers, and composers who experience diurnal variations of mood and have a choice of working hours learn to use their best hours for their creative work. Beethoven conceived his compositions during summer highs and did the more mechanical work of orchestration during winter lows.

On the whole, however, extreme mood changes are disruptive to the life of the manic-depressive and distressing for those who try to live with him. When this is compounded with the bizarre things he does, some problems can arise and his life can rapidly deteriorate. We will see this process at work in the lives of our subjects. More than most, the manic-depressive is the creator of his own disasters—and the one least able to cope with them.

SYMPTOMS AND TRAITS

DEPRESSION	MANIA

Mental Function

DEPRESSION	MANIA
Poverty of ideas	Flight of ideas, rhyming, punning, clang associations
Slow thinking	Rapid thinking
Distractibility	Distractibility
Self-doubt, defeatism	Overconfidence, competitiveness
Fear	Daring, blindness to danger
Somberness	Cheerfulness
Pessimism	Optimism
Apathy, boredom	Excitement, eagerness
Scrupulousness	Unscrupulousness, malice
Modesty	Arrogance
Renunciation, timidity	Ambition, no sense of limits
Fear of deprivation	Acquisitiveness
Oversensitivity to criticism	Addiction to praise and flattery
Loneliness, fear of strangers	Sociability, loving crowds
Envy, insecurity	Good will, jealousy
Stinginess	Generosity
Despair at criticism, opposition, or frustration	Intolerance of criticism, opposition, or frustration

Delusions

Sin	Nihilism
Ugliness	Attractiveness
Guilt	Innocence
Failure and incompetence	Achievements and ability
Poverty	Wealth or money to come
Being unloved, unwanted, rejected	Being loved, desired, accepted
Negative grandeur: being the worst of mankind	Grandeur: being a great person or the best of mankind
Hypochondriasis, expectation of imminent death	Invulnerability
Worthlessness	Perfection of self and insignificance of others
Physical and mental defects	Superhuman powers

Ways of Responding to People

Avoidance of people, shyness	Gregariousness, hospitality, friendliness
Asking advice	Volunteering advice
Complaints	Flattery, criticism, ridicule, teasing
Aloofness	Familiarity
Ignoring people	Charming and persuading people
Indifference or hostility	Love, hostility, hatred
Self-depreciation	Boasting
Diminished sexual interest and activity (occasionally increased)	Increased sexual interest and activity
Trying to escape notice	Ostentation
Submissiveness, passivity	Dominance, aggressiveness, manipulation, deception
	Vengefulness, threatening, shifting blame to others, lawsuits
Reduced communication	Increased communication

Behavior

Lack of will, indecision	Willfulness, impulsivity
Slow, laconic speech	Rapid speech, pressure of speech, jokes, witty remarks, puns
Quiet voice	Loud voice

Reliance on routine	Creativity, resourcefulness
Abandonment of interests and activity	Frequent change of activity and interests, taking on too much
Reduction and slowing of mental and physical activity	Hyperactivity, quickness
Procrastination	Haste
Crying	Laughing
Avoidance of change	Pursuit of novelty
Parsimony, self-denial	Extravagance, hedonism, playfulness
Self-neglect	Self-adornment
Cautiousness	Carelessness, risk-taking
Conformity, obedience	Nonconformity, disobedience, mischievousness, practical jokes, illegal acts
Inhibition	Lack of inhibition
Suicide attempts	
Suicide	Playfulness
Homicide	Homicide

Physical State

Fatigue, lethargy	Energy, restlessness
Malaise	Physical well-being
Digestive disorders, headache, chest pains	Reduced awareness of hunger, pain, fatigue

Appearance

Unattractive, aged	Attractive, youthful
Haggard, ill	Vigorous, glowing
Negligent dress	Fashionable, conspicuous dress
Lack of expression or look of suffering	Intense expressiveness

SYMPTOMS COMMON TO BOTH DEPRESSION AND MANIA

Thoughts and behavior dominated by mood, lack of moderation, bizarre behavior, exaggerated moods, reduced concentration, poor memory, labile mood, irritability, hostility, jealousy, faultfinding, violence, destructiveness, rage, paranoia, increased or decreased appetite, ideas of reference, alcoholism, insomnia, egocentrism, religiosity, alcoholism, drug abuse, job loss, marital discord, bankruptcy, compulsive gambling, and automobile accidents are more prevalent among manic-depressives than among others.

SYMPTOMS COMMON TO THE EXTREME STAGES OF DEPRESSION AND MANIA

Hallucinations, delusions, disorientation, confusion, violence against self and others, catatonia, and suicide (particularly in depression).

3

Newton

A CHILD OF HIS CENTURY

The seventeenth century, as much as any, was a century in which Europe seethed with war: peace reigned on the continent for only seven years of the hundred. For England it was a century of change and revolution, both peaceful and bloodstained. James I died in 1625, to be succeeded by his son Charles I, who was beheaded in 1649 after seven years of civil war. For the following four years England was a republic until Oliver Cromwell took power. Eventually he assumed dictatorial powers and ruled until his death in September of 1658. Cromwell was succeeded by his son, who resigned the following May. A year later the son of Charles I, Charles II, was proclaimed king by Parliament and died without legitimate issue in 1685. His younger brother, James II, a Catholic, assumed the throne but was driven from it three years later, to be replaced by William and Mary, who were crowned in 1689. The previous year Parliament had assumed many of the powers of the Crown and made England a constitutional monarchy. On Mary's death in 1694, William continued to rule alone until his death in 1702.

Newton's life was also filled with warfare, primarily against his fellow scientists, and with change. He followed the trend of his century in another respect: he had one foot in the modern world and one in the medieval. For the average European, religion was an integral part of everyday life that both explained reality and directed personal conduct. In England heretics and blasphemers were executed as late as 1612, and they continued to be killed in France until 1748. Newton's own interest in religion amounted to an obsession, and his writings on religious subjects would fill seventeen books, exceeding the total of his scientific writings. While his colleague Robert Hooke realized that fossils were evidence that the earth was much older than the Bible suggested, Newton took the Bible literally. His colleague Robert Boyle did genuine chemical experimentation, but Newton was involved in the alchemist's search for a substance that would give eternal life. He believed in both mathematics and miracles. In the course of the century, however, secular forces began to replace religious influences, as politics, philosophy, and science lost their religious content. This too was reflected in Newton's life, for he chose a career in science instead of entering the church, as had members of his family.

The medieval outlook on the world still predominated among most of the inhabitants of Europe and England. Both witchcraft and the persecution of witches increased, not to subside in Europe and England until the century's last decades. The execution of witches continued in England into the following century, and laws against sorcery were not repealed until 1736. So long as belief in the supernatural retained its hold on people's minds, there would remain great resistance to scientific ideas. The Inquisition censured Galileo in 1633 for supporting the new thesis that the earth revolved around the sun. Even some of the freest minds of the century led science into blind alleys, as had the scholastics, by relying too much on logic. The philosopher and mathematician Descartes, while advancing mathematics, retarded the progress of physics by denying the existence of vacuums, gravity, and magnetism. Science was also impeded by the lack of or primitive state of scientific instruments: microscopes and telescopes were crude and accurate thermometers did not yet exist. Chemistry was a collection of recipes without a coherent theory to explain them, and the life sciences were largely as the classical Greeks had left them.

Yet in the midst of this confusion, a new scientific age was dawning. Suddenly, science became fashionable for aristocrats and royalty, the latter founding scientific societies and the former joining and financially supporting them. Money was being invested in the first scientific museums and in zoological and botanical gardens, and for the first time careful records with illustrations were made of zoological and botanical specimens and of experiments of all kinds. Underlying this activity was a fundamental change of attitude: it no longer sufficed to refer to ancient authorities to describe reality, for facts, experiments, and proofs based on them were becoming the constituents of science. Perhaps because the other sciences required a technology that was not yet sufficiently developed, the rising scientific spirit found its greatest expression in mathematics during this first of the scientific centuries. And mathematics, in its rigor and exactness, became the model for other intellectual disciplines, including philosophy. Two of the century's leading philosophers, Descartes and Spinoza, gave their works a mathematical style. Descartes and the philosopher Leibniz also made major contributions to mathematics.

The scientific society became a phenomenon of the century. The Accademia dei Lincei was founded in Italy in 1603, the Royal Society was established in London in 1660, and similar institutions arose throughout Europe. The Royal Society, which played as large a part in Newton's life as he did in it, was a loose organization in which people came together to read scientific papers, present experiments, and discuss all matters of scientific interest, including the latest scientific news from abroad. Perhaps more significant was the society's function as an institution run by and for intellectuals. Its membership included poets, an architect, and aristocrats as well as scientists. The scientists themselves were men of broad interests, such as Robert Hooke who was a painter, organist, chemist, astronomer, physicist, and wrote a major work on microscopy.

Until this century the intellectual life of England and the Continent had been dominated by religious institutions: the universities themselves were created and controlled by Catholic and Protestant interests. Now, with the rise of the scientific societies and the growing secularization of the universities, it was possible for intellectuals to find recognition and financial support outside of the churches. For the first time since the fall of classical civilization, the rise of a secular intelligentsia became possible. Outside of the churches there had always been scattered savants who relied on the generosity of their aristocratic or noble patrons, and writers remained in this dependency until growing literacy and cheaper printing created a reading market that could support them. However, already, especially in England, the scholar and the scientist could do as Newton did: make a living free of the restrictions imposed by both church and the ruling classes and their need for a "good press." The new, free intellectuals were achieving status on their own and living in the style of those who possessed wealth and power. Newton, for one, amassed a respectable fortune.

Besides the growth of secular institutions that could support increasing numbers of intellectuals, the development of an international community of the learned in this century was furthered by the spread of postal systems. The flood of mail that crossed international borders made it almost impossible for governments to restrict the flow of information, or even to keep track of it, for the number of letters now being sent precluded government inspection of all but a small percentage of them. People linked themselves across national boundaries in confidential networks for the sharing of political, commercial, and other types of information. The growing need for information sharing created such novelties as scientific journals and less specialized magazines. The first English newspaper was published in 1621, and by the time the first daily paper was published in 1702, journalism had become a mature profession. Intellectuals came together socially in the salons of the wealthy and aristocratic, but some, like Newton, also had their own salons. It was a century of opportunity for genius, for people to rise from any social level to the heights of achievement.

THE FAMILY AND YOUTH OF A PRODIGY

Newton's family was one unlikely to make history. Only two members were memorable, and that in a way was regrettable. Newton's father was remembered as being "a wild, extravagant, and weak man." It is not unusual for manic-depressives of high achievement to have similar fathers, ne'er-do-wells of manic temperament, as did Napoleon, Beethoven, and Dickens. Newton's half-nephew, possibly another manic type, was a scandalous clergyman, often rebuked in strong language by his famous uncle.

The prodigy was born prematurely on Christmas Day, 1642, three months after his father died, and was so small and weak that he seemed unlikely to survive. His date of birth into a fatherless family and his survival against odds later contributed to Newton's grandiose conviction of having been predestined for greatness. When he was three, his mother remarried and, in a sense, orphaned him a second time, for she moved to another town with her new husband. She left the toddler in the charge of his grandmother, as the only child in her household. Even as a youngster, Newton displayed manic-depressive traits. Once, when visiting his mother and stepfather, he experienced an attack of rage such as those that were to plague him for the rest of his years. He described it later as "Threatening my father and mother Smith to burne them and the house over them." At age ten he himself left home for boarding school. The following year, his mother, having been widowed a second time, returned with the three children of her second marriage.

Symptoms of depression that remained with Newton for most of his life appeared during these years. A woman who knew him recalled him as one who "was a sober, silent, thinking lad, and was never known scarce to play with the boys abroad, at their silly amusements; but would rather chose to be at home, even among the girls," his half-sisters. He never learned to seek out other children, nor did he make equivalent efforts when a man. Manic attributes contributed to his isolation by making him unpopular. When he did play with other children, he continually outwitted them and insisted on dominating them.

The boy spent his manic energy on building miniature mills, carts, machines, and inventions of his own. He devoted every penny he received toward the purchase of tools of all sorts, and during his free time, his room was filled with the noise of sawing and hammering. His constructions gave him early training in developing dexterity, using tools, and turning concepts into objects, all these capabilities essential to physicists of that time, who had to make much of their own equipment. Despite the chidings of his conscience, he could not desist from these activities even on the day of rest, the Sabbath. At boarding school his ceaseless activity was directed toward drawing, which he did on the walls of his room, covering them with birds and other animals, plants, men, ships, and fragments of mathematics.

The ability to bring all of one's powers to bear on one's work during long periods of hard labor is important for achievement of the highest order. It is essential that a manic-depressive have superior powers of concentration if he is to accomplish anything that is complicated, particularly because concentration is one of the first abilities to give way in both mania and depression. Newton had an extraordinary capacity for concentration even as a child, as his later friend and first biographer, William Stukely, relates: "On going home from Grantham, 'tis usual at the town end to lead a horse up Spittlegate hill, being very steep. Sir Isaac had been so intent in his meditations that he never thought of remounting, at the top of the hill, and so had led his horse home all the way, being five miles. . . . The horse by chance slipt his bridle and went home: but Sir Isaac walked on with the bridle in his hand, never missing the horse."

Newton's parents, like those of many other geniuses, did not recognize their child's talent and made plans contrary to their offspring's special gifts. His mother wanted him to run the family farm and resented his reading so many books. It took considerable persistence on the part of Newton's teacher to persuade her that her son should be tutored by him in preparation for university, and she agreed to this only because she would not have to pay for the instruction. One might wonder why she wanted to keep him at home: when he was seventeen, Newton's violent temper made him a trial to the household. He recorded: "Striking many." "Peevishness with my mother." "With my sister." "Falling out with the servants." "Punching my sister." To injury he often added insults. The servants rejoiced when he left for university.

GRAVITY AND A BACHELOR'S DEGREE

At Cambridge Newton earned his way as a sizar, performing some of the duties of a servant. He rarely departed from a hardworking, abstemious existence, and a depressive temperament underlay his excessively puritanical nature. The rare occasions on which he joined his fellow students at taverns and gambled at cards may have been due to brief episodes of mania. His notebooks of the college years document his sadness, anxiety, fear, and low opinion of himself. On the whole, he maintained isolation from his fellow students and immersed himself in his studies. For amusement, he made scientific instruments and ground and polished lenses for them. He made only one friend among his fellow students, who describes Newton as being, when they first met, "solitary and dejected."

In 1662, Newton underwent a depressive crisis that took the religious form of an obsession with sins, real and imaginary. He listed all that he could remember committing from his childhood on, and kept a ledger of current sins until the mood passed. His problems with rage, and a suicidal thought are expressed in this cryptic entry: "wishing death and hoping it to some." In 1664 he had a breakdown caused, he believed, by overwork and his staying up late too many nights to observe a comet. It is more likely that the overwork and sleeplessness were caused by a manic or hypomanic episode followed, as is often the case, by a collapse into depression.

In January of 1665, Newton was awarded his bachelor's degree. Because bubonic plague was by then spreading from London and the university was closed, he went home. He stayed there for two years, until the plague had subsided. This is the period during which the apple fell and suggested to Newton the law of gravity. Without doubt, the years 1665 and 1666, when he was home with his mother, were the most creative of his life. He conceived the basic theories of gravitation and light that, even had he not also invented differential and integral calculus, would have made him the greatest genius of science until Einstein. Looking back on his life at the age of seventy, Newton said: "All this was in the two plague years of 1665 and 1666 for in those days I was in the prime of my age for invention and minded Mathematics and Philosophy more than any time since."

THE HERMIT OF CAMBRIDGE

Soon after Newton returned to Cambridge, he began to advance in the ranks of the university. His appointment as Fellow of the University in 1667, which began his progress towards security and status, made him temporarily manic. He suddenly purchased a handsome wardrobe and bought new furniture for his quarters, which he remodeled and redecorated at considerable expense. He entertained guests in this new splendor and displayed his sartorial elegance at the taverns. Twenty years passed before he returned to this style of living. Within the following two years, Newton invented the reflecting telescope and was appointed Lucasian Professor of Mathematics, a position that doubled his salary and required that he give only one lecture per week. Using the time that was now available. Newton became a polymath like da Vinci. Stukely states: "He knew anatomy very well. He was indeed a master of every science; he studied everything."

There may always have been a seasonal mood cycle in Newton's life, but it was not recorded until his emanuensis. Humphrey Newton noted that his master's activity was at its peak in spring and autumn. Humphrey reports:

> He very rarely went to bed till 2 or 3 of the clock, sometimes not until 5 or 6, lying [in bed] about four or five hours, especially at spring or fall of the leaf, at which times he used to employ about 6 weeks in his elaboratory, the fire scarcely going out either night or day; he sitting up, one night as I did another, till he had finished his chemical experiments, in the performance of

which he was the most accurate, strict, exact. What his aim might be I was not able to penetrate, but his pains, his diligence . . . made me think he aimed at something beyond the reach of human art and industry.

Mania not only kept him going night and day, but it also kept Newton from feeling hunger and deprived him of the patience to sit down for a meal. Humphrey continues: "So intent, so serious upon his studies that he ate very sparingly, nay, oftimes he has forgot to eat at all, so that, going into his chamber, I have found his mess untouched, of which, when I have reminded him, he would reply—'Have I!' and then making to the table, would eat a bite or two standing, for I cannot say I ever say him sit at table by himself." Even in his later years Newton would not pause to eat his dinner until he had worked through the night if he was working on something that interested him.

In addition to the seasons, another factor set Newton's cycles from mania to depression: his scientific work. He began a new project or ventured into a new field of inquiry in a manic state that flooded him with ideas and energy. Apparently his intellect worked night and day, for he claimed that many ideas came to him in his sleep. Mania gave him the confidence to undertake the largest and most difficult problems: universal gravitation, the nature and behavior of light, and a new mathematics. Humphrey describes the effects of Newton's manic inspiration, "When he has sometimes taken a turn or two [in his garden for a walk] he has made a sudden stand, turn'd himself about, run up ye stairs like another Archimedes, with an eureka, fall to write on his desk standing, without giving himself the leisure to draw a chair to sit down on." Sometimes, at the discovery of a solution for which he was searching, Newton's euphoria overwhelmed him to the point where he was temporarily unable to continue with his work.

The intense concentration that Newton maintained during these manic states made him quite absentminded. Humphrey notes, "At some seldom times when he designed to dine in ye hall, he would turn to the left hand and go out into the street, when making a stop when he found his mistake, would hastily turn back and then sometimes instead of going into ye hall, would return to his chamber again." As mania dimmed his awareness of hunger, Newton often failed to notice that he had missed his meal. Even if he reached the dining hall, he might sit down, lost in thought, while the courses came and went without his noticing them. During his manic periods he invited people to his rooms for a glass of wine, but if an idea came to him while he was fetching the wine from another room, he would sit down to work on it, completely forgetting the guests who were waiting for him. His ability to concentrate did not always protect him from the confusion caused by mania: when he was doing alchemy, he lost track of the days and recorded impossible dates for some of his experiments.

In the course of his scientific career, Newton developed a pattern of manic inspiration and tireless work, which sometimes passed into depression before the work was completed. Then he might leave the work unfinished unless constantly urged by friends. If depression did not arrive until the work was done, it arrived in time to interfere with publication, which was often delayed. When criticism inevitably came, Newton would become enraged, refuse to continue work in that field, and retreat from the scientific community. Depression made criticism discouraging and controversy unbearable. Despite a successful career and early eminence, only continual prodding could induce Newton to publish his work and expose it to the attacks of his fellow scientists. Thus, he kept his calculus secret until Leibniz made a claim to prior discovery. Without the repeated exhortations of his friend, astronomer Edmund Halley, Newton would not have published his major work, the *Principia*.

Except for 1667–1668, the years at Cambridge were years of asceticism. Newton worked incessantly when manic, and almost as energetically when depressed, for the constant occupation of his mind provided an escape from melancholy. Depression also took the pleasure out of leisure activities, and Newton withdrew from social contact, so nothing was left to fill his time except work and study. Humphrey describes it, "I never knew him to take any recreation or pastime either in riding out to take the air, walking, bowling, or any other exercise whatever, thinking all hours lost that was not spent in his studies, to which he kept so close that he seldom left his chamber." John Conduitt, who married Newton's niece, attests to both the solitude of Newton's university years, and to his compulsive studying, "At the University he spent the greatest part of his time in his closet [private chamber] and when he was tired with his severer studies of Philosophy his only relief and amusement was to go to some other study as History, Chronology, Divinity and Chymistry all which he examined and searched thoroughly as appears by the many papers he has left on those subjects." The consequence of Newton's choice of activities was a monotonous life with vast increases in learning and productivity.

Stukely describes Newton as "one so intirely immers'd in solitude, inactivity, meditation and study; in an incredible expense of mind; and that thro' a long series of years." Teaching did not interfere with Newton's isolation for, as Humphrey explains, "so few went to hear him, and fewer understood him, that oftimes he did in a manner for want of hearers, read to the walls." If no one appeared to hear him, Newton would return to his chambers without lecturing. There is no evidence, however, that Newton suffered from this minimal social contact during his Cambridge years. Nor did he show any sign of sexual interest or activity. He was not interested in other people, rarely asking how anyone was, or how other scientists were progressing in their work unless it affected his own. All of this could have been caused by depression alone, but the nature of his work may have contributed to his solitude, for he had a more normal social life when the years of scientific creativity were over. In any event, his relationships with others were so insignificant that very few who were with him at Cambridge had any reminiscences about him, though less famous men were well remembered. His colleagues had little chance to even see him. Humphrey Newton reports on his master's solitary habits: "He always kept close to his studies, very rarely went visiting, and had as few visitors, excepting two or three persons." Humphrey adds, "He very rarely went to dine in the hall except on some public days, and then if he had not been minded, would go very carelessly, with shoes down at heels, stockings untied, surplice on, and his head scarcely combed."

On the rare occasions when Newton was in the company of others, he kept his interactions to a minimum. Like other depressives, he contributed little to conversations. Humphrey observes, "He would with great acuteness answer a Question, but would very seldom start one." Only one personal letter to a colleague exists from the nearly two decades Newton spent as a faculty member at Cambridge. Depression also made him a somber man: according to Humphrey, he heard Newton laugh only once in the five years they were together, and that was when someone asked what on earth geometry was good for. Newton's depressive avoidance of people contributed to his revulsion of fame. He requested that one of his papers be published anonymously because "I see not what there is desirable in public esteem, were I able to acquire and maintain it. It would perhaps increase my acquaintance, the thing which I chiefly study to decline." He wrote this in 1669, before any of his bruising contacts with members of the scientific community.

THE BURNT CHILD: NEWTON AND THE ROYAL SOCIETY, 1672–1674

Newton sent an exposition of his theory of color to the Royal Society in 1672 and was invited to joint the group. His approach to light and color was so revolutionary, however, that he spent the next four years defending it against attacks by fellow scientists in England and Europe. By 1674, Newton had turned his back on science and involved himself in the occult intricacies of alchemy. A friend, John Collins, wrote the following year, "Mr. Newton, I have not writ to or seen these 11 or 12 months, not troubling him as being intent upon chemical studies and practices." Discouraged by the controversy, Newton tried to resign from the Royal Society that year and wrote to its secretary, "Sir—I desire that you procure that I may be put out from being any longer a member of the Royal Society; for though I honor that body, yet, since I shall neither profit them, nor by reason of this distance, can partake of their assemblies, I desire to withdraw." Distance, the excuse Newton gave for withdrawing, convinced no one: distance had not been a problem when he joined the society, and the distance had not changed. Instead of accepting Newton's resignation, the society exempted him from paying dues, and the matter died. Newton's real reason for withdrawing was expressed in a letter he wrote to the philosopher Leibniz, who was not then an antagonist, "I was so persecuted in discussions arising out of my theory of light that I blame my own imprudence for parting with so substantial a blessing as my quiet to run after a shadow [recognition]."

A year later Newton was depressed and dispirited to the point where he gave up science. He wrote: "I intend to be no farther solicitous about philosophy [science], and therefore I hope you will not take it ill if you never find me doing anything more in that kind; or rather that you will favor me in my determination, by preventing, so far as you can conveniently, any objections of other philosophical letters that may concern me." In another letter he added: "I see I have made myself a slave to philosophy; but . . . I will resolutely bid adieu to it eternally, excepting what I do for my private satisfaction, or leave it come out after me; [he intended to leave publication of his work until after his death] for I see a man must either resolve to put out nothing new, or become a slave to defend it." During this period of despair, Newton tried to exchange his professorship of mathematics for one of law, but the vacancy went to someone else.

During the following two years Newton's letters reached levels of rage and paranoia that presaged the major psychotic episode of 1693 in which his illness was revealed to the scientific community. While in this period of delusion, 1677–1678, he threw himself into alchemy with the same fervor that he had brought to rational science, doing fantastic experiments while collecting multitudinous extracts from the bizarre writings of medieval madmen and mountebanks. His interest in religion now became a lifelong obsession, a not-uncommon development in the lives of manic-depressives. Among the authors who interested him was the mystic Jakob Boehme. When Newton left Cambridge in 1696, he devoted much time to interpreting the phantasmagorical prophecies of the books of Daniel and the Apocalypse, and he used biblical writings to compute how many generations had been born since the Creation. One of his friends, John Craig, thought that Newton, in the course of his life, gave much more time and effort to religion than to science. It was not until August 1684, when asked a question about planetary motion by his astronomer friend, Edmund Halley, that Newton undertook another major scientific project.

A "SUSPICIOUS TEMPER"

Newton's relationships with people, particularly scientists, were not usually productive and tended to bring out his tyrannical manic traits. Those who dared to disagree with him about anything, or failed to flatter him, courted trouble. His friend Richard Bentley disagreed with Newton over a biblical interpretation, and Newton refused to speak to the man for a year. William

Whiston, Newton's choice as successor to the Lucasian professorship at Cambridge, was dropped. Whiston explains: "So did I enjoy a large portion of his favor for 20 years together. But he then perceiving that I could not do as his other darling friends did, that is learn of him, without contradicting him, when I differed in opinion from him, he could not . . . bear such contradiction." Newton became so domineering that he insisted on his friends having only attitudes he approved. He turned against his loyal friend Halley for a while because the astronomer was not, in Newton's opinion, sufficiently serious about religion. Like other tyrannical manics, Newton became enraged when his friends took any independent action. Dr. Stukeley was banished from Newton's acquaintance for trying to become secretary of the Royal Society without first asking for approval. Stukeley reports, "Sir Isaac show'd a coolness toward me for 2 or 3 years, but as I did not alter in my carriage and respect toward him, after that he began to be friendly to me again." Other friends were rebuked for having quarrels with each other that had nothing to do with Newton. He also insisted that people do things precisely his way. If he could not dominate a group without fear of challenge, his involvement with it was limited. He refused to become president of the Royal Society until his adversary and fellow member Robert Hooke died.

Paranoia became a disrupting element in Newton's relationships. He kept his friends at a distance, and they learned to be wary of him. His friend Locke advised people to be very careful with Newton lest they offend one who was "a little too apt to raise in himself suspicions where there was no ground." Whiston said that Newton "was of the most fearful, cautious, and suspicious temper, that I ever knew." Often friendships were suspended for years because Newton imagined some slight or injury. When people failed to meet his demands, he assumed that they had turned against him. He was secretive and cold and formal in his manner. Friend and enemy alike experienced Newton's rages, which became proverbial in his family because of their frequency.

While friends often found Newton difficult, enemies found him ruthless. He was considered by them to be deceitful, unjust, and cruel. He began by refusing to acknowledge their scientific work and ended by giving them no quarter. He took a manic delight in vengeance, attacking the living, the dead, and institutions, all, he repeatedly claimed, "liars," "corrupters of truth," and "imposters." He derived great satisfaction in later years from punishing the counterfeiters and coin clippers placed at his mercy through his position at the mint. Newton seemed to have a continual need of targets for his wrath. When Hooke died, Newton took on Leibniz. After surviving Leibniz, who died in 1716, Newton took on the French academicians in a quarrel over biblical chronology. In his later, more manic years he reversed the attitude of his depressive years and became aggressive, seeming to seek out quarrels.

THE CREATION OF A MATHEMATICAL UNIVERSE

In 1865, Newton entered another period of manic activity. He became sociable enough to want to start his own scientific society at Cambridge but failed for lack of supporters. Had the project gone forward, it might have interfered with the most momentous scientific work he ever undertook. For eighteen miraculous months, during 1685 and 1686, Newton resumed his manic pattern of sleeping very little and neglecting to eat, while writing a work of 550 pages. In response to encouragement from Halley and competing claims from Robert Hooke, Newton took the ideas that had come to him twenty years earlier and, using the mathematics he had developed in the meantime, he described the physical world, ranging from small bits of matter to the solar system, from gravity to space and time, in terms of formulae and proofs. Two of the three volumes were so difficult that only the most advanced mathematicians could comprehend them. This extraordinary monument to human intelligence was not superseded until Einstein wrote his theory of relativity some two-and-a-half centuries later. Though few could at first understand *The Mathematical Principles of Natural Philosophy,* published in 1687, the work transformed Newton from a physicist and mathematician known only to a few fellow scientists to an international celebrity. His life was never the same. Fame changed Newton from a depressive to a manic, bringing him out of his shell and into the world of the powerful and wealthy.

The year his magnum opus the *Principia* (from its Latin title) was published, he emerged from his depressive isolation and took an interest in public affairs, a change that indicated the continuation of this manic phase. James II had engaged in a ploy to place Protestant Cambridge under Catholic control. Newton joined the small group of faculty that protested this attempt and stiffened resistance to it, successfully frustrating the king. In 1689 the new Newton spent his first year away from the university since he had become a fellow. He was elected the university's representative to the Convention Parliament and lived in London during the thirteen months of the Parliament's existence. This period saw the commencement of several important friendships for Newton, among them those with the writer Samuel Pepys, philosopher John Locke, and a young scientist, Fatio de Duillier. This last friendship was the most indicative of the changes in Newton, for it was the most affectionate relationship that he had had as an adult with anyone outside of his family. In the same year his family was diminished by the death of his mother. The quiet life he had led at Cambridge no longer sufficed, and Newton commissioned his new friends to obtain for him some kind of secure, well-paying government position.

"DERANGED IN HIS MIND"

During 1690 and 1691 Newton's life continued to be filled with manic activity and creativity, including increased involvement with his religious studies, but the euphoria came to an end in January of 1692. The first sign of the impending storm was a period of paranoia. He accused Charles Montagu, an old friend who had so far been unsuccessful in getting Newton the desired new post, of being "false to me," and of deliberate neglect, "upon an old grudge." Three weeks later Newton abandoned that unjust suspicion, but he did not return to serenity. According to an entry in the diary of a Cambridge student, Abraham de la Prynne, a fire accidentally burned some of Newton's work on optics in February, while he was at chapel, and his distress led to a breakdown. Prynne wrote, "When Mr. Newton came from Chapel and had seen what was done everyone thought he would have run mad, he was so troubled therat that he was not himself for a month after." Newton was fast approaching the greatest mental crisis of his life. That autumn, as his fiftieth birthday drew near, he began a year during which his insomnia and reduction in food intake were so great that even he commented on them. In the spring and summer of the next year, he wrote five chapters of a work that he grandiosely expected to do for alchemy what his *Principia* had done for physics. However, alchemy was a pseudoscience with impossible goals, such as changing base metals into gold, and no genuine success was possible. It is curious that Newton spent so much time and effort on an occupation that verged on witchcraft when others were engaged in rational chemical experiments. In his frustration, he began scratching out parts that he had written and finally left the work unfinished. Adding to his disappointment was the stress of breaking the relationship with Fatio, to whom he had drawn so close.

The crisis occurred during two weeks of the same summer, 1693. During this period Newton hallucinated conversations with absent people, suffered confusion, memory loss, anorexia, acute insomnia, rage, and paranoia. Humphrey, describing the same period, adds that Newton alternated between periods of immobility and periods of restlessness, during which he sometimes worked furiously or paced his room. These are the symptoms of a psychotic episode in which mania causes extreme insomnia and hyperactivity, while depression causes immobility. During the crisis there were also times when the illness improved enough for Newton to write logically on mathematics, chemistry, and theology. This is consistent with milder states of depression and mania.

When the agitation subsided, Newton passed into a deep, despairing depression. He tried to break with every friend he had and began making paranoid accusations, becoming enraged to the point of wishing dead his friend John Locke. All of this was revealed in letters he wrote to Pepys and Locke. In the letter to Pepys, Newton said: "I am extremely troubled at the embroilment I am in, and have neither ate nor slept well this 12 month, nor have my former consistency of mind." He had sufficient insight to realize that he had not been mentally normal for a year and still did not feel well. He then added that he wanted to have nothing more to do with anyone, a feeling typical of intense depression: "[I] am now sensible that I must withdraw from your acquaintance, and see neither you nor the rest of my friends any more, if I may but leave them quietly." Three days later he wrote to John Locke and apologized for some of his delusions:

> Being of opinion that you endeavored to embroil me with women and by other means I was so much affected with it that when one told me you were sickly and would not live I answered 'twere better if you were dead. I desire you to forgive me for this uncharitableness. For I am now satisfied that what you have done is just and I beg your pardon for my having hard thoughts of you for it and for representing that you struck at the root of morality in a principle you laid down in your book of Ideas and designed to pursue in another book and that I took you for a Hobbist. I beg your pardon also for saying or thinking that there was a design to sell me an office, or to embroil me.

Later, Newton could not remember what he had written to Locke and sent him another explanation for his mental collapse: "Last winter by sleeping too often by my fire I got an ill habit of sleeping [insomnia] and a distemper which this summer has been epidemical put me further out of order [that may be fiction], so that when I wrote to you I had not slept an hour a night for a fortnight together and for 5 nights together not a wink. I remember I wrote to you but what I said of your book ["of Ideas"] I remember not."

Soon after Pepys received his disturbing letter, he wrote to a mutual friend, Millington, in his anxiety about Newton's sanity: "I had lately received a letter from him so surprising to me from the inconsistency of every part of it, as to be put in great disorder by it, from the concernment I have for him, lest it should arise from that which of all mankind I should least dread from him and most lament for, I mean a discomposure in head, or mind, or both." Millington went to see what Newton's condition was and reported to Pepys:

> Before I had time to ask him [Newton] any questions he told me that he had writ to you a very odd letter, at which he was much concerned; added that it was in a distemper [illness] that much seized his head, and that kept him awake for 5 nights together, which upon occasion he desired I would represent to you, and beg your pardon, he being very much ashamed he should be so rude to a person for whom he hath so great an honour. He is now very well, and, though I fear he is under some small degree of melancholy, yet I think there is no reason to suspect it hath at all touched his understanding, and I hope never will.

Newton did not immediately recover from his "small degree of melancholy," and five years would pass before he felt the desire to take on another major project.

Meanwhile, rumors that Newton had lost his mind began to circulate in the English and European scientific communities. The Dutch physicist Christian Huygens heard from a Scotsman in May 1694 "that Isaac Newton, the celebrated mathematician, 18 months previously, had become deranged in his mind." Huygens added, "He has lately so far recovered his health as to begin again to understand his own Principia." In May of 1694, Newton was so depressed that his friends could not cajole him into publishing another edition of the *Principia.*

THE FANTASIES OF A RATIONALIST

Those who undergo the severer states of mania often develop grandiose delusions about their own importance, and they believe themselves to be so far above their fellow men that other human beings appear negligible to them. It is not uncommon for their delusions to have religious content, inclining them to see themselves as prophets or messiahs, divinely ordained to fulfill some great mission. Newton not only developed these ideas when he was intensely ill, but for most of his life he also retained them among his beliefs about reality. He believed that legend and folklore had predicted his greatness. Identifying himself as the only living scientist whose work had truth or significance, he felt that the work of other scientists was either trivial, addenda to his own findings, or plagiarisms of it. In his alchemical and religious writings he indicated that he alone among his contemporaries was appointed by God to bring His truth to the world. Newton further held that everything worth knowing would be revealed to him. This may explain why he expected to accomplish the miracles at which the alchemists aimed.

While severe depression held sway over him, Newton developed several delusions characteristic of that state. As his notations on Revelation and the Book of Daniel reveal, he was fascinated by biblical prophecies of doomsday and invented his own version. He convinced himself that the comet of 1680 had almost hit the earth and would fall into the sun fairly soon, raising solar temperatures enough to kill all life on our planet. No other scientist held these opinions, and Newton kept them to himself. Like many who experience depression, he had delusions of ill health and dosed himself for nonexistent tuberculosis. As Stukeley notes, Newton was unusually hale, "Sir Isaac by his great prudence and naturally good constitution, had preserved his health to old age." Paranoid delusions, to which many manic depressives are susceptible, accompanied Newton throughout his life and ruined many of his relationships.

A KNIGHT IN LONDON

The office of Warden of the Mint was offered to Newton in 1696, and he accepted this remunerative post, the like of which he had been seeking for seven years. He moved to London, where he was joined by his niece, Catherine Barton. She was then seventeen, and her father had died three years previously. Newton became a father to her, taking care of her and educating her. The warmth of their relationship can be felt in a letter he wrote to her when she went to the country to recover from smallpox: "I had your 2 letters and am glad the air agrees with you and though the fever is loathe to leave you yet I hope it abates and that the remains of the small pox are dropping off apace. . . . [I] intend to send you some wine by the next carrier. . . . Pray let me know by your next how your face is and if your fever be gone. Perhaps warm milk from the cow may [help] abate it." This was signed "your very loving uncle."

His way of life changed completely when Newton moved to London and the manic traits in his personality became predominant: the gloomy recluse of Cambridge was replaced by the courtier. He played the host on many occasions, with his niece acting as the hostess and mistress of the house. His home became the scene of large gatherings of the intellectual elite of London and was visited by foreign savants as well. He hobnobbed with the nobility and became a court favorite. Moreover, the nobility became favorites with him, and he brought more nonscientist aristocrats into membership in the Royal Society than anyone had before. Stukeley describes Newton's sociability, "He could be very agreeable in company, and even sometimes talkative." Stukeley found that Newton now "had in his disposition a natural pleasantness of temper and much good nature. . . . He used a good many sayings, bordering on joke and wit. In company he behaved very agreeably; courteous, affable, he was easily made to smile, if not to laugh."

The generosity of the manic also appeared. Newton promoted the careers— once at considerable expense—of many young mathematicians and arranged to get a pardon from the government for James Sterling so that the mathematician could reenter England. Stukeley praised his philanthropy and gives an account of his generosity to his family: "All his relations, who were numerous enough, largely partook of his bounty. He was generally present at the marriages of his relations, when conveniently he could be. He would on those occasions lay aside gravity, be free, pleasant, and unbended. He generally made a present of £100 to the females, and set up the men to trade and business."

In 1697 the flame of mathematics again burned brightly, if briefly, for Newton. He was sent two challenge problems by the Swiss mathematician Johann Bernoulli. His niece recorded that her uncle returned from the mint that day at 4 P.M., "very much tired, but did not sleep till he had solved it which was by 4 in the morning." Instead of going to sleep, Newton immediately wrote a long letter to the president of the Royal Society in which he presented the solutions. That year he was still capable of responding to an intellectual challenge with a manic excitement that kept him up all night. His manic restlessness stayed with him during his London years, and instead of resting during spare minutes, he would fill them with unnecessary copying. However, mania never again brought him to the creative heights of his Cambridge years, and it failed him completely in 1668, when he attempted to return to scientific work while fully active at the mint.

Years earlier, Newton had begun work on a study of the physical forces determining the motions of the moon. He worked in conjunction with the astronomer Flamsteed, whose observations provided Newton's data. This project had been ended by a quarrel between the two scientists. In 1698, Newton decided to finish the work on his lunar theory and Flamsteed again agreed to furnish data. However, paranoia and a depression that made his mind sluggish created more difficulties for Newton. He complained that the lunar calculations made his head ache and kept him from sleeping. Newton became increasingly irritable and impatient, developing the paranoid delusion that Flamsteed was deliberately sabotaging him and withholding the information needed to complete the work. Periods of lethargy and despair also interfered with Newton's efforts. He was undergoing another mental and emotional crisis, and rumors to that effect began to circulate. Flamsteed even heard that Newton was dead and wrote to him, "I pray for your perfect health." Although Newton told some people that he had abandoned the lunar theory because of his headaches and insomnia, he persecuted Flamsteed as though the astronomer had been at fault. He had Flamsteed expelled from the Royal Society and finally wrested from his victim control over the astronomer's life work.

The return of manic moods is evidenced by Newton's again running for Parliament from the University of Cambridge. He served from February 1701 until the parliament was dissolved in July 1702. Newton again offered himself as a candidate in 1705 but on being rejected by the voters departed permanently from politics.

The mint was no sinecure when Newton arrived. The government decided at that time to replace all the coinage in the realm with newly minted silver, and it had to be done rapidly to avoid economic disruption. Newton opened several auxiliary mints, multiplied the production at the London establishment, and accomplished the herculean task. He was promoted to Master of the Mint three years after he began there. In 1703 he was elected to the presidency of the Royal Society, which he ruled like an absolute monarch. In 1704 his work on optics, written largely in his Cambridge years, was published, adding to his glory. He was knighted by Queen Anne in 1705. Though he lived an additional twenty-two years, his major scientific achievements lay behind him. He devoted his energies to the dispute with Leibniz over which of them had invented calculus.

NEWTON'S POLARITIES

Newton's character, like that of many manic-depressives, is remarkable for its opposing traits. His biographers claim that he was stingy and generous, modest and megalomaniacal, high principled and unscrupulous. He was a man of rigorous logic, an exemplar in the use of scientific method, while simultaneously an alchemist who cherished strange delusions. His conduct was as contrasting as his moods and opinions. He raged at the prisoners who had been debasing the coinage and counterfeiting, and he showed no mercy when they were beaten and executed. Nevertheless, as John Conduitt reports, "A melancholy story would often draw tears from him, and he was exceedingly shocked by any act of cruelty to man or beast; mercy to both being the topic he loved to dwell upon." His grandniece who knew him in his later years was impressed with his love of children and thought him cheerful.

His contradictory personality traits developed in the course of a life that took Newton through extremes of both depression and mania, each with its own way of perceiving reality and responding to it, each with its own desires and delusions. The first sign of mood abnormality of which there is record is Newton's childhood rage, when he threatened to kill his parents and burn their house down. As a university student, he exhibited many depressive symptoms. During these years he had a breakdown preceded by manic insomnia and overwork. The "plague years," 1665-1666, were the most creative of his life, and in this brief period he originated most of the ideas that he developed during the rest of his scientific career. In 1674-1675 he was depressed enough to try to resign from the Royal Society, to give up science, and to attempt to secure a professorship in law. Another eighteen months of manic creativity concluded in 1686 with the completion of Newton's greatest work, the *Principia*. For six years thereafter, manic behavior was manifest as Newton joined the defense of Cambridge against King James and became involved in politics, serving in Parliament from 1689 to 1690. His most acute crisis arrived two years later, when an episode of paranoid manic psychosis turned to severe depression, from which he did not fully recover for two years. Mania returned Newton to politics in 1701.

Throughout his adult life Newton displayed recurrent paranoia, irritability, and attacks of rage. Though in the latter part of his life he received rewards and honors and led a sociable life as a celebrity in London, he still had periods of severe depression, such as the breakdown of 1698 that caused him to abandon his lunar theory.

The final image of Newton at age eighty-five, his years of quarreling over, his hours of rage, despair, and loneliness ended, is one of a brave man dying. Conduitt recorded: "He had violent fits of pain with very short intermissions; and though the drops of sweat ran down from his face with anguish, he never complained, or cried out, or showed the least peevishness or impatience, and during the short intervals from that violent torture, would smile and talk with his usual cheerfulness." The torture ended on March 20, 1727.

At the end of his life Newton saw beyond his delusion of having been given the key to the secrets of the universe and said, "I do not know what I may appear to the world; but to myself I seem to have been only a boy, playing on the sea shore, and diverting myself, in now and then finding a smoother pebble or a prettier shell than ordinary, whilst the great ocean of truth lay all undiscovered before me."

We will never know whether Newton could have made his discoveries and done the immense work needed to prove them without the energies of mania and the solitude that his depressive personality imposed upon him. What can be seen is that his manic-depression, with its rage and paranoia, set him apart from the rest of mankind as inexorably as did his great intellectual gifts, and he was, as Wordsworth wrote, "a mind for ever voyaging through strange seas of thought alone."

4

Beethoven

Napoleon and Beethoven were contemporaries, and the times were as revolutionary for music as they were for the nations of Europe. In fact, the Napoleonic wars undermined the economic foundations of music, forcing composers to play a new role in society and to find new sources of income.

Johann Sebastian Bach had a career typical of the prerevolutionary composer. He was a salaried employee of either a church or a member of the nobility. His responsibilities included training the singers and musicians who performed for the church or court, performing himself whenever required, and composing all the music that might be needed for any occasion, birthdays, funerals, or whatever his patron desired.

Kapellmeisters, as church composers were called, served as organists and had to provide compositions for every church service. Bach even had to teach Latin and give music training to the choir boys. While working for his employer, whether court or church, the composer wrote very little on his own initiative.

In the early eighteenth century music was laboriously copied by hand and, for the most part, stayed where it was written, so that court and church alike had music libraries consisting mainly of works their own composers had provided over the years. When Bach was born, there were some 340 composers working at the courts and churches of the German-speaking states. The music-publishing industry was rudimentary in his day, and most of Bach's music was not published until many years after his death. Bach was known to other musicians, but his audience was local and he was never a celebrity.

Some of the court composers like Haydn were constantly busy, for they had to prepare some kind of performance, ranging from small chamber music concerts to operas and symphonies, almost every day. Training in music was an essential part of an aristocratic education in the German states of the eighteenth century, so the court composer also had to give music lessons. His work could not be copied or performed elsewhere without his patron's permission, nor could he accept commissions to compose from anyone else unless his patron agreed to it. The court composer held the rank of valet; Mozart, as such, was expected to take his meals with the other servants. Beethoven was the first to refuse to do that. Beethoven, as proud, audacious, and autocratic as the French emperor, conquered the Viennese nobility as thoroughly in their salons as Napoleon did on the battlefield. The composer's patrons became his toadies, running errands and begging him to play for them while they treated him as an honored guest. Like that of the emperor, Beethoven's power could not be passed on to his successors, but he won composers a prestige and respect that the best still command.

In the course of Beethoven's lifetime several important changes took place. The harpsichord was replaced by the piano, a much more flexible and powerful instrument, and the orchestra increased its number and variety of instruments as the salon gave way to the concert hall. As metalworking developed, its techniques were applied to the wind instruments and brass, improving their sound, extending their range, and making their pitch more reliable. Composers were freed to write bigger, louder, and more complex works than before. Beethoven had the aggressiveness and self-confidence to lead the musical revolution.

Music-publishing companies sprang up everywhere in Europe. Composers were not protected by copyright laws, so publishers might pay them a lump sum for compositions or simply pirate works published elsewhere. At times, famous names that sold well were placed on pieces written by less popular composers, without the knowledge of the actual composer or the supposed one.

The widespread publishing of music did not guarantee the financial security of the composer, but those of the rank of Beethoven, Haydn, and Mozart were able to reach an international audience through their printed works. At the same time, the demand for new pieces declined. Since it now became possible to compile libraries of the published compositions of others, musicians who were employed at courts and churches no longer had to compose works for every musical occasion. Instead, composition gave way to their responsibilities as teachers, conductors, and managers of orchestras or choruses.

While those changes were in progress, most of the salaried positions for musicians disappeared. During the century following Bach's death, the map of Europe was redrawn several times. Some 120 small German states were incorporated into their larger neighbors, reducing the number of courts and court positions for composers, musicians, and singers. In addition, the Napoleonic wars depleted the wealth of the nobility that survived them, and most courts could no longer afford to maintain their own orchestras and composers. With the advance of the industrial revolution, wealth passed from landed aristocrats to those plebian entrepreneurs who became industrialists. The latter did not support musicians as part of their households. While patronage did not completely disappear, most composers, including Mozart and Beethoven, had to become freelancers, although they sought a salaried position and the financial security that went with it. Both of them did quite well on their own. Mozart died impoverished, largely because he was an incorrigible spendthrift, but Beethoven left a respectable legacy in bank shares.

Early in his career, Beethoven got income from several sources. Local aristocrats provided him with a stipend, and he received the profits from conducting concerts of his own music and royalties from his published works. He performed at musical soirees of the nobility and gave music lessons, though he did not always accept payment for these activities. After he became completely deaf, he had to give up everything except composing, but by then publishers vied for his manuscripts, and he could live quite well on his income from publication.

Once composers became freelancers, they were relieved of the responsibilities that had bound them at court and church. They no longer had to perform, conduct, give lessons, hire and fire musicians, train and rehearse choirs and orchestras, or write music unless they chose to do so, a situation that suited the independent Beethoven quite well. However, composers also lost their audiences when their music fell out of fashion. The large body of published works could suffice even if very little new material was added to it. When the artist lost his connection with the audience and his work became an ornament to life, rather than an integral part of it, he turned his back on the public. Part of the Romantic revolt was the artist's decision to please himself and his peers, leaving a puzzled and sometimes hostile audience behind. Beethoven's work found a large audience in his day, but even he wrote some pieces strictly for the market. He later gave this up, deciding, toward the end of his life, that it did not matter if his work was not understood. Some of it was not, but he wrote, he said, for the future. A century and a half later, the mass audience still has not caught up with him, but his daring was justified; he produced some of our greatest music.

PRELUDE

Beethoven led a comparatively uneventful life. His move to Vienna at the age of twenty-two, his gradually increasing deafness, and his entanglement with his nephew are the noteworthy occurrences in his biography, outside of his music. Once he was settled in Vienna where, for the most part, he spent the remainder of his years, his life had a curious sameness of texture. Themes and variations on them are played again and again. Throughout his life, Beethoven was prone to outbursts of anger, baseless suspicions, quarrels and reconciliations, fruitless infatuations, physical ills, changes of residences (which averaged better than two per year from 1792 on), and the hiring and firing of servants. Typical of the last is this sentence written to a friend, "I came here with a ruined stomach and a horrible cold, the former thanks to that arch-swine, my housekeeper, the latter handed on to me by a beast of a kitchen maid whom I had already chucked out once and then taken on again."

Beethoven's life, with its relatively minor and repetitious problems, does not lend itself to historical narrative. Therefore, a brief chronology of Beethoven's life will be followed by a description, arranged by symptom, of Beethoven's behavior.

Ludwig van Beethoven was born in Bonn, Germany, on December 16, 1770. His father started to teach him the violin when he was five. At age nine, he began to study piano and organ. Two years later, he played well enough to substitute for the court organist. In 1783, his first composition was published and the thirteen-year-old got a job as a pianist at a local theater. The next year he became assistant to the court organist. In 1787 he visited Vienna for three months, played for Mozart, and returned to Bonn when his mother died. From 1787 to 1792 he supported his father and two younger brothers in Bonn, where he held a post as court musician. He moved to Vienna in 1792, then and for many years that followed a Mecca for music. He studied briefly with Haydn and others and wrote his First Symphony in 1801. Signs of oncoming deafness had already been present for three years. In 1815 his brother Caspar died, and Beethoven took on the guardianship of his nephew, Karl. By 1819 Beethoven's hearing loss was so great that it became necessary for people to address him by writing their remarks. On March 20, 1827, Beethoven died in Vienna.

Beethoven may have inherited mental abnormalities from both sides of his family. His maternal grandmother was an alcoholic who suffered a mental breakdown, starved herself, slept outside in the cold and rain, and died as a result. His father, a musician with minor talent and little self-control, was an alcoholic and given to rages. He went so far into debt that Beethoven's mother had to sell some of her clothing and find work to keep bread on the table. If Father Beethoven managed to find his way home after a night of drinking, he would drag his son out of bed and make him play piano till morning, striking him for misplayed notes. He beat the child almost every day and would shut him away in the cellar.

Beethoven's mother was the most stable member of the family. To her went all of Beethoven's love and respect. However, she often neglected her three sons. The boys would be left in the care of servants, and no one bothered to keep them clean. She died when Beethoven was seventeen and he became the head of the family. Beethoven's brother Johann had the most even temperament of the three boys. Caspar, on the other hand, had a passionate and violent personality.

The three brothers could not tolerate each other for any length of time.

The composer hated both of his sisters-in-law. After Caspar's wife became a widow, she had a child out of wedlock. Caspar's son Karl, whom Beethoven took into his home, was expelled from school. The child became the rope in a tug-of-war between his mother and the composer. Beethoven won, but then conflict developed between uncle and nephew. Although Karl tried to be agreeable, the composer was often irascible and made life difficult for anyone who lived in his proximity. When Karl was twenty, he shot himself in the head but survived. Such are the unstable characters and irregular doings that commonly show up in the families of manic-depressives.

OSCILLATIONS OF MOOD

If an individual's life gives no indication of extreme changes of mood, then either the evidence is incomplete, or the person is not a manic-depressive. In Beethoven's case there is an abundance of evidence of mood shifts. He wrote to a friend on November 16, 1801, about a depression of two years' duration. His unhappiness had just ended because he has fallen in love. He has switched from misery and social withdrawal to euphoria, optimism, and a sense of physical well-being with improved mental function:

> I am living more pleasantly now, since I mingle more with people. You will scarcely believe how lonely and sad my life has been for the last two years. My bad hearing haunted me everywhere like a ghost and I fled mankind. . . . This change has been wrought by a dear fascinating girl who loves me and whom I love. . . . Unfortunately she is not of my station now—it would be impossible for me to marry. . . . Really, I feel that my youth is just beginning, for have I not always been in poor health? My physical strength has for some time past been steadily gaining and also my mental powers. . . . Oh! Life is so beautiful, would I could have a thousand lives!

The next oscillation, a year later, is from a happy summer to a wretched autumn. Beethoven begs God for one more day not of ordinary happiness, but of "pure joy." What manic-depressive would settle for less? He finishes his petition in the overwrought style of the Romantic. "As the leaves of Autumn fall and are withered—so likewise has my hope been blighted . . . even high courage—which often inspired me in the beautiful days of summer—has disappeared—Oh Providence—grant me at last but one day of pure joy—it is so long since real joy echoed in my heart—Oh when—Oh when, Oh Divine One—shall I feel it again. . . . Never?—No—Oh that would be too hard!"

Indications of Beethoven's extreme changes of mood appear in other letters, too. He writes of "the wretched yet frequently happy existence of us mortals" as though there was nothing in betweeen. Or he says, "Your report plunged me again from the regions of the highest rapture into the depths." For Beethoven that was a common trajectory.

In 1811 he reports: "I only came back from a Bacchanalian festival at 4 o'clock this morning, at which, indeed, I was forced to laugh a great deal, with the result that I have to weep almost as much today. Noisy joy often drives me powerfully back into myself." Beethoven was one of those who often pass directly from mania into depression without a normal phase in between.

His wild shifts of mood were no secret to his friends. Their comments about their friend's chameleon emotions span the period from when he was thirty to the end of his life. Fellow composer Czerny states, "Aside from the times when he was in one of the melancholy moods which occasionally overtook him . . . he was always merry, mischievous, full of witticisms and jokes." Another friend observed Beethoven's fluctuating moods and pressured speech, "When, on occasion, he did seem in good spirits, he usually went to extremes." Either there was a "cloud of melancholy that hung over his spirit," or "His conversation . . . became highly animated, and he was extremely loquacious." Eventually, Beethoven's companions learned to be wary of his emotional instability. "Nothing can possibly be more lively," one said, "more energetic than his conversation when you have succeeded in getting him into a good humor; but one unlucky question, one ill-judged piece of advice . . . is quite sufficient to estrange him from you forever." His manic anger and paranoia often disrupted the composer's relationships.

On another occasion, a friend relates, "Beethoven became very chatty, which surprised the company, as he was generally taciturn, and sat gazing listlessly before him." Apparently the morose image of Beethoven is the one that finally prevailed, despite his ebullient moments. Often, when he was depressed, he would hide until the mood passed, but his dark side was seen frequently enough for people to call him "a person of bad character, churlish and eccentric, a dog, vicious and prone to bite." Beethoven had so many depressive traits that one may conclude depression was his basic state.

The appearance of a manic-depressive is usually a reliable clue to his emotional condition. This was certainly true for the composer. His appearance varied as much as his moods. He went through periods when he dressed elegantly, was well-groomed, and looked in blooming health. That was the case in 1805. In 1810 he blossomed again and cared enough about his grooming to ask his baron, Zmeskall, to bring him a mirror. Beethoven had broken the only one he had. It was not unusual for the composer to break things. He was unusually clumsy for a pianist: he knocked inkwells onto his piano and he stained, overturned, and finally broke any furniture in his way. He never could learn to dance to the rhythm of the music that was playing. And, a friend remarks, "How he ever managed to shave himself is hard to understand, even making allowances for the many cuts on his cheeks."

Beethoven's handwriting also varied according to his moods, as it does with many manic-depressives, and his emotions were too intense to hide: his facial expressions always betrayed what state he was in.

Despite his lack of dexterity, the composer succeeded in looking presentable during the period 1813–1814. For the most part, however, Beethoven was as ill-groomed as he was talented, and he was not always clean. People noted that when he was depressed, he was even messier. There were moments when he might feel a bit better, but they did not last long enough for him to spruce himself up. His hairdo was famous. "When he put his hand through it," a friend remembers, "it remained standing in all directions which often looked comical. Once when he came, we noticed a hole in the elbow when he was taking his overcoat off; he must have remembered it for he wanted it on again, but said, laughing, taking it completely off, 'You've already seen it.'" Even at best, Beethoven was not handsome. According to one of the ladies of Vienna, "He was short and insignificant, with an ugly red face full of pockmarks."

In 1821 Beethoven's utter neglect of his attire got him into trouble with the police. He went for a walk in his usual ragged condition and lost his way. He began peering in windows in the hope of recognizing something familiar. Alarmed householders fetched a policeman. When Beethoven was arrested, he gave his name, but the policeman did not believe him and said "You're a tramp. Beethoven does not look so." Beethoven was taken to jail and could not obtain his release until an acquaintance identified him.

The composer's manic disorganization was not limited to his apparel: "My affairs are not always in the best order—perhaps the only mark of genius of which I can boast." The modesty was uncharacteristic, but the chaos was real. Descriptions by people who visited him bear this out: "Picture to yourself the dirtiest, most disorderly place imaginable . . . an oldish grand piano, on which the dust disputed the place with various pieces of engraved and manuscript music; under the piano (I do not exaggerate) an unemptied pot de nuit . . . a quantity of pens encrusted with ink . . . then more music. The chairs . . . were covered with plates bearing the remains of last night's supper, and with wearing apparel, etc." Another visitor saw "Books and music scattered in every corner . . . sealed or half-emptied bottles . . . friendly and business letters covering the floor. . . . [Sometimes it] became necessary to spend days, . . . weeks, in finding something necessary." Apparently Beethoven was not bothered by the smell of a full chamber pot when he composed.

Manic-depressives change the way they treat people as their moods change, and consequently, their treatment of people varies radically. This can make life very confusing for their children, because the rules keep changing. If a child commits an offense on a day when the parent is euphoric, the offense will be overlooked or even found amusing. When the parent is irritable or depressed, the same offense may provoke severe punishment. Beethoven was a thirty-five-year-old bachelor when he took his nephew, age nine, into his home, a difficult situation even without manic-depression to complicate it. The composer failed as a foster parent. He was inconsistent, bad tempered, and so starved for love that no child could satisfy his needs. One moment he spoiled Karl, the next, he hit him.

In a letter Beethoven wrote to a friend four years after Karl first came to him, there are obvious changes of mood and mind. The letter begins with rage because Karl "withdrew his hand from mine. . . . I have thrust him out of my heart, wept many tears for him, this good-for-nothing." Beethoven says in an agony of affection, "My love for him is gone." The next moment he adds, "I want to have nothing more to do with him except that I pay his expenses and otherwise look after him." A little further on he reverses completely. "I still love him as before . . . even more, I can in truth say that I often weep for him." And then, back to anger, "He shall not see me as long as I live, this monster; and the pestilential mother, who has trained him this way; now once again practices her intrigues with the boarding-school headmaster." There is a lot there: rejection, love, rejection again, paranoid suspicions about Karl's mother and the headmaster, and through it all, the inability to cut loose from Karl, whom he needed so desperately.

The same mood shifts and paranoia run through Beethoven's letters to Karl. The boy is now sixteen as his uncle writes to him: "I have been informed by somebody that again there have been meetings between you and your mother. . . . Have I once more to suffer the most abominable gratitude? . . . . If the tie between us is to be broken, let it be so, but you will be hated by all impartial people who hear about it." Then a little farther down he says, "Do not be afraid to come to me tomorrow, I still only suspect." A few days later he writes, "I can never trust you any more." Again he reverses himself: "My dear Son . . . only come to my arms, you shall hear no harsh word. . . . Only come—come to the faithful heart of your father."

Despite his fear and hatred of Karl's mother, when Beethoven heard that she was ill, he aided her financially and wrote: "Since her illness and misery are so great, help must be forthcoming at once. . . . I will see to it that I induce my stingy brother as well to make a contribution to her." As soon as she recovered, however, his compassion departed, and he resumed his persecution of her.

Beethoven once wrote: "He who wishes to reap tears will sow love." He proved this himself. His love for Karl made him, Karl, and Frau Beethoven miserable. Struggles over custody of the boy even reached the law courts. One judge took Karl out of his uncle's custody because the latter had made the child change schools so many times. Unfortunately, Beethoven got Karl back when the case was heard in a higher court. As the years passed by, the quarrels between uncle and nephew became so noisy that landlords had to evict them.

Either because he was a manic-depressive also, or because of what he had been through, or both, Karl tried to kill himself in 1826. After Beethoven was gone from his life, Karl appeared to settle down to a peaceful existence.

PENURY AND EXTRAVAGANCE

Like many other manic-depressives, Beethoven was as confused and confusing in his financial affairs as he was in many things. In depression, he became miserly, tried to borrow money, and thought of himself as a poor man, though he was not. This is a common delusion of depression. At other times he might rent three lodgings at once. Meals at restaurants could be costly because he would order at random and then send the food back. Yet careless though he sometimes was about spending money, he was not casual about making it. He did not allow publishers to take advantage of him and would even pit them against each other, getting good prices for work that was too difficult to perform to be commercially viable. However, the composer seems to have been motivated by pride rather than avarice.

Money was not one of Beethoven's deep interests. He said: "There ought to be an art depot in the world where the artist need only bring his work and take what he needs. As it is, one must be half a business man, and how can one understand—good God! that's what I call a nuisance!"

INCOMPATIBILITY OF MOODS WITH EVENTS

Beethoven often blamed his depressions on the loss of his hearing. This was a tragedy for him, as it would be for any musician. But, though his deafness kept worsening until it was total, his melancholy did not. Deafness did not destroy him either as a musician or as a person. It ended his career as a pianist and conductor, but because it forced him to concentrate on composing, posterity is the richer for his misfortune.

Beethoven's manic-depression may have saved him from the overwhelming despair that a normal musician would have felt on going deaf. He said "Only artists and free scholars carry their happiness within themselves." Whether that is true or not for others, it certainly is true for manic-depressives because their moods are often independent of what happens to them. They can be happy without cause, or even in the face of misfortune. It may be that Beethoven survived as a creator because he was brave or because his love of music kept him going. What he did have are the manic days of "pure joy" that he prayed for, and manias triggered by the process of working, along with the confidence and optimism that mania entrains. Those days came even when life was trying, and they permitted Beethoven to be creative under almost any circumstances.

The only things that could bring him down were ill health and depression, which usually arrived close together.

By 1822 people who knew Beethoven were aware that his moods were often out of phase with reality. This is what one of the composer's friends told a young man who wanted to meet Beethoven: "He knows that you want to visit him; he wishes to make your personal acquaintance; but at the same time we cannot be sure but that, when he sees us arrive, he will not run away because, just as he is sometimes full of the most spontaneous merriment, so he often is seized by the profoundest melancholy. It strikes him out of the blue, without any cause, and he is unable to make head against it."

MANIC EPISODES

In 1822 Beethoven had a manic spell that is recounted here by one of his friends. The composer's appearance matched his mood. He was well dressed, merry, friendly, excited, joking, talkative, and seemed to be having a marvelous time for no particular reason. The friend says:

> He came here to Baden, this time looking quite neat and clean and even elegant. . . . During the entire visit he was uncommonly gay and at times most amusing, and all that entered his mind had to come out. . . . His talk and his actions all formed a chain of eccentricities, in part most peculiar. Yet they all radiated a truly child-like amiability, carelessness, and confidence in everyone who approached him. Even his barking tirades . . . are only explosions of his fanciful imagination and his momentary excitement . . . the offsprings of a mad, humorous mood. . . . Once he is in the vein, rough, striking witticisms, droll conceits, surprising and exciting paradoxes suggest themselves to him in a continuous flow. . . . After all, I realized that he also had his hours of great gladness and perfect happiness.

EGOTISM AND GRANDIOSITY

Only a small minority of geniuses, it seems, are ever surprised to be recognized as such. Most wonder why it took so long. When a genius thinks that he is a genius, one can hardly call that opinion a delusion. For lack of a better word, "grandiosity" here refers to Beethoven's belief in his greatness, because he believed in his genius before there was any objective reason to do so.

The belief appeared quite early, before there was any evidence on which to base it, which is grandiose. When he was a boy and a neighbor complained about his sloppy dress, he replied, "When I'm famous no one will notice." In his twenties, he expected others to share his faith in his gifts—more than that, he demanded it. "With men who do not believe in me because I am not yet famous I cannot associate." At age thirty, he wrote to a friend: "You will only see me again when I am really great, not only great as an artist, but as a man. . . . I will only use my art for the benefit of the poor." This was one of those fleeting impulses of generosity that are forgotten as soon as manic inspiration is gone. By the time Beethoven was thirty-six, he felt, in his manic moments, that he had reached the pinnacle of achievement. When someone told him that "the great hero Napoleon" had just beaten the Prussians, Beethoven took this personally and exclaimed, "It's a pity that I do not understand the art of war as I do the art of music, I would conquer him!" About the same time he wrote to one of his patrons: "Prince! what you are, you are through accident and birth. What I am, I am through my own efforts. There are princes, and there will be thousands of princes more, but there is only one Beethoven." This was extraordinary effrontery for the day, even though it was true.

In 1815, Beethoven was becoming overweening. "Have you heard any of my great works there?" he wrote to a friend. To cover this display of grandiosity, he commits a bigger one, measuring himself against God. "Great say I—but compared with the works of the Highest everything is small. . . .When you write me the only address you need is my name."

Normal people often feel uncomfortable in the company of geniuses because they suspect that the genius looks down on them as members of an inferior species. Unfortunately, this is sometimes the case. The genius may try to disguise his attitude. Beethoven wrote in his diary, "Never let people notice the contempt you feel for them, for you never know when you may need them." Arrogance is another characteristic of the manic.

HYPERACTIVITY AND INSOMNIA, ECSTASY AND INSENSITIVITY TO DISCOMFORT

Wandering about all day and all night is a symptom that appears only as mania intensifies. A friend recorded that Beethoven was still engaged in such marathons when he was fifty-three years old. He adds that the composer sometimes would not return to his home "for several days." In the last year of his life, Beethoven was dying of cirrhosis of the liver, which caused intense physical discomfort, but his doctor recorded, "Often, with rare endurance, he worked at his compositions on a wooded hillside and his work done, still aglow with reflection, he would not infrequently run about for hours in the most inhospitable surroundings, denying every change of temperature, and often during the heaviest snowfalls." Usually these episodes of intense mania took place in the summer rather than in the winter. When he was manic in the city, Beethoven would take long, rapid walks through the city streets and exhaust anyone who tried to keep up with him.

Manic euphoria sometimes generates mystic states in which the manic feels filled with love, at one with all creation, and in touch with God. Beethoven's woodland manias were sometimes of this kind. He wrote in 1810, "It seems as if in the country, every tree said to me Holy! Holy! Who can give complete expression to the ecstasy of the woods?" It seems unlikely that one could achieve works of emotional range and intensity comparable to those of Beethoven without such extraordinary emotional experiences.

Even when he was only giving lessons, Beethoven experienced manic episodes during which he was inexhaustible and oblivious to physical discomfort. He would amaze and exhaust his students. One of them, Countess Brunswick, tells us: "Instead of remaining for an hour, from 1 o'clock on, he would often stay until 4 or 5 and never wearied of holding down and bending my fingers, which I had learned to stretch up and hold flatly [over the piano keys]. The great man must have been well content! For 16 days in succession he did not once fail to appear." One could argue that he was concentrating on the countess and not on the music, for he was quite susceptible to aristocratic ladies. However, he made the same kind of effort when he was teaching those to whom he was less attracted.

FLIGHT OF IDEAS

When an ordinary manic has flight of ideas, he is deluged with thoughts that have little to do with each other, and each one distracts him from the preceding one. For the manic who is talented, trained, and obsessed with his work, it is quite different. His ideas may come in the same rush and plenitude, but when he is working, the ideas are focused on his project and one thought develops from the preceding one, creating an organic whole. The result is not always perfection and may require extensive revision. Beethoven did a lot of such labor. He never lacked ideas when he was manic. "They come to me uninvited," he said, "out in Nature's open, in the woods, during my promenades, in the silence of the night, at the earliest dawn." What he could not use at once, he stored in his notebooks for later development.

Like many artists, he had flights of creative ideas in the middle of the night and, thus inspired, could not go back to sleep until he had written them down. Beethoven's mania could occur at any time. Sometimes the mood struck when he was being sociable, as witnesses have indicated, and then his flights of ideas were not in the form of fragments of music. "At such moments . . . the wealth of ideas which escaped his mouth appeared truly astonishing," an observer says. The flights of ideas and rapid-fire speech of a manic who is intelligent and educated can be dazzling. Samuel Johnson left that impression on people, as did the poets Coleridge and Delmore Schwartz.

SOCIABILITY

Usually, Beethoven did not involve himself with people unless he was feeling somewhat manic. Then he let out all the stops. When the composer Carl Maria von Weber met him for the first time, Beethoven treated him like a long-lost brother, although he did not like von Weber's music or respect him as a musician. Von Weber says that his host "received me with the most touching affection: he embraced me at least 6 or 7 times in the heartiest fashion and finally, full of enthusiasm, cried 'Yes, you are a devil of a fellow, a fine fellow!' We spent the noon-hour together, very merrily and happily. This rough, repellent man actually paid court to me, served me at table as carefully as though I were his lady, etc. . . . It gave me quite a special exaltation to see myself overwhelmed with such affectionate attention by this great spirit." Manic affection cannot be relied upon. It is like the momentary affection of a drunk and may be equally unrelated to the person on whom it is lavished. The elated manic is simply overflowing with love and happiness, and for the instant, he treasures the person or person in his company. But when his mood changes, he wonders what he ever saw in those he appreciated so much before. Manic-depressives are capable of sustained love that continues even during their depressions, but their moods influence the fervor of their devotion.

In the last year of his life, Beethoven could still be manic and sociable. As a witness reports, "In general . . . he was exceptionally merry and laughed at every jest . . . something not to have been expected in view of the generally current rumor that Beethoven was very gloomy and shy." At times Beethoven's social manias would turn into working manias. His companion Schindler saw the composer roll his eyes or stare upward or downward, eyes bulging, when inspiration struck. Schindler adds, "These moments of sudden inspiration often would surprise him in the midst of the gayest company or in the street, and usually attracted the liveliest attention of all passers-by."

JOKES AND PLAYFULNESS

Beethoven's friends would get notes from him such as: "Dear little Ignacious of my heart." . . . Come, then, to me this afternoon. You will find Schuppanzigh here also and we two will bump, thump, and pump you to your heart's delight. A kiss from your Beethoven, also called soup dumpling."

There were times when Beethoven's attempts at humor became cruel. He composed this song for his friend Schuppanzigh, a violinist of generous proportions. "Homage to Fatty/Schuppanzigh is a dope, dope, dope! . . . The fat and greedy hog, the egotistical imbecile! You dope, Schuppanzigh, You jackass. . . . Let us chime in: you are the greatest jackass! You dope! You jackass! Hi hi ha!" Sometimes Beethoven's humor was scatological and his judgment appalling, both common in mania. To the representative of a group called Friends of Music who offered him a commission to compose a piece for their society, Beethoven wrote: "First and best member of the Society of Enemies . . . I wish you open bowels and the handsomest of close stools." In the same mood he would address his patron Baron von Zmeskall: "My Cheapest Baron!" or "Pasha of various rotten fortresses !!!!!" "Rotten fortresses" were their code words for the prostitutes that they visited together. Another patron was addressed as "Dearest Victorious and yet occasionally blundering Count!"

When the manic becomes irritable, wit turns to sarcasm. Beethoven claimed that one of his servants "has the heavenly privilege of being one of the chief asses of the Imperial State (which is saying a good deal)" (Beethoven's parenthesis).

MANIC AGGRESSION, QUARRELS AND RECONCILIATIONS, IRRITABILITY AND RAGE

The composer's hair-trigger temper constantly involved him in domestic difficulties. His paranoia made him expect the worst from servants and landlords, while his irritability made him explode over trifles. A friend remarked, "He feels the need of changing his lodging every 6 months and his servants every 6 weeks." This was not random eccentricity. Beethoven moved frequently because he often quarreled with his landlords and was evicted, or he departed in anger. None of his servants could please him for long; if his unreasonable demands did not drive them off, he would throw them out, sometimes bodily, when rage overcame him.

It was not necessary to live with Beethoven in order to have a fight with him, verbal or otherwise. Friendship would make that not only possible, but also likely. By the time he was thirty-four, he could claim "I have found only 2 friends in the world with whom I have never had a misunderstanding."

Eventually Beethoven's mood changed, and these ruptured relationships were repaired. Beethoven's involvements with people show a typical manic-depressive pattern. During outbursts of anger, he broke off the relationship. Later, after the anger passed, he would feel remorseful and go to any extreme to effect a reconciliation. In one instance, Beethoven had been living with a friend, Stephan von Breuning, whom he had known for years. They quarreled over trivial matters but von Breuning was so angry that he moved out. Afterwards Beethoven told people, "I have nothing more to say to Breuning. . . . there never ought to have been a friendly relationship between us, and such will certainly not exist in the future." Some time later, however, his perspective changed, and he sent von Breuning a miniature of himself with a note: "I know that I broke your heart, but the feelings within me which you must have noticed, have sufficiently punished me for that. . . . My portrait was long ago intended for you. You know well that I always intended it for somebody; to whom could I give it with so warm a heart as you, faithful, good, noble Stephan—Forgive me if I have given you pain. I suffered no less myself. Only when I no longer saw you near me for such a long time did I feel to the full how dear to my heart you are and always will be." Von Breuning could not resist that, and the friendship resumed, though the two no longer attempted to live together.

Following a conflict with another friend, Beethoven was quite childlike in his distress and need for reassurance. "I was always good," he wrote, "and always strove to be upright and true in my actions. Otherwise how could you have loved me? . . . Ah! for 8 weeks I have displeased my best and noblest friend. . . . It was an inexcusable thoughtfulness. . . . Oh how ashamed I am. . . . I scarcely dare to ask you for your friendship any more." Beethoven concluded with his usual passion: "O God!—I must myself come to you and throw myself in your arms."

Despite his touchiness, ungovernable temper, and unjust suspicions, Beethoven had a great capacity for love and must have been rather lovable. His talent alone would not have made people care for him and take care of him as they did. Friends forgave him again and again because, as one of them said, "all in all, he was a dear, good fellow; only his variable humor and his violence where others were concerned, often did him disservice."

"Blessed is he who restrains his passions," Beethoven wrote. That was a blessing he did not know at first hand. Of all his manic symptoms, rage was the one that hurt others the most and did him the greatest damage. Irascibility also complicated his professional life. In 1808 he decided to arrange a concert of his own works as a way of augmenting his income, which he thought necessary. But he treated the members of the orchestra so roughly during rehearsal that they refused to play unless he was kept away. One of the singers was so incensed that she refused to perform under any circumstances, and a substitute had to be found.

Beethoven also became suddenly and unpredictably explosive when he was not working. According to one of his companions,

> One day, at noon, we were eating dinner in the "Swan" tavern when the waiter brought him the wrong dish. No sooner had Beethoven remarked about it and received a somewhat uncivil reply, that he took the platter—it was calf's lights with an abundance of gravy—and flung it at the waiter's head. The poor fellow was carrying a whole slew of other portions intended for other guests, on his arm . . . and was quite helpless. The gravy ran down his face and he and Beethoven shouted and abused each other while all the other guests burst into laughter.

This confrontation took place when Beethoven was in his early thirties, a period in his life in which he had fist fights with his brothers.

In his last decade, when age should have weakened if not mellowed him, reports of his rages became more frequent, while his behavior was just as violent and somewhat more bizarre. One of the composer's pupils was the six-year-old son of a friend. Beethoven hit the child on the knuckles with a knitting needle and thus lost a pupil. Though quite deaf in 1817, Beethoven still had one student left. He could not hear him play but he watched the young man's hands to see if they hit the wrong keys of the piano. When that happened, Beethoven became frenzied. His face turned red, his forehead swelled, and the veins bulged. He would pinch the unfortunate student very hard and once bit him in the shoulder. Pinching and biting are not forms of punishment, they are signs of rage. With the manic-depressive's rapid shift of mood, Beethoven was quite charming as soon as the lesson was over. During another fit of violence, he choked his nephew Karl. In his rages Beethoven would throw books at his servants.

Beethoven could lose his temper without any rational provocation. One day while he was having a few drinks in a tavern, he took a dislike to the person sitting nearest to him for no reason at all. When glaring at the individual did not dislodge him, Beethoven spat on the floor. He alternated spitting and staring until at last he said loudly, "What a scoundrelly face!" and ran out of the room.

Two years later, Beethoven again had an episode of irritable mania. Although he was supposed to be posing for his portrait, he was too agitated to hold still. The restlessness of mania makes immobility almost impossible. At times Beethoven walked out of the room while the painter was working on him. The artist worked as quickly as he could, trying to oblige his impatient sitter. As soon as the sitting was over Beethoven unleashed his rage, castigating the painter for the unforgivable crime of making his sitter face a window.

WORK MANIA

The dedicated artist tries to work whenever he can, regardless of his mental and physical condition, provided that he is not so ill that his efforts are substandard. It is possible to accomplish something, even in depression and illness, if one is not completely incapacitated. Mechanical work can be done then. The creative part of artistic production, if the result is to have value, requires that all one's physical and mental resources be available. If the work is to be truly exceptional, then even more is wanted. One needs inspiration: the energy, power, and flow of ideas that mania can bring.

Many artists have discovered that in certain moods the work comes easily and is of the highest quality. So they try to reproduce the circumstances that give rise to those fertile moods. Before the conditioned response was discovered by psychologists, artists were trying to induce it in themselves. A painter may find that putting on his smock and smelling paint or turpentine helps to induce his working mania. Beethoven relied on walking out of doors. Even with such aids, however, nothing is certain. The mania may not come, or it may arrive but not last long enough, or it may come at a time when to do any work is impossible. But it is so valuable to the artist that he tries to seize it whenever it arrives. Therefore, when he is inspired, everything else must be put aside until the work is done, or the mania subsides, whichever happens first. For Beethoven, the inspiration of his manic states took precedence over his physical needs, his obligations to students, and the company of friends.

In 1804 Beethoven was on a long walk with a student, who later wrote:

> We went so far astray that we did not get back . . . until nearly 8 o'clock . . . He had been all the time humming and sometimes howling, always up and down, without singing any definite notes. In answer to my question what it was he said "A theme for the last movement of the sonata has occurred to me." When we entered the room he ran to the pianoforte without taking off his hat. I took a seat in the corner and he soon forgot all about me. Now he stormed for at least an hour with the beautiful finale of the sonata. Finally he got up, was surprised to see me and said: "I cannot give you a lesson today. I must do some more work."

Now and then the composer was caught by inspiration while visiting friends. One of them describes Beethoven's transports in 1814. "He . . . tore open the pianoforte, . . . began to improvise marvelously. . . . The hours went by, but Beethoven improvised on. Supper, which he had purposed to eat with us, was served, but—he would not permit himself to be disturbed. It was late when he embraced me, and declining the meal, he hurried home. The next day the admirable composition was finished."

While Beethoven was composing, his head would become hot, and he found it necessary to cool off from time to time. He did this by dousing himself with water, which would run onto the floor and through the ceiling of the room below. When Beethoven had a musical idea but no paper, he would write on the window shutters. The scribbling and inundations contributed to his difficulties with landlords.

The composer could not work continually, though he would have liked to, as he did not have mania at his beck and call. Sometimes he took time off from work for recreation; at other times, he was forced to relax by a period of sterility. "Not on my life," he wrote, "would I have believed that I could be so lazy as I am here. If it is followed by an outburst of industry, something worthwhile may be accomplished." He was waiting for mania to return.

Although Beethoven was at his most creative during periods of mania, his works express a tremendous range of moods, from the humorous and the joyous to the most despairing. Sometimes this range of emotion occurs within a single piece. Mood changes can be as abrupt and extreme in the music as they were in the musician. However, there is no simple connection between the mood of the artist as he works and the mood his work expresses. Much of what he does comes from memory of what he has felt, from emotions that lie buried like veins of ore, far from the light of awareness.

WORK PERIODS AND PRODUCTIVITY

When Beethoven spent the summer at his brother Johann's country home in 1826, he would start composing at 5:30 in the morning. Presumably the whole household woke then, because Beethoven would sing and noisily keep time with his hands and feet during the process of creation. After breakfast with the family at 7:30, he would take to the fields with his notebook, composing as he went along at a fast jog. From noon until 3:00, he had lunch and then wrote music in his room. At 3:00 he again went outside, composing and rambling until supper at 7:30. After that was over he composed in his room until bedtime at 10:00 P.M. Anyone who has done creative work knows that this is a staggering schedule even for a young man, and Beethoven was fifty-six, only a year away from his death. Mania overcame both his age and poor health.

When he was two years younger, he had even more energy. Then his mania limited him to four or five hours of sleep nightly, and he would regularly compose from midnight until 3:00 A.M. Mania not only gave him extra working hours, it gave him the confidence and appetite for works on the grand scale, and the energy to attend to the smallest detail of his creations. No effort was too great, no revision too tedious. At the same time, his manic excitement and hunger for work kept him from going stale before a large project was completed. It may be that major works of art can not be accomplished without the aid of mania and what it supplies. One of Beethoven's friends called him "one of the most active men that ever lived."

Eighteen hundred and one was another fertile year. Beethoven recorded: "I live entirely in my music; and hardly have I completed one composition when I have already begun another. At my present rate of composing, I often produce 3 or 4 works at the same time." People who can work on two or more projects concurrently have high productivity. If they tire of one work, they can take up one of the others, forestalling boredom. Since a change of activity can renew a working mania, it may be that depression is warded off as well. If nothing else intervenes, one can work continually for very long periods.

Beethoven, however, did not compose round the calendar. Winter was a relatively fallow season, partly because he was often sick and depressed then, partly because his most intense manias took place during the summer months. In 1825 he wrote, "In winter I do but little. I only elaborate and score what I have written during the summer. Yet even that consumes a great deal of time." He could still accomplish the more mechanical phases of his work when manic inspiration was missing. However at times of illness, he abandoned even the mechanical work. He wrote in the latter part of his life: "So long as I am sick, I will do no work no matter how much Diabelli and Haslinger [his publishers] may urge me; for I have to be in the mood for it. Often I have been unable to compose for a long time and then all at once the desire returned to me." He recognized that he too had blocks. They particularly afflicted him during depressions. As a friend noted, "He composed, or was unable to compose, according to the moods of happiness, vexation and sorrow."

PERFORMING

Beethoven could pass into varied levels of mania when he was creating music and when he was enjoying the company of friends and admirers. Performing combined both of those incitements. His performances were often as creative as his work with pen and paper. In that era it was expected that musicians be able to compose while performing: to create new music as they played. In Beethoven's case, some of the material from his improvisations was later incorporated into written compositions. He would improvise, we are told, "especially when he was in good humor or excited. . . . The wealth of ideas which crowed in upon him, the moods to which he surrendered himself, the variety of treatment . . . were inexhaustible." These are indicators of mania: excitement, happiness, and flight of ideas. The same thing is repeated twenty years later. Beethoven was quite deaf but "delightfully gay" at a dinner party. A new acquaintance, an Englishman, furnishes this account of Beethoven giving a musical improvisation. "After dinner, he was coaxed to play extempore . . . he played for about 20 minutes in a most extraordinary manner, sometimes very fortissimo, but full of genius. When he rose at the conclusion of his playing he appeared quite agitated. No one could be more agreeable than he was— plenty of jokes."

It is easier for the composer, writer, or painter to work around his moods, to wait out depressions and make up for lost time during manias, than it is for the performer. The performer must try to do his best when the audience is there, regardless of how he may feel. One would expect that a man of such intense moods as Beethoven would be an uneven performer, and this was the case. Fellow musicians noted "the unreliable reading of one and the same composition—one day intellectually brilliant and full of characteristic expression, the next freakish to the verge of unclearness: often confused." As a musician becomes more excited, he tends to play louder and faster, with diminishing subtlety. Beethoven performed with such manic energy that he literally assaulted the keys and was a menace to the pianos of his day.

Sir John Russell, forebear of the English philosopher, furnishes this final picture of Beethoven in the throes of a manic improvisation: "The moment that he is seated at the piano, he is evidently unconscious that there is anything in existence but himself and his instrument. . . . He ran on during half an hour in a fantasy, in a style extremely varied, and marked, above all, by the most abrupt transitions. . . . The muscles of the face swell, and its veins stand out; the wild eye rolls doubly wild, the mouth quivers, and Beethoven looks like a wizard, over-powered by the demons whom he himself has called up." No one who saw Beethoven improvising could mistake him for a normal individual.

DEPRESSIVE EPISODES

This was the dark side of Beethoven's life. One might conclude that he paid for his manic energy, inspiration, and productivity with the suffering of depression and ill health. His first depression was a payment in advance, as it came when he was seventeen. There may have been previous depressions, but this was the first of which there is record. Beethoven had rushed home from Vienna just in time to see his mother before she died of tuberculosis. He wrote: "Since I have been here I have enjoyed only a few pleasant hours; during the whole time I have been troubled with asthma and I much fear that it will lead to consumption." That was depressive hypochondriasis. "I also suffer from melancholy, which for me is almost as great an evil as my illness itself."

The next illustration is from 1804. A friend writes about one of Beethoven's depressions in which misery, paranoia, social withdrawal, and indecisiveness occur. "You cannot conceive . . . what an indescribable, I might say, fearful effect the gradual loss of his hearing has had upon him. Think of the feeling of being unhappy in one of such violent temperament; in addition reservedness, mistrust, often towards his best friends, in many things want of decision."

In 1808 things were not much improved. Beethoven almost lost a finger. A friend implies that Beethoven was depressed most of the time. "He escaped a great misfortune which, added to his deafness, would have completely ruined his good humor, which, as it is, is of rare occurrency."

In 1813 the composer was in such a severe depression that he could not take care of himself. He no longer had a decent coat or a shirt without holes, though he certainly could afford to dress well. Friends noticed that he was, at times, "positively dirty" and was in a state of "almost continual melancholy." He admitted that "my condition . . . is probably the unhappiest of my life."

Karl's entry into Beethoven's life made it, on balance, even more wretched. He was now completely deaf and wrote: "God help me . . . hear my supplication, but to be with Karl in the future, when now no possibility can be found. Oh harsh fate, oh cruel destiny, no, no, my unhappy condition will never end." A year later, in 1816, Beethoven called himself "the most unhappy of all mortals." Between 1814 and 1819 Beethoven was relatively unproductive and did not complete any major works. In 1817, again in depression, he wrote that he was sick of life: "I appear destined to drain the bitter cup of all sorrow. If only it could once and for all be brought to an end!" Ruminations on death are symptoms of depression. The following year he was again waiting for spring with despondency, "and so many circumstances, and my health so bad at the time all made me so discouraged." In winter he was often ill and depressed. Depression lowers resistance to various physical ailments and being ill can intensify depression. Beethoven, in common with many depressives, suffered through many winters of successive onslaughts of depression and illness.

A close companion, Anton Schindler, relates what deafness was doing to the composer in 1822. Beethoven was trying to conduct the orchestra in a performance of his opera *Fidelio*. He could not hear the orchestra at all, could not tell what measure they were playing, and the confusion was so great that the musicians finally gave up. Beethoven turned to ask Schindler why the musicians were still. Schindler tells us:

> Hastily I wrote in effect "Please do not go on; more at home." With a bound he was on the parterre and said merely "Out, quick!". Without stopping he ran towards his lodgings. Inside he threw himself on the sofa, covered his face with his hands and remained in this attitude till we sat down to eat. During the meal not a sound came from his lips; he was the picture of profound melancholy and depression. When I tried to get away from the meal he begged me not to leave until it was time to go to the theater.

SOCIAL WITHDRAWAL

A neighbor remembered Beethoven being reclusive even in boyhood. "His happiest hours were when he was free from the company of his parents, which was seldom the case—when all the family were away and he was alone by himself." This does not prove that Beethoven had boyhood depressions, but it does add him to the long list of geniuses who, even as children, learned to look for their chief satisfactions not in the social milieu, but within themselves. The neighbor adds, "One could not say that Ludwig cared much for companions or society."

No one who knew Beethoven as a child could remember him playing. At age eleven he appeared to others thus: "Outside of music he understood nothing of social life; consequently he was ill-humored with other people, did not know how to converse with them, and withdrew into himself, so that he was looked upon as a misanthrope."

When Beethoven was forty-one, people were making the same observations about him, "The strange man lives completely in his art, is very industrious, and is unconcerned about other people." For the most part, Beethoven's happiest hours were still those he spent at his work. It is a behavior often attributed to geniuses, and it may be a contributing factor to high achievement. In 1815, while Karl made his disturbing entry into Beethoven's life, the composer was depressed and disgusted with the world: "Let them stab me and strike me! God will help me. I am so tired of contact with people that I hardly want to see or hear another one." For Beethoven, social withdrawal sometimes became tinged with paranoia. In 1804 he wrote, "I am not safe from people; I must flee in order to be alone."

It is difficult for a manic-depressive to recognize that his moods dictate his behavior, but Beethoven was able to do this from time to time. Though he could not force himself to act contrary to his moods, he was able to maintain friendships even when he had to withdraw from people. He would reassure his friends, "If you do not see me, put it down to my customary solitariness." Or he would explain, "I often have my hours of gloom when I tell those about me [his servants] to admit no one." Both of those statements confirm that depression, with its social withdrawal, was the state in which Beethoven spent much of his time. In his later years he achieved another difficult feat. He learned to live with his illness and accepted himself as he was.

THOUGHTS OF DEATH AND SUICIDE

Beethoven was suicidal on a number of occasions. In 1802 he wrote a will that was also an evaluation of his character and existence. In it he speaks of past temptations to take his own life, and also of his present longing for death, which is almost unendurable.

> How humiliating was it, when someone standing close to me heard a distant flute, and I heard nothing. . . . Such incidents almost drove me to despair; at times I was on the point of putting an end to my life—art alone restrained my hand. Oh! it seemed as if I could not quit this earth until I had produced all I felt within me, so I continued this wretched life—. . . I joyfully hasten to meet death. If it come before I have had opportunity to develop all my artistic faculties, it will come . . . too soon, and I should probably wish it later— yet even then I shall be happy, for will it not deliver me from a state of endless suffering?

Eight years later he was forty and again resisted the temptation to commit suicide because of his duty to music, without which, he says, "I should have long ago been no more—and indeed by my own hand."

There is a possible suicide attempt in 1813. According to Beethoven, "A number of unfortunate incidents occurring one after the other have really driven me into a state bordering on mental confusion." This may have been a stuporous depression. His brother Caspar was dying of tuberculosis, and Beethoven had just ended the most serious love affair of his life. While visiting Countess Erdody, an old friend, Beethoven disappeared and was found wandering on her estate three days later. It was thought that he wanted to starve himself to death, but he may have been stopped by the overwhelming disorganization that the most severe depression can cause. There is no conclusive evidence that Beethoven tried to kill himself. He appeared to have been able to find a reason for staying alive. In 1816 his nephew Karl gave him a motive: "During the last six weeks my health has been very shaky, so that I often think of death, but without fear, only for my poor Karl would my death come too soon."

Beethoven's last recorded statements about death were made in 1817. Apparently death was much on Beethoven's mind. "As for me, I am in despair so often and would like to end my life, for there is never an end to all these afflictions. God have pity on me, I consider myself as good as lost." To another correspondent he wrote, "I only say to you that I am better; last night I often thought about my death, also such thoughts are not unusual to me even in the daytime."

In depression people often become convinced that death is rapidly approaching them, a belief that Beethoven also held. Two years prematurely he wrote: "If my condition does not improve I shall not be in London next year—perhaps in my grave. Thank God the part is nearly played." His depression was so painful that he welcomed death as a release from torment that seemed to have no other relief.

WORK AND ILLNESS

While illness depressed Beethoven, mania may have contributed to his ill health. His disregard of physical consequences began, as Czerny tells us, in youth. "He had, as he often said, practiced day and night during his youth, and worked so hard that his health had suffered." Driven by the energy of mania, he periodically overworked throughout his life.

At age seventeen, Beethoven began to have asthma attacks that, together with a bad cough and sinus headaches, plagued him every winter. There was no aspirin or other medication to relieve his pain. By the time he was thirty, his digestive system was disordered with, as his doctor recorded, "loss of appetite . . . indigestion, and annoying belching, and alternating obstinate constipation and frequent diarrhea." These symptoms may have had other causes, but they are often concomitants of depression.

By 1817 winter-long illness was a regular part of Beethoven's life. "Since October 16," he wrote five months later, "I have been very ill with a feverish cold, from the effects of which I am still suffering; I shall probably not recover until the end of spring or even the summer. . . . For the past year up to the present I have been continually ill; likewise during the summer I had an attack of jaundice, which lasted until the end of August." He adds, "Thank God things are better and it appears that I am to be cheered up by the return of health and may live again for my art, which for the last 2 years has certainly not been the case."

Beethoven's body continued to disintegrate. His mania propelled him through illnesses in the summer of 1823, but he had painful problems with his eyes from April into July. In August he wrote, "I am feeling really badly and not only because of my eyes." Thanks to the magic of mania, that was one of his most inspired summers, filled with ecstatic rambles in the woods and writing music all day long. So much of Beethoven's life was spent in sickness and pain, weakness, and depression that it is remarkable that he accomplished anything at all. Given the pervasiveness of his misery, his work is all the more miraculous.

DEAFNESS

Beethoven's manias fueled his creativity, gave him courage, and saved him from the total despair that his deafness could have imposed on him. We must also give him credit for unusual persistence and total dedication to his art. His hearing abnormality began with a loss of ability to hear high tones and ringing in the ears when he was only eighteen. Tinnitus can be reduced or extinguished by antidepressant medicines; thus, had they been available at the time, Beethoven might have enjoyed many benefits from antidepressant therapy. It is one of history's crueler jokes that Beethoven, as a mature musician, could not hear normally. As his talent developed, as his mastery increased, his hearing diminished. When he was thirty he wrote: "My hearing has become weaker during the last 3 years . . . the humming in my ears continues day and night without ceasing. I may truly say that my life is a wretched one. For the last 2 years I have avoided all society, for it is impossible for me to say to people, 'I am deaf'." "Often I can scarcely hear anyone speaking to me; the tones, yes, but not the actual words; yet as soon as anyone shouts it is unbearable. What will come of this heaven only knows. . . . If nothing else is possible [to save him from deafness] I will defy my fate, although there will be moments in my life when I shall be God's most wretched creature."

After 1817 Beethoven never again heard his own compositions, or music of any kind. During Beethoven's last ten years, music, the beauty and joy of his life, the reason for his existence, continued only in his imagination and memory.

DELUSIONS OF POVERTY

Beethoven neither lived nor died a poor man. He had a good, if irregular, income from his compositions and also, for years, from regular contributions by the local nobility. However, in periods of depression he had the delusion that destitution was imminent and would needlessly borrow money.

PARANOIA

Loss of hearing can make even normal people develop paranoid tendencies. Therefore, a deaf manic-depressive may be inclined to paranoia on two accounts. Beethoven would argue with waiters about the number of rolls he was served because he expected servants to take advantage of his deafness. However, he thought he was being cheated long before he was deaf, as recorded by someone who knew him in 1801. "Easily excited, he would call people cheats to their faces. . . . Finally, in the taverns which he was most accustomed to frequent, all came to know his oddities and his absent-mindedness, and let him say or do as he wished, even permitting him to leave without paying his bill." Beethoven reserved his greatest distrust for members of his own family. He called Johann's wife a "fat son of a bitch and bastard." Beethoven made the life of his other sister-in-law, Karl's mother, quite difficult. Defying the terms of his brother's will, Beethoven took her son from her and denied her any access to the boy. He did not even permit her to give her son a hat. Beethoven never referred to her without calling her, at the least, "bestial." Certain that she poisoned her husband, Beethoven insisted on an autopsy. The autopsy indicated tuberculosis as the cause of death.

Beethoven's delusions peaked in 1816. He decided that Karl's mother was a prostitute and that she constantly spied on him and Karl. Then came delusions of grandeur. Beethoven discovered that he was on a mission from God, a "holy cause." That is a common delusion of the psychotic stage of mania. Beethoven also announced, "I am now the real physical father of my deceased brother's child," which he meant literally.

In later years, these delusions gave way to the more common fantasies of paranoia. Beethoven expected to be poisoned and in his last years insisted that his nephew and friends taste everything he ate or drank. The composer continually fired servants because he thought that that they were always playing "infernal tricks" on him, for which he threw chairs at them. Paranoia led him to change publishers several times in the belief that they were out to cheat him. Manic-depressive writers, among them Dickens, have been known to develop the same delusion.

Anything and everything made Beethoven suspicious of his friends. When they dared to disagree with him he would tell them, "I must say it occurs to me that you are as much my enemy as my friend." If they merely stayed around helping him for any length of time they would be told, "I have a certain fear that some great misfortune will befall me through you." He changed doctors more than once because he thought they "had strong designs" on him and "lacked honesty." While some of his suspicions about people may have been justified, it seems unlikely that he was always surrounded by schemers.

DELUSIONS OF REJECTION BY THE MUSIC WORLD

Beethoven's paranoia was not limited to distrust of friends, relatives, servants, doctors, landlords, music publishers, and strangers. He also expected to be mistreated by fellow musicians and the audience. The first musician to receive, but not deserve, his distrust was Haydn, who taught him for a while in 1793. Beethoven believed that Haydn did not like him. In actuality, Haydn wrote: "Experts and amateur alike cannot but admit that Beethoven will in time become one of the greatest musical artists in Europe. I shall be proud to call myself his teacher. I only wish that he might remain with me for some time yet. . . . In hundreds of situations I have always found that he is prepared, of his own accord, to sacrifice everything for his art." Haydn wrote this encomium to the elector at Bonn, Beethoven's former employer, and also requested financial assistance for his student.

In 1824 Beethoven, who always deplored the state of music in Vienna, decided that he would premiere his Ninth Symphony elsewhere because, he felt, it would not be appreciated in town. His friends had to work hard to convince him otherwise.

THE ETHICS OF GENIUS

Beethoven looked on himself as a high priest of art. The gifted, he felt, were called upon to make every sacrifice that art demanded, and the less gifted were obliged to make every sacrifice to the more gifted. "Power is the morality of men who stand out from the rest, and it is also mine," he said, as though he were a student of Napoleon. In his more grandiose moments Beethoven bragged, "I value them [friends] only as instruments upon which I play." As his letters of contrition testify, Beethoven cared more for his friends than that, but he did use them. He required that his friend Baron Zmeskall give him wine, lend him money, deal with his publishers, hire his domestics, assemble performers to play music with him, keep him supplied with quill pens, and finally, fill in on the cello. Such self-centeredness is a major feature of the manic character.

Beethoven, far from being society's victim, acted as though the artist could do no wrong. He would promise work and not do it, promise dedications that he subsequently gave to others, and sell the same piece to three different publishers. Anyone else would have been prosecuted for such conduct, but Beethoven was saved by his fame and reputation for insanity. His disregard of commitments he had made, and of social and ethical guidelines, is characteristic of manics.

The myth of the solitary genius disprized by a philistine public was created when composers lost their patrons and salaried positions. This was happening in Beethoven's day, and his uninhibited paranoia strengthened the myth. His colleague, Czerny, was there to see the truth:

> It has been repeatedly said in foreign lands that Beethoven was not respected in Vienna and was suppressed. The truth is that already as a youth he received all manner of support from high aristocracy and enjoyed as much care and respect as ever fell to the lot of a young artist. . . . Later, too, when he estranged many by his hypochondria [depression] nothing was charged against his often very striking peculiarities . . . and it is doubtful if he would have been left so undisturbed in any other country. It is true that as an artist he had to fight cabals, but the public was innocent in this. He was always marvelled at and respected as an extraordinary being and his greatness was suspected even by those who did not understand him.

Indeed, Beethoven did not have to wait long for success. By the time he was thirty he had five publishers and international fame. This is not now, and never was, the common lot of composers. At that time Beethoven was pleased enough to boast, "My art is winning me friends and renown, and what more do I want?" He added, "And this time I shall make a good deal of money."

OBJECTIVITY ABOUT HIMSELF AND HIS WORK

Lesser artists fail to rise above their own egos and, heavily encumbered by their self-esteem, they cease to criticize their work, to grow in their craft, to undertake what is worthwhile regardless of risk to fame and finances. It is rare to find a man like Rembrandt, who relinquished a popular style and a prospering career in order to go deeper into his art. Beethoven took the same plunges. While he sometimes wrote for the music market, he refused to limit his work to the measure of what amateurs, the main support of the music-publishing business, would like or to be able to play. In his last years he even departed from what professionals could understand, and his work still challenges their technique.

Beethoven had the temperament of an explorer. He did not know where he was going or what he would find, but the important thing was to move on, to leave behind what was familiar and safe. It never bothered him to criticize his own work, and he was confident that he could do better the next time. He was willing to take chances, to fail. Even as he was dying he was excited by the challenge of his oratorio, which he did not survive to write. In 1806, after hearing a friend practice an early Beethoven composition, the composer asked "By whom is that?" The performer answered "By you." To which Beethoven responded, "Such nonsense by me? Oh, Beethoven, what an ass you were!" He was not saying that to be amusing. He explained once that as he moved forward, he no longer cared for his early work. He did not value compositions simply because they were his. "You yourself know what changes a few years produce in an artist who is constantly advancing; the greater the progress he makes in his art the less do his works satisfy him." In 1815 he was more critical than his critics. When another musician told him how popular his sonatas and chamber pieces were in England, Beethoven said "That's damned stuff. I wish it were burned!" Although he was objective about his music, he was not emotionally divorced from it. For instance, when he wrote his B-flat Quartet in 1826, it moved him tremendously; just the memory of it—he could never hear it—would make him weep again.

Beethoven had his moments of grandiosity, but in reading his letters and quotations from his conversation, one does not feel the weight of a sprawling, overbearing ego as one does with Napoleon. "Good God!" Beethoven would say, "how pestered one is when one has such a wretched face as I have!" Or, "To do something like putting my papers in order, I need a dreadful amount of patience which, however, when it does make its appearance, anyone like myself must hold on to, because usually it is never there."

ALCOHOLISM

By the time he was thirty, his physicians recognized that Beethoven had a drinking problem. Four years later the composer indicated how important drinking was to him when he complained to a friend, "That my brother hasn't yet attended to the wine is unforgivable, since it is so necessary and beneficial for me." Beneficial it was not. Johann Beethoven, who was slow with the wine, describes what it did to his brother. "He would eat nothing at lunch except soft-boiled eggs, but he would drink more wine so that he often suffered diarrhea, thereby his belly became bigger and bigger, and he·wore a bandage over it for a long time." Beethoven was unwilling to give up wine even when his doctors prohibited it. Alcohol had become a regular part of his day, consumed at meals—"a great deal at table," a friend says—and if Beethoven went out at night, "He sometimes became tipsy."

His doctors learned that the composer went on binges, in addition to daily drinking. The precipitant might be emotional stress or hypochondriasis. Whenever he had attacks of asthma, Beethoven was sure that it was tuberculosis. He then drank to calm his fear. He also got drunk to celebrate performances of his music. According to his physician, Beethoven began to drink even more heavily during the last seven years of his life.

By December 1826, there were many syptoms of liver failure resulting from excessive alcohol consumption: jaundice, edema, and pain in the liver, which was lumpy. Dr. Warwich observed: "On my morning visit I found him quite upset; his entire body jaundiced; while a terrible fit of vomiting and diarrhea during the night had threatened to kill him. Shaking and trembling, he writhed with the pain which raged in his liver and intestines; and his feet, hitherto only moderately puffed up, were now greatly swollen. From this time on his dropsy developed; his secretions decreased in quantity, his liver gave convincing evidence of the presence of hard knots, his jaundice grew worse." In the course of his final illness, Beethoven had a brief manic episode during which he drank too much spiked punch. During this brief mania, "He grew lively," the doctor noted, and "often all sorts of witty ideas occurred to him, and he even dreamt of being able to complete the oratorio 'Saul and David' which he had commenced. Yet, as was to have been foreseen his joy was of short duration. . . . He wandered in his talk. . . . He grew more violent."

In February 1827, with only two weeks of life left, Beethoven wrote two letters to Schotts, his publishers, requesting wine. They sent him sixteen bottles. He also wrote to ask Baron Pasqualati, an old friend, for more, though the man just sent him some. In that letter Beethoven mentioned that he had also received "several bottles" of wine from his physicians. He was additionally being supplied by his friends Streicher and von Breuning. Alcoholic dependence is evidenced not only by the large amounts Beethoven requested, but also by the efforts he expended to secure a supply of wine when his physical suffering was intense and his strength nonexistent.

Evidently, Beethoven drank himself to death. Many manic-depressives die from the consequences of abuse of alcohols or drugs, both of which are taken as self-medicants. Until recently, alcohol and opium were the only mood modifiers available to the general public, and Beethoven used the local drug.

MANIC ROMANCE

Beethoven remained a bachelor. However, his friends attest that "there never was a time when Beethoven was not in love, and that in the highest degree," though "as a rule, only for a short time." That is exactly what one would expect of a person whose moods reversed themselves as quickly as Beethoven's did. Some of his friends even claimed that he was a bit of a Don Juan, despite his homeliness, though they may have been joking. In any case, he was interested in quality, not quantity; he wanted love. "Sensual enjoyment," he said, "without a union of souls is bestial; after it, one experiences not a trace of noble sentiment but rather regret."

Perhaps love belongs on the list of essentials for the great artist. If so, mania will be helpful, making him feel attractive, eliminating inhibitions, and bringing his sexual feelings to fever pitch. It will even provide him with the delusion that he is loved, at least for a while, and his confidence will advance his cause. Some of Beethoven's most beautiful songs are charged with his ardor. That he was passionate, he admits: "I am not wicked, ardent blood is all my failing . . . many a wild impulse assails my heart."

One of them assailed his heart in the spring of 1805. Beethoven was a snob and reserved his infatuations for aristocratic ladies. Unfortunately, they were also snobs, looking for something more suitable than a deaf musician. There is enough recorded in Beethoven's letters to Countess Deyn to outline the entire sequence of their affair, from infatuation through rejection. Beethoven begins: "Oh, beloved J, it is no desire for the other sex that draws me to you, no, it is just you, your whole self. . . . When I came to you—it was with the firm resolve not to let a single spark of love be kindled in me. But you have conquered me—The question is whether you wanted to do so?" She answers some time later, "The pleasure of your company could have been the finest ornament of my life if you had been able to love me less sensuously— that I cannot satisfy this sensuous love—does this cause you anger—I would have to break holy vows were I to listen to your desire—." In September he wrote, "A thousand voices are constantly whispering to me that you are my only friend, my only beloved." But he was not successful with that line, and the situation deteriorated. "Is it really a fact—" he wrote, "that you do not want to see me any more—if so—do be frank—I certainly deserve that you should be frank with me."

That was not the end of love for Beethoven. In 1810 he wanted to marry a girl twenty-two years his junior and even sent for his birth certificate, but her parents did not consider him acceptable. She married someone else. Five years later he told new friends that "he was unhappy in love" and that it was "now as on the first day," even though there was no hope. He may have been referring to a mysterious love whom his biographers call "the immortal beloved" for lack of a real name. He wrote but did not mail to her: "Much as you love me—I love you more—But do not ever conceal yourself from me . . . Oh God— so near! so far!" "You make me at once the happiest and unhappiest of men—At my age I need a steady, quiet life—can that be so in our connection?" He did not seem inclined to find out.

Women who loved Beethoven had much to overlook. One of those to whom he paid court found him quite resistible because, she said, "Beethoven's habit of expectorating in the room, his negligent clothing and his extravagant behavior were not particularly attractive." One refused his proposal of marriage, she said, "Because he was so ugly and half crazy!" Another was put off by his "Loud voice and his indifference towards others." She was embarrassed when people "stopped and took him for a madman; his laugh was particularly loud and ringing. What is more, when Beethoven saw people in the street that he did not want to speak to, he broke into a run." His friends said he was "half crazy," and when enraged, that "he became like a wild animal." "Some say he is a lunatic," and "I learned yesterday that Beethoven had become crazy" are the remarks that were making the rounds. They were enough to deter any prospective bride.

Eventually, Beethoven told himself: "There is no longer happiness except in thyself, in thy art—O God, give me strength to conquer myself, nothing must chain me to life." This cry of pain came with Beethoven's realization that he would never marry, would spend his life alone, and, he told himself, "Thou mayest no longer be a man."

MANIC REBELLION

Beethoven made his own rules in life as he did in music. He resented the elaborate etiquette required of the courtiers of his day. He could never have kept a position as court composer for very long: he would have walked out or been thrown out. When he was staying for a while at Prince Lichnowsky's demesne, Beethoven was annoyed that he was required to be clean at dinner. "Now every day I must be home at half-past 3 to change my clothes, shave and so on—I can't stand it!" When Beethoven was staying with another nobleman, his host, after hearing Beethoven's B-minor Mass, said "But my dear Beethoven, what in the world have you done now?" Beethoven not only left the castle at once, he left the city.

He was too proud to accept money for music lessons. A countess tells us: "He would accept no payment though he was very poor; but accepted linen under the pretext that it had been hand-sewn by the countess.—In the same way he taught Princess Odescalci and Baroness Ertmann." Beethoven's attitude was "don't forget that I, too, am a knight, even though not by title." He took a special delight in humbling the aristocracy. A witness says: "He was unmannererly both in demeanor and behavior. He was very proud; I have seen Countess Thun . . . lying on her knees before him [the composer was seated on the sofa] and begging him to play something—and Beethoven would not do it. But then, Countess Thun was a very eccentric woman." When Beethoven visited people, he would survey the room before entering and then enter only if he approved of all the other guests.

In matters of music, he was even more unyielding. If anyone, regardless how exalted, talked while he was playing, he would say, "I will not play for such swine" and leave. After a difference with Prince Lobkowitz over some bassoons, Beethoven yelled at the palace doors, "Lobkowitz is an ass!" The fervently music-loving aristocracy had no defense against him.

The government was equally tolerant and did nothing even when Beethoven said about the emperor, "Such a rascal ought to be hanged to the first tree!" On another occasion the composer remarked, "From the Emperor to the bootblack, all Viennese are worthless. I have only one pupil, and I'd like to get rid of him if I could—it is the Archduke." Free speech was not allowed in the empire, but Beethoven was excepted. Anyone else saying what he did in public would have been jailed.

Beethoven had no room in his soul for authority of any kind, not even that of his teachers. A friend tells us that all of them "had the highest esteem for Beethoven [but] they were agreed with regard to their opinion of him as a student. Each said that Beethoven was so obstinate and bent on having his own way, that he had to learn much which he refused to accept . . . through bitter personal experience." This is a common manic attitude.

ART VERSUS EGO

Art is a form of communication, but it is not like a billboard, which is designed to catch your attention and immediately deliver its message. Works of art have many levels of meaning. They are bearers of significance. They tell us what it is to be a human being, moving through time in the world we have. But art does not simply tell us: it makes us feel it, live it, with clarity and beauty that ordinary experience can not provide. When other messages are imposed on a work of art, it becomes trivial. Art cannot tell us about God, or love, or death, and at the same time sell us a bar of soap. Art is also ruined when it indicates to us: "The man who made this thinks he is wonderful." Art and ego are antithetical. Let the artist be as egomaniacal as he likes at leisure; but when he works, he must forget himself or he will never accomplish anything of much value. Beethoven was successful in the struggle against ego. He adhered to principles that maintained the purity of his music. Only when the work for the day was done did he let his ego take over. Egocentricity is an acute problem for the manic-depressive, both in mania and depression. Beethoven was self-centered in both states, but when he composed, he put all that behind him.

He was able to rise above egotism because he had an idol. In his last years, after having achieved international renown, he still believed that there was a composer greater than himself. This attitude is essential to the continued growth of an artist. If he recognizes no one as his superior, he begins to feel that nothing greater than what he has already done can be, or need be, achieved. His effort slackens, he stagnates, and eventually he decays. Beethoven never made that deadly error. When asked "Whom do you consider the greatest composer that ever lived?" he answered without hesitation, "Handel. To him I bow the knee." And he proceeded to do so. Two years later, during Beethoven's terminal illness, the works of Handel were sent to him. "I have long wanted them," he said, "for Handel is the ablest composer who ever lived. I can still learn from him." Whether or not Beethoven was correct about Handel does not matter. The essential thing is that he felt he could still learn from someone, that his work still had room for improvement.

Another attitude that preserved Beethoven from hypertrophy of the ego was a dedication to music that excluded everything else from importance. He wrote this to a little piano student who had sent him a letter: "The artist has no pride . . . he sees that art has no limits; he senses darkly how far he is from the goal."

Unlike the amateur, the professional artist does not intend to have fun when he works, though he often does. His aim is to do the best that he can, no matter how much patience and effort are required, no matter how much boredom and discouragement afflict him. In addition to patience and hard work, Beethoven demanded of himself a total commitment of feeling and intelligence to his art. He relentlessly drove himself toward perfection.

His attitude toward fame allowed him to maintain his independence as an artist. "I never thought of writing for reputation and honors; what is in my heart must out and so I write it down." He gave his life to climbing as close as possible to the summit of his art. He did not expect the masses to follow him that high. "Even if only a few understand me," he said, "I am satisfied."

PORTRAIT OF AN ARTIST

Beethoven's illness left its stamp on his music. His teacher Haydn was aware of the intensity of the mood, the manic rebelliousness and depressive coloration in Beethoven's compositions. Haydn said to his former pupil:

> You will accomplish more than has ever been accomplished; have thoughts that no other has had. You will never sacrifice a beautiful idea to a tyrannical rule, and in that you will be right. But you will sacrifice rules to your moods, for

you seem to me to be a man of many heads and hearts. One will always find something irregular in your compositions, things of beauty, but rather dark and strange, because you, too, are rather obscure and strange. In my works you will more often find something jovial, because that is what I am. Nothing could shake my natural cheerfulness, not even my wife.

This excellent analysis and prediction was made at the beginning of Beethoven's career. It proves that his manic-depressive traits were visible even then and were not the result of his subsequent deafness and alcoholism.

His music was even too manic-depressive for his fellow composer, Franz Schubert. Though Schubert was an admirer of Beethoven's, he was disturbed by the extreme contradicions of mood in Beethoven's work. Schubert complained of Beethoven's "eccentricity, which unites the tragic with the comic, the pleasant with the repulsive, heroism with rant, the very saint with the harlequin, unites, exchanges, and even confuses them." But of course, all of that describes Beethoven's character too. His music is the best portrait ever made of him.

5

Dickens

"THE PERILS OF CERTAIN ENGLISHFOLK"

Charles Dickens should have been a happy man. The father went to debtors' prison, but the son left an estate of over one million dollars (1952 value). Dickens, called by Tolstoy "a genius such as is met but once in a century," left school to work at age fifteen and became famous at age twenty-four, finishing his years as the most famous writer of his time. His was the greatest success story of the nineteenth century, but he died a tormented man, a man running to meet death head-on, driven by manic-depression. Dickens was like an engine that could not be turned off. By the time he was fifty-seven, his body was breaking down, his brain bleeding and dying.

Dickens was a man of his time, one might even say *the* man of his time, very much a part of his age. He was Victorian England, and no doubt that was part of the reason for his success as a writer: he dreamed the dreams of the century and its nightmares too. He lived in an ugly era when England, Europe, and America industrialized. Previously, England had been a nation of farmers, many of them on their own small holdings. Industry was largely confined to what families made in their own cottages, though a few water-powered factories existed. The population was only some eight million at the beginning of the nineteenth century. It ballooned to twenty-two million by 1850, despite massive emigration to all parts of the British Empire and the United States. Within England there was huge dislocation, and hamlets and villages died as the countryside emptied out. Company towns—built, owned, and run by factory owners for their profit—sprouted wherever money could be made by working people for long hours at low pay. The cities became engorged, and slums proliferated. People piled into rotting buildings without water, heat, light. Home was not a place to live in, just a place to starve and sleep in when the twelve-hour working day was done. The slums had no pavement or police, but they did have plenty of rats, crime, and disease.

Half the farm population vanished into dirty, dangerous, dead-end industrial towns. Millions of innocent people were sentenced to a lifetime of hard labor, prisoners of their poverty. The beginning of the nineteenth century saw things grow worse. Laws were passed that promoted the accumulation of land by the wealthy, and landless farm laborers had to take what wages were given them. Unions and strikes were illegal, public meetings outlawed, rioters killed without hesitation. Voting rights were limited largely to the privileged classes, and Parliament was a weapon of the rich against the rest. The wealthy wrote the laws and exempted themselves from most of the tax burden. The English had seen the French Revolution turn into a bloody "Terror," liberalism was dead, and the government practiced espionage against radical leaders. There *were* some who dared to protest against these cruel times.

Meanwhile, factories were roaring, smokestacks darkening the sky with their exhalations, and the new industrial entrepreneurs were building pseudocastles, while piling up fortunes that made aristocrats blanch. As wealth overflowed, it was reinvested in technology and science. The new mingled with the old. In 1850 cattle were still driven through the streets of London, but shopwindows were getting plate glass, the nights were bright with gas-lit street lamps, and steamships moved up and down the Thames. The country was crisscrossed by railway lines and canals, stage coaches were disappearing, and wireless telegraphy opened a new age of communication. Photographers were recording this double exposure: a vanishing world and a new one. Scientists such as Darwin brought the human species out of mythology and into science. Scientific thought had immediate consequences, such as antiseptic surgery and urban sanitation.

The working poor could not afford much of this progress, but together in the cities now, instead of scattered across the countryside, they constituted something new: a mass audience. Even though many could not read, and the government put a tax on newspapers to discourage those who could, newspapers and periodicals of all kinds were a growing phenomenon. The popular press made Dickens. His novels appeared in monthly installments in magazines. People who did not have the money for a book could buy a magazine, read it to those who could not read, and lend it to their friends. Dickens became that rare creature, an artist for all classes. Everyone could read him, but like other journalists of his day, he spoke for the lower classes. He knew the sufferings of the poor from personal experience. "I have been the champion and friend of the working man all through my career," he said, and it was true. He did not turn his back on poverty in his own days of prosperity. He went to the cotton mills, the mines, the slums, the jails, hospitals, "ragged schools," writing about what he saw. Because he wrote about the victims of society, he gave the middle and upper classes of England a knowledge of English life that they would never have sought out for themselves. England did not have a bloody revolution in the nineteenth century, partly because it developed a conscience as the century wore on, and a voice of that conscience was Dickens.

Victoria's reign was one in which laws were written and institutions established that did more for the welfare of the English people than in any previous part of their history. The secret ballot was brought into use, the right to vote much extended, and Parliament was reformed into a representative legislative body. Local government was also reformed, taking power away from the aristocracy. A civil service was developed that required entry by examination instead of by political connection. London and other large cities established police forces, making city life much less hazardous. Some one hundred crimes were removed from the list requiring the death penalty. Slavery was abolished in the British Empire. Factory hours were reduced and unions made legal. All of these reforms were agonizingly slow in coming, and women and children were not limited to a ten-hour work day until 1847. The victories were hard-won, but they did come. The other England, working England, was claiming a place for itself and developing a sense of itself, and Dickens was a part of this. He cared about the millhands and shopkeepers and clerks, servants, and orphans. He gave them names and faces and lives and made them unforgettable, and the world loved him for it. Good storytellers there had been before Dickens, but he brought a whole world out of the shadow. In return, everything: riches, fame, honor, love, all was given to him as to no man before him. Why was it not enough? Dickens himself is the answer.

"THE POOR RELATION'S STORY"

Everything with Charles Dickens was a family affair. Financial success is a case in point. His parents, his many brothers, their wives and children, his own sons and daughters, his sisters-in-law, all depended on him not only to bail them out of debt, but many of them also relied on him for full financial support. His manic-depression was also a family affair and a large factor in his family's flawed lives. Without the benefit of modern drug treatment, most manic-depressives have lives ruined by their illness. Only a tiny fraction are driven by it to achievement or success. So it was with the Dickens family.

John, the father, was a typical manic. "Chatty, lively and agreeable," an acquaintance called him. John not only liked to talk, but he also did so with flourishes. Charles imitated his father's talk in *David Copperfield,* where he put it into the mouth of Mr. Micawber. John's pressure of speech came out like icing through a pastry tube: fancy curlicues of sweet fluff. He loved to be with people, tell jokes, and host lavish parties. He was a thoroughly entertaining fellow, and his famous son would be much like him as an adult. All of this was benign enough, but John had one fatal manic flaw that opened a chasm beneath his feet. He loved to spend money, not only his own, but also everyone else's, including, eventually, that of Charles's publishers. John became a chronic bankrupt, and Charles's contributions kept him out of jail more than once. His father was imprisoned for bankruptcy when Charles was only twelve. In the course of his financial downfall, John took Charles out of school and did not give his son's future any further consideration. Charles felt that he was being abandoned, literally reduced to a nonentity, and never forgave his father for it. The pain is still fresh in these words written by Charles Dickens many years after the event:

> I know my father to be as kindhearted and generous a man as ever lived in the world. Everything that I can remember of his conduct to his wife, or children, or friends, in sickness or affection, is beyond all praise. By me, as a child, he has watched night and day, unweariedly and patiently, many nights and days. He never undertook any business, charge or trust, that he did not zealously, conscientiously, punctually, honorably discharge. His industry has always been untiring. He was proud of me, in his way . . . but, . . . he appeared to have utterly lost at this time any idea of educating me at all, and to have utterly put from him the notion that I had any claim upon him, in that regard, whatever. So I degenerated into cleaning his boots of a morning.

This negligence had fateful consequences for Charles's own sons.

Mrs. Dickens seems to have been equally well intentioned, equally irresponsible, and perhaps nearly as manic as her husband. She too had a fondness for jokes, conviviality, and parties. She was out dancing a few hours before Charles was born. She taught him to read but passed him to the maid as other babies came along. He did not learn to love well or wisely from her.

As the family fortunes were collapsing, Mrs. Dickens had a fanciful solution to the financial crisis and executed her plan with typical manic impetuosity. She moved the family into a large house at twice the rent they had been failing to pay, then she put out a brass sign designating the place as a school. She had never run one, but that did not matter for, as Charles relates, "Nobody ever came to the school, nor do I recollect that anybody ever proposed to come, or that the least preparation was made to receive anybody."

Mrs. Dickens's father also could not manage on his income, but he turned to embezzling to make up the lack. He avoided imprisonment only by permanently leaving England. Charles had a dangerous inheritance: his mother, however, was the only Dickens to die insane. He would, for other reasons, hold a lifelong grudge against her.

Charles's sisters had minor roles in his life, but all his brothers became a tribulation to him as soon as they were adults. They shared with their father faults that appear often in manics: lying, financial irresponsibility, impulsivity, and drinking to excess. They, too, tried to get money from Charles's publishers and expected their successful brother to support them as he did their parents. Charles said that Augustus had a "certain insupportable arrogance," "so stupid in a singular combination of vanity and overreaching . . . I have no hope for him." Augustus deserted his wife (leaving her for Charles to support) and decamped to America with a mistress. No sooner was he settled than he wrote Charles demanding money. He died there, leaving the mistress and three children in Charles's care. Brother Alfred died also, leaving his wife and five children to Charles. When Charles was forty-four, he was still writing to brother Frederik: "I have already done more for you than most dispassionate persons would consider right or reasonable in itself. But, considered with any fair reference to the great expenses I have sustained for other relations, it becomes little else than monstrous. The possibility of your having any further expenses from me, is absolutely and finally past." After what Charles called "a wasted life," Frederik died too. Frederik's widow, whom he had deserted when she had become blind, was thenceforth supported by Charles, the solvent member of the family.

The family fecklessness passed on to Charles's sons. "I can't get my hat on in consequence of the extent to which my hair stands on end at the costs and charges of these boys," he wrote, having "brought up the largest family ever known with the smallest disposition to do anything for themselves." "Why did the kings in the fairy tales want children? I suppose in the weakness of the royal intellect." Sidney joined the navy at thirteen, sank deep into debt, and behaved so badly otherwise that his father broke off seeing him. Walter ("He had always been in debt, poor boy," said his dad) died in debt in India at age seventeen. Alfred failed at a military career, went into debt, failed to become a doctor, failed in business, and was at last shipped off to Australia. Charles went into a business that went bankrupt. Frank was no good at his father's magazine and was sent to India to join the Bengal Mounted Police. He returned to England after his father's death but lost his inheritance through extravagance and bad investments. Then he became a Canadian Mountie. In these blighted lives we may again be seeing the disorganizing effects of manic-depression. The one success was Harry, who won scholarships to Cambridge and had a career in law.

Dicken's wife, Catherine, was also a manic-depressive. He was most comfortable among such people, being one himself and having grown up among them. Catherine had frequent, unprovoked depressions even when Dickens was courting her. Instead of the usual flattery of courtship, he warned her that she must change: "If a hasty temper produces this strange behavior . . .

overcome it: it will never make you more amiable, I more fond, or either of us more happy."

In 1851 Catherine was stricken, Charles wrote, "with a tendency of blood to the head," "giddiness and dimness of sight," plus "an alarming confusion and nervousness." Her treatment was "a rigorous discipline of exercise, air, and cold water" from which she also recovered. Whatever was wrong with her, Dickens in later years claimed that she was mentally ill, but by then he was saying this to justify his separation from her. A few years after he married Catherine, her sister Georgina moved in with them and seems to have been the stablest member of the household. Though her sister moved out, Georgina stayed on with Dickens despite the current rumors of an affair between her and her brother-in-law.

GOING INTO SOCIETY

Dickens once remarked: "There seems to be an attraction in me for mad people. They *will* take me into their confidence. One woman in Scotland has left me such an immense amount of imaginary property that I think of retiring on it." He should have added that the attraction was mutual. Walter Savage Landor, the godfather of one of Dickens's sons, was quite mad and lived up to his name. Another friend, the painter Edwin Landseer, had a mental breakdown in his forties. Charles's two closest companions, Wilkie Collins and John Forster, were at least mildly manic-depressive. Collins was also an alcoholic and later an opium addict. The author Thackeray, another Dickens crony, was just as manic as he was. We have testimony from their American publisher, Fields: "During Thackeray's visit to America his jollity knew no bounds, and it became necessary to repress him when he was walking in the street. I well remember his uproarious shouting and dancing when he was told that the tickets to his first course of readings were all sold, and when we rode together from his hotel to the lecture-hall he insisted on thrusting both his long legs out of the carriage window, in deference, as he said, to his magnanimous ticket-holders." Fields cites "the astounding spirits of both Thackeray and Dickens. They always seemed to me to be standing in the sunshine."

Charles befriended a Mrs. de la Rue and tried to cure her of her frightful hallucinations by hypnosis. Most people find that others like them suit them best, whatever the common element—social background, education, profession, etc.—may be. As Dickens amply demonstrates, this is true for manic-depressives too. They do clump together.

"A CHILD'S HISTORY": 1812–1824

Dickens started a brief autobiography: "I was born at Portsmouth on the 7th of February, 1812; . . . my father was in the Navy Pay Office; . . . I was taken by him to Chatham when I was very young, and lived and was educated there 'til I was 12 or 13, I suppose."

Charles was a tender little fellow, too fragile, too frequently ill to play with other children. Instead, he would watch them from his bedroom window while he sucked his thumb and rubbed his wrist. He was "reading as if for life," he later remembered. "I have been a Tom Jones [a child's Tom Jones, a harmless creature] for a week together. I have sustained my own idea of Roderick Random for a month at stretch." Like Newton and many others who achieve eminence with works of the mind, he was a shy, sickly child with a passion for reading.

Charles's solitary preoccupation with books might have turned him towards scholarly pursuits in later life, but there were other influences in his childhood that inclined him towards the sometimes macabre fictional adventures of which he eventually wrote. When he was five, a sister was born, the third child in the family, and he was turned over to a maid who told him horror stories every night. An impressionable child, he never forgot them, and patches of horror would darken his own stories decades later. The theater also made an early entry into Charles's life. He had a gift for comic songs and his dad would show him off, performing on table tops. A theater-loving family friend also took the boy frequently to the Theater Royal. His happy years drew to a close when Charles turned ten. Successive moves were made to cheaper lodgings as the family slid into poverty.

"HARD TIMES": 1824

The books Charles treasured were sold, along with almost all of the furniture and smaller items that Charles carried to the pawnbroker. His family was hounded by tradesmen who had to be paid and were not. "I know that we got on very badly with the butcher and the baker," Charles remembered, "that very often we had not too much for dinner."

Charles's older sister was able to continue her education through a scholarship to the Royal Academy of Music, but he was considered to be done with school at age twelve. He felt it a cruel betrayal by his parents and recorded with fresh bitterness many years later:

> It is wonderful to me that, even after my descent into the poor little drudge
> I had been since we came to London, no one had compassion enough on me—
> a child of singular abilities, quick, eager, delicate, and soon hurt, bodily or

mentally, to suggest that something might have been spared, as it certainly might have been, to place me at any common school. . . . My father and mother were quite satisfied. They could hardly have been more so, if I had been 20 years of age . . . and going to Cambridge.

Finally, all of the Dickens family, excluding Charles, moved together into debtors' prison, something not uncommon at that time. Charles alone was placed in a boardinghouse and given a 8 A.M. to 8 P.M. job of preparing bottles of shoe polish. He was expected to be self-supporting. "I certainly had no other assistance whatever (the making of my clothes, I think, excepted) from Monday morning until Saturday night. No advice, no counsel, no encouragement, no consolation, no support, from anyone that I can call to mind, so help me God." "I know that I tried, but ineffectually, not to anticipate my money, and to make it last the week through by putting it away in a drawer I had in the counting house, wrapped up in 6 little parcels, each parcel containing the same amount, and labelled with a different day." "I was so young and childish, so little qualified . . . to undertake the whole charge of my own existence, that . . . I could not resist the stale pastry put out at half price . . . and I often spent in that, the money I should have kept for my dinner." "[The blacking warehouse] was a crazy, tumble-down old house, abutting . . . on the river, and literally overrun with rats. . . . its rotten floors and staircase, and the old grey rats swarming down in the cellars, and the sound of their squeaking and scuffling coming up the stairs at all times, and the dirt and decay of the place, rise up visibly before me, as if I were there again." "My work was to cover the pots of paste-blacking; first with a piece of oil-paper, and then with a piece of blue paper; to tie them round with a string; and then to clip the paper close and neat, all round. . . . When a certain number of grosses of pots had attained this pitch of perfection, I was to paste on each a printed label; and then go on with more pots." "My rescue from this kind of existence I considered quite hopeless. . . . I felt keenly, however, the being so cut off from my parents, my brothers and sisters; and *that*, I thought, might be corrected. One Sunday night I remonstrated to my father on this head, so pathetically, and with so many tears that his kind nature gave way. He began to think that it was not quite right. I do believe he had never thought so before, or thought about it. . . . A back attic was found for me [near the prison]. . . . A bed and bedding were sent over for me and made up on the floor."

In these four or five months of complete despair and bewilderment, Charles's sister won a prize at the academy of music. The contrast with his own prospects was sharp and cutting: "I could not bear to think of myself beyond the reach of all such honorable emulation and success. The tears ran down my face. I prayed when I went to bed that night, to be lifted out of the humiliation and neglect in which I was." "I . . . felt my early hopes of

growing up to be a learned and distinguished man crushed in my breast.
. . . the misery it was to . . . believe that, day by day, what I had learned,
and thought, and delighted in . . . was passing away from me, never to be
brought back any more; cannot be written. My whole nature was so penetrated
with . . . grief . . . that even now, famous and caressed and happy, I often
forget in my dreams that I have a dear wife and children; even that I am
a man; and wander desolately back to that time of my life."

Mr. Dickens had a sudden inheritance that was enough to pay his debts
and release him from prison, but he kept Charles at the factory. By chance
Mr. Dickens quarreled with Charles's employer. Then he decided to take his
son from the factory and put him back in school. Mrs. Dickens, however,
wanted her husband to patch up the quarrel and send Charles back to his
work. "I never afterwards forgot," he later said, "I never shall forget, I never
can forget, that my mother was warm for my being sent back." That was
a wound that never healed, and the pain of those hopeless months never
left him: "From that hour until this at which I write, no word of that part
of my childhood . . . has passed my lips to any human being." "I have never
had the courage to go back to the place where my servitude began. I never
saw it. I could not endure to go near it. For many years . . . I crossed over
the opposite side of the way, to avoid a certain smell of the cement they
put upon the blacking corks. . . . My old way home by the borough made
me cry [even] after my eldest child could speak."

For the rest of his years Charles remained fascinated by crime and criminal
acts. He went to public hangings and paid several visits to the Paris Morgue.
He toured prisons in America, Switzerland, and France, as well as in England.
In his novel *Bleak House,* there are nine different varieties of violent death.
Such fatal terminations occur in many other Dickens stories as well.

"THE SCHOOLBOY'S STORY": 1824–1827

Mr. Dickens prevailed over his wife, and so their son returned to school for
three more years. Charles entered a manic phase, with only brief or moderate
depressions, that lasted until his return from America. He became very sociable,
was generally in humorous mood, and was given to telling jokes and singing
comic songs whenever the opportunity offered. His gaiety was so excessive at
times as to embarrass school friends. His laughter would become uncontrollable,
almost hysterical. Dickens did not, in those three years, give any sign of the
trials he had endured. Rather, he played pranks and acted the clown. A schoolmate
describes Charles as "a handsome, curly-headed lad, full of animation." "I quite
remember Dickens on one occasion heading us in Drummond street pretending
to be poor boys, and asking passers-by for charity." None of his friends knew
that the Dickens family had borne the stigma of destitution.

Charles at this time resumed his interest in fiction and theater. "Dickens took to writing small tales," the classmate continues, "and we had a sort of club for lending and circulating them." "We were very strong, too, in theatricals. . . . Dickens was always a leader at these plays." He was not granted much time for childhood: at age fifteen Charles took on the responsibilities of an adult and went out in the world to work.

"THE BATTLE OF LIFE": 1827–1833

The worst that life would do to Charles was done when he was twelve. The rest, he would do to himself. For the next five years, he did not know quite where he was going, but he was moving up in the world. He reports, "I was put in the office of a solicitor, a friend of my father's, and didn't much like it: and after a couple of years (as well as I can remember) applied myself with a celestial or diabolical energy to the study of such things as would qualify me to be a first-rate parliamentary reporter—at that time a calling pursued by many clever men who were young at the Bar."

Charles was more than ever entranced by the stage. He and a fellow clerk haunted a local theater, sometimes even acting small parts in the productions. He went every night to watch or act. Free hours at home were given to rehearsing parts. Finally he decided to become a professional actor and requested an audition. "I wrote to Barthy, who was stage manager, and told him how young I was, and exactly what I thought I could do; and that I believed I had a strong perception of character and oddity, and a natural power of reproducing in my own person what I observed in others." He was manic in the very tone of his words: self-confident to an unwarranted degree, boastful, and innocent of any sense that he was overweening. "I was laid up when the [audition] day came. . . . I wrote to say so, and added that I would resume my application next season. I made a great splash in the gallery [as a reporter] soon afterwards; I had a distinction in the little world of the newspaper, which made one like it; began to write; didn't want money; had never thought of the stage but as a means of getting it; gradually left off turning my thoughts that way, and never resumed the idea. . . . See how near I may have been to another sort of life."

At age eighteen Charles was hired as a reporter by *The Mirror* of Parliament. He soon moved on to a better position at the *Morning Chronicle:* "I was liberally paid there and handsomely acknowledged." "I left the reputation behind me of being the best and most rapid reporter ever known, and that I could do anything in that way under any sort of circumstances, and often did (I daresay I am at this present writing the best shorthand writer in the world)."

"GREAT EXPECTATIONS": 1833–1842

Charles's career as a writer of fiction began when he was twenty-one, when he submitted a story to a magazine that printed such donations anonymously and without payment. He followed this effort with a succession of genre paintings of English life. The *Sketches by "Boz,"* as some of his work-in-progress was titled, brought the young man to public attention. He blossomed into a dandy, a characteristic manic transformation. It was a natural time for high spirits. The future glistened with promise, and he was a free man, having just recovered from four years of unrequited love. His freedom lasted eighteen months, until he became engaged to Catherine Hogarth, the pretty daughter of a newspaper editor. During this period Charles had, in manic fashion, taken on a haystack of writing projects, including an operetta.

One evening he made the kind of visit that few but manics make, to the home of his fiancee and her parents. Bursting through their open French windows, wearing a sailor's outfit, he danced a hornpipe to his own whistled accompaniment and vanished without a word. Moments later, dressed in his own clothes, he reappeared at the front door and acted as though he knew nothing of the previous visitor.

Charles became fame's captive once and for all when he was twenty-four. His new series, "The Posthumous Papers of the Pickwick Club," became widely popular. Pickwick graced stages and song books. Manufacturers supplied a ravening public with Pickwick hats, coats, canes, cigars. The common people of England went Pickwick-mad. The fashionable people of London took Charles to their hearts and drawing rooms. Fellow author Leigh Hunt saw Charles thus in those exhilirating days: "What a face is his to meet in a drawing—room! It has the life and soul in it of 50 human beings." "He is a fine fellow . . . a face of the most extreme *mobility,* which he shuttles about—eyebrows, eyes, mouth, and all—in a very singular manner while speaking." The fast flow of strong emotion made Dickens's face a miniature theater. Even in repose, he rarely looked bland or calm.

The manic pace continued: Dickens married Catherine on April 2, 1836. Within the next year he became an author with an international readership, editor of *Bentley's Miscellany,* a father, and while continuing *Pickwick,* he began to write *Oliver Twist.* He filled every spare minute with friends and social events.

In quieter moments he fell in love with his sixteen-year-old sister-in-law Mary, who had joined the household when he married. She died suddenly in his arms in May of 1837, another love ended in sorrow. Charles was quite overcome, and for the first time, unable to write. *Pickwick Papers's* May installment was not published on time, and the June chapter of *Oliver Twist* did not appear until later.

But life moves on, and the manic life moves on very quickly. Soon the fantastic flood of words poured forth again. Before *Oliver Twist* was finished, Charles began his third novel, *Life and Adventures of Nicholas Nickleby.* To this was added the *The Old Curiosity Shop* in 1841 and *Barnaby Rudge.* Meanwhile, Charles left the *Miscellany* to found and edit his own magazine.

The day's work done, he often went to the slums to do what he could for the education and welfare of the children of the poor. In these years he also inaugurated the typical Dickens summer: renting a spacious house at the seashore, rearranging all the furniture (a favorite activity for manics), and filling the place with guests. These he exhausted with twenty-mile hikes, parties, dances, and all the games he had missed as a child.

During this, the ascending curve of his life, his confidence was Napoleonic. He felt that nothing could resist him and wrote to his friend Forster: "I wonder, if I went to a new colony with my head, hands, legs, and health, I should force myself to the top of the social milk-pot and live upon the cream! What do you think? Upon my word I believe I should." He was doing so where he was.

Looking for new worlds of adventure, Charles decided to go to America. Manic that he was, his impulse of the moment, like a wall of fire, drove him before it. A whole continent was waiting to adore him. As though madly in love, he could not put his mind to his work and lost appetite and sleep. Prior to departing, he took out a life insurance policy but first had to convince the insurance company that rumors of his insanity were false. By this time, Charles Dickens was widely recognized as an extraordinary phenomenon, not merely for his talent. His intensity, his manic energy and wild mood swings, set him apart.

"STRANGE GENTLEMAN"

The claim that Charles Dickens was a manic-depressive has been made before. Lord Brain, the British neurologist, mentions Dickens's "general mood of elation, associated with hyperactivity and broken by short recurrent periods of depression." Though the first to make a diagnosis of manic-depression, Lord Brain was not the first to notice Charles's oscillations of mood. In 1838 a family friend wrote about the effect of Dickens's emotional instability on those around him: "His own family appeared to be less at ease with Charles than anyone else and seemed in fear of offending him. There was a subdued manner, a kind of restraint in his presence, not merely the result of admiration of his genius or respect for his opinion, but because his moods were very variable. Sometimes so genial and gay . . . at other times abstracted and even morose." Dickens's son, Henry adds, "He was of course a man of moods, highly strung and very emotional, full of confidence at times and depressed in another."

Dickens began adolescence and went through early adulthood on the bright side of mania, often elated, pleased with himself, and happy with what he was making of his life. After his return from America he began to become acquainted with the painful aspects of mania: unbearable restlessness and agitation, irritability, and an increasing drive towards total control of the people around him, particularly his family. In his later years his depressions became burdensome too. These, combined with the agitation and incessant activity of mania, sometimes made him frantic. Throughout his life, though, he retained the personality and attitudes of a manic.

He also retained, for the most part, a manic appearance: he was sparkling with joy and energy, colorful in his dress. Novelist Richard Henry Dana saw Dickens in America: "I never saw a face fuller of light. He has the finest eyes; and his whole countenance speaks *life* and *action*—the face seems to flicker with the *heart's* and *mind's* activity. You cannot tell how dead the faces near him seemed." Charles was also, as many manics are, a show-off. He had to be the center of attention. No shrinking violet would have worn his petals. "Yes, the beggar is as beautiful as a butterfly," Thackeray said.

Like many manics, Charles Dickens was charming and amusing. With his songs, jokes, and pantomimes, he was a one-man variety show. At a political dinner during his first trip to the United States, he gave a speech pushing the candidacy of his manager on the grounds that the manager had less hair than the other candidates. According to one of those present, "We roared and writhed . . . and the candidates themselves were literally weeping and crying." Dickens had the manic's verbal urges and was given to sudden monologues. He would often write twelve letters a day when he finished his professional writing. His generosity was so well known that he was constantly plagued with demands for money. He always tried to do too many things at once. He never imagined the possibility of failure, or recognized the impossible as a limit to his desires. Forster said he had "A too great confidence in himself, a sense that everything was possible to the will that would make it so."

Dickens had the defects of manic personalities: he was self-centered and took it for granted that he was the chief interest of everyone around him. According to his daughter: "In his letters . . . he never forgot anything that he knew would be of interest about his work, his successes, his hopes or fears. And there was a sweet simplicity in his belief that such news would most certainly be acceptable to all, that is wonderfully touching and child-like coming from a man of genius." Dickens would remark: "By the by, I recommenced [the readings] last Tuesday evening with the greatest brilliancy."

Like many manics, Dickens did not have much regard for the wishes and opinions of others. A friend says, "His life was conducted on the . . . principle . . . that everything gave way before him. . . . The opinions which he held, his likes and dislikes, his ideas of what should or should not be, were all settled by himself, not merely for himself, but for all those brought into connection with him."

Dickens was a small-scale tyrant. After his initial literary successes, he refused to be part of any undertaking, be it financial, literary, charitable, or even travel, unless he was the sole source of decisions. His need to control others led him to learn hypnosis. His daughter notes: "He was always . . . much interested in mesmerism, and curious influence exercised by one personality over another."

Dickens was not satisfied with a monopoly of power, he had to control everything within his reach, down to the most trivial details. This is a common manic compulsion, and in some lines of work it is quite useful, but it intimidates people who have to obey. Dickens made inspections of his house and grounds three times a day. He examined his childrens' bureau drawers and saw to it that their coats and hats were on the hook assigned to each child. A bit of eggshell on the grass after a picnic made him quite disagreeable. The household schedule, daily menu, everything was decided by him. "If a chair was out of its place," his daughter adds, "or a blind not quite straight, or a crumb left on the floor, woe betide the offender." In addition to his irritability, which he attributed to his fellow humans' imperfection, Charles had the manic-depressive's abrupt, irrational furies. "I am still feeble," he wrote after a depression, "and liable to sudden outbursts of causeless rage."

On the one hand, he wanted to eliminate impulsive behavior in his family (an ambition he never realized). On the other, he brooked no restraint of his own. "I am going off, I don't know where or how far, to ponder about I don't know what. . . . I made a compact with a great Spanish authority last week, and vowed I would go to Spain. Two days afterwards Lagard and I agreed to go to Constantinople. . . . Tomorrow I shall probably discuss with somebody else the idea of going to Greenland or the North Pole." His wife was neither consulted nor invited along.

Dickens's brain, more than that of most manics, was a machine that ran day and night. It would not allow him to escape into sleep and often drove him for many dark hours thorugh the streets of whatever city he happened to be visiting. He was extraordinarily hyperactive. He did not work, he overworked: the Dickens oeuvre includes books, innumerable short stories, articles, speeches, a play, and an operetta. He also edited magazines, gave lectures, went on reading tours, and acted in and directed fifteen plays. He was very active on behalf of others, raising funds for orphaned children, setting up a home for "fallen women," and working out plans for improved sanitation in tenement areas. This list is not exhaustive.

He played as vigorously as he worked. When he learned a new dance step, he would rise from bed in the middle of the night to practice it, or astound passers-by by doing it in the city streets. No one around him, regardless of age, could match him for output of energy in games of all kinds, or on the long hikes and horseback rides he took daily regardless of weather. Dickens used strenuous activity not only as a safety valve, but he would also take hikes to relieve agitated depressions. He said: "If I couldn't walk so fast and far, I should just explode and perish." "I am incapable of rest."

His hunger for change and his flights from depression made him a compulsive traveler. He went to America in 1842 and again in 1867, to Italy in 1844, Switzerland in 1846, and back to both again. He rebounded between Paris and London countless times. Besides his reading tours, there were also trips up and down the British Isles and short trips too numerous and confusing to mention. Dickens did all of this when travel was uncomfortable, inconvenient, and often perilous. When he stayed in one country, Dickens traveled from town to town. Located for a time in one city, he would change his place of residence. His need for doing and going finally verged on the suicidal, shortened his life, and filled it with misery. At age forty-four he wrote, "How strange it is to be never at rest, and never satisfied, and ever trying after something that is never reached, and to be always laden with plot and plan and care and worry . . . that one is driven by an irresistible might until the journey is worked out!"

Dickens's illness, which was so severe, affected not only his life but also his writing. Lord Russell Brain holds that mild mania makes an artist fecund without confusing him (as more advanced states of mania may do), and furthermore, "The untiring energy and flight of ideas . . . add greatly to the productivity of the artist, as was the case with Dickens." Dickens's manic impatience kept his narratives moving briskly along, and his intense emotional life was the model for his work. Poet Walter de la Mare points out that Dickens was weakest "in portraying normal, somewhat commonplace and sensible persons." The novelist spent time with eccentric people and gave his stories the heat and tempo of his own experience. For manics, a life filled with forceful emotions, busy doings, and assorted crises *is* the norm; therefore, a placid existence is difficult for them to imagine or understand. The depressive, on the other hand, assumes that inertia, monotony, drudgery, and alienation from the day-to-day world are the major features of the human condition. One can recognize both of these versions of reality as the groundcolor for much fiction.

"THE HAUNTED MAN": 1842–1857

Charles Dickens burst on the American scene like a supernova. He was at the height of youth and fame. He was at the stage of mania that made him the ideal version of himself: his joy, energy, intelligence, and creativity were at their apogee and his skin glowed with health. Dickens had the rare blessing of spending much of his life in that condition. A witness describes him at thirty: "He ran, or rather flew, up the steps of the hotel, sprang into the hall. He seemed all on fire with curiosity, and alive as I never saw mortal

before. From top to toe every fibre of his body was unrestrained and alert.
. . . He laughed all over and did not care who heard him! He seemed like
the Emperor of Cheerfulness."

As soon as the chance arrived, Dickens transplanted his daily eight- or
ten-mile hikes to American soil. He took people along, telling funny stories
as he strolled, impersonating characters from his books, and acting out the
scenes in them. Several saw what a witness relates: "Dickens kept up one continual
shout of uproarious laughter as he went rapidly forward, reading the signs
on the shops. . . . When the two (Dickens and the Earl of M——) arrived
opposite the 'Old south Church' Dickens screamed. To this day I could not
tell why." The scream is a sign of intense manic excitement. What brought
Dickens to these pitches might have made anyone drunk with glory. He received
the kind of reception today reserved for popular rock stars. He saw it thus:

> There never was a king or emperor upon the earth so cheered and followed
> by crowds and entertained in public at splendid balls and dinners, and waited
> on by public bodies and deputations of all kinds. . . . If I go out in a carriage,
> the crowd surrounds it and escorts me home; if I go to the theater, the whole
> house (crowded to the roof) rises as a man. . . . I have . . . invitations from
> every town and village and city in the States. . . I have deputations from the
> Far West, who have come from more than 2,000 miles distance. . . . I have
> heard from the universities, congress, senate.

The fireworks ceased abruptly, however. Charles told the public what
he thought about the American printers who pirated his works and took
all the profit, giving nothing to the author. He called for a copyright law
to protect all writers. This aroused a storm of hostility among Americans
at the time, though such laws were later seen to be fair. About six weeks
after his arrival, Charles wrote: "I am sick to death of the life I have been
living here—worn out in mind and body—and quite weary and distressed.
I have declined all future invitations of a public nature. . . . I have never
in my life been so shocked and disgusted or made so sick and sore at heart
as I have been by the treatment I have received here (in America, I mean)
in reference to the International Copyright question." "I vow to heaven that
the scorn and indignation I have felt under this unmanly and ungenerous
treatment have been to me an amount of agony such as I have never experienced
since my birth."

Dickens was distressed by the anger he aroused, but he may also have been
rebounding from weeks of intense mania. Such states are usually followed by
depressions, which is precisely what happened during his second American tour.

A month later Dickens had become his usual manic self, doing everything
and prying into everything. He writes: "Parties—parties—parties—of course,
every day and night. But it's not all parties. I go into the prisons, the police-

offices, . . . the hospitals, the workhouses. I was out half the night in New York with 20 of their most famous constables; started at midnight and went into every brothel, thieves' house, murdering hovel, sailors' dancing place, and abode of villainy . . . in the town." He combined social conscience with insomnia.

The first crack in the Dickens's marriage appeared that May. Charles wrote about "the baggage—I mean the trunks; not Kate." He was finding her a nuisance. "In landing and going abroad, in getting in and out of coaches, Kate has fallen down perhaps 743 times. Once in going over a coaching road which is made by throwing trunks of trees into a marsh, she very nearly had her head broken off. It was a very hot day, she was lying in a languishing manner with her neck upon the open window. Bang-Crash! It is a little on one side to this hour." The gaiety of mania went on, as is evident in a letter that Dickens wrote on May 1 about his recent voyage on a paddle-wheeler:

It was blowing hard; and I was holding on to something—I don't know what. I think it was a pump—or a man—or the cow (brought for the milk) I can't say for certain, which. My stomach, with its contents, appeared to be in my forehead. I couldn't understand which was the sea and which the sky; and was endeavoring to form an opinion, or a thought, or to get some distant glimmering of anything approaching an idea, when I beheld standing before me, a small figure with a speaking trumpet. It waved, and fluctuated, and came and went, as if smoke were passing between it and me, but I knew by its very good-natured face that it was the captain. It waved its trumpet, moved its jaws, and evidently spoke very loud. I no more heard it than if it had been a dumb man, but I felt that it remonstrated with me for standing up to my knees in the water.— I was, in fact, doing so. Of course I don't know why. Sir, I tried to smile. Yes— Such is the affability of my disposition that even in that moment I tried to smile. Not being able to do so, and being perfectly sensible that the attempt faded into a sickly hiccough, I tried to speak—to jest—at all events to explain. But I could only get out 2 words. They bore reference to the kind of boots I wore, and were these—"Cork soles!"—"Cork soles,"—perhaps a hundred times (for I couldn't stop; it was a part of the disease)—The captain, seeing that I was quite childish, and for the time a maniac, had me taken below to my berth.

In some states of mania, even driving rain and wet feet are the stuff of humor.

Dickens was tired of the United States by the time he left for home six months later, but the mere fact of departure was enough to trigger a spell of mania. He recorded: "On board that ship coming home I established a club, called the United Vagabonds, to the amusement of the rest of the passengers. This holy brotherhood committed all kinds of absurdities." "We were really very merry all the way." That was no longer true about his life: he was leaving the careless years behind.

Dickens settled down for the summer at a pleasant seaside resort and sent a friend a description of his average day: four hours of writing, and the rest of the day to spend as he pleased, in the sunshine and salt air, no one daring to need him. It would have been paradise for most people:

> In a bay window . . . sits, from 9 o'clock to one, a gentleman with rather long hair and no neckcloth, who writes and grins as if he thought he were very funny indeed. At one he disappears, presently emerges from a bathing-machine, and may be seen, a kind of salmon-colored porpoise, splashing about in the ocean. After that he may be viewed in another bay window on the ground floor, eating a strong lunch; and after that, walking a dozen miles or so, or lying on his back reading a book. Nobody bothers him unless they know he is disposed to be talked to; and I am told he is very comfortable indeed. He's brown as a berry, and they do say, is in a small fortune to the innkeeper who sells beer and cold [alcoholic] punch. But this is mere rumour. Sometimes he goes up to London and then I'm told there is a sound in Lincoln's-inn-fields at night, as of men laughing together with a clinking of knives and forks and wine glasses.

This is the sketch of a man perfectly content with life, but it is no longer Dickens. For the writer, and many other manics, the good was no longer good enough. He would know wild, surging happiness, but no satisfaction, for peace became foreign to him. In October Dickens was on his way again, to Cornwall, just for amusement, and he found it. "Sometimes we travelled all night, sometimes all day, sometimes both. . . . Heavens! If you could have seen the necks of bottles, distracting in their immense varieties of shape, peering out of the carriage pockets!" "I never laughed in all my life as I did on this journey." "I was choking and gasping and bursting out of the back of my stock all the way."

In November he was into a new novel, *The Life and Adventures of Martin Chuzzlewit*, and a new element was emerging in his creative process: the writer's block. Dickens had suffered a period of prostration after his sister-in-law Mary died, and during those weeks he could not write. But throughout the first ten years of his life as a writer, mania was for him an ever-flowing spring of inspiration. Now it began to go dry, for depression, often agitated depression, would afflict him whenever he began a new work. Henceforth Dickens would have trouble starting most of what he wrote. "Men have been chained to hideous walls and other strange anchors," he wrote a friend, "but few have known such suffering and bitterness at one time or other as those who have been bound to Pens!" There were many days of retreat when he was shut away in his room, during which he remained unable to put down a word, and when he ventured into the rest of the house, he was "so horribly cross and surly that the boldest fly at my approach."

Charles Dickens lived the Faust legend. Mania was his personal demon that gave him the energy, the aspirations, and self-confidence to write, to grasp opportunities or invent them, to make the right friends, and to charm the world.

Combined with his own great talent, mania brought him wealth, companionship, as much fame as any man could want, and the fulfillment of his most extravagant ambitions, but he would pay the devil from now on with his soul, his body, and his life. He would weave a spiderweb of discontent all over Europe and Britain, as he ran from both depression and the agonizing restlessness of his mania like a man trying to escape the fire burning his own clothes.

Dickens launched 1843 with a hilarious Twelfth Night party, spellbinding children and adults both with his skill as a magician. According to Jane Carlyle, "Forster helped Dickens with the conjuring and they exerted themselves till the perspiration was pouring down and they seemed drunk with their efforts!" "Dickens did all but go down on his knees to make me waltz with him!" "In fact the thing was rising into something not unlike the rape of the Sabines!"

The year went on with the usual abundance of parties, charitable activities, and writing, but the road grew rougher. Painful mood changes would sometimes strike Dickens even when a book was past the initial dragging stage, and writing would become impossible again. He began at this time to punish his body for the suffering of his mind. In later years his body would have its revenge. He wrote in August of a day of "terrific heat" in which "I performed an insane match against time of 18 miles by the milestones in 4 hours and a half, under a burning sun the whole way. I could get no sleep at night, and really began to be afraid I was going to have a fever. Your may judge in what kind of authorship-training I am in today. I could as soon eat the cliff as write about anything."

In October another period of manic inspiration arrived and Dickens, in a blaze of emotion, began the story known today as *A Christmas Carol.* He pictures himself thus: he "wept and laughed, and wept again and excited himself in a most extraordinary manner in the composition; and thinking whereof he walked about the back streets of London 15 or 20 miles many a night when all sober folks had gone to bed." The story was done in less than two months, after which Charles, as he says, "broke out like a madman!" with "such dinings, such dancings, such conjurings, such blind man's buffings, such theatre goings, such kissings-out of the old years and kissings-in of new ones."

On January 15, Dickens's son Francis arrived in the world, along with a serious depression for the father. From this time on the births of his children, and the financial burden he saw in them, would provide Dickens with additional reasons for disliking his wife, as though her fecundity had nothing to do with him. During this period of depression the *Christmas Carol* did not bring in as much as he had counted on, making him feel "not only on my beam-ends, but tilted over the other side. Nothing so unexpected and utterly disappointing has ever befallen me!" Even in depression he maintained the manic style of multiple exclamation points and the constant use of the superlative degree. At this time he developed two depressive delusions, paranoia and the delusion of poverty. Certain that he was financially ruined, he determined to move his family where he could live more cheaply. He also became convinced that his publishers were cheating him, a conviction that would visit him from time to time regardless of who was his publisher or what was actually happening. In February he began to bring his work to another publisher.

That July Dickens took his wife, five small children, and a crew of servants to Genoa. The Palazzo Peschiere was rented, and he settled down to write another story, "The Chimes," in the autumn. However, it did not come easily, and for a week and a half it did not come at all. Then it arrived like an avalanche: "I am in a regular ferocious excitement with the Chimes; get up at 7; have a cold bath before breakfast; and blaze away, wrathful and red hot until 3 o'clock or so, when I usually knock off." Frequently, writing, for Dickens, was a distillation of his life as a manic-depressive. While he wrote "The Chimes," the emotional surges he experienced dwarfed those that he lived: "I have undergone as much sorrow as if the thing were real; I have wakened up with it at night. I was obliged to lock myself in when I finished it yesterday for my face was swollen for the time to twice its proper size, and was hugely ridiculous!" "I have had what women call a 'real good cry!' " "I am as nervous as a man who is dying of drink, and as haggard as a murderer." "I have worn myself to death in the month I have been at work."

As always, the end of a piece of writing left Charles in a high state. "I believe I have written a tremendous book. . . . It will make a great uproar, I have no doubt." He always felt afterwards that the emotional wrenchings and sleepless nights were worth it. This time his end-phase mania was so intense that it sent him, in the full howl of winter, across France and the English Channel to London so that he could read "The Chimes" to his friends. That, too, was worth it. He wrote his wife: "If you had seen Macready [a famous actor friend] last night undisguisedly sobbing, and crying on the sofa as I read, you would have felt, as I did, what a thing it is to have power."

Before moving back from Italy to London the next summer, Dickens made a tour that included Venice. The visit to that city inspired him to express the full dimension of his ambition, which was somewhat grandiose but helped him to continually surpass his previous achievements: "Ah! when I saw those palaces, how I thought that to leave one's hand upon time, lastingly upon the time, with tender touch for the mass of toiling people that nothing could obliterate, would be to lift oneself above the dust of all the Doges in their graves, and stand upon a giant's staircase that Sampson couldn't overthrow."

One of the fateful changes in Charles's life took place soon after his return to England: he again took up the theater. He wrote Forster, "I do not know if I have ever told you seriously, but I have often thought that I should certainly have been as successful on the boards as I have been between them." His friend Forster became most impressed with Dickens's capacity for all aspects of play production:

> He took everything on himself, and did the whole of it without effort. He was stage-director, very often stage-carpenter, scene-arranger, property-man, prompter, and band-master. Without offending anyone he kept everyone in order. . . . He adjusted scenes, assisted carpenters, invented costumes, devised playbills. . . . Such a chaos of dirt, confusion, and noise, as the little theatre was the day we entered it, and such a cosmos as he made it of cleanliness, order, and silence, before the rehearsals were over.

In addition, from all accounts, Dickens was an actor of professional caliber.

In September and November he gave performances of *Every Man in His Humor.* Many more plays would be done, often as escapes from depression, and it would be in the production of a melodrama called *The Frozen Deep* that Dickens would meet the girl for whom he left his wife. In the autumn he was also putting together a new newspaper, *The Daily News,* and having his usual birth pangs writing a story: "Sick, bothered and depressed. . . . I never was in such bad writing . . . [form] as I am this week, in all my life." In January, Dickens performed in two more of his productions of plays and left *The Daily News* when it was three weeks old because of a quarrel with its owners.

The next June Dickens removed his menage to Lauzanne, Switzerland. He began his new novel, *Dealings with the Firm of Dombey and Son,* at the end of the month but became mired in a depression that lasted longer than the half year of his stay at Lauzanne. This was his longest spontaneous depression so far, and it made him fear that he would suffer some sort of a breakdown. During this difficult period he had an uncharacteristic religious phase and decided to write a children's version of the New Testament. He also started going to Sunday services in Catholic and various Protestant churches. Tolstoy went through the same sort of search during a long depression. Unlike Tolstoy, Dickens was fundamentally a secular type and eventually would say, "As to the Church, my friend, I am sick of it."

In Lauzanne Dickens was supposed to produce a story for Christmas publication at the same time that he was turning out monthly episodes of *Dombey.* It was typical manic overcommitment, but unfortunately the mania did not stay on to help him with the work. "I . . . am subject to 2 descriptions in reference to the Christmas book: of the suddenest and wildest enthusiasm; and of solitary and anxious consideration."

The Christmas story, "The Battle of Life," was completed on October 17. Henceforth there would be other titles as grim as this. Dickens returned to Geneva, where he was able to work a bit more on *Dombey,* but then depression again clogged his mind. He thought a move to Paris would solve everything and made the move in November. "The agonies of house-hunting were frightfully severe," he recorded. "It was one paroxysm for 4 mortal days. I am proud to express my belief that we are lodged at last in the most preposterous house in the world."

This time the strategy against depression did not work, and the writer's block accompanied him to the City of Light. Instead of going on with *Dombey,* he "took a violent dislike to my study, and came into the drawing-room; couldn't find a corner that would answer my purpose; fell into a black contemplation of the waning month; sat 6 hours as a stretch" (during which time he produced only six lines). He would walk the streets of Paris till daylight and see how things were going in the morgue.

Dickens next paid a brief visit to London, in nasty December weather, carrying his depression along. He saw the city in a "hideous state of mud and darkness. Everybody is laid up with the influenza except all the disagreeable people." "I am in a dreadful state of mental imbecility myself and am pursuing Dombey under difficulties."

He was back in Paris on January 12, 1847, writing to Forster: "Irritable very mouldy and dull. Hardly able to work. . . . Disposed to go to New Zealand and start a magazine." But the light soon flickered on again and the writing went forward. At one point in the story Dickens had to kill his favorite character, Paul Dombey. Even the people and events in his books could upset his emotional equilibrium, and with the misery of this one, "I went out, and walked about Paris until breakfast time next morning." He painted Paris red when Forster visited but soon returned to parental burdens. Son Charles fell ill at school in England. Dickens and his wife rushed to him, the rest of the family remaining temporarily with Georgina in Paris. By March 9, Dickens had not yet found a house for the family in London, and he was still having a hard time grinding out the monthly installments of *Dombey.* He was caught in a vicious cycle: a depression that made writing and the practical tasks of living difficult, and the consequences of his inability to cope that aggravated his depression. He admitted, "My wretchedness, just now, is inconceivable." The next month a horse gave him a bad bite on the arm, an event that left him feeling "hideously queer." His wife had child number seven on April 18. In May he went with her to Brighton for a month. "I have been very unwell these last few days, with a low dull nervousness of a most distressing kind. . . . But I hope I am getting over it and seem to have a faint consciousness of myself again this morning."

In June he took off for another resort, Broadstairs. He had become involved in play production again, was manic and writing, he said, "About 100 letters a day, about these plays." The manic lift brought on by preparing a play was always followed, after the last performance, by some form of depression that was quite painful and in which he was often shaken by agitation. Charles wrote in August, "I am at a great loss for means of blowing my superfluous steam off, now that the play is over—but that is always my misfortune—and find myself compelled to tear up and down between this and London by express trains."

Another of his projects for 1847 was the establishment of a home for reforming prostitutes financed by his friend, heiress Angela Coutts. He went about it with his usual manic attention to detail, very like Napoleon ran France. Dickens reported to his philanthropist: "I have laid in all the dresses and linen of every sort for the whole house, purchasing the materials . . . at wholesale prices. I have made them as cheerful in appearance as they reasonably could be. . . . In their living room I have put up 2 inscriptions selected from sermons. . . . Also a little inscription of my own, referring to the advantages of order, punctuality, and good temper, and our duty towards God, and our duty towards our neighbors." Both his reforming zeal and fascination with forbidden sex were expressions of mania.

Dickens was able to ward off depression and remain manic for the first five months of 1848 by preparing two more plays. He staged these in May for Queen Victoria, among others. By July he was in black gloom again, and there is much marital dissatisfaction in his complaint. "I loathe domestic hearths. I yearn to be a vagabond. "Why can't I marry Mary [a character in a play]!" "Why have I seven children. . . . I am deeply miserable." His depression also made everything appear in its worst aspect to him. In August he felt no improvement: "I am completely blase—literally used up. I am dying for excitement. Is it possible that no one can suggest anything to make my heart beat violently, my hair stand on end." Dickens wrote "The Haunted Man and the Ghost's Bargain" in an agitated depression in November. He walked the chill streets at night and wept when he ended the story, which was full of "phantoms of past and present despondency."

Son Henry was born in January 15, 1849. The next month Dickens began to create a life of another kind, a fictional double of himself, a person who had his initials in reverse. He started *The Personal History of David Copperfield*. There was the usual spell of inertia at the beginning, and then the rush of inspiration. By June Dickens was in Brighton and merrily calling for his friend Mark Lemon: "Oh, my Lemon, round and fat,/Oh my bright, my right, my tight'un./Think a little what you're at—/Don't stay home, but come to Brighton!"

But the good times were fading sooner and sooner: August found Charles gone for a change of scene to Bonchurch. Instead of brightening, he had a stuporous depression so severe that he wrote about himself as "the Patient." "An extraordinary disposition to sleep except at night . . . is always present . . . and if he have anything to do requiring thought and attention," Charles wrote, "this overpowers him to such a degree that he can only do it in snatches, lying down on beds in the fitful intervals. Extreme depression of mind, a disposition to shed tears from morning to night." Dickens blamed his state on the place where he was; later, when he was "sufficiently rollicking," having "great games at rounders every afternoon, with all Bonchurch looking on," he did not notice the inconsistency of his claim that Bonchurch was depressing. He was quite recovered by September.

Dickens never thought himself beaten by life. He had been living on a mental roller coaster since he went to Lauzanne in 1844, and there was more dizzying instability at Paris. Stress was unrelenting: the struggles writing *Dombey,* a marriage becoming a drudgery, the acute, paralyzing depression at Bonchurch, the feverish excitement of play production and the inevitable crashes afterwards. But however sick and horrible he felt, he still tried to wrench himself out of his condition and carry on his responsibilities, even if he could only sit up for minutes at a time. Such tremendous courage and discipline is often essential if manic-depressives are to have year after year of achievement. Mania cannot carry them indefinitely; when it runs out they must fight to continue their work, until their illness has mercy on them. Dickens was one of the great ones: he was unconquerable.

In 1850 he achieved a long-desired dream: to run his own magazine, in which he could express his own social philosophy. He could write for everyone, not just the traditional reading classes. He wanted to do what he could to make England a better place for ordinary people. *Household Words* appeared in March, and *David Copperfield* was completed in the autumn. As he wrote the last pages he told Forster: "I am strangely divided, as usual in such cases, between sorrow and joy. Oh, my dear Forster, if I were to say half of what Copperfield makes me feel tonight. . . . I seem to be sending some part of myself into the Shadowy World."

Having survived a series of writer's blocks, Dickens was in full stride as a writer, but both mania and depression were affecting his creativity. As a writer he was very much the puppet of his moods. By the time he was twenty-three he had known that. "I never can write with effect . . . until I have got my steam up, or in other words, until I have become so excited with my subject that I cannot leave off." He had to be in an intense working high in order to write more than the few forced sentences a day that depression allowed him. He developed two methods of inducing the working high. Like many artists, Dickens conditioned himself to work in the presence of certain objects: in his case, some bronze figurines. This is not a wholly reliable procedure, as it fails in severe depressions. Dickens could depend on another resource for inducing a working high, however: like Beethoven, he would walk. Being a city lover rather than a nature lover, he preferred London or Paris to Beethoven's wooded hills. Dickens needed the stimulation and excitement of cities on a regular basis: "For a week or fortnight I can write prodigiously in a retired place, a day in London setting me and starting me up again. But the toil and labor of writing day after day without that magic is immense!"

Intense mania, unlike hypomania, is a miserable state to endure. The mental unease is like that of the addict deprived of his drug: a torture of desire, but without object; a being driven one knows not where. Dickens described it as "3 parts mad and the 4th delirious with perpetual rushing," and he would suffer when it was over. Whether the cause was stress, insomnia, or something less obvious, Dickens usually paid a high price for the power of his working highs. "It is impossible to go on working the brain to that extent forever." "On Saturday night I do not think I slept an hour. . . . The mental distress is quite horrible." "I am sick, giddy, and capriciously despondent," he remarked in the descent from his mania.

One consequence of needing intense mania in order to write was that Dickens often wrote, literally, in a state of transport. Therefore, previous calculations would go out the window, and he could not follow his own plan in writing a story. Hidden need and the force of strong emotions took over, as they do in mania. Dickens attests that when "I sit down to my book, some beneficent power shows it all to me, and tempts me to be interested, and I don't invent it—really do not—but see it, and write it down." His working highs were so strong that they could anesthetize him to all discomfort: "It is only when it all fades away and is gone, that I begin to suspect that its momentary relief has cost me something."

There was something hallucinatory about Dickens's state of being when he was deep in a story. He would swear that his characters followed him around after working hours. He complained especially about Fagin, Tiny Tim, and Little Nell. He would become quite devoted to his characters by the time he finished a story. "It makes me very melancholy," he once said, "to think that all of these people are lost to me forever, and I feel as if I never could become attached to any new set of charcters." There was no membrane separating Dickens's life from his art. When he had to describe the death of Little Nell, it was for him the ripping open of the badly healed memories of his sister-in-law's death: "I went to bed last night utterly dispirited and done up. All night I have been pursued by the child; this morning I am unrefreshed and miserable. I don't know what to do with myself." "I think it [the story] will come famously—but I am the wretchedest of the wretched. It casts the most horrible shadows upon me, and it is as much as I can do to keep moving at all." "I shan't recover for a long time. Nobody will miss her like I shall. . . . Old wounds bleed afresh. . . . Dear Mary died yesterday when I think of this sad story." "I am, for the time, nearly dead with work and grief for the loss of my child." He would not say as much for the way he felt about his real children. He seems to have preferred the world he created on paper to the family he generated in matrimony.

His daughter gives us this description of Dickens at work. Only a manic has the emotional charge and energy for this to be his natural way of producing material.

> My father wrote busily and rapidly at his desk, when suddenly he jumped from his chair and rushed to a mirror which he hung near, and in which I could see the reflection of some extraordinary facial contortions which he was making. He returned speedily to his desk, wrote furiously for a few minutes, and then

went again to the mirror. The facial pantomime was resumed, and then turning toward, but evidently not seeing me, he began talking rapidly in a low voice. Ceasing this soon, he returned once more to his desk, where he remained silently writing until luncheon time.

"For the time being he had not only lost sight of has surroundings, but had actually become, in action, as in imagination, the character of his pen."

Like so many manics, Dickens could not bear criticism. Forster noted that he "was sensitive in a passionate degree to praise and blame, which he made it for the most part a point of pride to assume indifference to." For his own survival as a creator, Dickens had to do what many other artists find necessary: avoid negative responses to his work as much as possible. "When I first began to write," he said, ". . . I suffered intensely from reading reviews, and I made a solemn compact with myself, that I would only know them for the future, from such general report as might reach my ears. . . . I have never broken this rule once, and I am unquestionably the happier for it—and certainly lose no wisdom." Dickens was usually smothered with praise, but praise, too, can be dangerous if one takes it too seriously. Many manic-depressive artists feel the impact of good or bad reviews of their work so intensely that they prefer to avoid what is too emotionally unsettling and opt for ignorance, despite their interest in the opinions of others.

At times, Dickens found writing fun and especially enjoyed doing comic passages. He confessed that "though I have been reading it [one of his pieces] some hundred times in the course of working, I have never been able to look at it with the least composure, but have always roared in the most unblushing manner."

Mania may become as much a hazard to the creator as it is a source of power and ideas. If it goes too far, confusion replaces clarity, and the organization of the work breaks down, as parts proliferate in chaos. At least in his work, Dickens was able to consciously resist the manic restlessness that wrecked his life; he could direct his flights of ideas. His unceasing struggle to achieve discipline and order in his life was more successful in his writing than anywhere else. He wrote: "I never could have done what I have done, without the habits of punctuality, order and diligence, without the determination to concentrate myself on one object at a time no matter how quickly its successor should come upon its heels." Dickens also won his battles against manic tendencies towards impatience, carelessness, and reluctance to edit his work. "I should have never made my success in life if I had been shy of taking pains, or if I had not bestowed upon the least thing I have ever undertaken exactly the same care and attention that I have bestowed upon the greatest. Do everything at your best." If there is a secret of success for the manic, it is in the iron discipline with which Dickens did his writing throughout a rambling, impulsive life.

Finally, he followed the practice that makes high achievement most likely: he put his art before everything else in his distracting and distracted existence. "I hold my inventive capacity on the stern condition that it must master my whole life, often have complete possession of me, make its own demands upon me, and sometimes for months together put everything else away from me."

The year 1851 was a typical Dickens year. While his father was dying and his wife was undergoing some sort of emotional collapse, he was in good spirits preparing another play. "Carpenters, scene painters, tailors, bootmakers, musicians, all kinds of people require my constant attention." "I have but 3 days in the week to myself, and, in those I have the Household Words [his magazine] to write for and to think about." In April, his theatrical mania protected him so well that he could write "I am quite happy again," although "My wife has been, and is, far from well. My poor father's death caused me much distress." And, "I came to London last Monday to preside at a public dinner—played with little Dora, my youngest child, before I went, and was told when I left the chair that she had died in a moment."

He moved to Broadstairs in May for another hospitable summer, left the family there, and went on tour with his play from mid-May to August. As soon as the performances were done, he was seized by an agitated depression: "Still the victim of an intolerable restlessness, I shouldn't be at all surprised if I write you one of these mornings from under Mont Blanc."

Charles recovered with the help of a new project, the furnishing and remodeling of a sumptuous house. He was feeling quite frisky when he wrote to his brother-in-law, who was supervising the reconstruction: "I have torn all my hair off and constantly beat my unoffending family. Wild notions have occurred to me of sending my own plumber to do the drains." "The very postman becomes my enemy because he brings no letter from you." "To pursue this theme is madness. Where are you?" "O rescue me from my present condition!" "I hope you may be able to read this. My state of mind does not admit of coherence—Ever affectionately. P.S. No WORKMEN ON THE PREMISES! Ha! ha! ha! (I am laughing demoniacally)."

Dickens ensconced his family in November. The next year he started *Bleak House* and went through the by-now expected ordeals beginning it. But 1852 was, on the whole, a quiet year, compared to the following one, when Charles's restlessness bordered on frenzy. March saw him in Brighton. In June he could no longer stay put: "I really feel as if my head would split like a fired shell if I remained here." On March 12 he landed in Boulogne with his wife, a phalanx of servants, and now nine children. In the autumn, back in London, Charles wanted to leave again: "I am so restless to be doing . . ." He toured Switzerland and Italy with two friends. In 1854 the merry dance went on. Charles prepared a play during the early part of the year, for a performance in June. That done, he dashed back to Boulogne with the family for the summer and fall. Again he was having "the strangest nervous miseries." "I have had dreadful thoughts of getting away somewhere altogether by myself. . . . Whatever it is, it is always driving me." In October he took the family to Paris.

In March of 1855, Charles was, for all of his traveling, still in the same place: in an agitated depression—this time in London—starting *Little Dorrit.* "I sit down to work, do nothing, get up and walk a dozen miles, come back and sit down again next day, again do nothing." As he progresses into the work, he notes, "I am steeped in my story, and rise and fall by turns into enthusiasm and depression." In May it was no better: "Restlessness worse and worse. Don't know at all what to do with myself." He escaped to Paris in the fall but hastened to England for short stays in November and December. Back in Paris, he wrote in January: "I am setting to work again, and my horrible restlessness immediately assails me. . . . As I was writing the preceding page, it suddenly came into my head that I would get up and go to Calais. I don't know why; the moment I got there I should want to go somewhere else." In February Charles briefly fled to London again. Agitated depression made him like a caged tiger. "Prowling about the rooms, sitting down, getting up, stirring the fire, looking out the window, tearing my hair, sitting down to write, writing nothing, writing something and tearing it up, going out, coming in, a Monster to my family, a dread Phaenomenon to myself, etc., etc., etc."

March of 1856 caught him back in London again. In that month he bought his dream house, which he first saw as a child, when it represented unattainable wealth and happiness. His devil was still keeping its part of the bargain, realizing all Charles's fantasies of fame and wealth, as it would do until the contract was fulfilled. Dickens went to Paris, then returned to London in May. On to Boulogne in the summer, with a visit in July to his other house in London: "I have wandered through the spectral halls of the Tavistock mansion 2 nights, with feelings of the profoundest depression."

In August cholera sent the Dickens family back to the relative safety of London. "The old days—the old days! Shall I ever, I wonder, get the frame of mind back as it used to be then?" It could not be: it was too late. Charles was only forty-four but already aged by his hurricane life. "I find that the skeleton in my domestic closet is becoming pretty big." His marriage was reaching its final stage of disintegration. The constant motion of his pinball existence was both a result and cause of the debacle of his marriage. He made many of his trips alone, a fugitive from his own home, or he escaped into the fantasy world of the theater. He was becoming convinced that he had missed the most important thing in life, the one that made it all worthwhile: love.

In October Dickens found relief in preparing another play, a Victorian melodrama, *The Frozen Deep,* which was to be given in his own house. He wrote in December, as his home was being transformed into a theater, "There has been a painter's shop in the school-room; a gas-fitter's shop all over the basement, a dress-maker's shop at the top of the house." It was the kind of uproar in which he delighted. The first performances of *The Frozen Deep* were given on January 6, 8, 12, and 14. No sooner were they done than Charles was mired in misery again. However, hope was at hand: a revival of the play was to be staged in August. Some professional actresses were hired to replace the amateurs who would not be available the second time. One of the actresses was Ellen Ternan. Dickens fell in love with her.

To understand how this very proper Victorian and model family man left his wife amid flaming scandal for an actress younger than his daughter, one must see him as he really was: a Don Quixote with a harem of Dulcineas. Ellen Ternan was just the last in a series of more-or-less serious, though platonic, romances.

Dickens's first love was a flirtatious, shallow girl, Maria Beadnell, who was eighteen when the seventeen-year-old Charles met her. He was a reporter then, while her father and uncle were in banking. Maria loved to collect admirers and her parents were too polite to throw him out, so he pursued her with love that "excluded every other idea from my mind for 4 years." "There never was such a faithful and devoted poor fellow as I was." She never gave him much encouragement, and when she finally discarded him, he wrote to her, "I have been so long used to inward wretchedness and real, real misery, that it matters little, very little to me what others may think of or what become of me."

There is a postscript to this. When Dickens was forty-three and she forty-four, Maria wrote to the celebrated author. Immediately, his love revived, and he wrote to her, "I have never been so good a man since, as I was when you made me wretchedly happy." They arranged to meet. Thus love dies. The charm of the young girl had gone rancid in the fat, middle-aged woman she had become.

Four years as love's victim were enough for Charles, and his next courtship, of his future wife, Kate, was somewhat like the obedience training of a dog, except that one rewards a dog with affection for good behavior. One looks in vain for hints of passion—on either side—in Charles and Kate's relationship. Perhaps so soon after his punishing years with Maria, he was too timid to offer his love to anyone who might refuse it. His next romance was with his sister-in-law Mary. Nothing had occurred when she was alive, but then "she sank under the attack and died—died in such a calm and gentle sleep that although I had held her in my arms for some time before, when she was certainly living (for she swallowed a little brandy from my hand) I continued to support her lifeless form, long after her soul had fled to heaven." Now she could not reject him. "I solemnly believe that so perfect a creature never breathed." "I have never had her ring off my finger by day or night, except for an instant at a time, to wash my hands, since she died. I have never had her sweetness and excellence absent from my mind so long." Twenty-six years later he wrote that she was still "as inseparable from my existence as the beating of my heart is." "I don't think there ever was a love like that I bear her." After Mary died, the marriage with Kate had no future.

Dickens began to window-shop. In 1839 he noticed a nineteen-year-old woman: "If I were a single man I should hate her husband mortally." He spoke of another as "the beautiful Mrs. F., whose eyelashes are in my memory."

The next year Dickens became madly infatuated with the newly wed Queen Victoria. After visiting her bedroom as a tourist, he "lay down," he said, "in the mud at the top of the Long Walk, and refused all comfort, to the immeasurable astonishment of a few straggling passengers who had survived the drunkenness of the previous night." He made of this quite a burlesque, writing of "starving myself to death," "hanging myself up in the pear-tree." He added: "I am very wretched, and think of leaving home. My wife makes me miserable, and when I hear the voices of my infant children I burst into tears." He wrote to another friend: "The presence of my wife aggravates me. I loathe my parents. I detest my house." In view of what he did later, this was not an idle jest.

Dickens's next romances were with two maiden laides that he met at Broadstairs in the summer of 1841. He went for a stroll on the pier with the younger one one night, and suddenly, seized by a manic urge for horseplay, he grabbed her and held her tight as the seawater rose to their knees. She called to his wife for help while the waves were sloshing them, but he only shouted, "Think of the sensation we shall create! Think of the road to celebrity which you are about to tread! No, not exactly to tread, but to flounder into. Let your mind dwell on the column in the Times wherein will be vividly described the pathetic fate of the lovely E. C., drowned by Dickens in a fit of dementia! Don't struggle, poor little bird." She shrieked back, "My dress, my best dress, my only silk dress will be ruined!" Mrs. Dickens contributed, "Charles! how can you be so silly?" The "lovely E. C." broke loose without any help, but on two other occasions he chased her to the same place, and she lost two bonnets. These were the golden years of Dickens's mania, and his romantic antics were quite playful. Later on there was more anguish than humor in them.

The following summer, Dickens was in the United States and found an attractive American to whom he sent designedly silly love letters. "My Better Angel,—if this should meet His eye, I trust you to throw dust in the same. His suspicions must not be aroused." She was married. "Be true to me, and we may defy His malice. When I think of futile attempts to tear 2 hearts asunder that are so closely knit together, I laugh like a Fiend. Ha! Ha! ha!" He enclosed a poem: "No artist in the world's broad ways/Could ever carve or mould'em/That might aspire to lace the stays? of charming Mrs. . . . [her name was Colden]." Back in England he wrote to her again: "It is more clear to me than ever that Kate is as near to being a Donkey, as one of that sex whose luminary and sun you are, *can* be." "At the present I will only add . . . sweet Foreigner, that I wish you would come and live next door; for the best part of my heart is in Laight Street, and I find it difficult to get on without it. . . . I am mournfully, and wholly faithfully—Yours—always—My Dear Mrs. Colden."

He was hers always until he met someone else who caught his fancy two years later. In February of 1844 Charles fell in love with Miss Christina Weller when she played the piano during one of his public apperances. He wrote that he was a "madman" with the "incredible feeling I have conceived for that girl." His next statement suggests that he identified her with his sister-in-law who had died at seventeen. "I cannot joke about Miss Weller; for she is too good; and interest in her (spiritual young creature that she is, and destined to an early death, I fear) has become a sentiment with me. Good God what a madman I should seem, if the incredible feeling I have conceived for that girl could be made plain to anyone! But for the recollection of Miss Weller (which has its tortures too) I don't know but I would as soon be comfortably suffocated as continue to live in this wearing, tearing . . . world." He is remarkably indiscreet for a married man of those days and even goes so far as to share his sentiments with her father. "I cannot help saying to you that your daughter's great gifts and uncommon character have inspired me with an interest which I should labor in vain to express." When Miss Weller became engaged to a friend of Charles's, he wrote that he would have liked to "run him through the body" "with good sharp steel." He predicted that the marriage "will all happen Wrong, and cannot be otherwise but Wrong; the undersigned being excluded from all chance of competition."

Later in the year Dickens took his family to Genoa. He became very friendly with a banker, de la Rue, and his pretty wife. Dickens spent hours every day, often late at night, practicing hypnosis with this lady. Charles's wife became very jealous of this ambiguous relationship, but he refused to break it off. Eventually geography separated the two couples.

In 1849 Dickens had another comic flirtation with a Mrs. Richard Watson, to whom he wrote that as he was toasting her,

> As the wine went down my throat I felt distinctly that it was "changing those thoughts to madness." On the way here I was a terror to my companions, and I am at present a blight and mildew on my home. Think of me sometimes, as I shall long think of our glorious dance last night. . . . P.S.—I am in such an incapable state, that after executing the foregoing usual flourish I swooned, and remained for some time insensible. Ha, ha, ha! Why was I ever restored to consciousness!!! . . . my recollection is incoherent and my mind wanders.

Dickens's longest involvement with a woman, excluding that with Miss

Ternan, was a playful one of eight years' duration, lasting from 1849 until he met Ellen. The object of his interest was Miss Mary Boyle. After he left her, he wrote, "Plunged in the deepest gloom. . . . On the way here I was a terror to my companions, and I am at present a blight and mildew on my home." This was the same year that Mrs. Watson had also caused a mildew. He kept up a correspondence in which he told Miss Boyle that he was "confoundedly miserable" and said such things as "o breezes waft . . . my Mary to my arms," "Ever Affectionately my darling," etc. They also managed to see each other from time to time, until Dickens gave himself to Ellen.

While manic types are capable of life-long fidelity to one person, their fondness for change and heightened sexual appetites do not encourage that behavior. Therefore, to have intense imaginings and feelings about the opposite sex—to flit from flower to flower, as it were—was quite normal for such as Dickens. It is possible that all the relationships were technically innocent. It was an age of sexual repression, especially for women. Ellen herself complained that the sexual relationship on which Dickens insisted was unwelcome to her.

While Dickens was totally miserable at home and blamed his discontent on his wife, he was convinced that the right woman was all he needed to be completely happy. Manic-depressives who have that delusion are often quite surprised to discover that their depressions return even after the "right" person has arrived. Some manic-depressives continue searching for happiness with a succession of "right" persons until senility or death ends it all. Dickens wrote to a friend about his suffering at home and love for Ellen, before he was separated from his wife:

> I am the modern embodiment of the old Enchanters, whose Familiars tore them to pieces. I weary of rest and have no satisfaction but in fatigue. Realities and idealities are always comparing themselves before me, and I don't like the Realities except when they are unattainable—*then,* I like them of all things. I wish I had been born in the days of Ogres and Dragon-guarded castles. I wish an ogre with 7 heads (and no particular evidence of brains in the whole lot of them) had taken the Princess whom I adore—you have no idea how intensely I love her!—to his stronghold on the top of a high series of mountains, and there tied her by the hair. Nothing would suit me half so well this day, as climbing after her, sword in hand and either winning her or being killed.— *There's* a frame of mind for you, in 1857.

After writing this letter, he moved out of the room he had shared with his wife.

If Dickens wrote to Ellen, she did not preserve his letters for posterity, so all that one can learn about their relationship is what outsiders observed. His daughter Mary gave an account of the affair: "She flattered him,—he was ever appreciative of praise—and though she was not a good actress she had brains, which she used to educate herself, to bring her mind more on a level with his own. Who could blame her? He had the world at his feet. She was a young girl of 18, elated and proud to be noticed by him. I do not blame *her.*" According to his daughter, Dickens and Ellen had a son. Either the child predeceased his father or Dickens was unaware of his existence, because money was bequeathed only to Ellen.

It was not so much that Kate was an unsuitable wife for Charles, though she may have been. The central problem was that Dickens was as restless in his loves as he was in all the other aspects of his life. Both mania and depression goaded him to keep changing everything. Unfortuantely, no change brought him tranquil contentment because he could not change what he was. Ellen, too, failed to make him live happily ever after, or even to stay at home.

"BLEAK HOUSE": 1857–1870

After the revival of *The Frozen Deep,* Dickens fell back into a severe, agitated depression. "I think I should sink in a corner and cry." "I want to escape from myself." "In the grim despair and restlessness of this subsidence from excitement . . . I want to cast about whether you and I can go anywhere—take any tour—see anything." He recognized to some extent that he was in a serious condition, and that it was an inherent part of his nature: "I have no relief but in action. I am become incapable of rest. I am quite confident I should rust, break, and die if I spared myself. Much better to die doing. What I am in that way, nature made me first." This was an isolated instance of insight. Soon he was blaming his condition on the profession that he had chosen: it was "restlessness which is the penalty of an imaginative life." Dickens managed to go on his tour, this time to Cumberland with Wilkie Collins, but returning home brought all the bad feelings back. Now he was blaming his unhappy condition on his marriage, oblivious of what he himself was doing to destroy his relationship with his wife.

> I don't get on better in these later times with a certain poor lady. . . . Much worse! Neither do the children, elder or younger. Neither can she get on with herself, or be anything but unhappy. (She has been excruciatingly jealous of, and has obtained positive proof of my being on the most intimate terms with, at least 15,000 women of various conditions in life, since we left Genoa. Please respect me for this vast experience.) What we should do, or what the girls would be, without Georgy [his sister-in-law who lived with them] I cannot imagine. She is the active spirit of the house and the children dote upon her.

Dickens was thinking of every possible reason to absolve himself from blame for wanting to rid himself of his wife. She did not get on with the children and contributed nothing to the household, she was jealous without cause, and he and she were simply incompatible. "Poor Catherine and I are not made for each other, and there is simply no help for it. . . . She is exactly what you know in the way of being amiable and complying; but we are strangely ill-sorted." He insisted that she was "the only person with whom I could not get on some how or another." His publishers might have disagreed with that. In late October he had a quarrel with Kate and at 2 A.M. walked thirty miles to his other home, Gad's Hill.

Over the years, Dickens had given readings of his work without fee to benefit various charities. These performances united both the actor and author in him. His daughter saw how much of himself was invested in them: "My father's public readings were an important part of his life, and into their performance and preparation he threw the best energy of his heart and soul, practicing and rehearsing at all times and places. The meadow near our home was a favorite place, and people passing through the lane, not knowing who he was, or what he was doing, must have thought him a madman for his reciting and gesticulation."

In March 1858 the author was seriously thinking of giving readings on a professional basis. He was always interested in making money. He also hoped that the travel and excitement of performing would provide a distraction from his depressions and troubles at home. "The domestic unhappiness remains so strong upon me that I can't write and . . . can't rest one minute. I have never known a moment's peace or content, since the last night of The Frozen Deep. . . . I have a turning notion that the mere physical effort and change of the Readings would be good, as another means of bearing it." "I must do something, or I shall wear my heart away." Even in his dreams he was trying to break out of his marriage. "Only last night, in my sleep, I was bent upon getting over a perspective of barriers, with my hands and feet bound. Pretty much what we are all about, waking, I think."

He began his reading tour in April. Meanwhile, the situation at home had become horrendous. A bracelet that Dickens had sent to Ellen Ternan arrived by mistake at his own residence and his wife opened the package. At this point her parents also became involved in the conflict. Now Charles blamed Kate for all the unhappiness in his life, and he intimated that she was mentally unsound besides. "I believe my marriage has been for years and years as miserable a one as ever was made. I believe that no 2 people were ever created, wih such an impossibility of interest, sympathy, confidence, sentiment, tender union of any kind between them, as there is between my wife and me." He does not explain why he impregnated her ten times. "You know that I have the many impulsive faults which belong to my impulsive way of life and exercise of fancy; but I am very patient and considerate at heart, and would have beaten out a path to a better journey's end than we have come to, if I could." She has "fallen into the most miserable weaknesses and jealousies, has, at times, been certainly confused besides."

The manic is wont to blame others for his own failures, and Dickens attributed to his wife the desire for separation. He said she felt herself too mentally unsound to continue the marriage. He appears to have convinced himself at least that his desires had nothing to do with the separation: "For some years past, Mrs. Dickens has been in the habit of representing to me that it would be better for her to go away and live apart; that her always increasing estrangement made a mental disorder under which she sometimes labors—more, that she felt herself unfit for the life she had to lead as my wife, and that she would be better far away." That would have been his dream come true. When friends tried to encourage a reconciliation, Dickens would have none of it: "It is not, with me, a matter of will, or trial, or sufferance, or good humour, or making the best of it, or making the worst of it, any longer. It is all despairingly over." He went further and accused his wife of not loving their children: "She does not—and she never did—care for the children, and the children do not—and they never did—care for her." It was not Kate, but Charles's own mother who was uncaring and sent her child out of their home to become a factory worker at age twelve. Dickens had become wrapped in delusions at this time. According to his daughter Kate, he himself was the uncaring one, not his wife: "My father was like a madman when my mother left home. This affair brought out all that was worst—all that was weakest in him. He did not care a damn what happened to any of us. Nothing could surpass the misery and unhappiness of our home." A separation was arranged on May 14. Everyone stayed in place except Kate and the oldest son, Charles, who moved out. Dickens never saw his wife again.

On May 29, at Dickens's insistence, the Hogarths, his in-laws, had to sign a statement claiming they made false accusations that Ellen Ternan was his mistress. Dickens himself was so irrational that he acted against his friends' pleadings and published his own denial of the mistress rumor on the front page of his magazine *Household Words,* a periodical that usually celebrated family harmony. He sent copies of this denial to all the newspapers. It was an unintended declaration of his love, in which he spoke of "misrepresentations, most grossly false, most monstrous, and most cruel—involving not only me, but innocent persons dear to my heart."

Now the paranoia of the manic-depressive became uppermost in Dickens's life. He had already shown signs of it. His usual response to literary criticism was to assume that it was a personal attack on him. He said of one unfavorable reviewer, "I think Hayward has rather visited upon me, his recollection of my disdaining his intimate acquaintance." Over the years Dickens turned against three of his publishing firms. He came to hate Bentley because the original terms of their contract no longer seemed adequate to a successful author.

He discarded Bradbury and Evans after their sixteen years of good service because Evans refused to print Dickens's rumor denial in *Punch* magazine. Next, the writer refused to have anything to do with anyone who had anything to do with his in-laws or wife. He broke with his dear old friends Thackeray and Mark Lemon in the mistaken belief that they had betrayed him. He saw himself as the victim of his marital drama and wrote on July 7: "I know very well that a man who has won a very conspicuous position, has incurred in the winning of it, a heavy debt to the knaves and fools, which he must be content to pay, over and over again, all through his life. Further, I know equally well that I can never hope that anyone out of my house can ever comprehend my domestic story. [One can infer that he was not receiving much sympathy.] I will not complain. I have been heavily wounded, but I have covered the wound up, and left it to heal." His responsibility for this episode of his life did not make the hurt any less painful, and his delusions do not appear to have given him much comfort. Nevertheless, Dickens did not collapse but continued his active life.

In August he began another tour that would carry him through England, Scotland, and Ireland. He did not set out in a very good state of mind, but the tour was the therapy he needed.

> I hope I may report that I am calming down again. It is no comfort for me to know that any man who wants to sell anything in print, has but to anatomize his finest nerves, and he is sure to do it. [The lament of the celebrity.] It is no comfort for me to know (as of course those dissectors do), that when I spoke in my own person it was not for myself but for the innocent and good, on whom I had unwittingly brought the foulest lies—Sometimes I *cannot* bear it. I had one of those fits yesterday, and was utterly desolate and lost. But it is gone, thank God, and the sky has brightened for me once more.

It was a relief to be able to share his audiences' good spirits: "They made me laugh so, that sometimes I could not compose my face to go on." The admiration that he received made him feel much better. "Our first week was an immense success. . . . It is a great sensation to have a large audience in one's hand." "The manner in which the people have everywhere delighted to express that they have a personal affection for me . . . is (especially at this time) high and far above all other considerations." During this period of acute distress Dickens developed his addiction to his reading tours.

Having left the publishers of *Household Words* because they would not print his rumor denial, he started publishing a rival magazine, *All The Year Round,* which debuted in April of 1859. He had wanted to call it *Household Harmony,* but friends objected. The year was relatively quiet. He began to write *A Tale of Two Cities.* In the following year, 1860, Dickens kept his spirits up with one of his manic hobbies: rebuilding and redecorating his home, Gad's Hill, in this case. He also began *Great Expectations.*

Ellen Ternan became a regular part of Dickens's life in this decade. He would rent a house in London for the spring season, where he and Ellen could spend two or three nights each week together. He also gave her a home at Peckham, and she became a regular visitor at Gad's Hill. Nonetheless, the last years were those in which the writer's depressive traits became noticeable. Most manic-depressives, even the manic types, have to endure longer, more frequent, and more severe depressions as they grow older. Dickens now found it difficult to start the day, lacking both the will for activity and any appetite for life. The merry raconteur was replaced by a silent man, withdrawn into himself. His daughter noted, "Often, when we were only our home party at Gad's Hill, he would come in, take something to eat in a mechanical way . . . and would return to his study to finish the work he had left, scarcely having spoken a word all this time." In 1866 he remarked, "Of course I am not so foolish as to suppose that all my work can have been achieved without *some* penalty, and I have noticed for some time a decided change in my buoyancy and hopefulness." This is evident in his letters of this period also. The gaiety and playfulness are gone. Longfellow visited Dickens in 1868 and was disturbed to see him so sad. A friend of Charles's told the poet, "Yes, yes, all his fame goes for nothing."

Dickens still resumed his manic ways from time to time. In 1863 he felt gay enough to turn a simple request to have his clock repaired into the following foolery: "Since my hall clock was sent to your establishment to be cleaned it has gone (as indeed it always has) perfectly well, but has struck the hours with great reluctance, and after enduring internal agonies of a most distressing nature, it has now ceased striking altogether. Though a happy release for the clock, this is not convenient to the household. If you can send down any confidential person with whom the clock can confer. . . ." The writer weathered the onset of grandfatherhood in 1864 quite well. "I once used to think what a horrible thing it was to be a grandfather. Finding that the calamity falls upon me without my perceiving any other change in myself, I bear it like a man."

He still liked to host complicated festivities of various sorts. In December of 1866 he arranged a day of footraces for the local lads and men, to be held on his own grounds, with cash prizes that he furnished. "We have been hard at work all day, building a course, making countless flags, and I don't know what else." The following day he exulted: "We had 2,000 people here. . . . There was not a dispute all day, and they went away at sunset rending the air with cheers."

Ever generous with time as well as money, Dickens even offered to stand in as a writer for a friend who had fallen ill, "I could do it, at a pinch, so like you that no one should find out the difference." However, he nursed the grudges formed when he sent his wife away. When his oldest son, Charles, married the daughter of Frederick Evans, the publisher with whom Dickens had broken completely during the separation crisis, the writer refused to go to the wedding because it was held at the Evans's house. The best Dickens could say upon the occasion was "I wish I could hope that Charlie's marriage may not be disastrous. . . . But I have a strong belief founded on careful observation of him that he cares nothing for the girl." Dickens's son's marriage was a success, but Dickens's own return to bachelorhood was not: he fled his home just as often as he had when his wife was still in it. "Indeed I suppose . . . that few men are more restless than I am, and that few sleep in more strange beds and dine at more new cook shops."

Dickens landed in many of these strange beds and cook shops while on his reading tours. These exhausting and sometimes hazardous adventures provided most of the drama in his remaining years. He traveled through England, Scotland, Wales, Ireland, the United States, and visited Paris, with hardly a year going by without one of these treks. The lure of them is visible in his comments about reading in Paris: "When David [Copperfield] proposed to Dora, gorgeous beauties all radiant with diamonds, clasped their fans between their hands and rolled about in ecstasy." Indeed, he gloried in the admiration of the female part of his audience: "Ladies stood all night with their chins against my platform. Other ladies sat all night upon my steps." "A lady whose face I had never seen stopped me yesterday in the street, and said to me, Mr. D, will you let me touch the hand that has filled my house with many friends!" The lonely little boy cast out of his own house was now embraced by the love and enthusiasm of thousands upon thousands, laughing, cheering, applauding him. "I must say that the intelligence and warmth of the audiences are an immense sustainment, and that always sets me up. Sometimes before I go down to read (especially when it is the day) I am so oppressed by having to do it that I feel perfectly unequal to the task. But the people lift me out of this directly." This is an example of the performing high that is, as he says, induced by the audience.

Almost from the start, the reading tours exacted a physical toll of him that he was increasingly unable to afford. As early as 1861 Dickens began to say: "The expenditure of lungs and spirits was . . . rather great; and to sleep well was out of the question. I am therefore rather fagged today." That pattern would repeat itself throughout the tour.

In June of 1863 a railway accident left Dickens with a panic disorder that would make any means of travel an ordeal, greatly enlarging the stress of his tours for the rest of his years. He had been aboard a train that went off a high bridge, with many cars falling to destruction. The writer survived because his car was left dangling from the bridge. He managed to get himself and Miss Ternan out of it safely, then he tried to help the wounded and dying who were scattered everywhere. He wrote later:

> My escape from the Staplehurst accident is not to be obliterated from my nervous system. To this hour I have sudden vague rushes of terror, even when riding in a hansom cab, which are perfectly unreasonable but quite insurmountable. I used to make nothing of driving a pair of horses habitually through the most crowded parts of London, I cannot now drive, with comfort to myself, on the country roads here; I doubt if I could ride at all in the saddle. My reading secretary and companion knows so well when one of these odd momentary seizures come upon me in a railway carriage that he instantly produces a dram of brandy.

In 1865 Dickens's foot became painful and swollen and would remain chronically so for the rest of his life, but he did not let it interfere with his long walks. Apparently it was more distressing to try to resist the manic impulsion to move than to hike on a damaged foot. On one occasion, he said, "I got frost-bitten by walking continually in the snow, and getting wet in the feet daily. . . . My left foot swelled, and I still forced the boot on; sat in it to write, half the day; walked in it through the snow the other half; forced the boot on again the next morning; sat and walked again. . . . At length, going on as usual, I fell lame on the walk, and had to limp home dead lame, through the snow, for the last 3 miles." His account illustrates the driving force of mania.

The next year, during a reading tour of the British Isles, Dickens developed a severe ache in his left eye, acute and sudden chest pains, and a pulse that indicated to his doctors that he had a heart ailment. Nevertheless, he went on a six-month reading tour of the United States, with serious consequences to his health. One of his reasons for undertaking this tour was that he could not resist a chance to live in his fantasy world: it was becoming so much more colorful and exciting than his own. "So real are my fictions to myself, that, after hundreds of nights, I come with a feeling of perfect freshness to that little red table [from which he read] and laugh and cry with my hearers as if I had never stood there before."

The manic's joie de vivre returned to Dickens during the early part of his American tour. A companion recorded: "Dickens was always planning something to interest and amuse his friends, and when in America he taught us several games arranged by himself, which we played again and again, he taking part as our instructor. While he was traveling from point to point, he was cogitating fresh charades to be acted when we should again meet." Ice and snow and even a bad case of influenza (catarrh) could not deter the writer from his daily twelve-mile hike when he was manic. He even wrote an announcement of a walking match between himself and one "Jemmy," describing himself as one "whose surprising performance . . . on that truly national instrument, the American Catarrh, have won for him the well-merited title of the Gad's Hill Gasper. Jemmy and the Gasper are . . . to walk out at the rate of not less than 4 miles an hour by the Gasper's watch for one hour and a half."

In front of his audience Dickens developed a performing high intense enough to banish all feeling of illness and exhaustion until he left the stage. "I not only read last Friday, when I was doubtful of being able to do so, but I read as I never did before, and astonished the audience quite as much as myself. You never saw such a scene of excitement." With such rewards for abusing his body, he was incapable of prudence. One afternoon he had no voice at all, but "after 5 minutes at the little table I was not (for the time) even hoarse." He did realize, though, that something about his "return of force when it is wanted" was not natural. "I am not at times without nervous dread that I may someday sink altogether," he admitted.

In the last months of the tour, Dickens became too nauseated to eat and consumed most of his calories in the form of alcohol. His diet was a nutritionist's nightmare: "At 7 in the morning, in bed, a tumbler of cream and 2 tablespoons of rum. At 12 a sherry cobbler and a biscuit. At 3 [dinnertime] a pint of champagne. At 5 minutes to 8, an egg beaten up with a glass of sherry. . . . At a quarter past 10, soup, and anything to drink I fancy. I don't eat more than half a pound of solid food in the whole 24 hours, if so much." There is not much information about Dickens's usual intake of alcohol, but during those weeks he was an alcoholic.

By March his only relief from depression was to go on stage: "I am nearly used up. Climate, distance, catarrh, travelling, and hard work have begun (I may say so, now they are nearly over) to tell heavily upon me." "I am beginning to be tired, and have been depressed all the time (except when reading) and have lost my appetite." His apparent vigor provided by mania during his performances gave people the false impression that he was in good health. "However sympathetic and devoted the people are about me, they *can not* be got to comprehend that one's being able to do the 2 hours with spirit when the time comes round, may be co-existent with the consciousness of great depression and fatigue."

When Dickens reached England again in April of 1868, he was quite ill. He was sick every morning and giddy throughout the day. He could only read from one side of his visual field. "My weakness and deadness are all on the left side," he said, "and if I don't look at anything I try to touch with my hand, I don't know where it is." This was the result of a stroke. His doctors warned him that another stroke, with total paralysis of the left side of his body, was sure to come if he continued his performances. Refusing to confront a reality that thwarted his will, he blamed his symptoms on his medications and planned the next tour.

Another tour of Britain was begun in December of 1868. This time Dickens included the reading of the scene in which Nancy Sikes is murdered. He gave this gruesome material a rendition that left the audience in shock. "I should think we had from a dozen to 20 ladies taken out stiff and rigid, at various times!" he boasted. The physical effect on the performer was even more traumatic: While he was doing the performance, his hands became almost black with blood, his face changed from red to white and back again, and his foot became too painfully swollen to walk on. After the performance he would need to lie down immediately and could not speak from sheer exhaustion, but the mania still enlivened him. Soon he would be overcome with hilarity, eager to return to the now-empty auditorium and perform the murder scene all over again.

One evening in February of 1869, while they were in Edinburgh, Dickens's manager, Dolby, asked him to recite the murder scene less often as it was so exhausting. Outraged, Dickens shouted, "Have you finished!" and slammed his knife and fork on the plate, smashing it. "Dolby! Your infernal caution will be your ruin one of these days!" Then the writer burst into tears and begged Dolby's forgiveness. On April 22, Dickens underwent total physical collapse. His foot was agonizingly painful, and he was nauseated, giddy, weak, and bleeding heavily from the intestines. The tour was interrupted; he was brought home and ordered to rest. In May he wrote his will.

That year, Dickens enjoyed one last manic summer, in which he seemed to be thirty again. A guest describes it:

> Every day we had out-of-doors games, . . . Dickens leading off with great spirit and fun. Billiards came after dinner, and during the evening we had charades and dancing. There was no end to the new divertisements our kind host was in the habit of proposing, so that constant cheerfulness reigned at Gad's Hill. He went into his work-room, as he called it, soon after breakfast and wrote till 12 o'clock; then he came out, ready for a long walk. . . . We went forth, rain or shine . . . 12, 15, even 20 miles were not too much for Dickens. . . . Then Dickens was at his best and talked.

Despite the objections of physicians, family, and friends, Dickens insisted that he do a few more readings in March of 1870 and set out again. His son Charlie went with him. The writer's doctor told Charlie: "I have had some steps put up at the side of the platform. You must be there every night, and if you see your father falter in the least, you must run and catch him and bring him off to me, or, by Heaven, he'll die before them all." That did not happen, but Dickens must have had another stroke, for he lost the ability to pronounce certain words. He resumed the struggle against depression.

"Though moody and dull the whole day," Dolby recorded, Dickens would not succumb to his emotional condition any more than he did to his physical state. He would not only give the reading, he would do it, Dolby said, "with his accustomed verve and vigor." When the tour concluded, Charles returned to Gad's Hill to work on his new novel, *The Mystery of Edwin Drood.* On June 9, the book unfinished, the author died of a stroke. The man who could not rest was finally at peace.

6

Van Gogh

Dickens was both a product of his time and a considerable influence on his period. Van Gogh was neither. He was out of step with his age. His chief involvement with contemporary art was his brief association with the Impressionists, some thirty painters who were rejected by the art establishment of Paris and denied participation in official exhibitions. They banded together to hold their own shows and ran counter to accepted tradition in several ways. Instead of painting pictures that told stories in a slick, photographic style, they presented images of ordinary people in the city or countryside. The Impressionists worked out of doors, trying to catch fleeting changes of light, the shimmer of summer haze, the poetry of weather. Academic art was conventionally colored, but the Impressionists loaded their canvases with brilliant hues, forcing the observer's eye to blend their dabs of blue and yellow into green, pink and blue to violet, etc. The academics were still mining the Renaissance for picture structure while the Impressionists borrowed from the off-center compositions of Japanese prints.

Van Gogh would learn all these things from the Impressionists and then leave them behind as he made his own work stronger, starker, even more expansive, more emotional, and more powerful. The Impressionists led him to a new universe of color, but he wrote his own cosmology. Art historians list him among the "Post-Impressionists." Tragically for him, he was too far ahead of his contemporaries for his work to find much acceptance and understanding during his own lifetime.

Van Gogh branched off from the Impressionists because, for him, blazing light and color were not ends in themselves, but merely the means toward an art of greater emotional force. "It is the painter's duty to be entirely absorbed by nature and to use all his intelligence to express sentiment in his work so that it becomes intelligible to other people." "One must feel what one draws." "For me, the drama of storm in nature, the drama of sorrow in life, is the most impressive." "Oh, there must be a little bit of light, a little bit of happiness, just enough to indicate the shape, to make the lines of the silhouette stand out, but let the whole be gloomy." These were his beliefs. Not all of his work is sorrow laden, however: some of his paintings are luminous with joy.

The Impressionists were involved in reinterpreting the visual world, making people see what was around them as it had never been seen before. Van Gogh, on the other hand, wanted his work to interpret the human soul. He wanted people to feel life as he did, to be aware of it in all its intensity. He believed that turning his feelings into art gave his work value and redeemed his life: "What am I in most people's eyes? A nonentity or an eccentric and disagreeable man—somebody who has no position in society and never will have, in short, the lowest of the low. Very well, even if this were true, I should want my work to show what is in the heart of such an eccentric, of such a nobody."

When he became an artist, Van Gogh chose for himself the role of victim. He set himself against the world, identifying himself with that section of society that suffered the most and was least able to defend itself: the poor. At work in the fields, the mines, at looms, or at their evening meal, the poor were his first subjects. "Being a laborer," he said, "I feel at home in the laboring class, and more and more I will try to take root there." He proved this when he set up housekeeping with a prostitute and her child; but his middle-class background stayed with him. He never went so far as to do any kind of common labor himself. Instead of taking time from his art to earn money, he would simply do without food, or whatever it was he could not pay for at the moment, until the money from his brother arrived.

Van Gogh was a Marxist in sympathies without ever having read Marx. The artist saw what the industrial revolution was doing to the poor and it horrified him: "Because I see so many weak ones trodden down, I greatly doubt the sincerity of much of what is called progress and civilization, I do believe in civilization, even in a time like this, but only in the kind that is founded on real humanity. I think whatever destroys human life is barbarous, and I do not respect it." His opinions notwithstanding, it never occurred to Van Gogh to start, or even to join, a revolutionary movement. He did not hope to change society, nor did he expect it to evolve into something better. His attitude towards the world was one of passive despair. This is often the orientation of the depressive personality.

Paradoxically, this avant-garde painter was a captive of the past. His concept of art and the artist came from a movement that was dead before he was born. It was Romanticism that furnished him with the belief that the artist must be a martyr, and his depressions confirmed such thoughts: Whatever the artist might accomplish in his art must be paid for with suffering. Van Gogh had assumed the role of martyr during his religious period, so it was natural for him to do so when he became a painter. In common with many Romantics, he believed himself to be the vessel of a special revelation: "I feel a power within me which I must develop, a fire that I may not quench, but must keep ablaze. Though I do not know to what end it will lead me, I should not be surprised if it were a gloomy one." The conviction that one is a seer or prophet can help to compensate for a lifetime of rejection. It also excuses one from the efforts necessary to achieve any worldly success.

Van Gogh willingly bore the stigmata of the Romantic artist even when it was not necessary. He spent money on art supplies and liquor that he should have spent on food. His malnutrition was so severe that he became weak, subject to frequent infection, and lost many teeth. He was often painfully hungry and would write to his brother, "I must tell you that I am literally starving." One might conclude from this that Van Gogh's brother, Theo, did not give him enough money to live on, but that was not the case.

Late in his brief life, Van Gogh saw his madness as another form of artists' martyrdom. "Am I to suffer imprisonment of the madhouse?" he asked and answered himself, "Why not?" Like most Romantics, Van Gogh came to look on the artist's agonies as a sign of greatness. "I think the history of great men is tragic . . . for usually they are no longer alive when their work is publicly acknowledged, and for a long time during their lives they are under a kind of depression because of the opposition and the difficulties of struggling through life." He surely qualified for that, because as he knew, "The more I am spent, ill, a broken pitcher, by so much more am I an artist." This is precisely the myth of genius that Van Gogh's own life helped to perpetuate, but it is *not* necessary to suffer hunger and illness in order to be a great artist. On the contrary, work of the highest quality requires all the energy and intelligence that one possesses. Any condition, such as hunger or illness, that reduces one's energy and alertness also diminishes the likelihood of producing work of much value. On the whole, misery terminates creativity and in some cases destroys the artist as well.

Van Gogh was not indifferent to success, he was completely hostile to it. He even extended that aversion to artists who were making a living at their trade. He said of them, "Now they try to devour each other and are big personages who have villas and scheme to get ahead." Speaking of their "fine houses," he adds, "That's no place for me, I won't go there any more."

The very thought of his own success was threatening. He was unhappy that he made no money from his work and had to rely on his brother's charity but felt that recognition would be worse. He said it was the equivalent of "ramming the live end of your cigar in your mouth." He tried to sabotage his own nascent fame by warning a critic who was going to review his work, "[Do] not go beyond a few words, because it is absolutely certain that I shall never do important things." It is no coincidence that Van Gogh ended his life just as his work was beginning to attract notice and be sold: it was one more unbearable stress for him. "As soon as I read that my work was having some success," he wrote, ". . . I feared at once that I will suffer for it; this is how things nearly always go in a painter's life: success is about the worst thing that can happen." With such beliefs, Van Gogh was programmed for tragedy.

THE SAINTLY SICKNESS

Vincent Van Gogh was a failed saint. Initially, when he was sixteen, he entered the more prosaic profession of art dealer, but this was a false start. He also tried several other occupations while his obsession with religion gradually engulfed him, a process that took nine years. Finally, at age twenty-five he decided to join his father's profession, the ministry. During the next two years he came to believe that his own version of Christianity was too radical for the established church. He took Christian ethics quite literally and gave all that he had to the poor, including, on one occasion, a brand new velvet suit. He was willing—even desperate—to give all of himself, all of his life, to meet what he thought were God's demands on him.

Every form of life was holy to Vincent, as it was to Saint Francis of Assisi. One family with whom Van Gogh boarded said that he would even rescue caterpillars from being trod upon. He loved to wander through the countryside, and the affectionate attention that he gave to all that he saw later enriched his paintings. For him nature was "everything that has brought you up and nourished you, everything you have loved," a vision of nature in the guise of an idealized mother. Van Gogh had warm feelings for every living creature except himself, however: he treated his own body with cruelty long before he cut off his ear.

Van Gogh's mental illness drove him to a martyrdom without meaning. He starved himself while living in rags and filth and cold. Manic-depression harried him across the frontier that separates generosity and sacrifice from self-destruction. Having failed to complete the required training for the ministry, Van Gogh tried to do missionary work, but two psychotic episodes made that impossible. He was too eccentric to be accepted for very long as a religious leader by any community. He was too sick to manage his own life, much less to guide anyone else. At that stage of his life Van Gogh did not recognize that he was mentally ill, so he blamed his inability to maintain a life of religious service on the decadence of Christianity. "Oh, I am no friend of the present Christianity, though its Founder was sublime," he came to say, and he spoke of Christianity's "bitter coldness." Having a truly religious cast of mind, however, Van Gogh had to build his life around worship: he had to dedicate his life to something. "I can very well do without a benevolent deity," he said, "in my life and also in my painting. But I can't do without something which is bigger than myself and constitutes my very life, the capacity to create." He gave to art the same total surrender of self that the saint gives to God. Art came before everything, and even physical survival was secondary.

Since religion was the center of the early part of Van Gogh's life, and the religion of art the center of his last ten years, we will pause briefly before tracing his life to survey that vast and fruitful field for research, the interpenetration of religion and manic-depression. Religious leaders have long been aware of connections between religious phenomena and the psychology of the individual. Saint John of the Cross was skeptical about those around him who aspired to sainthood: "I am really terrified by what passes among us these days. Anyone who has barely begun to meditate . . . goes about proclaiming 'God has told me this,' or 'I have heard that answer from God.' But all is illusion and fancy; such an one has only been speaking to himself." Gautama Buddha compared his own religious experience to that of the mentally afflicted. He said, "Like one who is driven mad by spells, I know not by whom I am crazed, or who possesses me."

For the most part, however, people interpret the claims of other religions as hallucination, delusions, confusion, or plain deceit, while taking their own beliefs for self-evident religious truth. Mohammed attempted suicide more than once, suffered from depressions and hallucinations, and thought he was possessed by a spirit, but all that did not damage his credibility with his followers. Martin Luther had depressions and hallucinations and states of manic confusion. "Not seldom," he said, "has it happened to me to awake at midnight and dispute with Satan concerning the Mass." He once threw an inkwell at what he thought was the devil. In 1527 he was on the verge of suicide. In 1503 he was in an abnormal state when he wrote: "When I try to work, my head becomes filled with all sorts of whizzing, buzzing, thundering noises, and if I did not leave off the instant, I should faint away. The day your letter came I had another visit from the Devil. I was alone, . . . and this time the Evil One got the better of me, drove me out of my bed, and compelled me to seek the face of man." Nevertheless, the opposition that rose against Luther was based on his doctrine, not his mental peculiarities. George Fox, the founder of Quakerism, believed that he had a special ability to "discern witches." He had visions and hallucinated a voice that he identified as God's. He also had recurrent and prolonged depressions. In his own words: "A strong temptation to despair came upon me. And sometimes I kept myself retired in my chamber, and often walked solitary . . . to wait upon the Lord." "And after some time I went into my own country again, and was there about a year, in great sorrows and troubles, and walked many nights by myself." "Now though I had great openings, yet great troubles and temptations came upon me, so that when it was day I wished for night, and when it was night I wished for day." In all this Fox was talking about endogenous moods, without external cause. The "great openings" were what he called his periods of mania when he was ecstatic.

One of the major Protestant mystics, Jakob Boehme, had manic ecstasies during which he thought he understood all creation, and "All creation now gave another smell beyond what words can utter." At other times he had prostrating depressions. Saint John of the Cross, whom we quoted earlier, was well acquainted with depression, which mystics called "the dark night of the soul." His description of it includes such symptoms of depression as pessimism, anxiety, the convictions of worthlessness, abandonment by God, and rejection by men, thoughts of death, and finally, terrible suffering. "That which this anguished soul feels most deeply," he wrote, "is the conviction that God has abandoned it, of which it has no doubt; that He has cast it away as an abominable thing. . . . The shadow of death and torments of hell are most acutely felt. . . . A terrible apprehension has come upon it that thus it will be forever. It has also the same sense of abandonment with respect to all creatures, and that it is an object of contempt to all, especially to its friends." The expectation of contempt indicates some degree of paranoia. San Juan de Dios behaved very much like Van Gogh. He dedicated his life to the poor, gave away all his belongings except the shirt he wore, and made a practice of fasting. Like Van Gogh, he too had a fit of frenzy, but instead of amputating his ear, he tore his clothing, pulled out his hair, destroyed all his secular books, ran through town yelling of his sins and hitting himself upon the chest, shouting for people to pray for him and for God to be merciful. Later in life, San Juan founded a mental asylum and a hospital that was quite innovative for its day in that there was only one patient per bed. The eighteenth-century religious leader Swedenborg hallucinated toads and beetles and thought he was the Messiah. He gave an eyewitness report that the natives of Jupiter walked on both hands and feet, while Martians spoke through their eyes and Saturians used their stomachs for the same purpose. Swedenborg claimed to have seen a man who said "I am God" and "Eat not so much." Swedenborg also averred: "I have spoken one whole year with St. Paul." "I have spoken 10 times with Luther. But with angels I have conversed these 22 years and continue to do so."

The experiences of diagnosed manic-depressives converge with that of saints and mystics. John Custance who was hospitalized for manic-depression said that during mania, "I feel a mystic sense of unity with all fellow creatures and the Universe as a whole; I am at peace." Other manic-depressives in the same state say they have a feeling of communion with God, a sense of direct contact. When a person in acute mania goes rigid in a rush of exaltation, he throws his head back, rolls his eyes heavenward, smiles ecstatically, and extends his arms as though to welcome bands of angels. This is remarkably like the pose and facial expression found for centuries in paintings of saints, the Virgin Mary, and other holy figures either on their way to or already in heaven. It seems that the look of a religious person in acute manic ecstasy was well known in less secular times than ours. Feelings and behavior that are considered peculiar to the religious life are found also in manic-depression, including its psychotic extremes. During his worst attacks, Van Gogh's delusions took religious form.

The delusions of both mania and depression may take on religious ideation. In depression people often feel that they have sinned and are consequently damned; that God rejects them, devils pursue them, and punishment awaits them. In mania, grandiosity may take the form of a conviction that God has designated the individual for special burdens and rewards, such as saving the world and being able to foretell the future. The manic may overflow with generosity, and his generosity is seen as irrational only when his philanthropic donations bring him to debt or poverty. John Custance's mania took this form:

> I gave money away [to prostitutes] until my bank warned me about my overdraft, but I was convinced that God would give me money to carry on the good work, and approached the Christian Science church in Curzon St. with a request for money for a particular girl in whom I was interested. Very naturally they refused, but I was so filled with righteous indignation that I pulled down in manical frenzy everything I could reach, with the idea of making myself a martyr, and thus showing up the meanness and hypocrisy of churches in general.

In mania there is sometimes an overwhelming temptation to do good. One overflows with love for all creatures, including humanity. One longs to devote one's life to some worthy cause, to make some meaningful sacrifice, no matter how painful. A man who speaks from his own experience is Clifford Beers, a manic-depressive who founded a clinic: "A man abnormally elated may be swayed irresistibly by his best instinct. . . . He may not only be willing but eager to assume risks and endure hardships which under normal conditions he would assume reluctantly if at all." Indeed, the courage, aggressiveness, and hope needed to preach a new faith, to found a new religion, are the same assets that mania contributes to the political leader and the social prophet.

A saint's or mystic's good deeds and religious insights are *not* invalid because their sources happen to be manic-depressives. Beethoven's music does not lose its beauty because he had the illness. Napoleon's conquests were not less real because he had the disease. The fact that Isaac Newton was a manic-depressive does not cancel the law of gravity. Truth can come from any person. Our comments are not intended as criticism of any of the people mentioned nor as an argument against their beliefs, but to demonstrate that Van Gogh's mix of religion with manic-depression has appeared at various times throughout religious history. He failed to be a saint not because he was a manic-depressive, but because he was too self-destructive.

THE VAN GOGHS

Napoleon, Beethoven, and Dickens all had ne'er-do-well fathers. As children, they, respectively, had to cope with civil war, alcoholism, and bankruptcy. Van Gogh, in contrast, had many advantages. His father was a clergyman, respected in his community. The family was externally stable, comfortably middle class. A career in a prospering family business awaited Vincent when he reached adulthood. There are no tales of horror in his chidhood, no tragedies, violence, deaths, or serious illness. His father took care of him and more than once rescued him from physical and mental disintegration. His brother gave him what every artist would like to have: money to live on without having to work for the art market. Yet, Van Gogh's life progressed through agony. The rejection of his work was not the reason. He was more afraid of success than of failure. Art was not to blame either. Van Gogh was even more miserable before he found himself as a painter than afterward. His own testimony tells us that art alone enabled him to endure life, art alone gave him a reason for existence. The terrible force that warped his personality, turned his life into a chain of disasters, and finally killed him was acute manic-depression. There are signs of it in his nearest relatives, too.

Vincent's mother loved drawing, and he probably inherited his talent from her. She also seems to have been a manic-depressive who would alternate between excitement and withdrawal. This, too, was part of his heritage. It is possible that Vincent inherited some of his traits from his father as well. According to Vincent, his father was autocratic, bad tempered, and domineering. Vincent wrote to his brother Theo: "Every time you say something to Father which he hasn't an answer for, . . . he will say 'You are murdering me,' meanwhile reading the paper and smoking his pipe in complete tranquility. . . . Or else Father will fly into a frightful rage; and as he is accustomed to people being scared of him under such circumstances, Father is surprised if somebody does not give way to his anger. Father is excessively touchy and irritable."

The other Van Gogh children may also have inherited manic-depression. One of Vincent's sisters spent thirty-eight years of her life in a mental hospital. His youngest brother, Cor, died at age thirty-three, a suicide. His brother Theo, always subject to severe attacks of anxiety and depression, became psychotic, threatened his wife and son, and was put in an asylum, where he died not long after Vincent did. Vincent took note of the similarity between them when he wrote to Theo, "Something of the same melancholy is in you, though less passionately and nervously than in me." Only two out of the six children were not suicides, or put into asylums, or both, so it seems that beneath a family life that was normal and conventional on the surface, something very strange was going on, and the outcome was frightful.

YOUTH: 1853–1873

Vincent was born on May 1, 1853, four years before his brother Theo. A servant in the household remembered the future artist as being the least likable of the six Van Gogh children. "Theodorus," she said, "was ordinary. But Vincent had something unusual; he was so childish, and not like anyone else; moreover, he had peculiar manners, and he was often punished accordingly." A visitor to the house found the boy extremely withdrawn. Vincent would not sit with others at the table for meals or speak to anyone when he came into the dining room. Instead, he ate his meal sitting in a corner, and even then, all he would take was bread. He had no close contact with anyone during his childhood. His sister Elizabeth said, "Brothers and sisters were strangers to him as well as his own youth." He avoided other children and would go off by himself with books on theology and philosophy. He was another gifted child who learned to substitute books for friends. When an adult, Vincent explained: "I have a more or less irresistible passion for books, and I continually want to instruct myself, to study if you like, just as much as I want to eat my bread." Vincent was also learning to draw by the time he was eight. A friend tells us he "would go all over the place to make his little sketches. This occupied him continually and was all he spoke of." Vincent did not enjoy his self-imposed isolation, though. He said, when an adult, "My own youth was gloomy and cold and sterile."

Of all the subjects in this book, Van Gogh is the one most crippled in his ability to understand and get along with others. He had no idea how to be nice to people, how to earn their love or friendship, and he never understood how he hurt them or why his behavior made them angry. He was an intelligent, sensitive, well-read man, but that is not enough. This was part of Van Gogh's tragedy. He had a tremendous need for love, but he did not know how to be human. Even in boyhood he was considered the odd one in what was an unusual family. What he was as an adult, he had already become as a child: lonely, irritable, subject to rages, ascetic, withdrawn, eccentric, gifted, and alternating between high spirits and long depressions. In severe cases of manic-depression, the symptoms may be noticeable even in childhood.

The love and comfort that Vincent's parents gave him, though it may have been inadequate, ended when he was eleven. He went off to boarding school and lived apart from the family from then on. At thirteen he changed boarding schools. At sixteen he went to The Hague to begin an apprenticeship at the Goupil Gallery. He did quite well, earning praise from clients, painters, and his employers, In May 1873, when he was twenty, he was transferred to the Goupil Gallery in London.

THE FAILURES BEGIN: 1873–1876

In London, Vincent initially functioned adequately although he was experiencing euphoria, which, for the manic-depressive, often presages sad times to come. In the gallery he would look at the paintings and feel "violent emotion, to the point of rapture." That summer he fell in love with his landlady's daughter and wrote home of his happiness: "Oh fullness of rich life, your gift, Oh God." He lapsed into deep depression when the girl, who was already engaged, rejected him. A change of scene seemed advisable, and in October of 1874 Vincent's uncle arranged for his transfer to the Goupil Gallery in Paris. Vincent's condition did not improve and by December he was back in London. He tried to escape his misery by drawing and by reading religious books. He kept to himself and began to impress people as an eccentric.

In May of 1875 he returned to the Goupil Gallery in Paris, but depression kept its grip on him. He began to feel out of place in the gallery, even though it was a family business and Theo would fit into it nicely later on. By March of the next year all concerned agreed that Vincent should leave the Goupil Gallery to find some work or profession that would make him happier. In this period he began to have paranoid thoughts. "It seems as if something were threatening me," he wrote.

When Vincent left the art business, it was suggested to him that he become a painter, but instead he applied for and was awarded a teaching position in England, starting in April. This job paid him with only room and board, so he soon changed to a school that paid him a salary. His depression continued undiminished, and he turned to religion for comfort. It made his failure as a teacher seem unimportant. At Christmas he left England to visit home, never to return. His uncle Vincent found him another job, this one in a bookstore in Dordrecht.

DORDRECHT: JANUARY–MAY 1877

Three people who knew Vincent in his twenty-third year provided the following information. Vincent would draw in his room at night and worry the landlord "because he was so queer" and might set the place on fire. The landlord adds: "Occasionally, well, speaking frankly, it was as if the fellow was out of his mind." "He avoided the other boys as much as possible; he always wanted to be alone." "Van Gogh, you ought to eat! How often I used to say this to him." The answer that came was "I am not in want of food; eating is a luxury."

A fellow clerk at the bookstore furnishes another picture of Vincent who, like many depressives, made the people around him uncomfortable. It is obvious that this witness did not like Van Gogh. "He always made a queer impression on me . . . instead of working, he was translating the Bible into French, German and English, in 4 columns, with the Dutch text in addition. . . . At other times when you happened to look, you caught him making little sketches. . . . No, he was not an attractive boy, with those small, narrowed, peering eyes of his and, in fact, he was always a bit unsociable. . . . He led an absolutely solitary life. He took many walks over the island, but always alone. In the shop he hardly spoke a word. In short, he was something of a recluse."

His roommate had more sympathy for Vincent and could see him as a human being but reports even more of Vincent's unhappiness and growing religious obsession.

> Van Gogh provoked laughter repeatedly by his attitude and behavior: for everything he did and thought and felt, and his way of living, was different from others of his age. At table he said lengthy prayers and ate like a penitent friar: for instance, he would not take meat, gravy, etc. And then his face had always an abstracted expression—pondering, deeply serious, melancholy. But when he laughed, he did so heartily and with gusto, and his whole face brightened. . . . Night after night Van Gogh sat reading the Bible, making abstracts from it, and writing sermons; for in those days . . . strict piety was the core of his being. . . . He not only went to the Dutch Reformed Church on Sunday, but also on the same day to the Jansenist, the Roman Catholic and the Lutheran churches. . . . Gradually he got more melancholy and his daily work cost him more and more effort. . . . And when he had to give ladies and other customers information about the prints exhibited . . . he paid no attention to his employer's interests, but said explicitly and unreservedly what he thought of their artistic value. . . . To be a minister of religion, that was his ideal, and it was an obsession with him. . . . So he struggled on, deluding his parents into thinking he was contented.

By this time in his life Vincent had worked in three galleries, held two jobs as a teacher, and been refused by the girl he wanted to marry. He had been continually depressed for almost four years. His family worried about him and, understandably enough, he looked on himself as a failure. He hoped that dedicating his life to God would salvage it. In March and April he wrote to Theo: "I hope and believe that my life will be changed somehow, and that my longing for Him will be satisfied." "Oh! Theo, Theo boy, if I might only succeed in this [becoming a preacher]! If that heavy depression because everything I have undertaken has failed and that torrent of reproaches which I have heard and felt might be taken from me. . ." His family agreed to help Vincent to prepare for the ministry.

AMSTERDAM: MAY 1877–JULY 1878

Vincent went to live with his uncle Jan in Amsterdam while he studied for a state examination that he was required to pass before he could enter the university. He started out bravely enough, with a sense of heavy obligation to all his family, but determined to succeed regardless of the difficulties. By now his younger brother Theo was launched on a promising career at the Goupil Gallery, but despite doing well, Theo too labored under melancholy and guilt. He wrote, "I wish I were far away from everything; I am the cause of all and bring only sorrow to everybody; I alone have brought all this misery on myself and others." Vincent answered him:

> The same feeling . . . is also on my conscience . . . when I think . . . of sorrow, disappointment, of the fear of failure, of disgrace—then I also know the longing. I wish I were far away from everything! . . . My head is somtimes heavy, and often it burns and my thoughts are confused. . . . There is much evil in the world and in ourselves—terrible things; one does not need to be far advanced in life to fear much, to feel the need of a firm faith in life hereafter and to know that without faith in God one cannot live—one cannot bear it.

His remarks about fear and evil, and his difficulty in thinking, are signs that the depression continued in its severity, even interfering with his efforts to study. He was trying to learn Greek and Latin with Dr. Mendes da Costa, who relates how Vincent went about it.

> Whenever Vincent felt that his thoughts had strayed further than they should have, he took a cudgel to bed with him and belabored his back with it; and whenever he was convinced he had forfeited the privilege of passing the night in his bed . . . [he would] lie on the floor of a little wooden shed without bed or blanket. He preferred to do this in winter, so that the punishment might be more severe. . . . [His face had] a pervading expression of incredible sadness and despair. And when he had come upstairs [for a lesson] there would sound again that singular, profoundly melancholy deep voice: "Don't be mad at me, Mendes [for Vincent's punishing himself again]: I have brought you some little flowers again because you are so good to me."

Latin and Greek were required of ministers, but Vincent did not manage to learn them. He would say "Mendes, do you seriously believe that such horrors are indispensable to a man who wants to do what I want to do: give peace to poor creatures and reconcile them to their existence here on earth?" He saw the function of the ministry in terms of his own needs. At this time he was moving in the direction of mysticism and wrote to his brother: "I am copying the whole of the Imitation of Christ . . . the book is sublime." He was also turning against the rules and official hierarchy of the church. Several years later, he explained why he failed to learn Latin and Greek and to progress in his preparation for a career in the ministry: "You understand that I, who have learned other languages, might have managed to master that miserable bit of Latin, etc.—which I declared, however, to be too much for me. This was a fake because I preferred not to explain to my protectors that the whole university . . . is in my eyes an inexpressible mess, a breeding place of Pharisaism." In retrospect, that thought must have been comforting to him, but at the time, Vincent was not ready to jettison the church. Seeing himself as a failure, he did not want another defeat, another cause for reproach. Vincent was intelligent enough to learn Greek and Latin; however, during the period in question, he was, as da Costa shows us, in an overriding depression. In that state many things happen: struggles with guilt, the unreliability of the will, endless pain take primacy while learning becomes very difficult. Concentrating is too taxing, and facts make only temporary ripples in one's memory. Fear—of the next day, of the next hour—is an added stress. A man sinking into severe depression is too impaired to learn Latin and Greek. Depression interfered with his learning, and his failure to learn kept Vincent depressed. Vincent looked on this period as the worst time of his life.

MISSIONARY SCHOOL IN BRUSSELS: AUGUST–NOVEMBER 1878

Vincent now decided to become an evangelist, a choice that required only three months of training at a missionary school, instead of the years of study needed for the ministry. The training was free; only board and lodging had to be paid for. By this time his parents had very little confidence in him. His mother wrote, "I am always afraid that wherever Vincent may be or whatever he may do, he will spoil everything by his eccentricity, his queer ideas and view of life." His father was equally discouraged: "It grieves us so when we see that he literally knows no joy of life, but always walks with bent head whilst we did all in our power to bring him to an honorable position."

Vincent was becoming increasingly odd and rebellious and would not accept authority of any kind. When asked during a lesson, "Van Gogh, is this dative or accusative?" he answered "I really don't care, sir." He had violent outbursts of rage in class. The other students found him obnoxious because of his unfriendliness, messy appearance, irritability, and unpredictable behavior and moods. He was a target for ridicule.

He did not pass the three-month course. The school notified his father to take his son home because Vincent was in poor mental and physical condition: thin, weak, nervous, excited, and unable to sleep. The young man was in a manic phase without euphoria. His father came to the rescue and arranged for Vincent to do religious work in the Borinage, an impoverished coal-mining district. Good work there would earn Vincent another chance to be certified by the missionary school.

THE BORINAGE: 1879–JULY 1880

Vincent's father took him to the town of Mons, in the Borinage, and established him in a boarding house. There, Vincent seemed much improved. He gave religious classes to the local children, lectured on the Bible, and visited the poor. He did so well that the evangelist committee gave him a six-month trial period in Wasmes, another Borinage coal-mining town. After he moved there, Vincent began to deteriorate again, becoming depressed and resuming his punitive asceticism. A M. Bonte who knew him there, describes the change that took place:

> [At first] he was well dressed, had excellent manners, and showed in his personal appearance all the characteristics of Dutch cleanliness. . . . [But as time went on] faced with the destitution he encountered on his visits, his pity induced him to give away nearly all his clothes; his money found its way into the hands of the poor, and . . . he kept nothing for himself. . . . He wanted to be even more destitute than the majority of the miners to whom he preached the gospel. . . . Soap was banished as a wicked luxury. . . . His face was usually dirtier than that of the miners. . . . The family which had taken him in had simple habits and lived like working people. . . . He left these people who had surrounded him with sympathy and went to live in a hovel. There he was all alone, he had no furniture; and people said that he slept crouched down in a corner of the hearth. Having arrived at the stage where he had no shirt and no socks on his feet we have seen him make shirts out of sacking.

A baker who knew Vincent continues:

> My kind-hearted mother said to him: "Monsieur, why do you deprive yourself of all your clothes like this—you who are descended from such a noble family of Dutch pastors!" He answered: "I am a friend of the poor like Jesus was." She answered: "You're no longer in a normal condition." One day when he came to our house, he started vomiting on the basement floor. . . . His food consisted of rice and treacle, no butter on his bread. . . . He was always at his studies; in a single night he read a volume of 100 pages; during the week he taught a school he had founded for the children, teaching them to fear God, and at the same time he was busy making drawings of . . . the mines.

In January Vincent was still sending happy letters home. By the end of February, a visiting chergyman found his condition so bad that it was necessary to inform the church council, which issued a warning: Vincent must behave in a normal fashion or leave. His father came to see him at Wasmes and found him lying on a sack, in an extreme state of malnutrition. He took his starving son out of the hovel and back to the boarding house, where Vincent seemed to improve, but without his father's supervision he deteriorated, and the council dismissed him.

Vincent made brief trips to Brussels and home to Etten, where he was withdrawn and hardly spoke. He did not know what to do next. Finally at his family's expense, he went to board with an evangelist at Cuesmes in the Borinage. Theo visited him there, and Vincent wrote to his brother afterwards: "If I had to believe that I were troublesome to you or to the people at home, or were in your way, of no good to anyone, and if I should be obliged to feel like an intruder or an outcast . . . I might wish that I had not much longer to live. . . . Perhaps it is only a terrible nightmare." Eventually he came to believe that all of those things *were* true, and after he came to this conclusion he shot himself.

Theo started to share his salary with his brother, a practice he continued for the rest of Vincent's life. Meanwhile, Vincent was starving himself again and spending the money he was given on Bibles, which he gave away every time he went out to sketch. His father made a trip to Cuesmes and tried to make Vincent behave more reasonably. The son did not become more reasonable; another change was occurring in him. He was shifting the foundation of his life from religion to art. He still spoke little and kept away from people, but now he drew all the time, even at meals.

Vincent visited home again in the spring of 1880, then returned to Cuesmes, where he moved in with a miner. He had lost his faith, had no work, no training, and did not know what to do with his life. He now saw himself as an exile from the family: "I have become . . . a kind of impossible and suspect personage in the family. . . . Therefore, . . . I think the best and most reasonable thing for me to do is to go away and keep a convenient distance, so that I cease to exist for you all." This was another agonized plea for acceptance and reassurance. His family was the only thing he had. He went on in this letter to Theo: "Now for more than 5 years—I do not know exactly how long—I have been more or less without employment, wandering here and there. . . . It is true that . . . my financial affairs are in a sad state; it is true that the future is only too gloomy; it is true that I might have done better. . . . If I don't do anything, if I don't study, if I don't go on seeking any longer, I am lost. . . . How can I be of use to the world? Can't I serve some purpose and be of any good?" Van Gogh did not give up "seeking" and, seeking, he found art. But before he did, he endured immeasurable anguish: "I feel imprisoned by poverty . . . one feels an emptiness where there might be friendship and strong, serious affections, and one feels a terrible discouragement . . . and a choking flood of disgust envelops one, and one exclaims 'How long, my God!'" His illness would shatter him again and again, but at last he found something he could use as a scaffold for his existence, to which he could attach the days that were left to him chipped and broken though they were. Art was to be the purpose of his life. Now he must prepare for it in earnest.

A LIFE IN ART BEGINS: OCTOBER 1880–1882

That fall Vincent moved to Brussels, where he met the painter Van Rappard, the only artist friend he made before he went to France. He stayed in Brussels for eight months, taking drawing classes and teaching himself anatomy. Then he went home again to Etten, where board and lodging cost him nothing, and he could spend all of his allowance on art supplies. This period began happily. Another painter, Mauve, gave Vincent some encouragement. The young man felt alive again and was well enough to fall in love. The woman he wanted was his widowed cousin, Kee. However, as soon as he told her his feelings, she refused to ever see him again. He came to visit her anyway, and when she did not appear, he held his hand over the flame of a lamp, insisting that he would keep it there until she stood before him. With his characteristic combination of stubbornness and masochism, he kept his hand over the flame until his skin began to burn, but Kee's father would have no more of that, blew out the lamp, and sent him away. As Vincent related later, this episode brought on another depression. "I had a strong, passionate love for her. . . . When I unexpectedly learned . . . that she had a kind of aversion to me . . . and refused even to see me, and that she left her house as soon as I entered it—then, but not before, that love for her received a death blow. . . . I then felt an inexpressible melancholy inside. . . . The emptiness, the unutterable misery within me made me think, Yes, I can understand people drowning themselves. But . . . I thought it much better to take heart and find a remedy in work." Unfortunately, the depression stayed on. Vincent became tense and irritable again, as well as miserably unhappy. He had a ferocious quarrel with his father. "I do not remember," he wrote to Theo, "ever having been in such a rage in my life." Following that explosion or conflict, it was impossible for Vincent to stay on, and he left town.

EXILE FROM SOCIETY: THE HAGUE, 1882–SEPTEMBER 1883

After Kee spurned him, Vincent never again tried to find a respectable wife or make a niche for himself in society. He gave up the conventional goals of life and henceforth concerned himself with only his progress as an artist. He identified with society's rejects while he stayed in Holland. His work was suffused with their suffering, which was his own, and his colors were as dark as their lives.

   This segment of Vincent's life began better than it ended. The letters that he wrote in the first half of 1882 are filled with enthusiasm for art. He wrote: "I feel ideas about color coming to me as I paint which I never had before. They're big and exciting!" In his exaltation, he was unaware of the wind and cold rain that occasionally pelted him when he painted out of doors.

He spoke of tracing "the outlines quickly as lightning." He worked with manic speed and impetuousity. Vincent usually became intensely manic while working at his art.

He was grateful for the occasional guidance of the painter Mauve, and he sought out other painters too, but Vincent could not keep friends. Either he withdrew from people, or he fought with them. One day Mauve gave him a plaster cast to use as a model, a common practice for artists at that time. In a rage, Vincent smashed it on the floor. His taking a prostitute into his home completed his estrangement from the community of artists in The Hague.

Four years earlier, Vincent stated that he would prefer a woman "who was ugly or old or poor or in some way unhappy, but who, through experience and sorrow, had gained a mind and a soul to one more attractive." The woman he chose was both poor and ugly, with one illegitimate child clinging to her and another in her womb. Her mind and soul proved to be disappointing to him, but by the time he met Christine, Vincent looked on himself as an outcast—another outcast would not look down on him. Her temperament was as difficult as his. He told Theo: "At times her temper is such that it is almost unbearable even for me—violent, mischievous, bad. I can tell you, I am sometimes in despair. She comes round again, and she has often told me afterwards: 'I myself do not know what I am doing then.'" During this period Theo was supporting his brother's household of three.

By midsummer Vincent was in the hospital with venereal disease contracted from Christine, and mania was again troubling him. He tried to reassure Theo that "the rest cure does me good and makes me so much calmer, and takes away the nervousness which has troubled me so much recently."

In July, Vincent had recovered from the infection but continued feeling depressed and rejected. He was unable to get along with anyone and miserable alone. He sent Theo an inventory of his personality:

> Do not imagine that I think myself perfect or that I think that people's taking me for a disagreeable character is no fault of mine. I am often terribly melancholy, irritable, hungering and thirsting, as it were, for sympathy . . . . I do not like to be in company, and often find it painful and difficult to mingle with people, to speak with them . . . confound it, I have a good side too, and can't they credit me with that also?

He had days of energy and optimism, with the insomnia that accompanied them, but those days cast before them the shadow of encroaching depression. Vincent seemed to sense the change from mania to depression: "I feel such creative power in myself . . . I have not slept well these last few nights. It is all that beautiful autumn scenery that I have on my mind . . . But I wish I could sleep at the right time, and I try my best, for it makes me nervous, but there is no help for it . . . I think if I were not in the open air so much and found less pleasure in my painting, I should soon become melancholy."

In November of 1882, everything was falling apart. Vincent wrote Theo that he was "dreadfully melancholy." He blamed it on his "dissatisfaction with bad work," on the need to "struggle on nothwithstanding thousands of short-comings and faults and the uncertainty of conquering them." His problems with his painting were really no greater than they had been during the previous months, when he was happy and eager. His winter depression brought despair, and despair enveloped everything. "One is afraid of making friends," he wrote, "one is afraid of moving, like the old leper. One would like to call from afar to the people: Don't come too near me, for intercourse with me brings you sorrow and loss."

The depression continued its reign through the winter. Vincent wrote in February: "I have been feeling very weak lately. I am afraid I have been overworking myself, and how miserable the 'dregs' of the work are, that depression after overexertion. Life is then the color of dishwater: it becomes something like an ash heap." His depression was getting worse, was immobilizing him. He was no longer seeking reasons for his condition. "There is no reason for it," he wrote Theo. "I have tried to work a little today, but suddenly I was overcome by a depression which I cannot exactly account for." "I am sorry that I did not fall ill and die in the Borinage that time instead of taking up painting, for I am only a burden to you." "Work is the only remedy; if that doesn't help, one breaks down." "Shall I be able to go on or not?" "I hope that a certain frenzy and rage for work may carry me through." That "frenzy" was his mania, but it would not return for some time. In the meantime, Vincent continued to disintegrate. In his desperation, he begged his brother to rescue him: "You must try to come soon, brother, for I do not know how long I shall be able to hold out. Things are getting too much for me . . . My constitution would be good enought if I hadn't had to fast so long, but it was always a question of fasting or working less, and I chose the former as much as possible, 'til I have become weak now." Vincent implies that he would not be in his malnourished state if Theo, who was supporting him and his companion and her child, had given him more money, but Theo was not at fault. Vincent was repeating the behavior of earlier depressions. He had starved himself in the Borinage, where his family paid for his room and board.

Theo came to the rescue that summer. He found his brother deep in debt, living in anguish and squalor. He advised Vincent to separate from Christine. There was nothing left of the relationship but quarrels and misery, compounded by conflict with Christine's family. However, she was the only companionship that Vincent had, the only person who had ever needed him, and it was difficult for him to turn his back on her.

Christine had her baby in July. In September Vincent left her and her children as well provided for as he could. Then he went to Drenthe alone, hoping that new surroundings would bring him some eagerness for living and working. It had helped before. Again he felt better for a while, enchanted by new scenery and new subjects to paint, but the charms of novelty wore off quickly: "I feel gloomy, notwithstanding the beautiful scenery." "I am overcome by a feeling of great anxiety, depression, . . . discouragement and despair more than I can tell. And if I cannot find comfort, it will be too overwhelming. I must work and work hard, I must forget myself in my work, otherwise it [melancholy] will crush me."

By this time Van Gogh's father had lost patience with Vincent. He was thirty years old, and for the last ten years had caused only endless pain for those who cared for him, forcing them to rescue him again and again from his frightful situations. For thanks, Vincent fought with them. His family never realized that he was ill—they thought he was merely an impossible person. While Vincent was in Drenthe, his father wrote to Theo: "It seems to me that Vincent is again in a wrong mood. . . . If only he had the courage to think of the possibility that the cause of much which has resulted from his eccentricity lies in himself. I don't think he ever feels any self-reproach, only spite against others. . . . We must be very careful with him, for he seems to be in a contrary mood." Vincent was aware of his parents' attitude toward him but he had nowhere else to go. When he realized that he could not survive alone, he went back to them.

NUENAN: JANUARY 1884–NOVEMBER 1885

Vincent returned to a Van Gogh household in the new town to which his father had sent him as minister. Although initially planning to keep his visit short, Vincent stayed on for two years. As usual, he was delighted with the fresh material for his art work: new scenes, new models. In January his mother broke her leg. Vincent took responsibility for her care until she recovered and made a good name for himself in the community while doing so. However, once he became secure in his relationship with his parents, he felt free to turn against his previous prop, his brother. He wrote to Theo: "You do absolutely nothing to procure me some distraction, which I need so badly now and then—of meeting people, and seeing things." "You do not understand me at all." "Brotherly or not brotherly, if you can give me nothing more than financial help, you may keep that too." "A wife you cannot give me, a child you cannot give me, work you cannot give me—money yes, but what is the use of it when I must miss all the rest!" Vincent seems to have had very little inclination to do anything for himself at that time. He added paranoia to ingratitude, accusing Theo of denying him success. "You belong to Goupil and Co., and Goupil and Co. will certainly not do anything with my work for years to come." "Your criticism of this past year and a half only seems like some kind of vitriol to me." If there was a saint in the family, it was the long-suffering Theo.

Through July and August of 1884, Vincent was involved with a local spinster, Margot Begemann, who had fallen in love with him. Her sisters refused to allow her to see him, once they knew what was afoot, and Miss Begemann responded to their restrictions by taking poison. It did not kill her, but it did kill the relationship. Vincent was blamed for her suicide attempt and treated like the village villain. None of this improved his state of mind. As 1884 wore on and the season for depression advanced, he became more and more irritable and paranoid, to the point of seeing any attempt to please him as an insult. According to one of his sisters, he never sat at the table with the family but kept to a corner with dry bread on the plate on his lap, as he had done in childhood. He crouched over it like a dog and masked his face with his hand, while studying a painting or a drawing that he kept on a chair beside him. He only spoke to the others when the conversation focused on books. Everyone found this degree of weirdness difficult to have in the house, and Vincent found it difficult to be there. He retreated as far as he could into art, working compulsively.

By January 1, 1885, his winter depression was again in full fury. Vincent wrote, "I never began a year of a more gloomy aspect." His father noted, "He seems to become more and more estranged from us." Vincent's father died suddenly on March 27 of that year, and Vincent perhaps believed the best thing he could do for his mother in her grief was to move out of the house. Whatever his motivation, two months after his father died, he moved into his studio, two rooms in the house of the sexton of the Catholic church. While there, he got along so badly with the priest that the cleric told his parishioners not to pose for Van Gogh. In November, after months of thinking about leaving, Vincent went to Antwerp. He left the work done in those two years to his mother, who was so careless with it that it disappeared forever.

ANTWERP: NOVEMBER 1885–FEBRUARY 1886

This time Vincent ran through his cycle in just three months. He started out quite manic, fascinated by the sights and sounds of town life after his two-year sojourn in the quiet of the country. He saw so many new types of people to paint that he could not get enough of painting. Again, he spent money without stinting on anything but food: "If I receive money my first hunger is not for food, though I have fasted ever so long, but the desire for painting is ever so much stronger, and I start at once hunting for models until there is nothing left."

In January he enrolled in the academy to spare the expense of hiring his own models, but as always, he could not conform. When the class had to draw a cast of the Venus de Milo, he exaggerated her already broad hips. The teacher was furious at this and destroyed Van Gogh's drawing while correcting it. In turn, Vincent screamed at his teacher, terrifying him: "So you don't know what a young woman is like, God damn you!"

Vincent would work on drawings far into the night. By the beginning of February, he had become exhausted by his manic pace, and a doctor told him he was suffering from complete prostration. Furthermore, Vincent was in trouble with all of his teachers at the academy and again decided to move. Theo suggested a return to the Brabant, but Van Gogh preferred to join his brother in Paris.

LIFE WITH THEO: PARIS, FEBRUARY 1886–FEBRUARY 1888

Theo made the best of the new living arrangements for Vincent's sake and wrote to his family in the summer of that year: "He is in much better spirits than before and many people like him. . . . He has friends who send him every week a lot of beautiful flowers which he uses for still life." During this period in Paris Vincent met and started learning from the Impressionists. For the first time he had the companionship of artists who were as fervent artistic and social rebels as he was. Even though he finally found himself a suitable milieu, he could not fit into it. He was trapped by the cycle of his illness: arrival in a new place would initiate a manic period filled with excitement, optimism, and energy; this mood changed by degrees into extreme irritability; and, finally, into depression and prostration. This is a familiar pattern to many manic-depressives, who learn to associate change of place, job, or even sexual partner with the good feelings of mania. When the inevitable depression returns, they make another change, which brings on another manic period. Some follow that cycle throughout their lives. They can never settle down, as each depression drives them away from where they are.

Vincent had another frantically productive summer. His mania, intensified by work, became as fervid as was possible to be and still paint. An art student who saw Vincent at work in early 1886 furnishes an account of a mania so fierce that Van Gogh could not even protect his work from smearing: "He worked in a spasmodic fury. . . . He scooped up the paint as though with a trowel and it trickled down the brush till his finger ends were sticky with it. He did not stop painting while the model took a rest. The turbulence of his study astonished the whole studio." When Vincent worked out of doors, his excitement was so overwhelming that he gesticulated and shouted to himself. He continued in the height of mania as he walked home from the day's work, and he was so out of control that in talking to someone he would wave the canvases in the air as he gestured and accidentally rub the wet pictures against passers-by.

Vincent became a regular customer of Le Tambourin tavern. Here he would argue with anyone who would listen to him, and people learned to avoid him because he was so unpleasant and explosive. One evening he was observed yelling his opinions at a man who was sleeping. In acute mania pressure of speech makes people talk to anything that remains stationary.

A portrait of Van Gogh during this period shows why people came to shun him: "He had an extraordinary way of pouring out sentences in Dutch, English and French, then glancing over his shoulder and hissing through his teeth. In fact when thus excited he looked more than a little mad; at other times he was apt to be morose, as if suspicious." He may well have been paranoid.

While Theo was trying to write reassuring letters to his family, he grew increasingly discouraged. The wear and tear of living with Vincent was excessive. Theo's friends worried about him, and one of them wrote: "Theo still looks frightfully ill. . . . The poor fellow has many cares. Moreover his brother is making life rather a burden to him, and reproaches him with all kinds of things of which he is quite innocent [a further sign of paranoia]. . . . The man [Vincent] hasn't the slightest notion of social conditions. He is always quarreling with everybody."

In the winter Vincent, in an agitated depression, found life almost intolerable and made it so for anyone misfortunate enough to be in his company. Vincent felt tired and, discouraged, found that everything was going wrong and that the world was sour. He prolonged his arguing far into the night, even haranguing Theo after the poor man settled in bed. Theo wrote to his sister: "My home life is almost unbearable. No one wants to come and see me any more because it always ends in quarrels, and besides, he is so untidy that the room looks far from attractive. I wish he would go and live by himself."

Theo's sister told him to ask Vincent to leave, but Theo could not bring himself to do so. However, after a particularly nasty series of quarrels, Vincent left and moved in with an English painter, Alexander Reid. The two of them decided to commit suicide together but changed their minds. Instead, Vincent returned to Theo.

Spring permitted Vincent to paint out of doors again, and it either coincided with or caused an improvement in his mental state. However, his irritability remained undiminished. On one occasion, when the sitter criticized a portrait he was doing, Vincent ran off in a rage and never resumed work on the painting.

He began a liaison with the proprietress of a cafe that he frequented. Although the relationship mitigated his loneliness and sexual hunger, it did not make him happy. He no longer looked to women for happiness: "As far as I myself am concerned, I still go on having the most impossible, and not very seemly love affairs, from which I emerge as a rule damaged and shamed and little else." Most of his relationships left him damaged. About the only things that could make him happy were the beauty of the visual world and his painting, when it was going well.

The winter of 1887 was even worse. Vincent's fits of rage were fiercer, his attacks on Theo merciless. He drove away his painter friends for whom he had so longed. Then he scorned them because they dropped him, just as he had done with the painters of The Hague and Antwerp. He felt excluded from his brother's life when Theo decided to marry, so Vincent again tried the old remedy for his ills, departure. Vincent left for Paris in February of 1888. The last and worst part of his life remained to be lived, the two years in which he would paint his greatest works.

PORTRAIT OF THE ARTIST AS A MANIC-DEPRESSIVE

Van Gogh's self-portraits have a frightening intensity, an alien quality that was visible in the actual person. His sister said that he had "a strange face— not the face of a young man. His forehead was already a little wrinkled, brows drawn together in a frown of concentration, eyes small and deep-set. . . . Despite this unprepossessing exterior, the unmistakable suggestion of inviolate depths gave a kind of strangeness to his whole person." Vincent's clothing and style of behavior contributed to the peculiar impression that he made on people. Theo wrote about it to his fiancee: "As you know, he has long since broken with what is called convention. His way of dressing and his manners show directly that he is an unusual personality, and people who see him say, 'He is mad.'" Even his fellow painters, a broad-minded group, thought he was crazy. One of them said that Vincent reminded him of the painting *Tasso in the Madhouse.* Another remembered that Vincent "would tear off his clothes and fall on his knees to make some point clear, and nothing could calm him down."

Van Gogh knew that he lived on a seesaw: "Some days I still suffer from unaccountable, involuntary fits of excitement, or else utter sluggishness." This was confirmed by people who knew him in his last days at Auvers. "He was erratic," they said, "cheerful one day and glum the next, talkative when he'd had a drop of drink, or silent for hours." Not only could his moods markedly alter from day to day, but they also fell into an annual cycle in which the worst and longest depressions took place in winter, and periods of mania occurred in summer. His manic periods were his most productive.

Manic-depressives often seem to have two or more personalities. As Theo wrote about Vincent: "It seems as if he were two persons; one, marvelously gifted, tender and refined, the other egoistic and hard-hearted. They present themselves in turns, so that one hears him talk first one way, then the other. . . . It is a pity that he is his own enemy, for he makes life hard not only for others, but also for himself." The egoistic personality was Vincent's manic side, the tender his depressed.

The manic personality was irritable and bad-tempered. Fellow painter

Van Rappard referred to Vincent as "the struggling and wrestling, fanatic, gloomy Vincent, who used to flare up so often." As Theo learned when Vincent lived with him in Paris, "It is difficult even for those who are his best friends to remain on good terms with him as he spares nobody's feelings." "Models would not pose for him and he was forbidden to paint in the streets; with his irascible temper this caused unpleasant scenes which excited him so much that he became completely unapproachable and at last developed a great aversion to Paris." "A quiet life is impossible for him; wherever he goes he leaves the trace of his passing," Theo lamented.

Impulsivity was another manic trait that Vincent exhibited. He admitted: "I am a man of passions, capable of and subject to doing more or less foolish things, which I happen to repent, more or less, afterward. Well, this being the case, what's to be done? Must I consider myself as a dangerous man, capable of anything?" His manic impulsivity sometimes took the form of extravagance. On one occasion he went on a frame-buying spree and had to subsist for four days on a diet "mainly of 23 cups of coffee, with bread that I still have to pay for."

A manic attribute that Vincent valued was what he called "hysterical excitement," or "the exaltation that comes to me at certain moments." Manic energy and insensitivity to fatigue or hunger permitted him, on occasion, to start a painting during the day, continue through the night, and through the next day, without stopping to rest or eat. When manic, he could not sleep, and on the nights that he did manage to sleep a bit, he said, "I became so eager [to paint] that many a morning I got up at 4 o'clock." He said that while working "one feels more energy and power than one was aware of, or rather, than one in fact possesses." This, of course, is the working high, which can keep people slaving away happily even when they are physically ill. It happened to Van Gogh. "I don't feel entirely well yet," he wrote to his brother after an illness, "but fortunately the work is so animating that as long as I am busy, I don't feel the weakness so much; but it overtakes me occasionally during the intervals when I am not in front of my easel." The effortlessness of manic production gives it a quality of unreality for the person doing it. Vincent mentioned this too: "I have a frightful ludicity at times when nature is so beautiful as it is now. Then I lose all awareness of myself. The picture comes to me as in a dream."

Though Van Gogh's working highs were unusually intense, they were no more dependable than those of anyone else. He says, "The emotions are sometimes so strong that one works without knowing one works: . . . [but] one must remember that it has not always been so, and that in time to come there will again be hard days, empty of inspiration."

Depression not only kept him from working, but it also made Van Gogh overcritical of the work he had done. "I am always filled with remorse," he said, "terribly so, when I think of my work being so little in harmony with what I should have liked to do. I hope that in the long run this will make me do better things, but we have not got to that yet." The perfectionism is sometimes dangerous for artists. It made Van Gogh careless about preserving his work, and a good portion of it was lost. Claude Monet went even further during his depressions—he destroyed perfectly good paintings.

Even for a depressive, Vincent was a solitary person. He met many people during his brief existence, but few of them became a part of his life, and fewer were permitted to penetrate his loneliness. He claimed that he preferred his work to anyone's company. "If I am alone—I can't help it, but honestly I have less need of company than of furiously hard work." At other times he complained bitterly of his loneliness and tried to get people to live with him. Beethoven did this too. Fundamentally, Van Gogh was not interested in people. He did not notice friends when he passed them on the street. Except for his deep involvement with the visual world, he lived within his mind. His letters to his brother are full of art, philosophy, religion, books he had read, and complaints about poverty. The few references he makes to other people show very little interest in their characters or in their existence apart from his own involvement with them.

Most of the delusions that Van Gogh entertained were the kind that occur in depression. Sometimes delusions of the mentally ill coincide with reality, but the delusions are nonetheless symptomatic of illness if the information available to the person does not justify the opinion held. A case in point is Van Gogh's belief that he would die young. "It may also be that I shall not live for so many years." Nothing in his physical or mental condition of which he was aware gave a foundation to his expectation of an early death. That idea was a product of depression combined with a fear of old age. Van Gogh feared that age would rob him of his creativity: "I also see the possibility of going to seed and seeing the day of one's capacity for artistic creation pass." Artistic creation was his only excuse for living. Vincent also had delusions of poverty while his brother was supporting him. The allowance Theo furnished him was twice what many schoolteachers earned in France at the time. However, Vincent's inability to budget his funds, combined with his punitive asceticism, led him, and many others since, to believe that Theo had stinted him.

Van Gogh had another typical manic-depressive delusion, or set of delusions: paranoia. Vincent barraged his brother Theo, his favorite target, with scolding, insults and threats: for not also becoming an artist, for not siding with Vincent against their parents, and for not arranging Vincent's success as a painter. He called Theo "cruel in your worldly wisdom," "too high and mighty to take the slightest notice . . . of my work." He wanted Theo to compel the public to buy his paintings. Paranoia also disrupted Vincent's friendships. He wrote this baseless accusation to Van Rappard: "Don't suppose that you are the only person to . . . criticize me to the point of crushing me out of existence with the result that I am in the state you know. On the contrary, something like this has always been my lot so far."

Besides standard manic-depressive delusions, Vincent also had an idiosyncratic one. He said that he was afraid of a normal diet because it would make him too strong, too dangerous. During his psychotic episodes, Van Gogh also had religious delusions: "I am astonished that with my modern ideas . . . I have attacks such as a superstitious man might have and that I get perverted and frightful ideas about religion." These would pass whenever his condition improved.

By the time Van Gogh was twenty years old, he had developed a strategy against depression. "Theo," he wrote,"I strongly advise you to smoke a pipe; it is a good remedy against the blues, which I happen to have now and then lately." Vincent went on to adopt two more remedies, nature and art. "I am doing very well here, but it is because I have my work here, and nature, and if I didn't have that, I should grow melancholy." Art became his lifeline. His despair reached such depths that he no longer worked with only the hope of doing great, or merely good, paintings. He wrote: "I almost dare to swear to you that my painting will improve. Because I have nothing left but that." "The desire to succeed is gone, and I work because I must, so as not to suffer too much mentally, so as to distract my mind." "It's the only time I feel I am alive, when I am drudging at my work." On those days when the working high did not arrive, painting still provided some relief from the despair and self-disgust of depression.

Drinking, one of the most widely used of all strategies against depression, played an important part in Van Gogh's life. He gave four reasons for drinking. Initially, he claimed that it afforded relief from the effort of painting: "Sheer work and calculation with one's mind strained to the utmost, . . . with a hundred things to think of all at once in a single half hour." "After that, the only thing to bring ease and distraction, in my case and other people's too, . . . is to stun oneself with a lot of drinking or heavy smoking." Next, he said, "If the storm within gets too loud I take a glass too much to stun myself." Van Gogh used alcohol not only to ease fatigue and reduce mania, but also to induce mania. He said that he needed to be in a state of exaltation in order to paint, and that alcohol and coffee were the means to achieve it: "Instead of eating enough and at regular times, I kept myself going on coffee and alcohol. I admit that, but all the same it is true that to attain the high yellow note that I attained last summer, I really had to be pretty well keyed up." Signac, a painter friend, stated that Vincent also drank after the day's work was done, when his manic state had no function. "Though he ate hardly anything, what he drank was always too much," Signac said. "Returning after spending the whole day in the blazing sun, in the torrid heat, and having no real home in the town, he would take his seat on the terrace of a cafe. And the absinthes and brandies would follow each other in quick succession." Perhaps Vincent ran short of grocery money because he spent it on drinks. It is not surprising that Van Gogh turned to alcohol for relief, as it was the most effective modulator of mood available in his time.

Some of the subjects in this book had more delusory ideas than Van Gogh; but if the severity of psychotic episodes is the criterion of illness, he was the sickest of them all. He had longer and more frequent attacks than the others. He suffered memory loss, delusions and hallucinations, disruptions of consciousness, and was disoriented to time and space. When his condition was at its worst, he was too confused, too mentally impaired, to paint. He must have been in a frightful state, because it is sometimes possible to paint works that have merit when moderately psychotic.

Van Gogh had at least thirteen psychotic episodes that lasted from one or two weeks up to two months. Generally, onset was sudden and, as he says, recovery slow: "The power of thought is coming back to me gradually, but I am much less able to manage practical things than hitherto. I am absent-minded and could not direct my own life just now."

A salutary feature of Vincent's psychotic episodes is that he could not remember much of what happened during them. This is characteristic of both mania and depression in their extreme stages. He also had periods of loss of consciousness, and in addition to his everyday paranoia, he acquired new delusions. He thought that he was being poisoned, that the police were pursuing him, and he once kicked a hospital attendant whom he mistook for a policeman. He was violent more than once. He was probably manic then, because two of his attacks occurred while he was painting, others while feeling intense emotion in the presence of beautiful scenery, and three more during trips into Arles while on leave from the hospital. He was more likely to have been excited on these occasions than depressed. He observed that his "madness" came on "in a state of excitement," in a "violent attack of exaltation or delirium." His mood in some of these acute manias must have been dysphoric, for at times he became suicidal. He made several attempts to kill himself by trying to eat oil paints or to drink turpentine or kerosene. Any of these would have been lethal if someone had not stopped him.

Many people in the arts have feared that they were losing their minds at one time or another, but few have had to live with the agonizing certainty of their insanity. Initially, Van Gogh thought that he was no more crazy than any other painter, and he wrote to Theo: "My poor boy, our neurosis, etc., comes, it's true, from our way of living, which is too purely the artist's life." He spoke of himself as "broke and crazy with this blasted painting," but he meant it humorously. By the time he wrote "Well, well, after all, there are so many painters who are cracked in one way or another that little by little I shall be reconciled to it," he had undergone several acute attacks and was trying to talk himself into accepting his condition. He developed uncommon insight into his illness: "I feel deeply that this has been at work within me for a very long time already, and that other people, seeing symptoms of mental derangement have naturally had apprehensions better founded than my unfounded certainty that I was thinking normally, which certainly was not the case." As long as he could paint, Vincent had something to live for, but his courage was beginning to run out. The prospect of slipping in and out of insanity for the rest of his life was becoming too much for him. "I am thinking of frankly accepting my role of madman," he wrote, "the way Degas acted the part of a notary. But there it is, I do not feel that altogether I have strength enough for such a part." Van Gogh would have suffered less had he not understood so well what was happening to him. The only thing worse than being mad is being mad and sane by turns, and that is what he was. The wonder is not that he killed himself at the peak of his powers, but that he endured his misery for thirty-seven years.

ARLES: FEBRUARY 1888–MAY 1889

When Vincent left Paris, he was, in his own words, "seriously sick at heart and in body," "going the right way for a stroke," "nearly an alcoholic." Not nearly: He *was* an alcoholic, and this time it took several weeks in the peace and quiet of a small town in southern France for him to recover. "When I began to think again instead of trying not to think, Good Lord, the depression and the prostration of it! Work in these magnificent natural surroundings has restored my morale, but even now some efforts are too much for me."

By early April, Vincent was again on the manic merry-go-round and boasting "I am in a fever of work!" That spring and summer were the most creative seasons of his whole life. The colors of his paintings were glorious and the distortions, the jagged lines, the violence of other periods were absent. He gives this exultant account of that period: "Ideas for my work are coming to me in swarms, so that though I'm alone, I have no time to think or feel. I go on painting like a steam engine. I think there will hardly ever be a standstill again." The manic always thinks like that. "I am so happy in the house and in my work." He was euphoric, inexhaustible in both senses of the word, working during the day "from 7 in the morning till 6 in the evening, only stopping once to take a bite around the corner." Even darkness did not slow him down! At night, he said, "I go out of doors . . . to paint the stars." The excitement, terrific pace, and ecstasy of mania shine through his words: "Nothing stops me working, I can't resist such beauty." "This coloured environment is quite new for me and I am extraordinarily elated by it. I'm never tired." He wanted his new home "to be a house of light for everybody."

One cannot live for long at such heights. By May 2, periods of depression began descending upon him again. He now worried about continuing to be a burden on Theo when his brother had his own family to care for. Vincent wrote: "Bear in mind, to go on spending money on this painting when things might come to such a pitch that you would be short of money for your own housekeeping would be atrocious, and you know well that the chances of success are abominable." "The money painting costs crushes me with a feeling of debt and worthlessness, and it would be a good thing if it were possible this should stop." "Now I as a painter shall never amount to anything important, I am sure of it." "If I had some acquaintance who would shove me into the [Foreign] Legion for 5 years, I should go. Only I do not want this to be thought a fresh act of madness on my part."

In July, Vincent blamed his "involuntary emotions" and "dullness on some days" on being alone. "Many days pass without speaking a word to anyone, only to ask for dinner or coffee." August was equally "disturbed and restless." He went back to his old remedy for depression and resumed heavy drinking. His diet now largely consisted of undercooked chick peas and alcohol. His appearance expressed his way of life. A witness says: "Vincent was a miserable, pitiful man, small of stature, . . . lean. He always wore a sort of overcoat, smeared all over with colors—he painted his thumb and then wiped it on his coat." Like Beethoven and Dickens, Vincent gave the impression of being not quite grown-up. The librarian at Arles said: "Vincent lives in my memory as an extremely timid man, a child. . . . To me he was an unhappy man, who suffered much. . . . There can be no doubt that his body was perpetually undernourished, and thin in conjunction with a productive energy intensified to frenzy. . . . Only one thing was important to him, his painting."

Most of the townspeople had no sympathy for this sad creature. Vincent became the town pariah. Even children were hostile, like animals who harry a sick or wounded member of the pack. One of them remembered: "People did not like to associate with Van Gogh, as he was always hanging about in the brothels. . . . Along with other young people I used to poke fun at this queer painter. . . . His appearance made a highly comical impression on us. His long smock, his gigantic hat, the man himself continually stooping and peering at things, excited our ridicule."

Vincent decided that the solution to his loneliness was to have an understanding soul, a fellow painter, come to share his home and studio. He failed to realize that his own temperament prevented him from living in peace with anyone for any length of time. The painter Gauguin was having difficulties of his own so, although the two did not know each other very well, Van Gogh finally convinced him to come to Arles. Gauguin could live there cheaply, as Theo would help with his expenses. After Gauguin agreed to join him, Vincent soared into another period of mania and frenzied activity that left him exhausted by the time his new roommate arrived, on October 23. Soon after his arrival, Gauguin reported to Theo, "Your brother is indeed a little agitated, and I hope to calm him by and by." Instead of calming him down, Vincent slipped into a routine of endless arguments with Gauguin. By the latter part of December, it was evident to Gauguin that he had to leave. He wrote to Theo: "I must go back to Paris. Vincent and I simply cannot live together in peace." Instead of leaving immediately, Gauguin stayed on, and the two artists resolved that particular quarrel. However, on December 23, Vincent, violently excited, cut off his ear and carried it to a girl in the local brothel. The postman took him home where the police later found him, lying on his bed, bleeding and unconscious. He was taken to the hospital.

Gauguin left the next day and Theo, who had been notified about Vincent's crisis, arrived. He stayed with his brother over the holidays and reported: "There were moments when he was well; but very soon after he fell back into his worries about philosophy and theology. It was painfully sad to witness, for at times all his suffering overwhelmed him and he tried to weep but he could not; poor fighter and poor, poor sufferer." While in the hospital, Vincent wrote about his condition: "Physically I am well, the wound is healing very well and the great loss of blood is being made up. . . . What is to be feared most is insomnia. . . . Now if I recover, I must begin [to paint] again and I shall not again reach the heights to which sickness partially led me." He was mistaken: he did reach the upper stratosphere of mania again. He left the hospital on January 7, 1889, though not for long.

On January 28, instability was returning or, rather, had not left: "I still have a sort of 'what is the good of getting better?' feeling." "The unbearable hallucinations have ceased, and are now reduced to a simple nightmare." "Once again, either shut me up in a madhouse right away—I shan't oppose it . . . or else let me work with all my strength." Vincent could not deny that he was mentally ill, but he tried to convince Theo and himself that he was no worse than most people. "Perhaps some day everyone will have neurosis, St. Vitus dance, or something else." "I must tell you this, that the neighbors, etc., are particularly kind to me, as everyone here is suffering either from fever, or hallucinations, or madness, we understand each other like members of the same family." That was his own fantasy, for the townspeople would soon cast him out. He was struggling to accept the idea that he was not sane, that he could not trust his mind ever again, that no one would ever trust *him*. "But as for considering myself as completely sane, we must not do it. People here who have been ill have told me the truth. You may be old or young, but there will always be moments when you lose your head." His next words, describing his pressure of speech during his recent attack, indicate that it was mania: "Well, well, there are moments when I am twisted by enthusiasm or prophecy, like a Greek oracle . . . and then I have a great readiness of speech." When he wrote this letter, he was not in a normal state. Theo was planing to marry, and Vincent felt that he was losing the central position he occupied in his brother's life. "But how come you are thinking at the same time of the clauses of your marriage settlement and the possibility of dying? Wouldn't it be simpler to stab your wife and be done with it?" Then he ominously wrote: "I always tell the people here that I shall begin by dying in their midst, and that then my malady will be dead." He had realized that death alone could free him of his terrifying illness.

The next day, after leaving the hospital, Van Gogh was again denying the seriousness of his condition: "I have just come home provisionally, I hope for good. I feel quite normal so often, and really I should think that . . . what I am suffering from is only a disease peculiar to this place." Six days later he was back in the hospital with the paranoid delusion that people were trying to poison him. He was mute and disoriented. Some time after he wrote: "I am feeling better, but again have had a few days like the others, when I did not know exactly what was going on and was upset." "At such times I don't know where I am and my mind wanders."

Ten days later he was released again, but by then his neighbors were afraid of him and insisted that the town government order his return to the hospital. He reentered confinement and had another attack, perhaps precipitated by his neighbors' action. His paranoia had been confirmed: he was being sacrificed for his neighbors' peace of mind. He informed Theo: "I write to you in the full possession of my faculties and not as a madman, but as the brother you know. This is the truth. A certain number of people here . . . addressed a petition to the Mayor . . . describing me as a man not fit to be at liberty, or something like that. The commissioner of police . . . then gave the order to shut me up again. Anyhow, here I am, shut up in a cell all the livelong day, under lock and key and with keepers, without my guilt being proved or even open to proof." "So you understand what a staggering blow between the eyes it was to find so many people here cowardly enough to join together against one man, and that man ill." Vincent had long suffered part of the horror of mental illness, the suffering caused by the illness itself. Now he was undergoing the other aspect of the horror, that caused by society's reaction to his illness. He was no longer free or safe anywhere. He could be imprisoned at any time, and for an indefinite period, without committing any crime. Indeed, he had fewer rights than a man who had broken the law. Vincent continued: "I answered roundly that I was quite prepared, for instance, to chuck myself into the water if that would please these good folk once and for all, but that in any case, if I had in fact inflicted a wound on myself, I had done nothing of the sort to them." "I really had done my best to be friendly with people."

Soon his resentment faded into the hopeless passivity of despair. He wrote: "I am only good for something intermediate, and second rate, and self-effaced. . . . I could never build an imposing structure on such a moldy, shattered past. So it is more or less all the same to me what happens to me—even staying here." However, in the hospital he was not allowed to paint, he had nothing with which to pass the time, and he was not even allowed to smoke. He said, "I would rather have died than have caused and suffered such trouble."

In a chaotic letter of March 29 he wrote that the only thing that clearly stood out was his flickering back and forth between mania and depression. By April 10 he was feeling better. He wanted to put all the horror behind him. "It is very probable that I shall have to suffer a great deal yet. And to tell the honest truth, this does not suit me at all." He wrote to his sister about the symptoms of his illness:

> I am unable to describe exactly what is the matter with me: now and then there are horrible fits of anxiety, apparently without cause, or otherwise a feeling of emptiness and fatigue in the head [a retarded depression] . . . and at times I have attacks of melancholy and of ferocious remorse . . . but . . . I am not exactly ashamed to tell myself that the remorse and all the other things that are wrong might possibly be caused by microbes. . . . Every day I take the remedy which the incomparable Dickens prescribes against suicide. It consists in a glass of wine, a piece of bread with cheese and a pipe of tobacco.

He was at home again, so he could smoke. He told his sister that he had had seven severe attacks so far: "I have had in all four great crises, during which I didn't in the least know what I said, what I wanted, and what I did. Not taking into account that I had previously had 3 fainting fits without any plausible reason, and without retaining the slightest remembrance of what I felt."

Theo married on April 17. Vincent wrote a bitter and ferocious letter to his friend Signac in which he referred to Theo as a "poor wretch" and the marriage festivities as "funereal pomp." It was actually Vincent's funeral. He depended on Theo more for emotional support than for financial support. Now that Theo had a life of his own, Vincent felt abandoned, and at a particularly bad time in his life, when he was broken and helpless. He was afraid and felt that he should not remain at large. Vincent wrote Theo on April 21: "I wish to remain shut up as much for my own peace of mind as for other people's. . . . Forgive me if I don't go into details and argue the pros and cons of such a step. Talking about it would be mental torture. It will be enough, I hope, if I tell you that I feel quite unable to take a new studio and stay there alone. . . . Not all my days are clear enough for me to write very logically."

Vincent was correct in thinking that he could not manage alone. Paul Signac visited him that spring while he was in the hospital at Arles. Signac saw that Vincent could shift from normalcy to a psychotic, suicidal state with frightening speed. Signac relates: "On the day of my visit he was quite sane, and the house physician gave me permission to go out with him. . . . He led me to his apartment . . . where I saw his marvelous pictures. . . . In the evening he was a little tired. . . . He wanted to drink about a quart of . . . turpentine from the bottle that was standing on the table. . . . It was high time to return him to the asylum. . . . I never saw him again." Signac did hear from Vincent again, when he wrote that he was having "seizures of despair of a pretty large caliber."

Indeed, Vincent had been having a very bad time during his last months at Arles. On some days he could not understand the letters he received. He was afraid his illness would put an end to his ability to paint. Then, what would there be left to live for?

SAINT REMY: MAY 8, 1889–MAY 16, 1890

Another problem that weighed more and more heavily on Vincent was that he was a burden for his brother. "It worries me a lot when I think that I have done so many pictures and drawings without selling one," he wrote on May 9. He was one of the very few men of genius who did not know how good he was. Had he known, he might have lived longer.

For the first time, Vincent accepted life in a place populated by the mentally ill. He admitted that he was one of them, and this enabled him to compare his experience of psychotic attacks with theirs. He was trying to understand the nature of his illness, to be calm and rational about the hell he went through: "I gather from others that during their attacks they have also heard strange sounds and voices as I did, and that in their eyes too things seemed to be changing. And that lessens the horror . . . which, when it comes on you unaware, cannot but frighten you beyond measure." He wanted to reassure Theo that he was improving, but he did not feel ready to resume life outside. "At present this horror of life is less strong already and the melancholy less acute. But I have no will, hardly any desires or none at all . . . for instance almost no desire to see my friends. . . . I have not yet reached the point where I ought to think of leaving here; I should have this depression anywhere."

By June Vincent was again deteriorating, having difficulties with his memory and thinking processes. "It is queer that every time I try to reason with myself to get a clear idea of things . . . a terrible dismay and horror seizes me and prevents me from thinking. . . . It is astounding to be afraid of nothing like this, and to be unable to remember things." The horror that floods the disordered mind is unrestrained by reason or philosophy, even if one retains the first and remembers the second. In psychosis one is a prisoner of the chemistry of terror, and there is no defense against it. Even a sane mind would succumb to terorr when all reality, one's life, the world, and everything in it become unreliable, and there is nothing to hold on to amid a swirl of metamorphoses. Vincent's terror was the harbinger of another serious attack, which struck while he was painting out of doors. For three weeks he alternated between "dementia" and "prostration." He stayed in his room the entire time, too mentally shattered to be able to paint.

He had gone so far away that it took a long time to come back. He recorded: "It is very difficult for me to write, my head is so disordered. . . . I am terribly distressed because the attacks have come back, when I was already beginning to hope that they would not return." Then he begged for permission to paint again, "for these days without anything to do . . . are almost unbearable."

As Vincent's mind cleared, the horror of his situation became evident to him. He was afraid of himself and the world in which he found himself. He wanted to leave: "First of all it is very expensive here, and . . . I am afraid of the other patients." His doctor claimed there was some improvement: "He has completely regained his lucidity of mind. . . . His thoughts of suicide have disappeared." Vincent's lucidity revealed to him a life of "poverty, sickness, old age, madness, and always exile."

In September he had a vague intimation that another attack loomed. "A more violent attack may destroy forever my ability to paint. During the attacks I feel a coward before the pain and the suffering. . . . I am now trying to recover like a man who has meant to commit suicide and, finding the water cold, tries to regain the bank." He wrote as though his life were already over: "I shall never do what I might have done and ought to have wished and pursued."

The cycle did begin again that month. "I am working like one actually possessed," he wrote Theo, "more than ever I am in a dumb fury of work." With the optimism of mania, he added, "I think that this will help cure me." He never recognized this stage as part of his illness, and that is the case with most manic-depressives. Theo, however, was alarmed, for he had seen this before and lived through what followed. He wrote to his brother: "I am always afraid when you are working that way, in a frenzy." It was useless to warn Vincent. The manic cannot voluntarily slow down.

As the mania began to darken into depression, Vincent's discouragement grew, and like many patients, he thought that leaving the hospital would make him feel better and be better for him. He said he was willing to "wait for the winter and the attack which will perhaps come back then." He now realized that he had an annual cycle. "But if it is a fit of religious exaltation again," he added, "then no delay, I would like to leave at once." Because Saint Remy was a Catholic hospital, Vincent thought it was the cause of the religious element in his attacks. However, manic-depressives can develop religious exaltations regardless of where they are confined. Vincent was grasping at anything that might help him. His next desperate remedy was to give up painting. "Very often terrible fits of depression come over me," so he said it seemed to him "a thing against all reason, to be doing this painting which costs so much and brings in nothing. . . . the trouble is that at my age it is damnable difficult to begin anything else." When the chemical trigger fired again, he was back at his easel: "Only when I stand before my easel do I feel somewhat alive."

The work of the last months of his life is curiously hollow. Nothing is left but agony, paint writhing off the canvas. Nothing holds its shape; reality is not fixed but wavers like the heated air above a fire. Without knowing it, Van Gogh was painting the world of psychosis, in which everything can warp and stretch and lose its identity.

When he wrote in January of the next year, he had gone through another psychotic episode and was again hard at work. That month a review of an exhibit that included his paintings offered Vincent his first praise. He was in no condition to feel joyous about it. He later wrote: "Please ask M. Aurier not to write any more articles on my painting, insist upon this . . . since I am too overwhelmed with grief to be able to face publicity."

Another stress at this time was the birth of Theo's child. As Theo's family and responsibilities grew, he had less room in his life for his brother: wife and child had to come first. In mid-February, while Vincent was visiting Arles, he had another psychotic episode that lasted until mid-April, the longest one so far. As he was coming out of it, Vincent wrote to Theo, "My head is so bad, without pain, it is true, but altogether stupefied." "What am I to say about these last 2 months?" "I am sadder and more wretched than I can say."

In May Vincent surrendered any thought of living outside of a hospital. "My mental condition is not only vague now, but has always been so, so that . . . I cannot think things out so as to balance my life." Then another fit of mania arrived. "In those last days at St. Remy," he recalled, "I still worked as in a frenzy. Great bunches of flowers, violet irises, big bouquets of roses, landscapes." In the same month, he left the relative safety of the hospital to go to his death.

AUVERS: MAY 21–JULY 29, 1890

Theo made arrangements for Vincent to stay with a Dr. Gachet, who was sympathetic to artists. Vincent would live at the doctor's home in Auvers, not far from Paris. On May 17 the painter arrived in Paris and went to his brother's home for a three-day visit before going on to Auvers. Leaving the hospital—or perhaps the time of year—had put Vincent in a rising mood. His sister-in-law was amazed at his apparent health and good humor. "He seems perfectly well, he looks much stronger than Theo," she noted. "He stayed with us 3 days and was all the time cheerful and lively."

Nevertheless there was no real improvement in Vincent. How could there be? In his first days at Auvers he flew into a fit of rage because he was not satisfied with the frame on another painter's picture. Vincent visited his brother again on July 1, but this trip did not go well. He became overexcited when talking with other painters, and Theo and his wife were anxious over an illness the baby was having. Vincent returned to Auvers in a state of depression. He next wrote to Theo: "I have since painted 3 big canvases already. They are vast stretches of corn under troubled skies, and I did not need to go out of my way to express sadness and the extreme of loneliness." That was early in July. Later that month he went after Dr. Gachet with a revolver.

Two days later Vincent shot himself. When Theo came to his bedside, he was conscious and said, "Don't weep. What I have done was best for all of us." When Theo protested, he answered, "No use. I shall never be rid of this depression." Theo stayed with his brother, thinking Vincent strong enough to survive the wound. Theo wrote to his wife, "Oh! If we could give him some new courage to live." Vincent held on for two days. Early in the morning of July 29, just before his life ended, Vincent said, "I wish I could die now." How few were the wishes granted to him.

After Vincent's death, people began to think that the world had lost a valuable man. Theo wrote about this to his mother: "Life was such a burden to him; but now, as so often happens, everybody is full of praise for his talents. . . . Oh Mother! he was so my own, my own brother." Theo died in a mental hospital six months later. Dr. Gachet wrote: "The more I think of it, the more I think Vincent was a giant. Not a day passes that I do not look at his pictures." "The word love of art is not exact, one must call it a faith to which Vincent fell a martyr." Art never made Vincent suffer. Instead it gave him most of the joy that he ever had. He fell a martyr to Dr. Gachet's carelessness in leaving a loaded gun where Vincent could get it.

POSTSCRIPT

Of all the artists who have led tragic lives, Van Gogh is probably the best known today. Many before him died mad: the poets Tasso, Cowper, and Hölderlin, the composer Robert Schumann, actor Edmund Kean, the dancer Nijinsky, writers de Maupassant and Swift. There have been many artists in the nineteenth and twentieth centuries whose work was not sufficiently appreciated during their lifetimes. Keats, Shelley, and Dickinson among poets, the painters Seurat and Gauguin, and the composer Franz Schubert come to mind. Among illustrious suicides we have Chatterton and Kleist in the nineteenth century, in the twentieth, Hemingway, Sylvia Plath, Hart Crane, Virginia Voolf, and others. But Van Gogh is the most famous of the few who were exemplars of all three kinds of tragedy: rejected endeavors, mental illness, and suicide.

However, it is not only his triple tragedy that has won eminence for Van Gogh. He produced an amazing quantity of great paintings in the short time allotted to him after he had mastered his craft. For a few years he was able to turn the ugliness and chaos of his life into beauty and controlled power. In his work there is more than originality and talent. These do not suffice to make great paintings. His best work is eternally alive: color has become passion and image has become spirit.

7

Diminishing Creativity

THE TORMENT OF PROMETHEUS

Biographies of creative manic-depressives are not cheering to read, and happy endings are few among them. Geniuses and lesser talents who are manic-depressives have the same problems, ranging from depressions that prevent work, to bankruptcies caused by manic extravagance. Ability alone does not guarantee financial success, except insofar as it increases the market value of one's work. Extraordinary talent enables people to do better work, and it may increase their satisfaction in their work, but it is no remedy for the vicissitudes of manic-depression. In case after case, much of the conflict, chaos, and pain in creative lives results from this illness.

Genius can be augmented by freeing creative manic-depressives from those effects of the disorder that are detrimental to creativity, and by helping them to maximize the advantages that the illness can provide.

Certain conditions must be met if creativity is to occur. One has to live long enough to receive training and produce work, just as it is essential to have time and the physical ability needed for one's work, the necessary material or equipment, and sufficient freedom from distraction. Severe physical illness or disability and extreme poverty make creative endeavor unlikely, if not impossible. However, those who meet the basic requirements may still find the way to creativity barred. Extreme states of manic-depression have detrimental effects on creativity regardless of external circumstances.

THE DISTORTED REALITY OF DEPRESSION

In stupor, depression is so overpowering as to reduce people to immobility. Jonathan Swift, the author of *Gulliver's Travels,* spent a year without reading or speaking to anyone or showing any awareness of anyone. The English writer Samuel Johnson describes the amnesia and reduced consciousness of his stupors: "A kind of strange oblivion has overspread me, so that I know not what became of last year, and perceive that incidents and intelligence pass over me without leaving any impression." Even the simplest tasks are difficult to do in this state, much less creative work. Johnson adds: "My time has been unprofitably spent, and seems as a dream that has left nothing behind. . . . I know not how the days pass over me." When the English poet Elizabeth Barrett Browning lost her father, she fell into a stuporous state that lasted for weeks. When her brother died, she suffered another depressive stupor, this one including hallucinations. She reports: "For more than 3 months I could not read—could understand little that was said to me. The mind seemed to myself broken up into fragments. And even after . . . the staring infantine faces, had gone back from my bed—to understand, to hold open to one thought for more than a moment, remained impossible."

Extreme depression can take a violently active form that is equally inimical to work. The Italian poet Torquato Tasso experienced depressions with hallucinations and paranoid rages, in which he once tried to stab a servant to death. The violence of extreme depression may be turned against oneself. The Russian writer Maxim Gorky attempted to shoot himself in the chest. During his recovery, his depression remained so severe that he experienced hallucinations.

Suicide attempts and suicidal thoughts are indicators of depression that appear in many creative lives. The French painter Gauguin survived an attempt with arsenic. The Hungarian composer Franz Liszt wrote a friend, "Look, if I ever fall into the water, let me sink to the bottom." The American philosopher William James wrote, "All last winter . . . I was on the continual verge of suicide." There is a long list of creative people who became suicidal during depressions. Even when a severe depression does not bring suicidal impulses, it may make the depressive too agitated to concentrate on work, or he may be so dejected that he cannot think of anything but his misery.

Delusions that one is worthless and life hopeless are often factors in suicide, and other delusions caused by depression also interfere with creative work. The German writer Heinrich von Kleist, in despair, burned his work and fatally shot his mistress and himself. The English painter Romney, even during his years of greatest success, fell into depressions during which he held the delusion that his talent was vanishing and that he must give up painting. The Italian composer Rossini developed the delusion that he had lost the ability to compose, as well as a delusion common to depression: that he was penniless. In the following notice the American writer Nathaniel Hawthorne tells his publisher that a work in progress cannot be finished, and a trace of hopelessness is evident through the humor. "Mr. Hawthorne's brain is addled at last, and much to our satisfaction, he tells us that he cannot possibly go on with the Romance announced on the cover of our January magazine. We consider him finally shelved, and shall take early occasion to bury him under a heavy article, carefully summing up his merits (such as they were) and his demerits, what few of them can be touched upon in our limited space."

Depression distorts the sufferer's judgment of himself and his work to a degree corresponding to the depth of mood. The worse he feels, the more he exaggerates the faults of his work. The creative person becomes pessimistic about everything and expects his work to meet with a harsh reception. Feeling no confidence in himself, he is loathe to begin new work for fear of failure, and current work may be abandoned as hopeless. Sometimes completed work is destroyed under the delusion that it is worthless. The French poet Rimbaud, who gave up poetry completely, burned all of his work in a fit of despair. Michelangelo, whose letters often contained complaints of depression, destroyed a pieta he had been carving from marble and left unfinished most of the work of his mature years.

The delusions caused by depression may give the depressive such a low opinion of his ability and work that the work is withheld to avoid criticism and rejection, or sold well below its worth. The depressive, having little faith in his own judgment, is too easily influenced by others, and criticism may lead him to give up his career for years, or to terminate it. The Italian painter Paolo Uccello was so depressed at a fellow artist's criticism of Uccello's painting that he became a recluse and did nothing except study perspective thenceforth. Another Italian painter, Carlo Dolci, on being criticized for working slowly, decided that he was the worst painter in the world and became too incapacitated by depression to work. According to the English poet Shelley, his colleague Keats reacted to criticism with such painful agitation that he bordered on psychosis.

Depression can nullify the benefits one might expect from praise. The English poet Stephen Spender expresses that negative reaction: "In common with other creative writers I pretend that I am not, and I am, exceedingly affected by unsympathetic criticism, whilst praise usually makes me suspect that the reviewer does not know what he is talking about."

As it intensifies, depression darkens one's view of everything, and an all-enveloping hopelessness can temporarily or permanently put an end to creative work. At fifty-one the French mathematician Lagrange decided that it was no longer possible to do anything significant in his field and neglected mathematics for years. The German composer Wagner said, "I feel it deep within me—if things continue thus, I'm done for; I've hope or trust in nothing more," at one of many despairing interruptions in his long career.

Anxieties arising from depression do not necessarily end careers, but they make both life and creative work more difficult. The Polish composer Chopin frequently complained of depression: "I wish I were dead," and "There are no words for my misery; how can I bear this feeling." He also had the typical depressive anxiety about imminent death, and when his mistress, the French writer George Sand, returned home late from a walk with her son, he was surprised to find them alive. Samuel Johnson felt intense anxiety about going berserk and bought fetters so that he could be chained when it happened. In calmer moments he recognized that he was prey to delusions: "O God! . . . Grant that I may be no longer distracted with doubts and harassed with vain terrors!"

Hypochondriacal delusions, as manifestations of depression, can convince people that they are too ill to work. Shelley, who experienced hallucinatory, suicidal, and stuporous depressions, developed the delusion that he had kidney stones and, when overwrought, would writhe on the floor, announcing, "I have the elephantiasis." Picasso, who had been in an automobile accident, did fewer paintings in 1936 because of imaginary injuries. Wagner, on the other hand, was spurred on to complete his work because, said he, "I'm always suffering from my nerves, and probably shall not last out much longer." That was thirty-one years before he died.

THE CRIPPLING EFFECTS OF DEPRESSION

The delusions common to depression may appear well before extreme stages, and that is also true of other symptoms that interfere with work or lower its quality. In the early stages of depression the sufferer may work compulsively, but invariably output diminishes as depression increases. He becomes bored easily and feels diminished pleasure in everything, including his work. Wagner describes this state: "My life is a succession of wan and spiritless days. . . . I can scarcely bring myself to write the most necessary letters! . . . I go out very little now—my distaste for everything is too great."

The depressive lacks energy, and feels an increasing need for rest and sleep. Consequently, he tends to work fewer hours per day. Loss of will power is another symptom that interferes with creativity, and it may appear in early stages of depression. The English poet Coleridge complained: "My case is a species of madness, only that it is a derangement, an utter impotence of the *Volition*, and not of the intellectual Faculties." Mozart experienced states of failure of will that kept him from finishing compositions until they were about to be performed and the musicians were anxiously waiting for them.

The depressive takes longer to finish work not only because he procrastinates and works less, but also because he is thinking more slowly, having trouble with memory, waiting in vain for words, for ideas, and for solutions to problems. Keats wrote to a friend, "I am now so depressed that I have not an idea to put to paper." Depression also interferes with concentration. The American painter Raphael Soyer attests: "I know that when I am depressed it's harder for me to work. . . . My wife gets a cold, or my daughter gets sick, or something like that. Those things depress me. And then it's hard for me to concentrate and work." In depression making decisions becomes increasingly difficult as well: one thought does not lead to another, and connections between ideas are not made. Mental effort becomes arduous and tiring.

When the creative person tries to remain productive during a depression, he tends to simplify his work, or omit important aspects of it, or reduce its dimensions: anything to make it easier as energy and thinking fail. Starting new projects becomes increasingly daunting and difficult. It is possible to perform what is habitual or routine, but as depression deepens, anything requiring originality or sustained thinking recedes from the realm of possibility.

Physical symptoms such as headache and digestive disorders are often concomitants of depression, and immune function is often compromised, so that physical illness may interfere with work. The mental agony that may accompany depression, like physical pain, can prevent work too. Many creative people have remarked on their experiences of agonizing depression. The Italian poet Tasso said in the sixteenth century, "My sadness is so deep and persistent that people often think me crazy, and I am forced to assent to the opinion myself." His colleague and fellow countryman Petrarch said, "A kind of melancholy grips me sometimes so tenaciously that I am tormented through long days and nights; for me this is a time without light or life—it is a dark inferno and most bitter death." The German writer Goethe remarked: "I have always been regarded as a man specially favored by fortune . . . But . . . I might go so far as to say that in my 75 years I have not known 4 weeks of genuine ease of mind."

Any of the symptoms of depression mentioned can be a roadblock to creativity. When several symptoms occur together, as is usually the case, the outcome may be a creative block. The German composer Robert Schumann spent an entire year depressed and unable to compose. Later he attempted to drown himself in the Rhine. He passed his last years in a mental hospital. The Italian painter Annibale Carracci had an artistic block lasting five years. The novelist I. B. Singer recounts:

> I had, myself, a number of years in which I could not write . . . When I did try to write, I suddenly discovered that I could not construct a sentence correctly. I was astonished because my language was always very fluent, but in this case of deep depression, my sentences became too abrupt, and sometimes not really correct from the point of view of syntax and this lasted for years. . . . I wrote and rewrote, and nothing came of it. . . . A real depression can make a writer impotent.

THE COMPLICATIONS OF MANIA

Mania can make one too restless, impatient, and energetic to accomplish anything. A friend of the Russian poet Pushkin describes him in this hyperactive state: "He could not sit sitll. He whirled about, hopped up and down, changed chairs, upset the sewing basket, tangled all the skeins of wool in my embroidery frame, moved the cards of a double solitaire my mother had begun to lay out." Insomnia usually accompanies this frantic pace, and the manic has busy nights as well as busy days. The American novelist Thomas Wolfe spent a manic three years writing his first novel and kept going night and day. "At the end of the day of savage labor," he reports, "my mind was still blazing with its effort, could by no opiate of reading, poetry, music alcohol, or any other pleasure be put at rest. I was unable to sleep, unable to subdue the tumult of these creative energies, and as a result of this condition, for 3 years I prowled the streets."

The manic may become irritable and hostile, and as he tends to act on every impulse, he may become aggressive, violent, and even homicidal. The Spanish painter Goya participated in street fights and left Zaragoza after someone died in one of the brawls. The American poet Robert Lowell describes a manic episode that resulted in his being straitjacketed and confined in a padded cell. "I ran about the streets of Bloomington Indiana crying out against devils and homosexuals. I believed I could stop cars and paralyze their forces by merely standing in the middle of the highway with my arms outspread. . . . I suspected I was a reincarnation of the Holy Ghost, and had become homicidally hallucinated."

When duels were in fashion, the aggressiveness of the manic could cut short his life. Pushkin was killed in his thirties while dueling, as was another Russian writer, Lermontov. The brilliant French mathematician Galois died the same way when he was twenty. The Italian painter Caravaggio, whose violence earned him a long police record, had to flee the authorities after killing an adversary. Manics often find themselves at odds with the government, and creative manics are no exception. Both Pushkin and Lermontov were exiled, Pushkin having written the tsar, "I debated whether I should kill myself or murder Your Majesty." The Italian artist Cellini, who hallucinated occasionally, committed murder, was jailed for theft, and frequently left town to avoid imprisonment. The Dutch painter Pieter Muller managed to keep working in prison, but as a rule manic combativeness and its consequences interfere with creative work.

The manic's excess energy can drive him into activity for its own sake. Inexhaustible, he may fail to recognize when a project is complete and spoil it by overelaboration. He may sacrifice quality to quantity, for he cannot stop to think about his work and the direction it is taking. The most prolific creators are not necessarily the best. Telemann, history's most prolific composer of classical music, is not the equal of his contemporary Bach. The English writer Southey, who poured out close to fifty volumes, is hardly remembered today. Volubility, both spoken and written, is a characteristic of mania that poses a particular hazard for the writer. Wolfe gives an account of its effect on him: "I not only wrote what was essential, but time and time again my enthusiasm for a good scene . . . would overpower me, and I would write thousands of words upon a scene which contributed nothing of vital importance to a book whose greatest need already was ruthless condensation." With manic enthusiasm, he felt "not only that everything had to be used, but that everything had to be told, that nothing could be implied." He hated cutting: "My soul recoiled before the carnage of so many lovely things cut out upon which my heart was set."

The fast-thinking, long-working, hyperactive, and self-confident manic can accomplish things requiring a tremendous expenditure of effort, and he loves to take on gigantic projects. The Flemish painter Rubens is an example. He said, "My talent is such that no undertaking, however vast in size or diversified in subject, has ever surpassed my courage." Impatience, however, makes some manics careless. The English poet Lord Byron said that he had to get a poem right at the first attempt: "I can't correct; I can't and I won't."

Creative works may become chaotic as mania intensifies, bringing a flood of unconnected thoughts and impulses that interferes with concentration and memory. The German author E. T. A. Hoffman declared: "Disorderly ideas seem to rise out of my mind like blood from opened veins." The English poet Coleridge remarked on his inability to think or speak in a logical sequence: "My thoughts bustle along like a Surinam toad, with little toads sprouting out of back, side and belly." He would speak nonstop for hours, leaving his listeners complaining, "I could not make head or tail of Coleridge's oration; pray, did you understand it?" If anyone could understand Coleridge, it should have been another poet, but Wordsworth replied, "Not one syllable of it."

The manic, unable to order his own thoughts in logical sequence, also finds it difficult to follow an argument or explanation, to listen to others talking without interrupting, or to read a book to its conclusion. He is unable to think through anything complex, for everything distracts him. Little of value can be done under these conditions.

Though he spends an impressive amount of time and energy on his work, his output may decrease because he starts something new before completing the current project. During one manic period of his life, the French novelist Balzac started several books without finishing any of them. Because the American inventor Edison often lacked the patience to produce and market some of his inventions such as the electric train, others profited from them.

Some manics spend their lives changing direction and consequently accomplish very little. The English scientist Robert Hooke was gifted and indefatigable and worked in several sciences but never stayed with one long enough to make major contributions. According to the American Nobel physicist Isidor Rabi, his colleague Robert Oppenheimer had a similar problem. Rabi says: "Oppenheimer wanted every experience. . . . I never ran into anyone who was brighter than he was. But to be more original and profound, I think you have to be more focused." Sometimes the manic, instead of trying to do too many things in sequence, does too many things simultaneously. Rubens once conversed with visitors while listening to a reading of Tacitus, painting, and dictating letters.

Mania increases sociability, which can, if carried too far, interfere with creativity. Byron observed, "If I go into society, I generally get, in the long run, into some scrapes of some kind or another, which don't occur in my solitude."

Most of Byron's "scrapes" were complicated and contentious love affairs: he usually chose temperamental women, or they chose him. The heightening of sexuality that often accompanies mania is yet another distraction that can reduce creative output. The Italian painter Raphael, though occasionally troubled by depression, was known for his amorous exploits. When one of his romances kept him from finishing a commission, his patron brought Raphael's lover to the house where the work was to be done. Balzac once conducted four love affairs simultaneously. People often fall in love when manic. This was Robert Lowell's pattern, resulting in engagements to four women and marriages to another three. Goethe, who became manic every seven years, fell in love with a new woman each time. Pushkin, who went to receptions and parties when manic, fell in love at each one and would say, "What a gorgeous creature! I can't live without her!" He was also a good customer of the prostitutes in Saint Petersburg.

THE DESTRUCTIVE FANTASIES OF THE CREATIVE MANIC

The delusions that develop in intense manic states can reduce both the amount and quality of creative work. Manics tend to undertake overambitious, or even impossible, projects because they are overly optimistic. They fail to realize that what they want to do is too expensive, too time consuming, too large, too complicated, or impractical for other reasons. Thomas Edison was particularly fond of grandiose enterprises, the more extravagant the better. He once announced: "I am spending more than my income getting up a set of 6,000 films to teach the 19 million children in the United States to do away entirely with books." On another occasion he tried to make a pendulum move with the force of his thought alone. As mania increases, one becomes increasingly unrealistic about what is possible.

Some manics waste time and resources on work for which they have neither talent nor training. Edison did this too. Despite never having studied music and being partially deaf, he claimed: "I am going to do for music

exactly what I did for electricity when I invented machines to measure it."
Picasso wrote poetry in time that he could have spent more productively.
Thackeray had the insight to recognize the deceptive nature of such confidence.
"When I have dined," he said, "sometimes I believe myself to be equal to
the greatest painters and poets. The delusion goes off; and then I know what
a small fiddle is mine and what small tunes I play upon it."

While work is in process, manic delusions may convince the creator that
work is much better than it is: consequently, necessary corrections or
improvements will not be made. The finished work is often seen through
rose-colored glasses if mania still prevails. The English poet Blake called one
of his creations "the Grandest Poem that this World contains." The financial
rewards to come are often overestimated also. Wagner admitted, "My sanguine
temperament is apt to suggest to me that the royalties to be expected are
nearer [in time] than they really are."

THE EFFECT OF MANIA AND DEPRESSION ON STYLE
AND ON OTHER CHARACTERISTICS OF CREATIVE WORK

Thought processes, ideas and opinions, emotions, and behavior are all affected
by mania and depression, the more so as these states intensify, and creative
work often displays characteristics that result directly from manic or depressive
symptoms. However, creative work is not always done at one sitting or in
one state: it may be gone over again and again, so that the end result is
a blend in which no simple correlation with mania or depression can be
discerned. Or, the form of creativity may be constrained by factors that eliminate
the marks of mania and depression. Creativity in physics has to conform
to natural law, and mathematics has to conform to its own inner structure.
But even in the freedom of painting and music, only some works are clearly
manic or depressed in style and content. More often a creative work is a
palimpsest of moods, particularly if it took weeks, months, or longer to produce.
The effect of mood on work is evident primarily to the person doing the
work, and to people who are present during the creative process, for they
can compare what the creator produces in different states of mind.

The driving energy of mania produces large-scale, intense, powerful, and
sometimes crude work. Because mania is the enemy of restraint, the work
often contains an excess of ideas and material, unnecessary elaboration, and
elements that do not belong. The manic has a preference for exaggeration,
overemphasis, and dramatic effects. He delights in startling, bizarre, exotic effects
and prefers to invent his own rules. His rapid thinking gives his work a fast,
exciting, sometimes frenetic pace. Musicians tend to play louder, less subtly,
and faster when manic. Manic writers, impelled by pressure of speech, are
prolix, create long, complicated sentences, and use foreign or unusual words.

Coleridge confessed that he would use five hundred illustrations to make a point, by which time no one knew what he wanted to prove. Manics like long strings of adjectives, and comic writers such as Mark Twain and Rabelais cite long lists of items. The manic tendency to digress adds to the shapeless sprawl of manic writing, and manic rambling shapes some comic novels.

The manic feels intensely, and his emotions shift rapidly from euphoria through anger and even anxiety. Manic art shows the same sudden changes of mood, content, and style. Some of the music of Robert Schumann is marked by stark contrasts and manic disorganization. Manic writing may be contradictory and illogical. The content of manic art parallels the content of manic conversation: it may be egocentric, confessional, contentious, rebellious, angry, merry, funny, sexual, scatological, mystical, or prophetic. Manic novels tend to be eventful, have elaborate plots and multiple settings, large casts of characters, much colorful detail, and are likely to cover long spans of time.

Depression produces works that are the antithesis of manic work. Depressive novels focus on hopeless relationships and situations, people who are doomed, and people who are physically or mentally damaged or handicapped. The plots are slow moving, the characters are few, and the action occurs in a relatively confined space. Depressive writing deals with ennui,· pain, ugliness, illness, poverty, destruction, and death. It is often obsessive, pessimistic, nihilistic, and nightmarish, or it may be introspective or philosophical. The emotional tone of depressive art is eitther flattened or ranges from irritated through sad to agonized. In 1768 Samuel Johnson was extremely depressed and managed to write only a prologue to a play called *Good-Natur'd Man.* The first lines of the prologue are: "Pressed with the load of life, the weary mind / Surveys the general toil of human kind." As his friend Boswell remarked, "Who could suppose it was to introduce a comedy . . . "

The effects of depression on style derive from the reduced energy and mental function that often occur in that state. "Poverty of ideas" is the term used for the mental vacancy that can occur. The effect of depression on writing is to simplify grammar and vocabulary to the point of monotony. Severe depression usually results in sterility, but if work is attempted, it tends to become disorganized, not because the extraneous is included, as in mania, but because essential connective material is missing. The inability to make decisions may leave work somewhat vague. Severe depression prevents original thought, and attempts at creative work are consequently somewhat mechanical, derivative, labored, and boring. When the depression causes anguish without reducing mental function, the effect on style is more subtle: painting becomes darker, and the colors tend to be cool and muted. Some of Picasso's blue-period paintings contain images as sad as the color of the palette implies.

The relationship between creative work and mania and depression is often not as clear as the preceding observations might suggest. Byron attests: "Some of my nearest approaches to the comic have been written under a deep depression of spirits." If he was not joking or mistaken, the paradox invites investigation.

From time to time attempts have been made to read the nature of the creature in the creation. In the sixteenth century Vicente Carducho stated that even the height of the painter could be guessed from the size of the figures he painted, "For he will let himself be carried away by his temperament and will imitate himself in his works." Some three centuries later William James said: "A philosophy is the expression of a man's character." While creative work indubitably reflects somewhat of the personality of the person who does it, there is no simple correspondence between the two. Who would guess that James, the inventor of such a down-to-earth philosophy as pragmatism, had hallucinations, or that Tchaikovsky composed "The Waltz of the Sugar Plum Fairies" while in a depression? The manic-depressive who has a predominantly depressed or manic personality will generally do work characterized by his predominant state, but that rule has exceptions.

TIME LOST TO INCAPACITATING MANIA AND DEPRESSION

It is impossible to establish how much creativity has been wasted because of mood disorders, but one could make a long list of creative manic-depressives who were hospitalized for mental illness. A trio of eighteenth-century English poets suffered that fate: William Collins, William Cowper, and Christopher Smart. The German mathematician Georg Cantor was hospitalized for manic-depression when he was forty and was in and out of hospitals for the rest of his life. Though he did some work between hospitalizations, the severity of his illness effectively ended his career. The French philosopher Auguste Comte spent a year in an asylum and, like Robert Schumann, tried to drown himself in a river. A French social philosopher, the Comte de Saint-Simon, who suffered from chronic and severe depressions, was hospitalized. The German philosopher Friederich Nietzsche was put in an asylum at the age of forty-five and never recovered sufficiently after his release to resume his work. The French painter Daumier spent four months in a mental hospital and two in a prison. Another French painter, Maurice Utrillo, was hospitalized at age eighteen and began his painting there. The Norwegian painter Edvard Munch was hospitalized for eighteen months. Robert Lowell did some of his most disorganized work in a mental hospital. For the French writer de Maupassant and the poet Baudelaire, syphilis of the brain contributed to the dementia that led to hospitalization. This small sample does not begin to indicate the extraordinary number of creative people who have been afflicted by manic-depression.

CLASSIC PROBLEMS OF THE CREATIVE INDIVIDUAL

Many of the difficulties that repeatedly appear in the lives of creative people have been directly or indirectly caused by manic-depression.

Poverty has long been considered a concomitant of the creative life, but an examination of biographical material leads to the conclusion that in many cases extravagance, rather than lack of income, caused constant debt, bankruptcies, and, in some cases, imprisonment for debt. Christopher Smart and the German painter Adam Elsheimer died after being imprisoned for debt. Painters appear prone to extravagance, especially in the sixteenth and seventeenth centuries. The Dutch painters Brouwer, Molenaer, de Witte, Hals, Vermeer, and Rembrandt were incapable of living within their means, and Rembrandt was declared bankrupt when he was fifty. The German painter Johann Rottenhammer, who was well paid by emperors, kings, and other wealthy patrons, had nothing left to cover the expenses of his burial. The same fate also befell Mozart. The Italian painter Bartolo Gagliardi, when told by his friends to save something for the lean years, always replied that all he needed was enough to cover the cost of a burial urn.

Some English writers were no less extravagant than Continental artists. Oliver Goldsmith and Richard Sheridan are among those who died in financial difficulties, as did the Welsh poet Dylan Thomas. His wife explains, "The valuable quality of moderation was totally lacking in both of us." The American publisher Fields furnishes a description of mania inducing extravagance. He describes the English writer Thackeray, who had a lifetime of financial insecurity despite a good income, as being on one occasion "wild with exultation," adding "all my efforts were necessary to restrain him from rushing in and ordering a pocketful of diamonds." The manic-depressive may become so elated when he receives money that he spends more in the succeeding mania than he acquired. Wagner provides an example: "You know that I cannot save. . . . If I get money it is certain that I've always spent 3 times as much and am in debt."

Gambling, often an expression of manic-depression, sometimes brings the creative person into poverty. The Russian writer Dostoyevsky, in debt all his life, was a manic-depressive compulsive gambler, as was de Musset. The French poet was also at times suicidal, given to frenzies, and subject to hallucinations.

Abuse of alcohol and drugs is another frequent accompaniment of manic-depression and is quite common in the lives of creative people. Many of them have used substances to relieve depression or reduce manic excitement. Keats took opium to calm his manic excitement. So did his fellow poet Shelley who, holding a bottle of the drug, said: "I never part from this." Liszt relied on alcohol.

Many manic-depressives tolerate or enjoy their manias but prefer to shorten or eliminate depressions. It is not surprising that it is more common to use drugs and alcohol to relieve depression than to diminish mania. The English playwright Addison drank to escape depression and became an alcoholic, as did the English poet Swinburne, who also had problems with paranoia. The Dutch painter Jongkind was an alcoholic who suffered depressions, paranoia, and debt. Eugene O'Neill would drink during the depressions that followed the completion of his plays. In his more suicidal moments he would imbibe varnish and a mixture of wood alcohol and camphor. De Quincey used opium to reduce his suffering from depression. He also had delusions of persecution. Byron gave up opium in preference to alcohol, saying, "The spirits (at least mine) need a little exhilaration, and I don't like laudanum [opium] now as I used to." Samuel Johnson tried to avoid drinking but would resort to it when depressed. He explained: "He who makes a *beast* of himself gets rid of the *pain of being a man*."

Some creative people resort to drugs and/or alcohol to stimulate creativity. The French writer Gautier tried to increase his creativity with hashish. Byron would keep writing all night on alcohol: "Gin-and-water is the source of all my inspiration," he said. The English playwright Sheridan felt that he could not write when sober, and the German playwright Schiller kept the creative juices flowing by priming the pump with wine, champagne, and coffee. His compatriot and fellow playwright Schlegel relied on opium. O'Neill was one playwright, however, who never drank while working, stating, "I don't think anything worth reading was ever written by anyone who was drunk or even half-drunk when he wrote it." The American poet Hart Crane used alcohol to launch him into a poem but made copious changes afterwards, when he was sober.

Drugs and alcohol may occasionally loosen the inhibitions that impede creativity, but they generally interfere with intellectual processes, while addictions to these substances limit the production of creative work and/or its quality. De Quincey was unable to complete a manuscript that he had already advertised because he resumed heavy opium consumption. Coleridge did most of his best work before his opium addiction developed. Sheridan's best work was done before alcoholism took over his life. The Russian composer Mussorgsky lost his ability to work to alcoholism. Dylan Thomas had his most creative period before his heaviest drinking. He summed up his situation: "Promiscuity, booze, . . . too much talk, too little work."

Abuse of alcohol and drugs has ruined many careers and also shortened lives. The American actor Edmund Kean would try to perform when drunk, with disastrous results, or would fail to appear at all, and people became wary of engaging him. He jumped off the roof of a house and died when he was forty-six. The Scottish poet Robert Burns, who spoke of "a deep incurable taint of melancholia which poisons my existence," died an alcoholic at the age of thirty-seven. The American writer Edgar Allen Poe, who was jailed for drunkenness, also tried to commit suicide by overdosing on opium, had periods of paranoia, and died at the age of forty, after being found unconscious in the street.

CONFLICTS IN WORK AND LOVE

Creative people frequently find themselves in conflict with those on whom they depend for recognition and financial reward. Invariably, they blame the philistine or conservative mentality, the venality, or the dishonesty of their adversaries. However, in many cases, paranoia and irritability originating in manic-depression are sources of conflict that interfere with work and sabotage careers.

To receive criticism is always painful, but many creative manic-depressives develop a hatred of critics that seems unjustified. O'Neill claimed: "Generally speaking the critic of any kind of art is simply a defeated, envious, inferior type who knows nothing whatever about his subject." Paranoia changes that hatred to the expectation of persecution, with personal motives such as jealousy or vengeance sometimes imputed to the critic. The English painter Rossetti thought that local critics were at fault: "Men of intelligence in England are ever a persecuted sect." The German poet Heine thought the problem with critics was a contemporary one: "You well know that greatness of character and talent is not forgiven in our time." O'Neill saw the critic as a universal and eternal problem: "I know enough history to realize that no one worth a damn ever escaped them. . . . When I'm generally approved of, I begin to look in the mirror very skeptically and contemplate taking up some other career."

Many a creative manic-depressive becomes paranoid about his colleagues and imagines that they are trying to wreck his work or interfere with its reception. Edison became so secretive that he would not tell the people working in his laboratory enough about his projects to allow them to accomplish anything. Robert Hooke thought that everyone, including Newton, stole his ideas. Paranoia can also instill delusions that one's colleagues are trying to prevent one from receiving recognition or financial reward. Such ideas can lead to vendettas. Rossetti, who was also suicidal and abused drugs and alcohol, imagined that his colleagues Browning and Lewis Carroll insulted him in their works.

Those who are intermediaries between creative people and the market for their work may become the targets of paranoia. Gauguin was convinced that all his art dealers were cheating him. Writers may go from one agent to another because of baseless suspicions. People who pay the creative person for his output also receive unjust accusations of swindling and, sometimes, are the target of needless lawsuits. The American writer Lafcadio Hearn broke his relationship with *Harper's Magazine* because of unjust suspicions. Poe walked out of his job at *Graham's Magazine* because he imagined he was about to be fired. Spurred by paranoia, creative people impede their careers and waste time and energy on needless conflict. Their delusory suspicions can also interfere with their work and careers by causing them to take flight. The Hungarian poet Lenau was driven from country to country by delusory fears. Walter Savage Landor needlessly exiled himself from England. Michelangelo uprooted himself several times without real cause.

Domestic problems loom large in the lives of creative people, and these may have their origin not only in the manic-depression of the person in question, but in manic-depression among members of his family.

The mood changes and, in some cases, changes of personality that are a hallmark of the illness are often disconcerting and baffling to those who witness them. One of de Musset's lovers recorded: "On one side there is the kind, tender, ardent man, . . . affable, uncomplicated, unpretentious, modest, sensitive, excitable, prone to weep over nothing at all, an artist in the full meaning of the word. . . . Then . . . you find yourself at grips with a man possessed by some sort of demon, weak, violent, arrogant, blindly obstinate, self-centered and egotistical to the extreme, blasphemous, . . . whipping himself into a frenzy of evil." The self-centeredness, delusions, and impetuosity of some creative manic-depressives make them hard to live with, as Elizabeth Hardwicke, one of the wives of Robert Lowell, attests: "The excitement, the unreal plans and demands, the unpredictability . . . the deep underlying unreality is there, the fact that no one else's feelings really exist, wild projects, etc."

During both mania and depression the creative person may become hostile, venting this feeling on those at hand. Carlyle would go for weeks without speaking to his wife. At other times he saw her only at meals and refused to travel in the same carriage with her. O'Neill alternated between treating his wife Agnes with passionate attention and antagonism. The paranoid Italian painter Gaspare Celio for forty-five years kept his wife locked in the house where he hid from the world.

Rages and violence are all too common in the lives of creative manic-depressives, and the person nearest to them may become their targets. The French writer Alexander Dumas, another extravagant and consequently penniless artist, attacked his wife during his rages, tearing at her hair. Sweden's leading playwright Strindberg, who expected to be killed because of his talent, had delusions of grandeur and hallucinations and oscillated between beating his wife and making love to her.

One of the most miserable marriages in the annals of creativity was that of Lord Byron, whose wife left him because she considered him mad. He had told her that he hoped she and the child they were expecting would die. She recorded: "He used to get up almost every night, and walk up and down the long Gallery in a state of horror and agitation which led me to apprehend he would realize his repeated threats of Suicide." When he got into bed with her, he would tell her, "'Don't touch me'—in a voice of raging detestation." He also dropped hints about his incestuous relationship with his half-sister.

The divorce and accompanying scandal drove Byron into permanent exile from England.

The French poet Verlaine, who was imprisoned for beating his mother, beat his wife and once bit through her cheek. He also slashed her with a knife, tried to strangle her, and nearly killed his infant son by throwing him against a wall. He left his wife to become the lover of Rimbaud, but this relationship was also violent. Verlaine shot Rimbaud through the wrist, and on another occasion, his lover cut Verlaine several times with a knife.

Some of the husbands, wives, and lovers of creative people have attempted suicide, as did the second husband of the English novelist George Eliot. He jumped into the Grand Canal in Venice. Rossetti's wife killed herself with opium.

Having a creative manic-depressive in the family has rarely been an unmitigated delight. Wagner's brother Albert once wrote to him: "I am used to seeing you respect people only if and *as long as* they can be useful to you; when the usefulness is over, the person also no longer exists for you. . . . Greatly as I value and love your talent, it is just the opposite as regards your character." Thomas de Quincey's oddities were a trial to his daughters. He occasionally set things, including his hair, on fire. When a daughter remarked, "Papa, your hair is on fire," he replied, "Is it, my love?" and absently rubbed the fire out with his hand. He piled his papers until every piece of furniture and every inch of floor were covered with them, leaving only a clear path to the door. He called this process "snowing up." When a room reached that condition, de Quincey locked the door and left it forever. He did this to six rooms.

In his study of genius, Francis Galton observed, "I have been surprised at finding out how often insanity . . . has appeared among the near relatives of exceptionally able men." Often one finds that the family member also has manic-depression, a common occurrence with this disorder. Byron said of his mother, "My poor mother was generally in a rage every day, and used to render me sometimes almost frantic." Both of the parents of the French writer Chateaubriand suffered from depression, and he became suicidal. Johnson's friend and biographer James Boswell, an alcoholic manic-depressive, had a brother and daughter who became psychotic.

Three generations of mental disturbance appear in the family of the French novelist George Sand. She was suicidal during her youth, and her father had suicidal tendencies. Her mother was delusional, believing that a Spanish doctor had removed the eyes of her infant son. When the baby died some time later, she thought he had been buried alive. Life among her grandchildren was not exactly serene. Sand was hit in the chest while trying to intervene when her son-in-law tried to hit her son with a hammer, and only the strenuous efforts of some guests prevented her son from shooting her son-in-law.

Many creative people have family members who are hospitalized for mental illness. The English writer Charles Lamb became psychotic during his adolescence but recalled it "with a gloomy kind of envy, for while it lasted, I had many hours of pure happiness." During his mania, he had to be confined. His sister became violently manic one day and attacked her aunt, mother, and father with a knife. Her mother and aunt died, and she was hospitalized intermittently for the rest of her life. When Lamb took her on trips during her good periods, he packed a straitjacket, never knowing when she would worsen. Henry James's father had a breakdown during which he saw "a damned shape squatting near" that kept him company for nearly two years. One of his sons, Bob, had a breakdown; William was suicidal and hallucinated; and his sister, also suicidal, had her first breakdown before she was eighteen. She died in an asylum.

The French novelist Victor Hugo had a brother who spent many years in an asylum, dying there at thirty-seven. The writer's daughter, after many years of psychosis, died in an asylum too. Robert Schumann's sister was psychotic when she died at the age of twenty-one. Goethe's sister was completely immobilized by depression for two years and died in a psychotic condition at the age of twenty-seven. Emerson, who had a brother who died while psychotic, called insanity "the constitutional calamity of my family." Sometimes the illness has culminated in suicide. The American writer Melville had a son who, after quarrelling with his father, shot and killed himself. Edison's son, an alcoholic manic-depressive, was hospitalized for mental illness and killed himself some years later.

Loneliness is a not-unusual complaint of creative people. The Austrian composer Franz Schubert, despite his many friends, lamented: "Every night when I go to sleep I hope never to wake again, and each morning I am only recalled to the griefs of yesterday. So I pass my days joyless and friendless." Clearly, depression colored his perception, but some manic-depressives do isolate themselves and become lonely. The Dutch writer Erasmus declared: "I have always wished to be alone . . . [I am] the most miserable of men, the thrice-wretched Erasmus." Nietzsche said: "I have 43 years behind me and am as alone as if I were a child." He never marrried, as is the case with many creative manic-depressives. Carlyle, who married but kept aloof from his wife, also complained: "My isolation, my feelings of loneliness . . . what tongue shall say? Alone, Alone!"

Depression makes some creative people withdraw from others, while paranoia makes others flee their former companions. Rossetti suspected all of his friends in his last years and saw no one. Heine first describes his depression and paranoia and then passes judgment on both: "Sick, alone, persecuted, unable to enjoy life—that's how I live here. Nowadays I write practically nothing. . . . I have almost no friends. A pack of scoundrels have allied themselves with all my would-be friends, etc." "Everywhere I hear my name, followed by derisive laughter." Later Heine sees the unreality of his delusions: "My inner life was nothing but brooding and immersion in the gloomy pits of a dream world, occasionally lighted up by fantastic lightening flashes." A Renaissance Italian painter, Francisci Bassano, died of his paranoia. In a severe depression, he fled his friends, servants, and the imaginary police and jumped out of a window to his death.

Mania can also create solitude around the person afflicted by it. Byron complained: "My friends are dead or estranged, and my existence a dreary void. I am quite alone, as these long letters sadly testify." Yet his charm, wit, good looks, and fame drew people to him. If they did not stay it was because, as he warned some of them, "When you know me better, you will find that I am the most selfish person in the world." The genius, as conceived by the Romantics, came to be known as a monster of selfishness, and often enough, a creative, egotistical manic-depressive came along to keep the image fresh. Heine said of Victor Hugo: "Almost all his old friends have abandoned him, and to tell the truth, it is through his own fault they have done so, because it is his egotism that has affronted them." The French painter Degas drove friends away with other manic characteristics. He was opinionated and said what he liked, regardless of whom he hurt. He never married, was contemptuous of women, and was very lonely.

In part, this loneliness results from the obnoxious behavior of some manics. The grandiose manic, overestimating his achievements, finds no appreciation sufficient. Insisting that he alone knows what is true and how things should be done, he is impossible to work with. He ends by dividing the world into two groups, his sycophants and his enemies.

THE HAZARDS OF SUCCESS

Success and fame may be enjoyable when they arrive, but they interfere with creativity in numerous ways. Elizabeth Barrett Browning describes the treatment given to George Sand, "Crowds of badly educated men adore her on their knees." Time given to receiving homage is largely time wasted and lost to creativity. Furthermore, for some, such attentions can become addicting. Byron, who was an idol before scandal caught up with him, attests to this: "A successful work makes a man a wretch for life: it engenders in him a thirst for notoriety and praise, that precludes the possibility of repose; this spurs him to attempt others, which are always expected to be superior to the first." He points to one of the pressures that success imposes: the need for greater success with each work. Fear of falling short can prevent people from producing anything at all and, at the very least, makes any creative effort much more difficult.

Arrival at the summits of success can place obstacles in the way of creativity by insulating people from the input they need to continue working. This is seen in the cases of many writers who, on becoming famous, leave the milieu and the people who furnished the material for their work. Thenceforth, they live the rarefied existence of the celebrity and are cut off from the larger world and its concerns, with their work becoming increasingly artificial and irrelevant. This is one of the reasons why, for many writers, their best novel is the first successful one.

By destroying the privacy and freedom from distraction needed for creative work, fame presents an additional obstacle. Loss of privacy is particularly trying for shy depressives like Tchaikovsky, who said: "I desire with all my soul that my music should be more widely known. . . . In this sense not only do I love fame, but it becomes the aim of all that is most earnest in my work. But alas! . . . the thought that someone may try to force the inner world of my thoughts and feelings, which all my life I have guarded so carefully from outsiders—this is sad and terrible. There is a tragic element . . . in this conflict between the desire for fame and the fear of its consequences."

The creative individual, even when he is not shy, is caught in a cruel dilemma. In order for him to fulfill his function as a creator, his work must find its audience. As Picasso observed, "Success is an important thing! It has often been said that an artist should work for himself, for the love of art, and scorn success. It is a false idea. An artist needs success. Not only to live, but primarily so that he can realize his work." However, if his success passes a certain point, it destroys the very conditions essential for him to continue his efforts. Picasso in his later years had to hide from the public. He said then, "Of all—hunger, extreme poverty, the incomprehension of the public—fame is by far the worst. It is the castigation by God of the artist."

The most damaging effect of fame, because it is the most difficult to remedy, is what it does to the character of the creative individual. It can bring out the worst in the manic-depressive. When the eighteenth-century French writer Voltaire was in his heyday, a contemporary says, "It was the custom for ladies to become agitated, grow pale, and even faint . . . ; they threw themselves into his arms, stammered and wept and adored." The treatment given to celebrities has not improved with time. It is difficult for most people to receive passionate adulation without becoming egotistical and grandiose; for the manic it is almost impossible. In his growing arrogance, not only does he domineer shamelessly, but he loses the ability to criticize himself and his work, or to learn from criticism, and thus ceases to grow. Success and fame may also make him increasingly manic, even to the point of precipitating psychosis.

8

Augmenting Genius

According to tradition, creative individuals must suffer beyond what ordinary mortals endure on the assumption that suffering is essential to creativity. The poet de Musset insisted: "Those who afford us our highest intellectual pleasures and our sweetest consolations appear doomed to weariness and melancholy." Some have held, as did the Goncourt brothers, that the suffering caused by mental illness is the price one must pay for creativity. "Talent," the Goncourts said, "exists only at the cost of our nervous condition." Manic-depression can give immense advantages to the creative person, but not when the disorder is in its more intense phases. Then it not only causes suffering, but the pathological behavior and the other problems it produces also tend to reduce both the quantity and quality of creative work. These problems can be mitigated or avoided if creative manic-depressives are spared the more intense states of the disorder. Some creative manic-depressives could become more productive were they to spend more of their lives within milder limits of mania and depression.

WHEN MOOD ENHANCES CREATIVITY

Mild mania and depression are the best states for creativity because they increase both the quantity of completed work and its quality. The American molecular chemist Paul Saltman describes the enthusiasm and productive energy of mild mania: "I really feel terrific. I just run down to the laboratory in the morning and just jump in. . . . I just want to get as much done every day as we possibly can." The milder states of mania allow one to be more disciplined and less impulsive than do severer states, thus improving the chances of carrying work to completion. Milder states induce less of the impatience and distractibility that interfere with work. During Nietzsche's milder states of mania, he says, "I used to walk through the hills 7 or 8 hours on end without a hint of fatigue," and "My creative energy flowed most freely." Had the mania been more intense, he would have had insomnia, but he says, "I slept well, laughed a good deal—I was perfectly vigorous and patient."

Patience is one of the contributions mild mania makes to quality. The person who is only mildly manic works quickly, but attends to details as well as to larger factors. He is inventive and resourceful but does not take as many foolish chances as the manic. He is also freer of the delusions of mania, better able to be realistic about his work and to correct it. Boswell reports that Johnson exemplified this: "When in a good humor, he would talk of his own writings with a wonderful frankness and candour, and would even criticize them with the closest severity."

Mild depression also contributes to creativity. It is not as fecund as mild mania, but it does not reduce the output of work below normal levels. Mozart attests, "I have done more work in 10 days since I came to these rooms than in 2 months at any other lodgings, and were I not visited so frequently by black thoughts (which I must forcibly banish), I should do still better." Some people are incited to higher productivity by mild depression. They may work from a sense of duty, which is intensified in mild depression, or they may use work to distract them from sadness. Mild depression can enhance the quality of work by making the creative person highly sensitive to criticism. To avoid the pain of negative comment, he becomes exceedingly careful and thorough, a perfectionist constantly looking for mistakes to correct.

The person who fluctuates between mild depression and mild mania profits from the best of both states. He is imaginative, original, insightful, conscientious, and willing to keep working until no further improvement can be made. His work is likely to be rich, deeply felt, of great range and scope, balanced between strength and subtlety.

MOOD CONTROL

The adroit administration of mood-stabilizing medications can help manic-depressives increase the time they spend creatively, and so can their choice of activities. Both are very individual matters: what is best for one person might not succeed with another.

Many creative manic-depressives have attempted to reduce their depressions to a tolerable level. Samuel Johnson gave considerable thought to this matter. He said, "To have the management of the mind is a great art, and it may be attained in a considerable degree by experience and habitual exercise." This is true only when mania or depression has not advanced too far. Johnson recommended distraction as one remedy for depression: "Let him [the depressed person] continue to have as many retreats for his mind as he can, as many things to which it can fly from itself." Johnson was also an advocate of exercise, moderation in eating—which he rarely practiced—and moderation in drink, in which he did not always succeed. "I have drunk many a bottle by myself," he said, "in the first place, because I had need of it to raise my spirits; in the second place, because I would have nobody to witness its effects upon me." He also would cheer himself by visiting the actresses at his friend David Garrick's theater. This, however, was too stimulating. "I'll come no more behind your scenes, David," he said, "for the silk stockings and white bosoms of your actresses excite my amorous propensities."

Michelangelo, who was often burdened by depression, found that a dinner party banished a dark mood: "This gave me exceeding great pleasure, since it drew me forth a little from my melancholy, or shall we call it my mad mood, not only did I enjoy the supper, which was most agreeable, but far more the conversation." Byron was not satisfied to escape depression and sought to invoke the excitement of mania. He suggested that one turn "to gaming—to battle—to travel—to intemperate, but keenly felt pursuits of any description, whose principal attraction is the agitation inseparable from their accomplishment." French painter Géricault claimed that the right attitude to the right event can generate a fertile mania: "If obstacles discourage the mediocre talent, they are, on the contrary, the necessary food of genius; they ripen and exalt it. . . . Everything that opposes the triumphant progress of genius irritates it, and induces that fever of exaltation that overthrows and conquers all to produce its masterpieces." Some manic-depressives who are not creative also respond to challenges, or even to crises, with a manic episode.

The friends of the Italian painter Carlo Dolci tried to rouse him from a depression so severe that he had completely lost faith in himself as an artist and no longer spoke to anyone. They begged him in vain to take a trip to the country. Finally, one of them brought Dolci's priest into their conspiracy. The priest insisted that Dolci finish part of a painting of the Virgin Mary, while a friend presented the painter with brushes and a prepared palette. The work turned out so well that the depression vanished. Work has long been recognized as a way to alleviate depression, and many creative manic-depressives experience mild manias from the process of working, provided they can become deeply involved in it. Stephen Spender observed, "There is no doubt that writing poetry, when a poem appears to succeed, results in an intense physical excitement, a sense of release and ecstasy." Even if the work is not a splendid success, one may still experience a rise of spirits while doing it.

Some creative people spend their ingenuity on moderating mania rather than depression. Wagner was one of these. He found that going to parties without his wife, and getting drunk at them, made him manic. He noted: "The extraordinary bird-like freedom of my existence has the effect of exciting me more and more. I was often frightened by the excessive outbursts of exaltation to which I was prone." He learned that the life of a conductor, with its pressured rehearsals and stimulating performances, made him intolerably manic. He said, "How little I am able to endure the permanent excitement which would be involved in my frequent public experiences I know full well." At times he was so manic that he had to ration the hours he spent working, for fear of becoming too excited to work at all: "Nowadays my nerves are so upset that if I work 2 hours before midday, I have to spend all the rest of the day and night carefully recovering from these 2 tempestuous hours in order to fit myself for another 2 hours' work the next day. I have to fear, and avoid, the least effort or excitement: I dare not read or do anything else to excite my brain."

FITTING WORK PHASE TO MOOD

The creative manic-depressive who cannot manage to stay within the milder states may find that some productive work can still be done in the more intense stages of depression and mania. However, as Wagner realized, mania can become too intense for one to remain in control of oneself or one's work. It can also increase one's desire to see people and have fun and seduce one from creativity. A poem, or some other work that can be completed during a fever of inspiration, may be a suitable project during mania, as is anything that gives outlet to the manic's need for physical activity. Nevertheless, any project requiring discipline, concentration, and protracted effort will be more safely done during mild mania.

The phases of creative work that are generally best done during mania are the conceptual and early phases, when confidence and a ready flow of ideas are most serviceable. The American mathematician Morris Kline describes a symptom of mania, the flight of ideas that can assist in creation: "Approaches and ideas are likely to occur with such rapidity and suddenness that one can't pursue each one seriously at the moment. A good thing to do is to jot these ideas down so as not to lose sight of them." Aaron Copland is familiar with this fertile flood during composition. "Writers probably have this same problem of writing fast enough so that they can get it all down while they are under the spell," he says. "You have a fear that you may be going to lose it at any moment. Outside interruption is definitely out. In music you have to get it down on score paper. Otherwise you might forget it." Such floods of ideas occur only during mania and are least chaotic during mild states.

Kline uses depression for revision. "A depressed state," he says, "affects one's willingness to think. One can force oneself to work only on something that's more routine or that really was worked out before and needs revision." He is speaking of something more intense than mild depression, for in that state creative thought is still possible.

A sufficiently painful depression may make one so critical that not even revision should be attempted. George Sand describes the Polish composer Chopin, first in hypomanic creativity, and then in a sabotaging depression:

> His creation was spontaneous, miraculous. It came to him without search or prescience, it came on his piano, sudden, complete, sublime, or it sang in his head during a walk; and he hurried back to hear it by throwing it on the piano, but then began the most heart-breaking labor I have ever seen. . . . He analyzed too much when he wanted to write it, and his regret at not finding it what he considered perfect threw him into despair. He would shut himself in his room for whole days, weeping, walking up and down, breaking his pens, repeating or changing a measure a hundred times, writing and defacing it as many times, and beginning again the next day with despairing and minute perseverance. He would spend six weeks on a single page.

Milder depression can be quite fertile and much less painful. Freud was among those who find a mild depression the best state for work, because it favors concentration and dedication. It is also the best state for polishing work and for the large-scale, critical review of one's work that points the way to new directions for growth.

Some creative manic-depressives have learned, by trial and error, to fit the phase of work to the mood they are in at the moment. It helps if one has regular mood cycles and can discover what time of day, month, or year is most likely to bring depressions or manias. The Italian writer Vittorio Alfieri believed that his moods varied with the hour, the season, and atmospheric conditions. He said, "I have always experienced more or less facility in writing according to the weight of the air—absolute stupidity in the great solstitial and equinoctal winds, infinitely less perspicacity in the evening than in the morning, and a much greater aptness for creation in the middle of winter and of summer than in the intermediate seasons." Goethe may not have been aware of periodicity in his moods, but he learned to use them nonetheless. He dedicated periods of mild mania to conceiving his works and spent days of mild depression attending to his business affairs.

Advantage can be taken of mood instability by checking the errors and defects of one mood when the opposite one arrives. Some creative manic-depressives have several works in progress in different stages, so that when depression arrives, in which work can be corrected, something in progress needs that attention, and when mania brings its cornucopia of ideas, a project in need of them awaits.

Tainted Verdicts

When mania lingers on beyond a work's completion it can skew the assessment of what has been accomplished. The writer Arthur Koestler notes, "You sometimes have false inspirations, and you write something in a state of euphoria, and the next day you look at it and it's lousy." A postmanic depression can be equally deceptive. Wagner could be overly critical when depressed. "Recently I glanced through my score of *Lohengrin,*" he confesses, "it filled me absolutely with disgust, and my intermittent fits of laughter were not of a cheerful kind." The American novelist Henry James observed: "Our judgments are all dictated by feeling—a feeling of undue elation or undue depression, and the verdict we come to is apt to be preposterous in either case alike."

Yet one cannot escape the necessity to make judgments about one's work, regardless of the distortions caused by intense moods. Mistaken opinions can be somewhat reduced by sinking anchors in external reality. The creative manic-depressive can attempt to be logical and list the reasons for his verdict in order to ascertain whether any of them have a basis other than his own mood of the moment. He is at an advantage if he waits until his mood changes to determine whether or not his judgment changes with it.

Some manic-depressives have been helped by the opinion of trustworthy, objective, and knowledgeable people. Thomas Wolfe was saved from despair over his work and received encouragement to complete it from his editor, Maxwell Perkins. Wolfe reports:

> A terrible doubt began to creep into my mind that . . . I had created a labor so large and impossible that the energy of a dozen lifetimes would not suffice for its accomplishment. During this time, however, I was sustained by one piece of inestimable good fortune. I had for a friend a man of immense and patient wisdom and a gentle but unyielding fortitude. I think that if I was not destroyed at this time by a sense of hopelessness . . . it was largely because of the patience and courage of this man.

Wolfe was unable to tell when he had written enough, so Perkins made this judgment for him. The editor arranged for the book's printing to begin while the author, uninformed, was away for two weeks.

Removing Blocks and Stimulating Creativity

The English writer Charlotte Bronte had to wait through long periods when it was better not to write. She told her fellow writer Harriet Martineau: "I think I would rather hire myself out again as a governess than write against the mood. I am not like you, who have no bad days. I have bad days, bad weeks, aye! bad months." Few and fortunate are those who have never felt their creativity blocked. Sometimes a remedy can be found. First, it is important to try to determine what is causing the block. The conditions in which one is trying to work may be unsuitable, and what is suitable depends very much on the individual. The Italian painter Vasari needed quiet and stated that the person who "wants to work well must keep away from cares and worries since mastery requires thought, solitude, and a tranquil, not a distracted mind." Kline holds that a mathematician must be fresh: "If he is tired . . . he will find that ideas do not present themselves."

Both a painful but alert depression and a stuporous depression can be the source of a creative block. The Scottish inventor James Watt was blocked by depressions in which he experienced a failing memory, as well as "laziness, stupefaction, and confusion of ideas." These are symptoms of a stuporous depression and signal that only the simplest, most mechanical work, if any, can be done. Pushkin was prey to the more active, but more painful, type of depression. He wrote, "Yesterday I was so depressed that I don't recall ever feeling anything like it." As a result of it, he wrote, "I am working slowly and with bad grace. The last few days I have had a headache and boredom has been gnawing at me." Picasso could become so depressed by external events or conditions that he would stop painting. Selling his work could bring on a depressive block at times.

Mania itself can lead to a depression that prevents or impedes creative effort. Byron would become manic in company and then fall into depression when the company was gone. He says: "An animated conversation has much the same effect on me as champagne—it elevates and makes me giddy, and I say a thousand foolish things while under its intoxicating influence . . . and I sink, under reaction, into a state of depression." Many creative manic-depressives, having worked intensely and tó the point of exhaustion during mania, lapse into a stuporous, anxious, or combined type of depression, as did Keats. He reports: "I went day by day at my poem for a month; at the end of which time . . . I found my brain so overwrought, that I had neither rhyme nor reason in it, so was obliged to give up for a few days. . . . Instead of poetry I have a swimming in my head, and feel the effects of a mental debauch, lowness of spirits, anxiety to go on, without the power to do so." Hawthorne was felled by a similar block. "I have been in a Slough of Despond," he says, "for some days past, and have written so fiercely that I came to a stand-still." It is particularly painful when manic creativity departs and crippling depression takes over before the work is completed. Many creative manic-depressives are surprised when the sense of accomplishment they expect to feel on completing a work is undermined by depression.

Some creative people take on their blocks and less productive phases as challenges to ingenuity and, regardless of mood, are always looking for ways to stimulate creativity. One means they employ is to try to increase the input on which their work depends. Scientists and scholars may benefit from the method Kline uses to generate mathematical ideas. He says: "Reading related material may be the best way to get the mind started on a new channel of thought and because the reading is related, this new thought may be the right one." The chemist Saltman gets stimulation from other people and from the instruments with which he works. "I really need someone else working with me who presents new ideas," he says, "or I need to find a new instrument to try out our problem, or I need to see an article by someone else in which I find the germ of an idea."

Another approach combines activities that raise one's mood with the elimination of distraction. Tchaikovsky was devoted to his evening walk, which he took alone. Then, says his brother, "He thought out the leading ideas, pondered over the construction of the work, and jotted down fundamental themes. The next morning he looked over these notes, and worked them out at the piano." Mozart found that solitude and the mood-raising activities of walking or traveling were good for musical flights of ideas. If he was already somewhat manic and unable to sleep, solitude permitted him to focus his thoughts on music: "When I am, as it were, completely myself, entirely alone, and of good cheer— say, travelling in a carriage, or walking after a good meal, or during the night when I cannot sleep; it is on such occasions that my ideas flow best and most abundantly."

Although lithium salts and antidepressant drugs have been intensively studied in terms of their therapeutic effects on mania and depression, relatively little attention has been focused on the ability of these agents to enhance creative intelligence. Mogens Schou, a prominent lithium researcher, interviewed twenty-four creative manic-depressives who had been treated with lithium. Half reported experiencing greater creativity while taking the medication. Additional research in this area would be of great interest.

GENIUS OR TYRANT?

There are some fundamental differences between manic-depressives who become tyrants and those who become geniuses. In our volume *Power Beyond Reason,* we explore the relationship between manic-depression and tyranny. The tyrant is a grandiose, paranoid manic-depressive who decides to pursue power and has an opportunity to do so in a country amenable to autocratic government. By contrast, the genius is a talented manic-depressive who chooses a career in a creative field, undergoes appropriate training, and produces work that is highly valued. Some people have the potential for both.

Geniuses such as Newton can be grandiose, paranoid manic-depressives who also develop tyrannical personalities. Tyrants like Hitler and Mao Tse-

Tung can develop interests in the arts and may also possess some creative ability. Hitler always claimed that he preferred art to politics. Had he been accepted into the Vienna Academy of Arts and won some success as an artist, he might have refrained from political activity altogether. Rubens combined a highly lucrative career as a painter with a successful career as a diplomat. Chance determines the type and degree of a manic-depressive's talent, the type and degree of his illness, and the career choices and opportunities open to him. Chance thus determines whether he will be a genius or a tyrant, if, indeed, he becomes either one.

Those who savor the fruits of creativity and wish to avoid the perils of having delusional dictators running amok need not leave the outcome entirely to chance. Awareness of the need to withold from grandiose, paranoid manic-depressives the opportunity to prey upon their countrymen and endanger the world will improve the prospects of a safe future. An increased understanding of the problems, as well as the assets, that manic-depression brings to creative people will make it easier for them to realize their potential.

TOWARD GREATER CREATIVITY

Whatever raises creative people to greater productivity and higher levels of achievement increases the likelihood that they will produce work that society values. Changes in attitude would of themselves create a better climate for creativity and genius. Many creative manic-depressives could benefit from losing their fear that their gifts would vanish if their moods were moderated. Their creativity and lives might improve were people who know them to encourage them to seek appropriate treatment for the destructive phases of their illness. A change in attitude is needed, no less within the medical profession than in society at large, towards viewing the potential value of lithium and antidepressants as enhancers of intelligence and creativity, rather than as remedies for illness alone.

Bibliography

Andreasen, N. C. "Creativity and Mental Illness: Prevalence Rates in Writers and Their First Degree Relatives." *American Journal of Psychiatry* 144 (1987): 1288-1292.

Atlas, James. *Delmore Schwartz: The Life of an American Poet.* New York: Avon Books, 1977.

Babbitt, Irving. *Rousseau and Romanticism.* Boston: Houghton Mifflin Co., Inc., 1947.

Barzun, Jacques. *Berlioz and the Romantic Century.* Boston: Little, Brown and Co., Inc., 1950.

———. *Romanticism and the Modern Ego.* Boston: Little, Brown and Co., Inc., 1945.

Bate, Walter Jackson. *The Achievement of Samuel Johnson.* New York: Oxford Press, 1961.

———. *Coleridge.* New York: Collier Books, 1973.

———. *From Classic to Romantic.* New York: Harper and Bros., 1961.

Beethoven, Ludwig. *Beethoven's Letters.* Edited by A. C. Kalishcher. New York: Dover Publications, Inc., 1972.

———. *The Letters of Beethoven.* Edited and translated by Emily Anderson. 3 vols. New York: St. Martin's Press, 1961.

———. *New Beethoven Letters.* Translated by Donald W. MacArdle and Ludwig Misch. Oklahoma: University of Oklahoma Press, 1957.

Behrs, C. A. *Recollections of Count Leo Tolstoy.* Translated by Charles Edward Turner. London: William Heinemann, 1893.

Bell, E. T. *Men of Mathematics.* New York: Simon and Schuster, 1965.

Bell, Quentin. *Virginia Woolf: A Biography.* New York: Harcourt Brace Jovanovich, Inc., 1972.

Belmaker, Robert H., and Van Praag, H. M. *Mania: An Evolving Concept.* New York: S. P. Medical and Scientific Books, 1980.

Berlioz, Hector. *Hector Berlioz: A Selection From His Letters.* Edited and translated by Humphrey Searle. New York: Vienna House, 1973.

———. *The Memoirs of Hector Berlioz.* Edited and translated by David Cairns. New York: Norton Press, 1975.

Bernbaum, Ernest. *Guide Through the Romantic Movement.* New York: The Ronald Press Co., 1949.

Bernstein, Jeremy. *Experiencing Science.* New York: Basic Books, Inc., 1978.

Birkenhead, Lord. *Rudyard Kipling.* New York: Random House, 1978.

Bittner, William. *Poe: A Biography.* Boston: Atlantic-Little, Brown, 1962.

Blair, Dierdre. *Samuel Beckett: A Biography.* New York: Harcourt Brace Jovanovich, 1978.

Blake, William. *The Portable Blake.* Edited by Alfred Kazin. New York: Viking Press, 1959.

Blessington, Lady. *Conversations of Lord Byron.* Edited by Ernest J. Lovell, Jr. Princeton, N.J.: Princeton University Press, 1969.

Boswell, James. *The Life of Samuel Johnson.* Edited by C. P. Chadsey. Garden City, N.Y.: Doubleday and Co., Inc., 1946.

Bowen, W. H. *Charles Dickens and His Family.* Cambridge, England: W. Heffer and Sons, Ltd., 1956.

Bowle, John. *The English Experience.* New York: Capricorn Books, 1972.

Brain, Lord Russell. *Some Reflections on Genius.* New York: Pitman Medical Publishing Co., 1960.

———. "Authors and Psychopaths." *British Medical Journal* 7 (1949): 1427.

Brandes, George. *Voltaire.* New York: Tudor Publishing Co., 1934.

Brasol, Boris. *Oscar Wilde The Man, The Artist, The Martyr.* New York: Charles Scribner's Sons, 1938.

Brewster, Sir David. *Memoirs of the Life, Writings, and Discoveries of Sir Isaac Newton.* 2 vols. Edinburgh, Scotland: Thomas Constable and Co., 1855.

Brod, Max. *Franz Kafka: A Biography.* Translated by G. Humphrey Roberts and Richard Winston. New York: Schocken Books, 1973.

Browne, Lewis, and Weihl, Elsa. *That Man Heine: A Biography.* New York: The MacMillan Co., Inc., 1929.

Bulgakov, V. F. *The Last Years of Tolstoy.* Translated by Ann Dunnigan. New York: Dial Press, 1971.

Burr, Anna Robeson. *Alice James: Her Brothers—Her Journal.* New York: Dodd, Mead and Co., 1935.

Burton, Elizabeth. *The Pageant of Early Victorian England.* New York: Charles Scribner's Sons, 1972.

Butscher, Edward. *Sylvia Plath: Method and Madness.* New York: The Seabury Press, 1976.

Byron, Lord George. *Byron's Letters.* London: Walter Scott, 1886.

——. *Letters and Journals of Lord Byron: With Notices of His Life.* Edited by Thomas Moore. 3 vols. London: John Murray, 1833.

——. *The Works of Lord Byron: Letters and Journals.* Edited by Rowland E. Prothero. 6 vols. New York: Charles Scribner's Sons, 1904.

Cabanne, Pierre, *Van Gogh.* Translated by Daphne Woodward. New York: Praeger Publications, 1963.

Carlyle, Thomas. *On Heroes and Hero Worship, and the Heroic in History.* Boston: Ginn and Co., 1902.

Carr, Virginia Spencer. *The Lonely Heart: A Biography of Carson McCullers.* Garden City, N.Y.: Doubleday and Co., Inc., 1975.

Chapman, John S. *Byron and the Honourable Augusta Leigh.* New Haven: Yale University Press, 1975.

"Characteristics of Men of Genius," selected chiefly from the *North American Review.* London: John Chapman, 1864.

Chateaubriand, Francois René. *The Memoirs of Chateaubriand.* Edited and translated by Robert Baldick, New York: Alfred Knopf, 1961.

Chekhov, Anton. *Anton Chekhov's Life and Thought: Selected Letters and Commentary.* Translated by Michael Henry Hein and Simon Karlinsky. Berkeley, Calif.: University of California Press, 1975.

Chopin, Frederick. *Chopin's Letters.* Edited by Henryk Opienski. Translated by E. L. Voynich. New York: Vienna House, 1973.

Christianson, Gale E. *In The Presence of The Creator: Isaac Newton and His Times.* New York: MacMillan, Inc., 1984.

Clark, [Sir] George. *The Seventeenth Century.* New York: The Oxford Press, 1961.

Clark, Ronald W. *Edison: The Man Who Made The Future.* New York: G. P. Putnam's Sons, 1977.

Conot, Robert. *A Streak of Luck: The Life and Legend of Thomas Alva Edison.* New York: Seaview Books, 1979.

Craddock, Thomas. *Rousseau as Described by Himself and Others.* London: Arthur Hall and Co., 1877.

Craft, Robert. *Stravinsky: Chronology of a Friendship 1948–1971. New York: Random House, 1973.*

Crick, Bernard. George Orwell: A Life. Boston: Little, Brown and Co, Inc., 1980.

Cruikshank, R. J. *Charles Dickens and Early Victorian England.* London: Sir Isaac Pitman and Sons, Ltd., 1949.

Dallas, R. C. *Recollections of the Life of Lord Byron.* London: Charles Knight, 1824.

David, Hans T., and Mendel, Arthur, eds. *The Bach Reader*. New York. W. W. Norton and Co., Inc., 1966.

Davies, Stan Gebler. *James Joyce: A Portrait of the Artist*. New York: Stein and Day, 1975.

Delacroix, Eugene. *The Journal of Eugene Delacroix*. Translated by Walter Pack. New York: Covici-Friede Publishers, 1937.

Dickens, Charles. *Charles Dickens' Letters to Charles Lever*. Edited by Flore V. Livingston. Cambridge, Mass.: Harvard University Press, 1933.

———. *Dickens to His Oldest Friends*. Edited by Walter Dexter. London: Putnam, 1932.

———. *The Letters of Charles Dickens*. Edited by Madeline House, Graham Storey, and Kathleen Tillotson. Oxford: Clarendon Press, 1974.

———. *The Letters of Charles Dickens* Edited by Walter Dexter. 3 vols. Bloomsbury: The Nonesuch Press, 1938.

———. *The Letters of Charles Dickens to Wilkie Collins*. Edited by Lawrence Hutton. New York: Harper and Bros. Publishers, 1892.

———. *The Love Romance of Charles Dickens*. Notes by Walter Dexter. London: Argonaut Press, 1936.

———. *Mr. and Mrs. Charles Dickens: His Letters to Her*. Edited by Walter Dexter. London: Constable and Co., Ltd., 1935.

———. *The Selected Letters of Charles Dickens*. Edited by F. W. Dupee. New York: Farrar, Straus, and Cudahy, Inc., 1960.

———. *The Unpublished Letters of Charles Dickens to Mark Lemon*. Edited by Walter Dexter. London: Halton and Truscott Smith, Ltd., 1927.

Dickens, Mamie. *My Father as I Recall Him*. New York: E. P. Dutton and Co.

Dolby, George. *Charles Dickens as I Knew Him*. London: T. Fisher Unwin, 1887.

Dostoyevsky, F. M. "The Diary of a Writer." Translated by Boris Brasol. New York: George Brasiller, 1954.

Edwards, Anne. *Vivien Leigh*. New York: Pocket Books, 1977.

Einstein, Alfred. *Music in the Romantic Era*. New York: W. W. Norton and Co., Inc., 1947.

Elgar, Frank. *Van Gogh*. Translated by James Cleugh. New York: Frederick A. Praeger, Publishers, 1966.

Ellis, Havelock. *A Study of British Genius*. New York: Houghton Mifflin Co., 1926.

Ellman, Richard. *James Joyce*. New York: Oxford University Press, 1982.

Elsna, Hebe. *Unwanted Wife: A Defense of Mrs. Charles Dickens*. London: Jarrolds, 1963.

Elwin, Malcolm. *Lord Byron's Wife*. New York: Harcourt, Brace and World, Inc., 1963.

D'Épinay. *Memoirs and Correspondence of Madame D'Épinay.* Translated by J. H. Freese. London: H. S. Nichols, Ltd., 1899.

Fido, Martin. *Charles Dickens.* London: The Hamlin Publishing Group.

Fields, James T. *Yesterdays With Authors.* Boston: Houghton, Mifflin and Co., 1900.

Fieve, Ronald R. *Moodswing: The Third Revolution in Psychiatry.* New York: Bantam, 1979.

Finney, Theodore M. *A History of Music.* New York: Harcourt, Brace and Co., 1950.

Fitsgibbon, Constantine. *The Life of Dylan Thomas.* Boston: Little, Brown and Co., Inc., 1956.

Forster, John. *The Life of Charles Dickens.* 2 vols. London: Chapman and Hall, Ltd., 1904.

Fowler, Gene. *Good Night, Sweet Prince: The Life and Times of John Barrymore.* New York: Viking Press, 1944.

Frye, Northrop. *Romanticism Reconsidered.* New York: Columbia University Press, 1966.

Furst, Lillian. *Romanticism in Perspective.* New York: St. Martin's Press, 1969.

Galton, Francis. *Hereditary Genius.* New York: World Publishing Co., 1962.

Gaskell, Elizabeth Cleghorn. *The Life of Charlotte Bronte.* London: J. M. Dent and Sons, 1971.

Gaunt, William. *The Pre-Raphaelite Dream.* New York: Schocken Books, 1972.

Gelb, Arthur, and Gelb, Barbara. *O'Neill.* New York: Harper and Brothers, 1962.

Gerin, Winifred. *Charlotte Bronte: The Evolution of Genius.* New York: Oxford University Press, 1969.

Gershon, Samuel, and Shopsin, Baron, eds. *Lithium: Its Role in Psychiatric Research and Treatment.* New York: Plenum Press, 1973.

Ghiselin, Brewster, ed. *The Creative Process.* New York: The New American Library, 1955.

Goertzel, Victor, and Goertzel, Mildred G. *Cradles of Eminence.* Boston: Little, Brown and Co., Inc., 1962.

Gogh, Vincent van. *The Complete Letters of Vincent van Gogh.* Translated by S. van Gogh-Bonger and C. de Dood. 3 vols. Greenwich, Conn.: New York Graphic Society, 1958.

Goldwater, Robert, and Treves, Marco, eds. *Artists on Art.* New York: Pantheon, 1945.

Good, Michael I. "Primary Affective Disorder, Aggression, and Criminality: A Review and Clinical Study." *Archives of General Psychiatry* 35 (1978).

Goncourt, Edmond de, and Goncourt, Jules de. *The Goncourt Journals 1851–1870.* Translated by Lewis Galantiere. Garden City, N.Y.: Doubleday-Anchor, 1958.

Gorky, Maxim. *The Autobiography of Maxim Gorky.* Translated by Isidor Schneider. Secaucus, N.J.: Citadel Press, 1973.

Graves, Alonso. *The Eclipse of a Mind.* New York: The Medical Journal Press, 1942.

Grimsley, Ronald. *Jean-Jacques Rousseau: A Study in Self-Awareness.* Cardiff, Wales: University of Wales Press, 1961.

Gulenno, Jean. *Jean Jacques Rousseau.* Translated by John and Doreen Weightman. 2 vols. New York: Columbia University Press, 1966.

Haight, Gordon S. *George Eliot: A Biography.* New York: Oxford University Press, 1968.

Hall, A. R. *The Scientific Revolution 1500–1800: The Formation of the Modern Scientific Attitude.* Boston: Beacon Press, 1954.

Hamilton, Ian. *Robert Lowell: A Biography.* New York: Random House, 1982.

Hanson, Lawrence, and Hanson, Elizabeth. *Noble Savage: The Life of Paul Gauguin.* New York: Random House, 1955.

Harding, James. *Gounod.* New York: Stein and Day, 1973.

Hayman, Ronald. *Kafka: A Biography.* New York: Oxford University Press, 1981.

Heine, Heinrich. *Heinrich Heine: Self-Portrait and Other Prose Writings.* Edited and translated by Frederick Ewen. Secaucus, N.J.: The Citadel Press, 1948.

Helge, Lundholm. *The Manic-depressive Psychosis.* Durham, N.C.: Duke University Press, 1931.

Heyman, C. David. *Ezra Pound: The Last Rower.* New York: Seaver Books, 1980.

Hibbert, Christopher. *The Making of Charles Dickens.* New York: Harper and Row, Publishers, 1967.

Houghton, Lord. *The Life and Letters of John Keats.* London: J. M. Dent and Sons, 1969.

Hussey, Dyneley. *Wolfgang Amade Mozart.* New York: Harper and Brothers, 1928.

James, Alice. *Alice James: Her Brothers—Her Journal.* Edited by Anna Robeson Burr. New York: Dodd, Mead and Co., 1935.

Johnson, Edgar. *Charles Dickens: His Tragedy and Triumph.* 2 vols. New York: Simon and Schuster, 1952.

———, ed. *The Heart of Charles Dickens.* Boston: Little, Brown and Co., 1952.

Jordan, Ruth. *Nocturne: A Life of Chopin.* New York: Taplinger Publishing Co., 1978.

Josephson, Mathew. *Jean Jacques Rousseau.* New York: Harcourt, Brace and Co., 1931.

———. *Stendhal: Or, the Pursuit of Happiness.* New York: Doubleday and Co., Inc., 1946.

Julian, Philippe. *Dreamers of Decadence.* Translated by Robert Baldick. New York: Praeger Publishers, 1971.

Kafka, Franz. *The Diaries of Franz Kafka 1910–1913.* Edited by Max Brod. Translated by Joseph Kresh. New York: Schocken Books, 1965.

———. *The Diaries of Franz Kafka 1914–1923.* Translated by Martin Greenberg. New York: Schocken Books, 1974.

———. *I Am A Memory Come Alive: Autobiographical Writings by Franz Kafka.* Edited by Nahum M. Glatzer. New York: Schocken Books, 1976.

———. *Letters to Felice.* Edited by Erich Heller and Jurgen Born. Translated by James Stern and Elizabeth Duckwood. New York: Schocken Books, 1973.

———. *Letters to Friends, Family and Editors.* Translated by Richard and Clara Winston. New York: Schocken Books, 1977.

———. *Letters to Milena.* Edited by Willi Hass. Translated by Tania and James Stern. New York: Schocken Books, 1953.

Kaplan, Bert, ed. *The Inner World of Mental Illness.* New York: Harper and Row, 1964.

Kaplan, Justin. *Walt Whitman: A Life.* New York: Simon and Schuster, 1980.

Kapp, Julius. *The Women in Wagner's Life.* Translated by Hannah Waller. New York: Alfred A. Knopf, 1931.

Karl, Frederick R. *Joseph Conrad: The Three Lives.* New York: Farrar, Straus and Giroux, 1979.

Kleist, Heinrich von. *The Major Works of Heinrich Von Kleist.* Edited by Robert E. Helbling. New York: New Directions Publishing Co., 1975.

Kraepelin, Emil. *Manic-Depressive Insanity and Paranoia.* Translated by R. Mary Barclay. Edited by George M. Robertson. Edinburgh, Scotland: E. and S. Livingstone, 1921.

Kretschmer, Ernst. *The Psychology of Men of Genius.* Translated by R. B. Cattell. New York: Harcourt, Brace and Co., 1931.

Kunitz, Stanley, J., and Colby, Vineta, eds. *European Authors 1000–1900.* New York: H. W. Wilson Co., 1967.

Lange-Eichbaum, Wilhelm. *The Problem of Genius.* Translated by Eden and Cedar Paul. New York: MacMillan Co., 1932.

Leinsdorf, Erich. *Cadenza: A Musical Career.* Boston: Houghton, Mifflin Co., 1976.

Logan, Joshua. *Josh: My Up and Down Life.* New York: Delacourt Press, 1976.

Longyear, Rey M. *19th Century Romanticism in Music*. Englewood Cliffs, N.J.: Prentice-Hall, Inc., 1969.

Ludwig, Emil. *Beethoven: Life of a Conqueror*. Translated by George Stewart McManus. New York: G. P. Putnam's Sons, 1943.

———. *Genius and Character*. Translated by Kenneth Burke. New York: Harcourt, Brace and Co., 1927.

———. *Goethe: The History of a Man*. Translated by Ethel Colburne Mayne. New York: G. P. Putnam's Sons, 1928.

Lundun, S. J. "Case Report of a Titan's Last Crisis." *Archives of Internal Medicine* 113 (1964): 442–48.

McCarthy, Patrick. *Camus*. New York: Random House, 1982.

Mahler, Gustav, and Mahler, Alma. *Gustav Mahler: Memories and Letters*. Edited by Donald Mitchall. Translated by Basil Creighton. Seattle: University of Washington Press, 1975.

Mankowitz, Wolf. *Dickens of London*. New York: MacMillan Publishing Co., Inc., 1977.

Manuel, Frank. *A Portrait of Isaac Newton*. Cambridge, Mass.: Harvard University Press, 1968.

Mareck, George. *Gentle Genius: The Story of Felix Mendelssohn*. New York: Thomas Y. Crowell Co., 1975.

Matson, Katenka. *Short Lives: Portraits in Creativity and Self-Destruction*. New York: William Morrow and Co., Inc., 1980.

Maude, Aylmer. *Leo Tolstoy*. New York: Haskell House Publishers, Ltd., 1975.

———, ed. *Family Views of Tolstoy*. Translated by Louise and Aylmer Maude. London: George Allen and Unwin, Ltd., 1926.

du Maurier, Daphne. *The Infernal World of Branwell Bronte*. Garden City, N.Y.: Doubleday and Co., Inc., 1961.

Maurois, André. *Ariel: The Life of Shelley*. Translated by Ella D'Arcy. New York: Frederick Ungar Publishing Co., 1952.

———. *Byron*. Translated by Hamish Miles. New York: D. Appleton and Co., 1930.

———. *Lelia*. Translated by Gerard Hopkins. New York: Harper and Brothers, 1953.

———. *Olympio: The Life of Victor Hugo*. Translated by Gerard Hopkins. New York: Harper and Brothers, 1956.

———. *Prometheus: The Life of Balzac*. Translated by Norman Denny. New York: Harper and Row, 1965.

Medurn, Thomas. *Conversations With Lord Byron*. London: Henry Colburn, 1824.

Mendels, Joseph. *Concepts of Depression*. New York: John Wiley and Sons, Inc., 1970.

Mendelssohn, Felix. *Felix Mendelssohn: Letters.* Edited by G. Selden-Goth. New York: Vienna House, 1972.

Meyers, Jeffrey. *Married to Genius.* New York: Harper and Row, 1977.

Milbanke, Ralph. *Astarte.* London: Christophers, 1921.

Miller, Betty. *Robert Browning: A Portrait.* New York: Charles Scribner's Sons, 1953.

Millgate, Michael. *Thomas Hardy: A Biography.* New York: Random House, 1982.

Moore, Harry. *The Priest of Love: A Life of D. H. Lawrence.* New York: Farrar, Straus and Giroux, 1974.

More, Louis Trenchard. *Isaac Newton.* New York: Charles Scribner's Sons, 1934.

Mozart, Wolfgang Amadeus. *Letters of Wolfgang Amadeus Mozart.* Edited by Hans Mersmann. Translated by M. M. Boyman. New York: Dover Publications, Inc., 1972.

Musset, Paul de. *The Biography of Alfred de Musset.* Translated by Harriet W. Preston. Boston: Roberts Brothers, 1877.

Nazaroff, Alexander I. *Tolstoy: The Inconstant Genius.* New York: Frederick A. Stokes Co., 1929.

Newman, Ernst. *The Life of Richard Wagner.* 2 vols. London: Cassell and Co., Ltd., 1933.

———. *Wagner as Man and Artist.* New York: Alfred A. Knopf, 1924.

Nietzsche, Friedrich, and Wagner, Richard. *The Nietzsche-Wagner Correspondence.* Edited by Elizabeth Foerster-Nietzsche. Translated by Caroline V. Kerr. New York: Liveright, 1949.

Nisbet, Ada. *Dickens and Ellen Ternan.* Berkeley, Calif.: University of California Press, 1952.

O'Brian, Patrick. *Pablo Ruiz Picasso: A Biography.* New York: G. P. Putnam's Sons, 1976.

Paykel, E. S., ed. *Handbook of Affective Disorders.* New York: The Guilford Press, 1982.

Pearson, Hesketh. *Dickens, His Character, Comedy and Career.* New York: Harper and Brothers, 1949.

Peckham, Morse. *The Triumph of Romanticism.* Columbia, S.C.: University of South Carolina Press, 1970.

Perenyi, Eleanor. *Liszt: The Artist as Romantic Hero.* Boston: Little, Brown and Co., Inc., 1974.

Praz, Mario. *The Romantic Agony.* Translated by Angus Davidson. New York: Oxford University Press, 1954.

Quennell, Peter. *Byron in Italy*. London: Collins Publishers, 1941.

———. *Byron: The Years of Fame*. London: Faber and Faber, 1935.

———. *Hogarth's Progress*. New York: Viking Press, 1955.

Raynor, Henry. *Music and Society Since 1815*. New York: Taplinger Publishing Co., 1978.

———. *A Social History of Music From the Middle Ages to Beethoven*. New York: Taplinger Publishing Co., 1978.

Richardson, Joanna. *Verlaine*. New York: Viking Press, 1971.

Roberts, Mark. *The Tradition of Romantic Morality*. London: MacMillan, 1973.

Rosner, Stanley, and Abt, Lawrence E. *The Creative Experience*. New York: Delta Publishing Co., Inc., 1970.

Rousseau, Jean-Jacques. *The Confessions of Jean-Jacques Rousseau*. New York: The Modern Library, 1945.

Rousseau, Jean-Jacques

———. *Original Correspondence of Jean-Jacques Rousseau With Mad. La Tour de Franqueville and M. Du Peyron*. London: J. Johnson, 1804.

Rubenstein, Arthur. *My Younger Years*. New York: Alfred A. Knopf, 1973.

Sadie, Stanley. *Mozart*. New York: Vienna House, 1965.

Sandors, Mary F. *George Sand*. London: Robert Holden and Co., Ltd., 1927.

Schorer, Mark. *Sinclair Lewis: An American Life*. New York: McGraw Hill Book Co., Inc., 1961.

Schou, M. "Artistic Productivity and Lithium Prophylaxis in Manic-depressive Illness." *British Journal of Psychiatry* 135 (1979): 97–103.

Schubert, Franz. *Franz Schubert: Letters and Other Writings*. Edited by Otto Erich Deutsch. Translated by Venetia Saville. New York: Vienna House, 1974.

Scott-Stokes, Henry. *The Life and Death of Yukio Mishima*. New York: Farrar, Straus and Giroux, 1974.

Shopsin, Baron. *Manic Illness*. New York: Raven Press, 1979.

Simons, Julian. *Thomas Carlyle: The Life and Ideas of a Prophet*. London: Victor Gollancz, Ltd., 1952.

Singer, Isaac Bashevis. *In My Father's Court: A Memoir*. New York: Farrar, Straus and Giroux, 1966.

Sitwell, Sacheverell. *Liszt*. New York: Dover Publishing Co., Inc., 1967.

Skinner, Cornelia Otis. *Madame Sarah*. Boston: Houghton, Mifflin Co., 1966.

Solomon, Maynard. *Beethoven*. New York: MacMillan Publishing Co., 1977.

Sonneck. O. G., ed. *Beethoven: Impressions by His Contemporaries*. New York: Dover Publishing, Inc., 1967.

Stael, Baroness de. *Letters on the Works and Character of J. J. Rousseau*. London: G. G. J. and J. Robinson, 1789.

Starkie, Enid. *Arthur Rimbaud*. New York: New Directions, 1968.

Steigmuller, Francis. *Maupassant: A Lion in the Path.* New York: Grosset and Dunlap, 1949.

Stendstedt, Ake. "A Study in Manic-Depressive Psychosis: Clinical, Social and Genetic Investigations." *Acta Psychologica et Neurologica* [supplement] (1952): 79–80.

Sterba, Editha, and Sterba, Richard. *Beethoven and His Nephew.* Translated by Willard R. Trask. New York: Schocken Books, 1971.

Stone, Irving. *Lust For Life.* New York: The Heritage Press, 1937.

Stowe, Harriet Beecher. *Lady Byron Vindicated.* Boston: Fields, Osgood and Co., 1870.

Stukeley, William. *Memoirs of Sir Isaac Newton's Life.* London: Taylor and Francis, 1936.

Sukholm-Tolstoy, Tatiana. *The Tolstoy Home: Diaries of Tatiana Sukholm-Tolstoy.* Translated by Alec Brown. London: Harvil Press, Ltd.

Swanberg, W. A. *Dreiser.* New York: Charles Scribner's Sons, 1965.

Tchaikovsky, Peter. *The Diaries of Tchaikovsky.* Translated by Wladimir Lakond. New York: W. W. Norton and Co., Inc., 1945.

Tchaikovsky, Peter, and Tchaikovsky, Modest. *Life and Letters of Tchaikovsky.* Edited by Rosa Newmark. New York: Vienna House, 1973.

Teichman, Howard. *George S. Kaufman: An Intimate Portrait.* New York: Atheneum, 1972.

Thayer, Alexander W. *Thayer's Life of Beethoven.* Edited by Elliot Forbes. Princeton, N.J.: Princeton University Press, 1973.

Thompson, Oscar. *Debussy: Man and Artist.* New York: Dover Publications, 1965.

Tolstoy, Alexandra. *Tolstoy: A Life of My Father.* Translated by Elizabeth Reynolds Hapgood. New York: Harper and Brothers, 1953.

Tolstoy, Count Ilya. *Reminiscences of Tolstoy.* Translated by George Calderon. New York: The Century Co., 1914.

Tolstoy, Leo. *The Diaries of Leo Tolstoy: Youth 1847–1852.* Translated by C. J. Hogarth and A. Sirnis. New York: E. P. Dutton and Co., 1917.

———. *The Journal of Leo Tolstoy 1895–1899.* Translated by Rose Strunsky. Alfred A. Knopf, 1918.

———. *The Letters of Tolstoy and His Cousin Countess Alexandra Tolstoy 1857–1903.* Translated by Leo Islavin. London: Metheuen and Co., Ltd., 1929.

———. *Miscellaneous Letters and Essays.* Translated by Leo Weiner. Boston: Dana Estes and Co., 1905.

———. *My Confessions and the Spirit of Christ's Teaching.* New York: Thomas Y. Crowell and Co., 1887.

Tolstoy, Leo. *The Private Diaries of Leo Tolstoy 1853–1857.* Edited by Aylmer Maude. Translated by Louise and Aylmer Maude. London: William Heinemann, 1927.

———. *Tolstoy Letters.* Edited and translated by R. F. Christian. 2 vols. New York: Charles Scribner's Sons, 1962.

———. *Tolstoy's Love Letters.* Edited by Paul Biryukov. Translated by S. S. Koteliansky and Virginia Woolf. London: Hogarth Press, 1923.

Tolstoy, Count Leon N. *The Truth About My Father.* London: John Murray, 1924.

Tolstoy, Sergei. *Tolstoy Remembered by His Son.* Translated by Moura Budberg. New York: Atheneum, 1962.

Tolstoy, Countess Sofya. *The Countess Tolstoy's Later Diary.* Translated by Alexander Werth. London: Victor Gollancz, Ltd., 1929.

———. *The Diary of Tolstoy's Wife 1860–1891.* Translated by Alexander Werth. London: Victor Gollancz, Ltd., 1928.

Toye, Francis. *Guiseppe Verdi: His Life and Works.* New York: Vintage Books, 1959.

Trevelyan, G. M. *History of England.* Vol. 3. Garden City, N.Y.: Doubleday and Co., Inc., 1953.

Troyat, Henri. *Pushkin.* Translated by Nancy Amphoux. Garden City, N.Y.: Doubleday and Co., Inc., 1970.

———. *Tolstoy.* Translated by Nancy Amphoux. Garden City, N.Y.: Doubleday and Co., Inc., 1967.

Turnbull, Andrew. *Scott Fitzgerald: A Biography.* New York: Charles Scribner's Sons, 1962.

———. *Thomas Wolfe.* New York: Charles Scribner's Sons, 1967.

Turner, Edward Raymond. *Europe Since 1870.* New York: Doubleday, Page and Co., Inc., 1927.

Turner, W. J. *Beethoven: The Search For Reality.* London: Ernest Benn, Ltd., 1927.

Twain, Mark. *The Autobiography of Mark Twain.* New York: Washington Square Press, Inc., 1961.

———. *Mark Twain's Letters to Mary.* Edited by Lewis Leary. New York: Columbia University Press, 1961.

Ulam, S. M. *Adventures of a Mathematician.* New York: Charles Scribner's Sons, 1976.

Underhill, Evelyn. *Mysticism.* New York: Meridian Books, 1960.

Van Loon, Hendrik Willem. *The Life of Rembrandt Van Rijn.* New York: Heritage Press, 1939.

Vasari, Giorgio. *Vasari's Lives of the Artists.* Edited by Betty Boroughs. New York: Simon and Schuster, 1946.

Vernon, P. E., ed. *Creativity*. Harmonsworth, England: Penguin Books, Ltd., 1973.

Wachhorst, Wyn. *Thomas Alva Edison: An American Myth*. Cambridge, Mass.: The MIT Press, 1981.

Wagner, Richart. *Art, Life and Theories of Richard Wagner*. Edited and translated by Edward L. Burlingame. New York: Henry Holt and Co., 1889.

———. *The Bayreuth Letters of Richard Wagner*. Edited and translated by Caroline V. Kerr. Boston: Small, Maynard and Co., 1912.

———. *Family Letters of Richard Wagner*. Translated by William Ashton Ellis. New York: Vienna House, 1971.

———. *Letters of Richard Wagner*. Edited by Wilhelm Altmann. Translated by M. M. Bozman. 2 vols. London: J. M. Dent and Sons, Ltd., 1925.

———. *Letters of Richard Wagner: The Burrell Collection*. Edited by John N. Burke. New York: MacMillan Co., 1950.

———. *The Letters of Richard Wagner to Anton Pusinalli*. Translated and edited by Elbert Lenrow. New York: Alfred N. Knopf, 1932.

———. *My Life*. New York: Dodd, Mead and Co., 1911.

———. *Richard to Minna Wagner*. Translated by William Ashton Ellis. New York: Vienna House, 1972.

———. *Richard Wagner's Letters to His Dresden Friends*. Translated by J. S. Shedlock. New York: Scribner and Welford, 1890.

———. *Richard Wagner to Mathilde Wesendonck*. Translated by William Ashton Ellis. Boston: Milford House, 1971.

Wagner, Richard, and Liszt, Franz. *Correspondence of Wagner and Liszt*. Translated by Francis Hwefer. Edited by W. Ashton Ellis. 2 vols. New York: Vienna House, 1973.

Weigler, Paul. *Genius in Love and Death*. Translated by Carl Raushenbush. New York: Albert and Charles Boni, 1929.

Weiner, Norbert. *I Am a Mathematician: The Later Life of a Prodigy*. Cambridge, Mass.: The MIT Press, 1956.

Weissman, Myrna M., Fox, Karen, and Klerman, Gerald L. "Hostility and Depression Associated with Suicide Attempts." *American Journal of Psychiatry* 130 (1973): 4.

Weissman, Myrna M., and Paykel, Eugene S. *The Depressed Woman: A Study of Social Relationships*. Chicago: The University of Chicago Press, 1974.

West, Jessamyn, ed. *The Quaker Reader*. New York: Viking Press, 1962.

Westfall, Richard S. *Never at Rest: A Biography of Isaac Newton*. Cambridge: Cambridge University Press, 1980.

Wettlin, Margaret, tr. *Reminiscences of Lev Tolstoy by His Contemporaries*. Moscow: Foreign Languages Publishing House, 1960.

Wilson, Angus. *The World of Charles Dickens*. New York: Viking Press, 1970.

Winoker, George, Clayton, Paula J., and Reich, Theodore. *Manic Depressive*

Illness. St. Louis: C. V. Mosby, 1969.

Wittkower, Rudolf, and Wittkower, Margot. *Born Under Saturn.* New York: W. W. Norton and Co., Inc., 1963.

Wolpert, Edward A., ed. *Manic-Depressive Illness: History of a Syndrome.* New York: International Universities Press, Inc., 1977.

Zoff, Otto, ed. *Great Composers Through the Eyes of Their Contemporaries.* Translated by Phoebe Rogoff. New York: E. P. Dutton and Co., Inc., 1951.

Zweig, Stefan. *Balzac.* Translated by William and Dorothy Rose. New York: Viking Press, 1946.

DATE DUE		
NOV. 1 2 1990		
~ 8 MAR 1995		
27 NOV 1995		
JUL 2 7 1999		